'A gr... ...

> Roz Watkins, author of *The Devil's Dice*

'A corking thriller'

> Ed James, author of *Kill The Messenger*

'Fast-paced and enthralling' C. L. Taylor, author of *Sleep*

'Fast, furious, fantastic . . . One killer thriller!'

> Mark Edwards, author of *Follow You Home*

'Edgy'   Clare Mackintosh, author of *Let Me Lie*

'Gritty and gripping'

> Kimberley Chambers, *Sunday Times* No.1 Bestseller

'Marnie Riches is already a leading light in the field of
Mancunian noir'   *Guardian*

'Gritty and great fun'   *Express*

Backlash

MARNIE RICHES

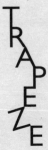

Marnie Riches grew up on a rough estate in north Manchester. Exchanging the spires of nearby Strangeways prison for those of Cambridge University, she gained a Masters in German & Dutch. She has been a punk, a trainee rock star, a pretend artist and professional fundraiser.

Her best-selling, award-winning George McKenzie crime thrillers, tackling the subject of trans-national trafficking, were inspired by her own time spent in the Netherlands. Dubbed the Martina Cole of the North, she is also the author of *Born Bad* and *The Cover-Up* – the critically acclaimed hit series about Manchester's notorious gangland.

Tightrope was the start of a brand-new series and *Backlash* picks up where this book left off. Set mainly in the famous footballer-belt of Hale, Cheshire, and introducing quirky northern PI, Bev Saunders, who risks everything to fight the corner of her vulnerable client, the series has been met with many positive reviews. So far, Marnie has sold an impressive 250,000 books and counting . . .

When she isn't writing gritty, twisty crime-thrillers, Marnie also regularly appears on BBC Radio Manchester, commenting about social media trends and discussing the world of crime fiction.

First published in Great Britain in 2020 by Trapeze Books,
an imprint of The Orion Publishing Group Ltd
Carmelite House, 50 Victoria Embankment,
London EC4Y 0DZ

An Hachette UK company

1 3 5 7 9 10 8 6 4 2

A CIP catalogue record for this book is
available from the British Library.

ISBN (Mass Market Paperback) 978 1 4091 8197 2
ISBN (eBook) 978 1 4091 8198 9

Typeset by Born Group

Printed and bound in Great Britain by Clays Ltd, Elcograf S.p.A.

FSC
www.fsc.org

MIX
Paper from
responsible sources
FSC® C104740

www.orionbooks.co.uk

To Sarah Stephens-Smith and Caro Bainbridge, for being the original and best Empress Dollies.

PROLOGUE
Mihal

It had been easy to escape while Terry wasn't watching. The bullying chump was too greedy to pay anyone to guard them all overnight. Just as it had been up north, under the watchful eye of the bossman bastard himself and his brute of a brother, the second-tier foreman depended on fear and withholding their IDs to make them stay put. It certainly worked on the Bulgarians. And if they were terrified of a paid lackey like Terry, who wasn't even on site, those spineless *bulangius* wouldn't dare challenge two Romanian real men like Mihal and Bogdan – especially when they were loaded with Spice. With drug-fuelled super-strength, Bogdan loosened a thick sheet of ply to let Mihal through the building-site fencing. They were out.

A short walk took them into the heart of Holland Park, where the elegance of one of London's most expensive neighbourhoods was tastefully spotlit in the early evening darkness and patrolled around the clock by infra-red, hi-res CCTV.

Mihal peered up at the three and four storey Victorian villas that surrounded them on either side of the tree-lined boulevard.

'This is a waste of time,' he said, eyeing the alarm boxes and CCTV orbs that festooned the eaves of every single house. He swayed like a whippy sapling in the October wind; made dizzy by the wealth on view and the pink clouds that scudded across black London skies. 'You might as well try to break into a bank. We'd do better in a crappier area. Let's head north and see what we find.'

But Bogdan grabbed a fistful of his filthy hoody and dragged him along the street. 'You've got no faith in your older brother.' He pointed at one of the houses where the paintwork was looking tired, even in the dark. 'See? No CCTV,' he said, grinning. 'And look at the bell-box for the alarm. It's ancient.'

'Maybe it's empty,' Mihal said, shivering not just with the cold but because of the paranoia that was just nibbling away at the edges of his high. The four-storey house loomed above him. With no lights on or curtains drawn, the windows were like watchful black eyes. Perhaps the house knew his and Bogdan's intentions. For a moment, even the sharp tangle of the tall holly hedging seemed enchanted, barring their entry with malicious intent. 'I bet there's nothing in there worth stealing. Let's just go back and smoke some more. If Terry finds out we—'

Bogdan pushed him through the gate and into the deep shadows of the front garden. 'Bet it's old people,' he whispered. 'They're lazy about security. Think they're immune to break-ins.'

'And they *never* have computers. What's the point if there's nothing we can sell in the pub?'

'There's bound to be food in the fridge at least. And jewellery, maybe.'

A security light came on, bright enough to make them both squint. That paranoia was taking a tight hold, now. Mihal imagined he could hear a dog barking inside the house. Perhaps the snap of a twig on the other side of the fence was the sound of a nosy neighbour watching their every move. 'We should have just gone through the bins at the back of Sainsbury's Local. I've got a bad feeling, Bogdan.'

In answer, his brother steered him round the back to some wood-framed French doors that, even in the dark, looked as though rot had taken hold after decades of neglect. He held his hand out, flexing his callused fingers.

'Give me the crowbar, for God's sake.'

Reluctantly, Mihal hoisted the tool from the waistband of his jeans. Snatched it from beyond Bogdan's reach and started to jemmy the patio door himself.

The lock on the rotten door popped with only a little encouragement, swinging open in the breeze. The room was shrouded in blackness. Bogdan pushed him aside, barrelling into the gloom.

'No dog,' he said, crashing into something.

Mihal hung back, regretting leaving the predictability of the building site. He felt the cold sweat rolling down his back, soaking into the grimy waistband of jeans that had grown baggy through weight loss. Were the sirens in the distance coming for them? Was the slamming door beyond the tall hedge a neighbour coming to see if there was an intruder?

Suddenly a strobe of light illuminated the room. Mihal jumped, thinking it the owner emerging from the blackness, shining a torch onto Bogdan. But his brother had merely opened the door to a refrigerator, revealing a dated kitchen.

'Aha!' Bogdan said, lifting a plate from the bottom shelf of the fridge. 'Chicken! Smells fresh, too.' He wrenched off the leg and bit into it hungrily. 'Come in and shut the damned door, you pussy!'

Salivating, his stomach growling, Mihal followed suit and ripped the second leg off the chicken.

'Come on!' Bogdan said, still chewing. 'Let's see what's worth nicking.'

'No. Let's just take whatever food we can find and leg it,' Mihal said, rifling fruitlessly through the vegetable drawer. He spied a block of cheese wrapped in cling film and rammed it into the pocket of his hoody. Belched. 'I don't feel right.'

But the creaking of floorboards beyond the kitchen said his older brother was already exploring. A light went on elsewhere, casting a yellow glow onto the faded splendour of the hallway. The sound of crockery smashing was deafening.

'Jesus Christ, Bogdan!' Mihal ran through to the living room to find him sweeping everything from an old mahogany sideboard onto the floor. 'At least shut the curtains, you fool! Anyone can see us.' He hastened to the window and yanked the dusty velvet curtains together, praying nobody had looked in whilst walking past.

'Nice candelabra,' Bogdan said, holding his tarnished silver trophy up to the cobweb-festooned chandelier. 'Weighs a tonne. I reckon it's solid.'

'It's too big. How the hell are you going to stick that inside your jacket? We need cash or small stuff that's easy to sell quickly.'

'The bedroom,' Bogdan said, hurling the candelabra onto the green draylon sofa. 'Rich old farts in places like this always have pearls and diamonds knocking about.'

With his heart thundering inside his chest and the blood rushing in his ears, as he climbed the stairs, Mihal could barely hear Bogdan's wager that there would be a cash-tin in the wardrobe. His hands were so slick with sweat, they slid from the bannister. But Bogdan lurched on into the master bedroom at the front of the house, crashing over to the dressing table, yanking drawers clean out of their

4

housings. The bed was made neatly, covered by an old-fashioned handmade quilt − the kind their mother used to sew in the summer evenings in readiness for the harsh Romanian winters. Old soft furnishings and yellowing wallpaper made Mihal sneeze with gusto as though his body wanted to expel the musty stench of age, damp and neglect.

'See? Look at the size of these gobstoppers! They'll be worth a packet, I'm telling you.' His brother lifted up a necklace, still clinging to a simple silver necklace tree planted on the dressing table − a flash of iridescence under the 100W glare of the centre light. But Bogdan's movements were Spice-clumsy; the spittle bubbling up at the corners of his mouth in excitement. He grabbed the pearls and tried to yank them free. The thread snapped and Mihal watched as they bounced like cheap children's beads across the thin carpet, rolling under the bed.

'Idiot!'

They scrabbled on their hands and knees to retrieve their precious bounty, each blaming the other. But sirens and the squeal of tyres outside interrupted their squabbling.

Mihal darted to the window. Stole a glance through the edge of the net curtain at the street below: two uniforms clambering out of two squad cars. Looking straight up at the window. Could they see him?

'Shit! It's the cops!' He retreated hastily, tripping over Bogdan's kneeling form. There was that rushing of blood in his ears again, so loud, he could barely hear himself speak. 'Turn the damn light off!'

With cracking knees, Bogdan rose, his fists full of pearls. He stood on his tiptoes, craning his neck to see the ambush that awaited them below. Plunging the pearls into his pockets, he started to run. 'Out the back. Before they come round.'

As Mihal followed him onto the landing, feeling he might vomit at any moment, he heard low voices in the kitchen. A man's and a woman's. No. Two men and a woman. Saw torchlight probing the darkest corners. The crackle of police radio. They were already inside.

Suddenly, a figure emerged into the hallway, clad in black and hi-viz green. A policewoman. She looked up and locked eyes immediately with Bogdan who stood like a statue on the galleried landing, peering down at her, transfixed.

'Police! Raise your hands where I can see them!' Her voice was confident and strong.

In an instant, she was flanked by the two men. They were thundering up the stairs, shouting.

Bogdan yelled something indistinct in their native Romanian, rooted to the spot as though the Spice had turned his feet to concrete. But Mihal was already running towards the staircase that led up; away from the cops.

'Run, Bogdan!' he cried.

Finally, his brother seemed to wake from his reverie. He pelted past Mihal on the stairs, almost sending him tumbling back down. The cops were almost upon them, now.

'Hold it right there!' the tallest of the policemen yelled. He reached out and grabbed Mihal's hoodie. 'It's over, mate. Put your hands where I can see them. You have the right to remain silent . . .'

Mihal stumbled and fell chin first onto the next stair up. He tasted the metallic tang of blood immediately as his teeth cut into his bottom lip.

Above him, Bogdan climbed on. Where the hell was he going?

'Give it up, bro!' Mihal called after him, straining to see his brother's ascent into the dark and the unknown. 'There's nowhere to go!'

But with the remaining cops only steps behind him, he watched in dismay as Bogdan yanked open the door to the attic. He heard footsteps across bare floorboards. The distinctive rattling sound of a sash window being hoisted open resounded through the house. Warnings, shouted from below by the police.

'Don't do anything stupid, Bogdan!' Mihal yelled, struggling in vain to be free of his captor.

He was answered only by his brother's guttural scream and the dull thud of a body hitting the patio outside.

CHAPTER 1
Bev

'Keep an eye on the time, will you?' Bev said, pressing the phone to her ear. She continued to peer through the windscreen at the entrance to the factory. It was a crumbling 1930s brick building with a tired 1970s makeover. She was sick of the sight of it. 'I've got to be out of here for half one. That Jim Higson is coming in at two.'

'So, set your alarm, man!' Doc's voice was muffled. The clack-clacking down the line was undoubtedly the sound of his molars, grinding away at food. She'd clearly caught her business partner mid-sausageroll.

Her own stomach rumbled. 'You're tech. So that means you're my alarm.'

'Tech, bollocks! You must be the only thirty-year-old I know who doesn't know how to set—'

'Call me at 1.30 p.m. on the dot. Right? We might be doing well right now, but we can't afford to lose new business. And don't forget, if someone calls, you're my posh, female receptionist. How do you answer the phone?'

'Beverley Saunders, Private Dick,' Doc said in a falsetto. 'How may I felch?'

'Say it properly, for God's sake.'

'Beverley Saunders Private Investigations. Mandy speaking. How may I help?'

'Better. Call me at 1.30 p.m. Don't screw up.'

At the sight of her first target emerging from the heavy glazed doors, she ended the call, flinging the phone onto the passenger seat of her Polo. Her pulse was pounding, her breath coming in short bursts. Bev lifted her camera to take photos of the man she had been observing for weeks. Dave Caruthers. Balding with a comb-over. Shiny trousers, pulled up over his gut. He seemed a picture of innocence but the camera didn't lie.

She zoomed in with the long-range lens, making sure she got a clean shot of the fat shopping bag he was carrying. It had been quite obviously empty when he'd gone in at 8.00 a.m. Now, it bulged. The boss said the company had been making a steady loss for a year. Could the contents of that bag provide damning evidence as to why?

'Where are you going with that, you sly old sod?' Bev asked, snapping away as he trudged across the factory's car park.

Looking over his shoulder, Dave Caruthers, the man who had played the role of faithful bookkeeper for the last thirteen years, sidled up to his old blue Nissan and stuck his key in the lock of the boot.

Bev knew it was time.

Snatching up her phone, she clambered out of her car and sprinted over to the Nissan. She needed to intercept him before it was too late.

'Excuse me!'

He was poised to open the boot. His questioning look was frozen somewhere between fear and a half-smile.

Bev beamed at him, knowing she had to put him at his ease long enough to avoid a nasty confrontation. 'Dave, isn't it?' She clocked a flash of the bounty inside the bag in his hand. All she needed was for him to hesitate for a moment longer and perhaps she'd be celebrating weeks of patient waiting and watching coming to fruition.

'Do I know you?' he asked.

'I'm Daisy,' she said. 'Don't you remember?'

She stretched out her hand to shake his. That look about him of a deer caught in a hunter's sights said he was considering his options.

Finally, he blushed, plonked the bag onto the boot lid of the car and wiped his hand on the seat of his trousers before thrusting it towards her in a move to reciprocate.

Bev looked from his hand to the bag; from his hand to the bag. Her heart thudding. *Now! Now!*

She snatched the bag from the boot lid and swung it out of his reach.

'Hey! Get off that! It's mine!'

She opened it to reveal packet upon cellophane packet filled with cheap, jewel-coloured bras. Finally! 'What? Are you going to cry, "thief"? That's a bit rich, isn't it?'

In her peripheral vision, she'd seen the vertical blinds hanging at one of the office windows twitch. Now, Bev's client – the owner of this backstreet lingerie packing factory – was marching towards them wearing an expression that could melt tarmac.

'Caught you, you thieving, lying . . .' Grabbing Dave Caruthers by the shirt sleeve, shaking like a brewing volcano, the boss's face grew redder and redder until he erupted definitively with a bellowed, 'Twat!'

Sensing even before her phone rang shrilly in her coat pocket that it was time to bow out and leave her client to it, Bev handed him the bag full of pilfered under-wear. 'Thanks for your business, Malcolm. I'll be in touch regarding payment.'

On the way back to the new office that she shared with Doc, Bev felt sunshine in her heart, though the A56 from the outskirts of Trafford back up to Altrincham was slick with falling rain.

'Ah. There you are,' Jim Higson said, before Bev had even had the opportunity to pull off her bobble hat and coat.

Her potential new client stood to attention in the waiting area of 'Beverley Saunders Private Investigations', which was little more than two second-hand leather armchairs that Doc had found on eBay, a thrift shop tea trolley containing well-thumbed copies of *PC Mag*, *Kerrang* and *Computer Weekly* and an IKEA yucca plant. Bev sized up Higson's Farah slacks, slightly too short in the leg, and his extremely shiny orthopaedic shoes, undoubtedly polished on a weekly basis by the woman sitting at his side.

Bev smiled warmly. 'Yes. Here I am. Bev Saunders, Private Investigator, at your service.' She spun her bobble hat in the air in a flourish and bowed at this uptight little man and his apparently demure wife. 'How did you know it was me?'

Jim Higson pointed to the picture that hung above the seats. It was a framed, blown-up copy of the article that had appeared in *The Times*, declaring Bev a 'Super-Snooper' for having outed a national hero as a thief who had been operating at a level Dave Caruthers, bra-burglar, could only ever dream of. 'You're famous.'

Feeling pride swell inside her like a small balloon filled with warm air, Bev unlocked the door to her office. Her cheeks flushed hot with the implied compliment. 'Guilty as charged.'

'We were ever so excited to read that someone local was behind all that,' Higson's wife finally said, smoothing down her A-line skirt as she rose from the leather chair. She was a good four inches taller than her husband. Looked like one of those rangy old birds who had been stunners in their day but who now shopped at the Edinburgh Woollen Mill and baked cakes for the WI. Except this woman wasn't that old. 'I said to Jim, *that's* the PI we need on our side! Didn't I, Jim?'

'That's right, Penny.' Jim Higson grabbed his grey anorak and marched towards the door that Bev held open. 'Are you the man for the job, Beverley Saunders?' Jim raised a bushy eyebrow and laughed knowingly, as though he was trying on being debonair like a pair of shoes that were beyond his budget.

'That depends on the job, doesn't it?' Bev said, trying to guess what could possibly have driven this drab couple to pay for a professional's services. A bad future son-in-law who needed to be exposed for the spendthrift he was? A workman who had walked away from a bodge-job, taking their life savings with him? Perhaps a ruckus with a parish councillor over the church Christmas fund?

She ushered them into the office that only marginally stank of mildew now that Doc had laid a new laminate floor (badly) and its walls had been treated to several coats of Damp Seal and white emulsion paint. Bidding them to sit, she disappeared into the kitchenette, making instant coffee in a cafetière and placing it on a tray, together with some Lidl shortbread biscuits which she piled into an impressive looking Fortnum & Mason tin that Doc had found in the charity shop. Two second-hand china mugs, a bowl of brown sugar cubes that she'd swiped from a café in Altrincham and milk in a small jug she'd liberated from Costa completed the appearance of corporate sophistication.

'Now, how can I help you?' Bev needlessly plunged the instant coffee in the cafetière with some ceremony, eyeing the Higsons surreptitiously. She then laced her hands together on her desk top, wearing her best confidante's expression, since most of her client's wanted a good half hour to unburden themselves before there was any hope of securing a paid contract.

With a mug of coffee steaming in front of him, and his wife sitting silently beside him fingering a biscuit on a side plate, Jim began.

'It's our neighbour. Anthony Anthony.' He paused, clearly expecting a reaction from Bev. 'What do you think of that for a name? I mean! Have you ever heard anything like it?'

When he spread his long fingers along the desk top, Bev remembered that when she'd done a background check on him, she'd discovered he was a piano technician. It figured, given the elegance of those fingers on an otherwise plain man.

Penny Higson tittered and tucked her mousy blonde hair behind her ear. Blinking hard. 'Very silly name. I'm sure it's made up. But if you met the man, you'd think it was right on the money, wouldn't you, Jim?'

'Well, I agree as names go, that's pretty daft, but it doesn't warrant private investigation at an hourly fee,' Bev said, making a silent wager with herself that this case would have its roots in a leylandii dispute. 'How about you tell me the full story and why you need my help?' She eyed the couple and noticed then the dark circles under Penny's eyes and the booze-reddened nose on her husband. Were these people at the end of their collective tether? Did she sit up at 3.00 a.m., sipping hot chocolate and fretting while he snored fitfully in a brandy-induced stupor?

Jim nodded. He was suddenly all serious. 'He's giving us a dog's life, is 2Tone – that's what his loutish mates call him. He has these parties 'til all hours. They're shouting and jeering and swearing. He's got one of those massive speaker systems like what you get at the Moss Side carnival. Notting Hill and that. I've seen them on the telly. All home-made sub-woofers in wooden cabinets with bass cones the size of Texas. I know my music. Classical music, obviously! And I mean . . . can you imagine the racket, pumping out rave music so that pictures are falling off the walls? Falling off the walls, like we're living by the runway at the blinking airport! You should see the rubbish all over the cul-de-sac after one of these parties, too.'

'Oh, yes. It's like the end of Glastonbury Festival,' Penny said. 'And he doesn't clean it up. Us other residents have to do it.'

'And sometimes, they have live bands. And they're cavorting in his pool in that back garden of his in the nip! The nip, I ask you. Like Sodom and Gomorrah. We live on a quiet cul-de-sac in a residential area, you know.'

'Very respectable,' Penny chimed in. 'Apart from Anthony, obviously. It's a little development of ten exclusive executive homes. We were the second family to move there when it was first built in 1996. The problem is . . .'

Jim leaned forwards, holding his wife back in a gesture that was both protective and domineering at the same time. 'Problem is, he built the blinking development. Anthony, I mean.'

'So, he's a builder,' Bev said, scribbling in her notepad whilst mentally patting herself on the back for having guessed correctly that a workman was involved, even if the connection was only tenuous.

'No,' Jim said. 'A landscaper by trade.'

14

'Is there a problem with the house?'

'Not at all,' Penny said quietly, shaking her head. 'It's lovely. Very solidly built.'

'Excellent pointing,' Jim said, nodding. 'My wife keeps the place like a show home, don't you, love? And you should see my workshop. But that's not why we're here. This man is a dangerous bully. Antisocial, like.' He tapped the desk top repeatedly. 'He's got this dog.'

'Soprano,' Penny said, her colour suddenly draining. Her finely plucked eyebrows beat a retreat towards her hairline. 'It's a German Shepherd. Big as a horse.'

Jim slapped the table, clasping those fingers into a fist. Pointing with a jab, jab, jab towards Bev; his lips pressed together so that they were almost white and bloodless as he seemingly fought over what to say first. 'It's not a dog. It's a hound. He hasn't got it trained, you know. It barks all day like a wolf.'

Wolves howl, Bev thought, but she merely nodded. 'Go on.'

'It jumps the fence. I'm sure he's goading it. It jumps the fence and . . . and . . .' He breathed in and out heavily through his nostrils. Lowered his voice to an almost-whisper. 'It goes toilet in my dahlias.'

'Yes,' Penny said. 'We've spoken to Mr Anthony several times about the . . . poo. We've got a tiny grandson, you see. He's into everything. So, I'm worried about toxoplasmawhatsit.'

Though the situation sounded grim, Bev held her fingertips to her mouth, trying to hold the giggle inside as she imagined a giant German Shepherd shitting in Jim Higson's undoubtedly pristine flower bed. 'Mmmn,' was all she could manage.

'But that's the least of it,' Jim said. 'The parties are a nightmare.'

Both nodded. Bev wrote *parties* in her pad and gestured they should tell her more.

'I'm semi-retired,' Jim said. 'I tune and refurbish pianos for the finest musical establishments. I do a lot of work at home in my workshop, and we like a quiet life, don't we, Penny?'

Penny nodded. 'Yes. I'm out a lot, giving piano lessons. At least I get a break, but Jim's at home much of the day. I'm worried about all the stress he's under.'

'Tell me about more about the nature of these parties,' Bev said, turning to Jim.

'Well, this 2Tone twit calls them, "fundraisers". That's how he gets away with it. It's every blinking weekend, if not twice a week. Half of Little Marshwicke descends on his house. Most of them seem like thugs – gangsters and their molls. Flashy cars and that. You know the type. And as if the loud music isn't bad enough, they're riding up and down near my perimeter fence on quad bikes! I ask you!'

'Oh yes. Quad bikes,' Penny corroborated. 'They chew up his lawn but he doesn't seem to care. They make such a racket. It's just the two of us these days, now that the kids have grown up. It's very intimidating.'

Bev folded her arms and sighed. Neighbour disputes. The bullying of an ageing couple by a wide-boy, by the sounds. It was a familiar story. She could imagine her ex, Rob the Knob doing exactly such a thing if he had a spine . . . or friends.

'They're diving into his pool 'til four in the morning. All the floodlights on. Shouting and whooping and the ladies half undressed. It's not respectable. It's . . .' Jim's shoulders started to heave and Bev was surprised when tears welled in his sad blue eyes and spilled onto his ruddy cheeks. He opened and closed his mouth, cocking his head to the side and frowning as though it was a struggle to say anything at all. Finally he managed, 'I'm at the end of my rope.'

'Have you been to the police?' Bev asked, pausing in taking notes.

Penny nodded. Smoothing her hand over her husband's shoulder. 'They won't touch it. They say there's no evidence. Police won't come out to a disturbance, now, you know. They tell you to keep a noise diary and complain to the council. The couple of times they did come out because that heathen's guests had vandalised my greenhouse, and then, one time, they car-keyed my car . . . both times, the party had been closed down before the coppers got there. Convenient, eh? No way of proving I wasn't lying. Same with the dog. Apparently a canine *movement* in a bag and some crushed dahlias isn't hard evidence of a crime. They told us to lodge a formal complaint with the Dog Warden.'

'And did you?' Bev asked.

'If we did, we'd have to declare it as a formal neighbour dispute and we'd never be able to sell our house.'

Bev turned back to Jim. 'Do you want to move? After all these years?'

He held his hands out, examining spotless short finger-nails. They shook slightly. 'It might come to that if we can't prove what a nuisance he is and how he's ruining our lives. The last thing I want is to be driven out of my own home when I should be gearing up for a quiet retire-ment. But unless Anthony is forced to admit his behaviour is . . .' He squeezed his eyes shut. His brow furrowed.

'Psychopathic,' Penny finished. 'If we can put together something we can take to the police and our solicitor, we can get him to stop. In the meantime, he's claiming harassment.'

'Oh,' Bev said. 'So, he's saying *you're* the nuisance

17

neighbours?!'

They looked at one another and nodded.

'Apparently so. Where's the justice in that?' Jim said. 'He's up to all sorts, if you ask me. He's got too much money to burn and he's a nasty type. But we're here because he's making our lives a misery. He's going to put me in an early grave. Can you help us?'

Bev narrowed her eyes, wondering if the Higsons could even afford the hours and hours of surveillance that this case would inevitably require. Then again, if she was ever to get a decent place where she could permanently accommodate her daughter, Hope, she'd need every penny she could get. 'Let me speak to my digital-research team.'

CHAPTER 2
Bev

'I don't like it,' Doc said, shaking his head, not looking up from the rose he was fashioning from red Lego bricks.

'Why? What now?!' Bev asked, throwing her hands up in exasperation as her 'digital-research team' vetoed yet another willing client. She stared at the delicate structure that was taking shape in Doc's nimble hands and stifled the urge to swipe it onto the floor. 'They seemed desperately, genuinely unhappy and stressed off their tits. I'm guessing they wouldn't have come if they hadn't thought they could pay. I personally can't see a problem.'

But Doc merely raised an eyebrow and shuffled further back into the cocoon of the wicker egg chair that he'd recently dragged in from the nearest charity shop on Altrincham's high street. 'Neighbour dispute,' he said without looking up. He blew a strand of his long, lank blond hair out of his eyes, grimacing as he pushed a particularly stubborn Lego block home.

'Since when was it a crime to need help with a neighbour dispute? How is that any worse than a wronged wife or jealous husband?' Bev felt her hands grow clammy. She visualised herself being stuck in the limbo of a poverty trap for the rest of her daughter's childhood, unable to afford, let alone win a custody battle against her ex, Rob.

That duplicitous turd was sitting pretty in the luxurious Didsbury pad he'd funded with her bloody money, while she was shacked up platonically in a commercial rental with a heavy-metal throwback who had a criminal record. Sharing a shower that spat rust from the showerhead, when the mood took it, wasn't much of a step up from Sophie's damp basement. 'Money's money, Doc. I can't turn away a new client when I've got so much at stake. If it's billable, I'm in. It's my name on the door.'

Finally Doc stopped assembling the Lego rose and met her gaze with those bloodshot blue eyes that attested to late nights spent gaming when he wasn't conducting online research. He sighed deeply. 'Neighbour disputes are trouble.'

Flinging herself onto his typing chair and spinning around slowly, Bev tried to bite back her irritation . . . and failed. 'What the hell do you know about them, James Shufflebotham? The nearest you've ever got to talking to your ex-neighbours was them calling the police because the weed farm in your loft was getting them high.'

Doc pursed his lips and looked back down at his rose. 'If you must know, my folks went to court with the people next door just before I went to college. It cost them thousands.' His eyes were suddenly wide. 'And I mean *thousands* . . . all over a hedge that next door wouldn't trim. My old man and the guy had been buddies for ten years – ten bloody years, man! You know what happened?' He rose from the egg chair, loped over to the high window with the depressing bars that gave his 'office' the air of a prison cell. Staring wistfully out at the industrial-sized bins, the litter-strewn alleyway and the bird-shit splattered old Morris Minor Traveller that lay beyond, he raised his eyebrows. Shook his head. 'Neighbour disputes can turn nasty very quickly – even more so than divorce. My dad's so-called buddy actually shot him in the arse with an air rifle. Mum was plucking buckshot out with tweezers for a month.'

'What happened to the neighbour? Was he arrested?'

But Doc didn't answer. He merely shooed her out of the typing chair so that she was forced to perch on the corner of his desk amid the crinkling Quavers bags and Ginsters pasty-wrappers.

'Does this say "2Tone"?' he asked, jabbing a long finger at the notepad she held on her lap.

'Yeah. Anthony Anthony. So irritating, they named him twice, if Jim Higson is to be believed.'

'2Tone's a bloody magnificent nickname. Sounds like a gangsta rapper.' Within a second, he was immersed in googling the object of the Higson's hatred; the story of his father's punctured bottom and pride already forgotten. 'It's like his parents knew he was going to be a wide boy.'

'How do you know he's a wide boy?' Bev asked, screwing up the crisp packet and throwing it into the wastepaper basket with practiced aplomb.

'I don't. But you know . . .? Nominative determinism and all that. Does 2Tone sound like a vicar or a social worker to you?' Doc scanned through the list of results. 'American. American. American. Here we go. Does your man live in Little Marshwicke?'

'Yep,' Bev said. 'That's the place. Home to the crème of Pennine high society. Gentleman farmers, construction moguls and the odd TV celebrity. It's all North Face jackets and Range Rovers up there, from what I gleaned when I was researching the Higsons. I once drove up there by mistake. The hairpin bends were terrifying and it did nothing but piss down. In fact, I think it's the place where clouds go to die.'

With a click of the mouse, Doc brought up a photo of a muscle-bound, mahogany-tanned man in his late forties or early fifties. He sported a black crew cut that almost looked like it had been drawn onto his skull with a Sharpie, receding only slightly. Flanked on one side by a man who appeared to be the Mayor, judging by the ceremonial chains around his neck, and on the other side by a woman in a floral skirt with Margaret Thatcher hair, it was clear that either the other two were giants or Anthony was tiny.

Doc started to chuckle. 'My spidey-senses are never wrong. Look at the state of our 2Tone. Napoleon on steroids. He's trouble, Bev. I'm telling you.'

Scanning the online article from local rag, *Pennine Weekly*, Bev absorbed the headline.

Paving the way to a brighter future – local landscaper helps kids flourish

'There's more to this bloke than Jim Higson made out,' she said softly as she read on.

The great and the good of Little Marshwicke's business community gathered at the luxury home of landscaper and Rotary Club member, Anthony Anthony last night for one of his famed fundraising dinners. The evening of fine food, music and dance raised an impressive £5,000 to help local charity, 'Full Marks'. The money will be spent on careers training for local youths at risk of offending.

Scanning the copy, she could see that rather than being a raucous thorn in the community's side, Anthony Anthony seemed highly regarded – by the local press, at least. 'Hero or zero? What do you reckon?'

Doc peered into the wastepaper bin and frowning at the balled-up Quavers bag. 'I've told you. It's a no from me.

Do you fancy playing me at Metal Gear Solid? I've got a second controller.'

'Are you flirting with me, James?' Bev folded her arms, irritated that Doc was trying to veto her taking on paid work for reasons that seemed personal at best, just plain spurious at worst. 'Because wearing out my thumbs on an Xbox console is not my idea of a fun Friday night.'

Doc spun his chair around so that he was facing her now. He stretched out his long legs and chewed the inside of his cheek. 'Why? Are you off out on the pull? Again? Where is it this time? Victor's in Hale? Alty Market? Goose Green? Where do the good-time boys go round here, Bev?'

Bev stood abruptly, snatched up an empty pizza box and flung it into Doc's midriff like a ninja's shuriken star. 'Cheeky bastard.'

'Ow!' Doc grabbed the box and rammed it home into the bin. 'No need to be so hostile.'

'Keep your beak out of my personal life, Doc. We may be sleeping under the same roof but we're not going out, right? I don't want to play Solid Metal Bollocks. I'm in the middle of an origami koi carp. That's excitement enough for me, if you *must* know. And I think turning this case down would be a mistake. I don't know what your problem is, anyway. You get to sit in here, all nice and safe and warm. It's me that gets a numb bum on stakeouts in my damp, cold Polo. I risk life and limb, wielding a zoom lens in the faces of ropey, lying twats. So, what exactly is your problem?'

Doc rolled his eyes. He yawned and stretched, his Iron Maiden T-shirt riding upwards, revealing the beginnings of a paunch, covered in blond navel hair. 'Oh, for Christ's sake. You met the Higsons. If you reckon you can handle this Anthony dick, go for it. OK? Let's do it. And stop being so bloody argumentative.'

CHAPTER 3
Bev

Angry knocking on the glass made her jump. She wound the window down and peered out into the darkness at a woman – in her seventies, perhaps – clutching a small white dog under her arm like a rolled up swimming towel.

'I'm sorry, young lady, but you'll have to move,' the woman said. The dog yapped its agreement. 'You're blocking my drive.' She stood over Bev expectantly, her fleece-clad bosom heaving with clear indignation; baggy grey jogging bottoms hanging from her ample lower portions. Her swollen feet were wrapped in fleecy socks and stuffed into fur-trimmed slippers. She certainly didn't look like she was about to drive off into the depressing mizzle and pre-dawn dark of the wintry Pennines at six in the morning. Were her cheeks florid because she was irritated by Bev or did she always look like her blood pressure was through the roof? '*Now!*'

Wanting to tell the interfering old dear to sod off, but realising she had to keep the residents sweet on a cul-de-sac if she was going to spy on one of their number, Bev smiled apologetically. 'Oh, I'm so sorry. I'm . . .' What excuse should she give, if any? 'Er, I'm doing a bit of work for—'

'I'm the head of the Neighbourhood Watch and I've been watching you. Just move it or I'll call the police.'

No explanation required. Mrs Nosy Slippers was already shuffling back up her drive, her dog's tail wagging just below her armpit. At a guess, she was an insomniac pensioner with nothing better to do than stare out of her front window, monitoring driveway access infractions in the early hours. She'd clearly been in the market for winning an argument, and Bev had delivered. Better not to attract her attention further.

Backing up, Bev sandwiched the Polo between two houses that were on the opposite side of the cul-de-sac to Anthony Anthony's house. They'd been built in the same pale stone that was typical of Pennine and West Yorkshire architecture and were now attractively spotlit. The style was nouveau-riche-nineties' ostentation with a faux-period twist. Given how the trees had grown up since the small development had been built, at a glance and in these light conditions, it could have been there since the early 1900s. Damn it. She'd been able to see much more a moment ago.

On the passenger seat, her phone pinged. It was a text from Doc, who had pulled an all-nighter and was apparently still up.

2Tone likes his ladies muscly and tattooed.

She replied, thumbing her text out deftly.

Look for dirt that's prosecutable, not his porn prefs. Unless he likes kids.

Hoisting her camera, she peered down the zoom lens to look for signs of life in Anthony's home, but a conifer in his front garden was obscuring her line of sight. There was nothing else for it. She'd have to get closer.

Clambering out of the car, she crept towards the house, praying she wouldn't be spotted in the dark of the early morning. Now that Mrs Nosy Slippers had retreated behind closed doors with her dog, the only sound on the cul-de-sac was that of Bev's breathing and the hum of electricity coming from the streetlights.

She approached iron railings that surrounded his plot. Peered through the chinks in some thick laurel hedging. A white Transit van was parked on the drive.

'What have you got in there?' she said softly, eyeing the three doors in a garaging block that was bigger than the entire house she and Rob had owned on the London/ Kent borders.

Her breath steamed; her face already felt damp. She could almost see the tiny droplets of water that hung in the air in a freezing mist. Little Marshwicke was in a cloud.

The rumble of a diesel engine growing louder punctuated the near-silence. There was a squeal of tyres as a long, black Mercedes Sprinter swung into the entrance to the cul-de-sac. Bev had to hide, and fast. She ran low through the open gates and into the garden of the Higsons' house, concealing herself in the shadows of Jim Higson's giant wooden work-shop just as the Sprinter bounced onto the kerb outside Anthony Anthony's house. Had she been spotted?

The driver gave two long, insistent toots on the horn.

Daring to stand on the edge of a large planter that contained a miniature Japanese maple, she peered over the fence to get a better look. Though she couldn't yet see her target emerging from his front door from this new vantage point, she could hear him above a barking dog.

'All right, dickhead!' 2Tone bellowed to the driver. 'What time do you call this? You're fucking late.'

Preceded by a bounding German shepherd that raced around the garden as though it had been freed after a long incarceration, finally, Anthony Anthony came into view.

He was striding the length of the drive like someone who owned a giant pair of balls or else was suffering from some pelvic disorder. She saw a stocky man in his middle years who wore stained jeans and a padded tartan shirt. Beige Timberland-style work-boots on his feet. In the pre-dawn murk, it was hard to tell if he was wearing a beanie on his head or if his hairline really was so unnaturally defined. He carried a flask in one hand and what appeared to be a heavy bag of tools in the other.

His colleague leaned out of the driver's window and said something that wasn't quite discernible with the hedge in the way. Raucous laughter ensued.

'Oh, what's this?' Bev said, spying movement in her peripheral vision at one of the Higsons' bedroom windows above her. She caught sight of Jim Higson, peering out at the scene below. He was scowling and either muttering to himself or talking to his wife, somewhere inside out of view. Hardly surprising since old 2Tone had a voice like a foghorn, loud enough to wake people in the adjacent streets.

Perhaps aware of his audience though he didn't show it, the landscaper's six-feet-tall electronic gates clanged shut behind him and he clambered into the passenger side of the Sprinter. Slammed the door shut with some force. The giant dog remained in the garden, untethered; flinging itself up against the fence and barking as though it were possessed. Either Anthony Anthony had no real handle on how noisy he was or else he was deliberately seeking to goad his neighbours.

Bev watched as the colleague revved the van and did a three-point-turn in the middle of the cul-de-sac, its head-lights butting right up against neighbouring garden walls; its tail lights following suit as it reversed. The Sprinter squealed back onto the road and was gone.

Waiting a moment, Bev saw Penny Higson join her husband and peer out, grey-faced, at the spot where 2Tone's colleague had been parked. She put her hand on Jim's shoulder and said something that looked placatory. Clutched her dressing gown close. Surprisingly, no other neighbours on the cul-de-sac, including those on the opposite side to Anthony Anthony's house, came to the window. No Mrs Nosy Slippers, now. Perhaps they hadn't heard the commotion. Perhaps they had just grown accustomed to being disturbed at an ungodly hour but were too scared to protest.

The Higsons retreated from view once again. The dog, however, streaked over to where Bev was perched on the planter at the boundary. It proceeded to snarl, hurling itself against the fence. The wood panel wobbled ominously, looking as if it might buckle and disintegrate at any moment, leaving Bev exposed – a handy, oversized dog-biscuit in the shape of a terrified woman.

'Good doggy. Bugger off, nice doggy!' Bev said stumbling off the planter, turning her ankle painfully as she did so.

With a clanging heart, she rammed her camera into her bag, crept back to her car and set off in the mist towards the main road. She needed to get on that Sprinter's tail. But where was it? At the junction, she looked up and down the almost deserted street. No sign of Anthony. She put her ineffectual wipers onto their highest setting in a bid to see beyond the yellow blur of streetlights punctuating the rain-soaked darkness.

There was no shine of headlamps or the glow of tail lights to be seen – even in the distance. Surely she hadn't already lost her target in such a tiny village. There was only one main road that led in or out, either down through a circuitous criss-cross of country roads towards Oldham or up, up and into the wilds of the moors, with West Yorkshire beyond and more rain-soaked villages that clung to the slopes of the Pennines. Either way, this was the stuff of Bev's nightmares. Roads that were too narrow to allow cars to comfortably pass one another. Ditches, sheer drops or stone-walling at her side that could total the Polo if she made one false move. Possibility of rogue sheep appearing from nowhere: high. Likelihood of yet another bloody crash: at least 80 per cent.

'Where are you, you little turd? Show yourself!'

If Anthony Anthony is off to work, chances are, he'll be heading towards Manchester and the M60.

Bev hit the indicator and opted to turn right towards the motorway. She passed the short run of shops that were still shuttered at this time in the morning. The lights of a solitary newsagent that was open for business shone out like a beacon. She turned away from the fluorescent dazzle.

There was still no sign of the black Mercedes Sprinter as she approached traffic lights that were turning to red. Only one car was waiting for green on the other side of the empty junction. She slowed, almost hypnotised by the hee-haw of her windscreen wipers that battled the steady downpour.

'Brilliant. First day on the job in a dead end, ghost-town shithole in the pissing wet, and I'm having to throw the towel in. Ah, to hell with it,' she told the red light. 'I'm going back.' She imagined working on her origami koi carp – the feel and smell of the smooth paper between her fingertips as she folded it with the expertise of the obsessively compelled and disordered to make intricate scales and fins. Already, she felt cheered. Then, she remembered there was an unopened pack of crumpets in the cupboard. Things were looking up. Maybe Doc had made an interesting discovery.

It was only as the amber lit up beneath the glow of the red that Bev finally glanced in her rear-view mirror. It took a split second to register the large Mercedes star, glinting against the black grille. Anthony Anthony and his colleague had slipped stealthily in behind the Polo. How the hell had that happened? Had they been parked up, waiting for her? Were they onto her already?

Bev's heartbeat quickened. This wasn't how her stakeout was meant to go. Damn!

Take a route they probably won't. Then, double back. Keep breathing, Bev. Stay calm. It's a coincidence.

The lights turned green, and Bev pulled away. She clicked on her indicator to turn left, heading for deepest countryside and in the opposite direction to the motorway. Silently, she bet that 2Tone's driver would honk his horn angrily at her and speed straight over the junction or take a right. But he didn't.

In her mirror, she could see the Sprinter's indicator click on. Turning left. He was following her.

'Oh, for God's sake. You're kidding me.'

Maybe at the next junction, she could throw him. Except Bev didn't know this place at all, and the Polo didn't have anything as luxurious as a Sat Nav. She'd researched her route up here in advance on Google maps and had written down directions in her notepad. Old skool Bev. What a woeful excuse for a PI she was! She didn't even have the price of basic navigational equipment, though she relied on finding her way around strange locations.

'Dick!' She gripped the steering wheel, feeling her lips prickle with dread.

Already the village had come to an end, and with no rising sun in sight, she was forced to put on her main beams. Whether she'd been rumbled or not, the Sprinter was driving aggressively close to her. Headlights flashed in her rear-view mirror, blinding her. Did he want her to pull over or get out of his way?

But there was nowhere to go. Drystone walls rose on either side of the narrow, winding country lane. Beyond those, only the ominous bulk of the Pennines stretched along the horizon like the spine of a sleeping dragon, merely waiting for an opportunity to devour city-folk who trespassed on its territory.

'Shitting Nora! He's going to run me off the road. Back off, you moron!'

Should she call the police?

Bev glanced down at her mobile phone. Snatched it up, trying to keep her eyes on the treacherous bend ahead. Registered that she had no bars this far out. And the Sprinter was honking now. It was no good. She might still get through to the emergency services, but there was no way she'd be able to use the phone and steer properly. She flung it back onto the seat, praying for a lay-by or passing place. The car felt like it was going to turn over as she took an S-shaped bend too fast.

'Come on, Bev! Think! Think!'

What might make them hang back? Brake lights! If she slammed them on, though, the Sprinter was so close behind her that it would definitely plough straight into her.

'Fog lights!' she shouted, triumphantly jabbing at the buttons.

Sure enough, the bright red glow of her rear fog lights caused the Sprinter to slow. The gap between them widened. Bev exhaled heavily.

'Yeah. I hope that put the fear of God into you! Serve you right, you road-hogging moron.'

But the Sprinter's driver must have realised her ruse. The van gained on her afresh, flashing its headlights aggressively, almost touching her bumper, now.

'No! No! No!' Bev could see the sign for a steep descent just up ahead. *30% incline: Low gear now!* it warned her. It was immediately followed by the sign for yet another sharp bend.

Failing to brake in time, Bev clipped the drystone wall on her passenger side with her wing mirror. She yelped as the impact sent it spinning off into the darkness. *Jesus. That's going to cost me to fix! Watch where you're going, dammit!*

The road straightened out and widened suddenly, with deep ditches appearing on both sides of the road. Which was worse? An unforgiving wall or a ditch that could swallow her little Polo whole?

The giant sheep seemed to come out of nowhere. Fifty metres ahead, the road was blocked by an impassive ball of wool the size of a small car. Forty metres, thirty . . . Bev slammed on her brakes, but the road was too wet. The van was upon her. She started to skid.

CHAPTER 4
Doc

When the phone rang, Doc jumped. He hadn't realised he'd fallen asleep, though it was hardly surprising, since he'd been awake for thirty-two hours straight. Utterly absorbed by hacking the browser history of Anthony Anthony's PC – the sort of information that was impossible to access if you weren't in the know. Easy for a seasoned pro like Doc. Turned out that a Computer Science degree from Oxford had its uses.

The list of visited sites had included Marshalls, the purveyor of fine block paving and flagstones for driveways and gardens. Several online dealers of building products as well as horticultural supplies had been bookmarked. Doc had counted two hundred and fifty-three visits to various koi carp specialist suppliers and aquatic centres. Scores of visits to the website of the youth charity that Anthony supported. He had an Amazon account and had bought high protein dietary supplements, vitamins to combat male-pattern baldness and football paraphernalia for Bolton Wanderers, as well as the odd HBO or Netflix series boxset. Doc had discovered he was a regular user of various vanilla porn sites, especially on a Monday and Tuesday evening – hardly surprising for a divorced man who perhaps had nothing better to do that early in the week. The only odd penchant his browser history had revealed had been an obsession with female bodybuilders. Anthony had googled and visited thousands of pages of women that would put Arnold Schwarzenegger into the shade with their rippling, oiled bodies and bull necks. And he definitely had a thing for ex-glamour model, Jodie Marsh, who was now mahogany brown and ripped like a twenty-year-old male surfer . . . with tits.

When Doc had googled Anthony Anthony's name, the local online press had been full of praise for this prodigious local businessman who saved more at-risk youths from the hell of prison with his proselytising zeal for honest graft, family and community, if their reports were to be believed, than the Catholic church had saved souls in the new world. Taking a closer look at the charity's website itself, Doc had skimmed over a raft of case studies of hard-bitten young teens, wearing hoodies and jeans or tracksuits, looking as though they had just taken a break from moped-mugging old ladies to pose for the photographer. Their backdrops had been rough concrete estates in Heywood or the run-down, red-brick slum-streets of Victorian terraces in Oldham and Rochdale, with the broken-windowed bulk of disused mills in the distance.

Reading the charity's mission statement was the last thing Doc remembered before sliding into an uncomfortable slumber with his keyboard as a pillow. And now a phone was ringing out in their suite of offices-cum-living accommodation.

How long had he been out exactly? An hour? Less?

Rubbing his painful stiff neck and wiping the drool from his chin, Doc wondered if it was his mobile. No. That was on the kitchenette worktop. Landline. It was the landline. He jogged through to Bev's office and picked up.

'Yeah?'

Then he remembered he had agreed to pretend to be a receptionist. He raised his voice by several octaves. 'I mean, good morning. Bev Saunders Investigations, Mandy speaking.'

'Is she there?' A man's voice on the other end. Insistent. Anally retentive, for sure.

Doc stretched and yawned, receiver still in hand. 'She's away from her desk at the moment. Who shall I say was—?'

'It's Jim Higson. Beverley was supposed to meet me at my house at 8.30 a.m. sharp for a briefing. She never showed. I've been calling and calling her mobile phone but she's not picking up.'

Doc blinked, yawned again and looked at the clock on the wall. Bev had left just after 5.00 a.m. in a bid to catch the landscaper going to work at crazy-o'clock.

Momentarily, he forgot he was supposed to be Mandy and let his voice drop. 'Dude, it's not even 9.00 a.m. yet. Are you sure she arranged to see you that early?'

'Dude? What kind of professional lingo is, "dude"?'

Shit! You're Mandy! Bev will kill you if you blow it. The falsetto returned. 'I'll say you called.'

Doc hung up. He was digital-research and as such, he was under no obligation to make nice with arrogant old farts like Higson beyond a cursory, 'Hello' and 'Goodbye' when he was being the fictitious receptionist. But it was strange that Bev had missed the briefing. Could she simply have got carried away during her surveillance of Anthony Anthony? Yes. That was probably it. And yet she also wasn't picking up an important client's calls . . .

Padding back towards his own office, Doc made a stop-off at the kitchenette to fix himself a strong instant coffee. As the kettle boiled, he pulled his mobile from his rear jeans pocket and dialled Bev. Surely she'd pick up if she saw it was him on the other end. But his call rang out until he was automatically sent to voicemail.

'Hi. It's me. Call me back. Higson's on your case about a missed appointment. So, just call me back.'

He took the milk from the small fridge and sniffed it. It smelled distinctly on the turn but he used it anyway. He threw his teaspoon into the sink which was fast becoming a mass grave for used cutlery and crockery. Bev would inevitably start yelling that the place was a mess, when Hope was due to come for an overnighter at the end of the week, but until then, they'd both studiously ignore the washing up. He smiled at the thought. Dialled Bev's number again, and yet again, was sent to voicemail.

'It's me again. Why aren't you picking up? Hit me back if there's a problem.'

Why would she have arranged to meet Higson if she was on a stakeout? It didn't make sense. Higson was almost certainly confused.

Advancing to her office, Doc spied her desk diary, lying open. Approaching her desk, he ran his finger over the diary's page – smooth but for the indent of her ballpoint pen where she had written the only entry for the day: 'Higson. 8.30 a.m.'

'Oh, Bev.'

Doc felt his pulse quicken as he sat in Bev's typing chair and dialled her number yet again. As he waited with dread for her voicemail message to kick in, he eyed the five most complex and beautiful of her origami creations that he'd had mounted for her in traditional oriental shadow boxes. His moving-in present to her, now proudly displayed on shelving he'd put up for her above second-hand filing cabinets that were still mainly empty, but for the files on the

Fitzwilliam case and a handful of new clients. Everything in the office told Bev's story. The punters would never guess that the stylish sofa was second-hand and doubled as her bed. They'd never imagine what pandemonium lay behind the door of her store cupboard. But that was Bev all over.

'Hi. You've reached the voicemail of Beverley Saunders, Private Investigator. Please leave a message after the tone and I'll call you as soon as I can.'

Dammit. Why wasn't she picking up? Was it possible she'd followed Anthony Anthony into the Pennine wilds where there was no signal? Yes. That might be it.

'I'm starting to worry about you, man. Call me, please.'

Doc rose from the chair and crossed the office, stopping in front of the store cupboard. He was tempted to open this Pandora's Box and look through her collection of hundreds upon hundreds of dusty origami pieces, kits still in their wrapping and abandoned half-completed structures. That's what she claimed the tiny windowless room contained, anyway.

His hand was on the storeroom handle. Would it hurt to take just one peek? The desire to know more about her than she would willingly reveal to a chump like him was strong. Who knew what she did or whom she did when she slipped out at night and didn't return 'til the small hours?

On the verge of stepping over this particular line, his phone bonged with two new notifications.

At last! Please let it be her.

Plucking it from his pocket, he saw there was a missed call from Bev and a voicemail recording left over an hour ago, though it was only now reaching him.

He backed away from her inner sanctum. Picked up the message as he padded through to his own office. The recording was terrible. Bev was shouting to make herself heard above what sounded like a hurricane, given all the crackling and hissing. She sounded fraught and frightened, but her words were unintelligible. What the hell was going on up there in the wilds of Little Marshwicke?

'OK. I've had enough of this. I'm sorry, Bev. But sometimes, if the stalker's cap fits, I'm gonna wear it.'

Flinging himself into his own desk chair, with trembling fingers rattling across his keyboard, Doc brought to life the business end of the GPS tracker he'd surreptitiously installed on her phone, after the previous case had almost seen her strangled in an Ealing penthouse. Her phone's signal had pinged off three masts in Little Marshwicke a good two hours earlier, showing her moving out of the general area where the Higsons and Anthony lived, towards the village and then out to the countryside, where it and she had seemingly been stationary for far too long. Something was amiss.

'Don't worry, Bev. I'm coming to find you,' Doc muttered, summoning an Uber.

As the cab driver texted to say he was only moments away, Doc pulled on his old grey ski jacket and tucked his laptop, tracking equipment and dongle inside, clutching them to his body and zipping them up like a baby in a papoose.

The balding, grey-faced driver tried to make small talk with him. 'I never driven up that way before,' he said in a strong Eastern European accent, glancing at Doc in the rear-view mirror. 'Little Marshwicke. Never even heard of it. How come you off there this time in morning?'

'UFO spotting,' Doc said, wishing the guy would leave him in peace while he triangulated the latest position of Bev's phone. The battery on his dongle was dead, however. Damn. He plugged it into his laptop to charge.

'What? Like spaceship and alien? *Independence Day* film?'

'Yeah. For real. Flying saucers over the Pennines. It's a thing. I'm going to offer myself to them for experimentation. But I'm in a rush, so . . .'

The driver fell silent then, merely stepping on the gas and offering a raised eyebrow in response.

The cab skirted past the beginnings of rush-hour congestion on the M60 and started to head out towards Stalybridge. A weak sun had started to clothe the foothills of the Pennines in pale grey light. Doc's ears had begun to pop, and every bend in the road that the cabbie took at speed made his stomach lurch. These were the rain-soaked wilds of the north – impoverished housing; carpet roll-end warehouses; pubs that had become vaping shops; newsagents that had become off licences; farmland. This was not the natural habitat of a Doc.

'You want Little Marshwicke. Library? Post Office? Rotary Club, maybe?' the cabbie asked, passing a 1960s brutalist school building – all aluminium windows and ugly coloured façade, with a cluster of phone masts stuck to its roof like a futuristic experiment.

Suddenly, Doc's dongle glowed bright green again. His software cranked up a notch and gave him a more precise location. His heart leaped.

'Can you hang a left at the next junction, please?' he asked. 'We need to go along that road for about two miles. Fast as you can, please.'

The cab driver was shaking his head, speaking rapidly in what sounded like Polish.

'I'm actually looking for my friend,' Doc said. 'She's stuck out here and she needs me.'

'No UFO?'

'No. Promise.'

Where was she? Would he find her, out here among the unyielding dry stone walls and the anonymous green fields?

'I'm coming, Bev,' he muttered.

They rounded a bend and almost ploughed headlong into a tangle of metal and flashing lights. Bev's Polo was lying on its side in a ditch.

CHAPTER 5
Mihal

'How do you feel you're coping with your addiction, Mihal?' the psychiatrist asked, cocking his head to the side as though his patient had his undivided attention. And yet, the shrink was busy writing the date in the margin of his notes, drawing over and over the numbers with his biro until they were heavily indented and shiny.

'Yes. OK. I have it under control.'

Finally they locked eyes. Dr Dreyfuss had switched his bullshit detector on, now. His gaze was so direct, Mihal was forced to study the hairs on the backs of his own hands.

'The antidepressants are really helping,' he offered, hoping to placate the psychiatrist. 'And keeping busy, also. My studies have changed everything.'

'Yes. I see you're excelling at your Open University course. Congratulations. We have quite the mathematician in our midst! Your English has improved beyond my wildest expectations since you arrived. You're clearly a very intelligent man, Mihal. But, I mean, with the other inmates using all around you, you're not tempted by them? Even with the stress of leaving?'

Outside, Mihal could hear shouting, whooping, jeering. His fellow inmates were enjoying their only hour of fresh air, while he was being assessed. His peers. What a goddamn joke. He had nothing in common with most of the residents of HMP Wandsworth apart from an address. The hard men of Clapham. The rude boys of Tooting.

'I keep myself to myself,' Mihal said, wrapping his Romanian tongue around the English with ease after three years of total immersion at Her Majesty's leisure. 'I was lucky that my solicitor stopped me from being extradited back home. I appreciate getting a second chance. Bogdan was not so lucky. It would have been pissing on my brother's memory to take a step backwards. I got clean. I'm staying clean.'

'You responded well to treatment.'

Mihal nodded, remembering spending weeks in his cell, sweating like a beast; on the floor with depression; crippled by nausea and diarrhoea; puking over his bedding. He'd taken beating after beating, once he'd been able to drag himself out of bed, as he'd refused protection from the various factions that ruled the roost inside. 'I was determined. I am strong, in here.' He tapped the side of his head emphatically.

The psychiatrist nodded. 'Your strength of character and good behaviour is precisely why you're up for early release. You'll be a free man next week, Mihal. Don't waste your liberty.'

His palms were clammy at the thought of being on the outside again. His passport, stolen by the man who'd bought him as slave labour from his trafficker, had been reissued. He was an almost-qualified man, allowed to stay in the UK. But he hadn't been in charge of his own life for a long, long time. And he was so alone, he could feel the solitude gnawing at his bones. He felt vulnerable like a newborn. 'I won't.'

The psychiatrist was smiling benignly but still studying him carefully, like the lab rat he was, for anomalies and signs of deceit. 'Good. But the biggest challenges you'll face will be drug-related. Mark my words. I see it time and again. Most of the addicts in here turn back to it straight away when they get out. They're out and back in again. It's like revolving doors. You know why?'

What does he want to hear? Think before you speak! Taking that step over the threshold of HMP Wandsworth's portico to breathe the free air outside again depended on Mihal being signed off by the shrink.

'They go straight back to hanging out with the same guys. Ex-cons,' he said, knowing by the psychiatrist's benign smile that he'd answered well. 'They end up doing Spice; breaking the law. Same old bad habits. I am not like those men. *Spune'mi cu cine te-nsoţeşti, ca să-ţi spun cine eşti.* It's a Romanian saying. You know what that means? You can tell a man by the company he keeps. Lay with dog, you get fleas.'

Dreyfuss nodded and wrote something in his pad. 'Very true. And what do you plan to do for money when you're a free man? Will you put your studies to good use?'

Mihal nodded. Grinned disarmingly. 'Oh yes. I will find a job . . . maybe teaching numeracy to other immigrants. I think I'd like to teach. Adult college. Lead a good, clean life.'

'Will you go home? Back to Romania?'

Mihal thought about what might await his return in his homeland. His mother was dead. His sister had run away when she was fifteen to Berlin to work as a cleaner, rather than stay in a shithole small Romanian town with zero prospects. The only thing that awaited Mihal if he returned home was the spectre of Vasile Andrescu – the man who had trafficked all three brothers to the UK, renting them out as slave labour on British building sites and finally selling them and leaving them to rot in perpetuity under the brutal jurisdiction of their new UK owner. 'No. Here is my home, now.'

He had ended the session on an optimistic note, only to find himself caught up in a scuffle on his wing.

'Give it back, you fucking thief! My girl sent me that!'

Stuart, one of the biggest guys in the place who was down for a five stretch, was snatching at a photo one of the other inmates clutched in his hand. He swung a punch at the grinning thief – a sinewy man with bright ginger hair. What was his name? Clive? Colin? Mihal couldn't recall. But he could tell they were all varying degrees of wasted. The place reeked of Spice, and yet the prison guards didn't seem to notice or else they were beyond caring in an over-stuffed prison where riot was always the unspoken possible outcome of any mild set-to. Things escalated quickly inside.

One of the guards strolled towards the fighting pair, all shiny shoes and crowd-controlling paraphernalia glinting on his utility belt, though he showed no signs of drawing his baton. 'Break it up, girls,' he said with little enthusiasm. He didn't get too close.

By now, Stuart had his scrawny ginger opponent in headlock. 'This little bastard nicked my girl's photo out my cell. That was private shit, man.' He even sounded high, slurring his speech.

The other inmates were jeering like punters around a boxing ring. They were openly smoking spliffs stuffed with the potent cannabinoid. Not caring that they were getting high in full view of the staff.

One man – Lying Dave – started to slump against the door frame to his cell. The attention turned from the brawling giant and the skinny thief to the spectacle of Lying Dave being propped by his cellmate, Greek George. Dave somehow plucked himself out of the slow slump and stood there, momentarily unsupported. He swayed to and fro with his eyes closed, drooling onto his trainers.

'He's going! He's going, man!' the others shouted, slow clapping and whooping at the prospect of his imminent collapse.

Mihal knew how this would play. There would be blood and vomit all over the floor in the next five minutes as Lying Dave battered his head against the hard floor. A fight would break out over who was to blame and things would only deteriorate from that point onwards, especially once the medical staff came up and the guards were compelled to calm everything down. He had to get back to his cell or risk getting embroiled in the mayhem.

One week. That's all he had to endure, and then, it could begin.

'So what are you going to do when you get out of here?' Kenny asked, as he shovelled lumpy mashed potatoes into his mouth. His eyes shone with vicarious excitement or else the prospect of getting a new cellmate after nine months of listening to a moody Romanian snoring every night.

Mihal looked around the dining room, carefully monitoring who might be paying attention to them or trying to eavesdrop. Other people's business was currency in a place like this. He lowered his voice. 'I'm going to find my little brother, Constantin. Alive or dead, I'll find him. And then, I'm going to track down Bogdan's killer.'

It was hard to read some of Kenny's facial expressions since alopecia had robbed him of all hair, including eyebrows – hell, the stress of being in a place like this could do that to a man – but he was definitely raising the ghost of his eyebrow then. 'Your big brother fell out of a window, didn't he?'

Nodding, Mihal wiped his mouth on the sleeve of his track suit top. 'Yes, but it's Spice that killed him. And maybe Constantin, too. It broke our family up. The shit that we were being fed was strong. A killer. Thai Dragon, they called it, after the guy that makes it.'

Kenny frowned and smiled quizzically. 'You can't take out a drug, mate.'

'But I *can* take out the bastard that got us all hooked on it.'

'Take him out?' Kenny asked, smiling quizzically. He started to rub the palms of his hands against the sides of his bald head. The bent accountant was clearly uncomfortable with the turn the conversation was taking. 'As in . . .?'

Mihal nodded. He drew a line with his index finger across his neck. 'I'll track him down and when I do, I'll slaughter him like a goat and watch him bleed out.'

CHAPTER 6
Bev

'I think you should go to A & E with that,' Doc said, grimacing at her head. He reached out to touch the graze with bony fingers. In the grey morning light on the rain-soaked hillside, he looked as though he might blow away in the stiff wind. 'Get them to do a CT scan or whatever.'

Bev shied away. 'Piss off, Doc. The paramedic cleaned it up. He said if I wasn't feeling right, I should go. But I feel fine. I'm fine.' She wasn't about to tell him that the florid green of the grassy fields was making her eyes smart and that the pitted asphalt of the country road felt like it was undulating beneath her. *Don't puke. Deep breaths.*

'You were driven off the road, into a ditch, Bev. How is that fine?' Her business partner took off his ski jacket and draped it around her shoulders. 'You're shaking.'

She shrugged him off and handed the coat back. 'I'm cold. That's all. It's the crack of dawn and we're on a mountainside. You'll catch pneumonia. Put the bloody thing on, for Christ's sake.'

Wearing a hangdog expression as though she'd just robbed him of his life savings, he pulled the jacket over his lanky frame. 'Let me buy you a cuppa, then. Tell me the full story.'

With a clunk, the beleaguered Polo was finally loaded onto the tow truck. A man in a hi-viz vest started to strap the wheels down to the ramp. The second time in less than twelve months.

'That car's jinxed,' she said softly, swallowing down bile. 'Maybe I'm jinxed.' She started to walk back down the road towards the village, staggering slightly.

'Are you sure you're all right?' Doc said, catching her up and grabbing her by the elbow.

In truth, Bev felt like she was about to pass out. But she wasn't going to let Doc know that. Nothing a slab of cake and a strong, hot coffee couldn't solve, as long as she could get it down her without delay.

Bev singled out the only café in Little Marshwicke that looked as though it would serve a great fry-up and a pint of strong tea, rather than smashed avocado on rye bread and a mug of steaming herbal piss. It was a tiny converted two-up, two-down house in the middle of a Victorian stone-built terrace, flanked by an organic vegetable co-op on one side and an antiques shop on the other. A doorbell tinkled as they entered, and the two stepped into a 1980s time warp of floral red, white and black wallpaper with different patterns above and below a matching paper border. It smelled of warm grease and vanilla. It looked like an ageing aunt's front room.

'This'll do,' Bev said, spotting a glass display cabinet rammed with giant cakes. Her head throbbed but her stomach was growling. 'Have you got fudge cake?' she asked the woman behind the counter. 'Please tell me you've got fudge cake.'

'Course we have, love.' The woman eyed the graze on Bev's forehead with undisguised curiosity. She breathed in sharply. 'That's nasty.'

As she shovelled a large slab of chocolate fudge cake onto a side plate, she treated Doc to a suspicious, appraising look.

48

Gave his knuckles the once-over, presumably checking for signs of bruising.

'I've just been in a car crash,' Bev said, wondering if it was worth quizzing this woman about Anthony Anthony. In a small place like Little Marshwicke though, a woman in her early sixties could be Anthony's mother or aunt, for all she knew. It was a risky move.

'Oh, you poor, poor love.' She poured black coffee from a large, steel urn into a plain mug and pushed it towards Bev. 'Where did it happen?'

Too many questions. Now Bev felt like she was the one being investigated. 'Sorry. I feel very wobbly.' She gripped the countertop. 'I just want to get sat down. Can we . . .?' She gesticulated towards an empty table by the window – furthest away from the counter where they wouldn't be overheard.

The café owner looked disappointed. Wiped her clean hands on her striped apron. 'Sit wherever you like, love. Shout me if you need anything.'

Bev carried her cake and coffee over to the Formica table, shooing Doc away when he tried to help her into her seat. 'Pack it in, will you? I'm not an invalid.' She glanced over to the only other customer in the tiny place – an elderly man with the biggest ears Bev had ever seen. He was shovelling down a full English, apparently studying a framed Beryl Cook print on the wall beside him. But just because he was staring intently at the colourful rendition of gleeful buxom women playing cards, it didn't mean he wouldn't be eavesdropping.

Doc sipped his black coffee and narrowed his eyes at Bev. 'OK. Out with it. What happened?'

'Keep your voice down.' Bev closed her eyes and exhaled heavily, already feeling the familiar whiplash burn in her shoulders and neck. 'I got run off the road by Anthony. Well, the feller driving him.'

'Jesus. How? I thought you'd be tailing him.'

Between mouthfuls of cake, Bev related how she had lost the Mercedes Sprinter in the dark and driving rain. 'So, I'm at a junction and I spot them, right up my arse. They followed me into open country, flashing and honking.' Out of the corner of her eye, Bev noticed the café owner using a dustpan and brush only two tables away. She dropped her voice to a near-whisper. 'I was crapping myself. You know how those country roads are?!' The woman was standing only one table away, now. Sweeping up dirt that wasn't there. Definitely earwigging. 'Next minute, there's a sheep the size of a horse in the middle of the road.'

'A sheep?'

'Yeah. Actually, a ram. I think it had horns and that. It's all a bit . . . Anyway, I do an emergency stop, right? But the Sprinter rear-ends me. The car skids and rolls and I'm in a ditch.' Without warning, tears pricked at the backs of her eyes and gushed onto her cheeks.

'Did you hit the sheep?'

Bev shook her head. She tried to speak, but only heaving sobs came out. Flashbacks to lying in hospital after her horrific crash on the A56 out of Manchester some months earlier. At that moment, Bev felt both the unluckiest and the most fortunate woman in the world.

'Oh, eh, love,' the café-owner said, suddenly standing over Bev and placing an arm around her. Uninvited, she took a seat at Bev's side, treating her to a sympathetic smile. Offering her a clean napkin as a handkerchief. 'The roads round here are a nightmare, especially when you're not used to them. There's traffic blackspots everywhere. A little kiddy got killed a couple of years ago. Hit and run.

Ooh, that was a bad do. The poor parents. We keep asking for them to widen the road and the pavements, but . . .' She shrugged. 'They've been here since horse and cart times, haven't they? Country roads. They're not meant to take vans and trucks side by side.'

Bev wanted to tell the woman that she hated the damned countryside; that village life was a pile of crap. She wanted to tell Doc that he'd been right all along; she shouldn't have taken this sodding case on. But Bev was not keen on admitting fault – a trait she'd inherited from her cow of a mother. And the mention of a hit and run piqued her interest. 'Did they catch the child's killer?' She wiped her eyes with the napkin. Visualised the Sprinter's driver and wondered if his bullying exploits extended to ploughing down innocent children.

'No, love. He's still out there, somewhere.'

'Or she?'

The woman bit her lower lip and smiled. 'Maybe. Call me Gaynor, by the way.' Glancing at their empty cups, she winked. 'Next ones are on me. So, go on! Who ran you off the road? Did you say it was a big van? A Mercedes. Not that I was listening, like.'

Dismissing the doubt that gnawed away in the pit of her stomach and ignoring the throbbing in her head that felt like a persistent alarm, Bev made a decision. It wouldn't hurt to see what this village gossip knew about her target. 'I wouldn't know who it was. I'm not from round here. I was on my way to Huddersfield for a job interview. I thought I was being clever, taking the back roads. All I wanted to do was avoid rush hour on the M62.'

'Yes, it's shocking on the tops. Especially in bad weather.'

'Anyway, I did catch a glimpse of the passenger, just as the van overtook me. He had dark stubble and was wearing a beanie hat. Ring any bells?'

Gaynor shook her head slowly. Her mouth arced downwards. She tapped the tabletop with her index finger. Then her nostrils flared and her eyes lit up. 'Anthony Anthony.' She folded her arms over her apron. 'He's big in gardens. High up in the Rotary Club. All funny handshakes and that. I've seen him riding around in that van when he's not burning up the tarmac with his daft Bentley.' Her features bunched up into a look of pure disgust. 'Thinks he's Charlie Potatoes, that one. He used to come in here for his butties. Roast beef and mustard, he liked.'

'Sounds like he's not top of your Christmas list,' Bev said. 'What happened?' Was this nosy café owner going to reveal something nefarious enough to warrant a police investigation? Had she heard tell of Saturday night GBH or Sunday morning sexual harassment?

'He brought that horrible mutt in here, didn't he? Soprano. What a name for a bloody dog. It's like an elephant! An elephant, I'm telling you.'

Out of the corner of her eye, Bev could see Doc's sullen face brighten with a grin. She kicked him beneath the table. 'Was the dog badly behaved?'

Gaynor stood abruptly, almost knocking her chair over. 'Badly behaved? It crapped right in the middle of my caf.' She pointed to a spot on the red lino between the tables and wrinkled her nose. 'He didn't even offer to clean it up! Dirty rotten thug. I don't know what he's feeding that dog, but its emissions were ungodly-smelling, I can tell you.'

'So you banned Anthony?'

She shook her head. 'No. Cheeky bugger started getting his butties from the new Waitrose that opened up at the far end of the village. My sister-in-law, Peggy . . . she works on the tills, so she tells me what's what. You know?' Blinking like she had a tic, her delivery was almost rapid

52

enough to heat up the café by several degrees. 'He calls himself community-minded, that jumped-up little Flash Harry, but he wasn't prepared to keep supporting a local business, was he? And to think, he did my daughter's drive . . . and he wasn't cheap!'

Bev had nothing useful from the exchange. Anthony Anthony was brash, loud and selfish. She'd observed that much for herself in the few moments it had taken him to get into his workmate's van at 6.00 a.m. Spooning the last piece of fudge cake into her mouth, feeling the ground pitch and roll beneath her as though she was on a wayward ferry, she realised she needed to go home and sleep until she felt normal again.

'Our Peggy actually went for a job at his house last week,' Gaynor said, returning to her position behind the counter.

'Oh?' Bev said, feeling the gossip machine that was Gaynor might finally reveal something of interest.

'Yeah. He's after a new cleaner. Pays well. He's not stingy, I'll give him that much. But it's the dog. Peggy's asthmatic. She said there was that much dog hair, she could barely breathe.'

'So he's still looking?' Bev exchange a glance with Doc as she gathered up her bag and scarf.

Gaynor nodded and sat on a high stool by the coffee urn. 'Oh, aye. Advert's still in the newsagent's window. Nobody wants to work for him. Are you surprised?'

'Not one bit,' Bev said, ushering Doc out of the door. 'Thanks for everything! Bye!'

As soon as they were outside, Doc brought up the Uber app on his phone.

'Not so fast,' Bev said, wondering if she'd be able to keep her cake down. 'Before we head off, let's make a quick detour to the newsagent's.'

CHAPTER 7

Bev

'I've got a right to see where my daughter's sleeping,' Rob said, pushing past Bev and advancing down the hallway.

'How dare you?!' Bev mustered as much venom in her voice as she could, though she opted not to shout. The last thing she wanted was Hope overhearing the argument. Again. 'Hey! Come back here! I never invited you in.'

Her words fell on absent ears, however, since Rob had already disappeared into the small meeting room that had been allocated to Hope as a temporary bedroom. The space was empty but for some bright pictures on the wall, a camp bed and a few sticks of furniture. Bev jogged after Rob to find him running a finger over the side table that doubled as a nightstand.

'Get out!' Bev said, praying Hope was out of earshot in the toilet. 'You've no right—'

Rob held up a fingertip covered with a light film of dust. 'You want my daughter to sleep on a camp bed in this dump? You think that's appropriate parenting?'

Bev grabbed at the sleeve of his cashmere coat and tried to usher her ex-husband back out of the room but he easily shrugged her off.

'Are you assaulting me?' He grinned nastily.

'No. Just trying to remove a trespasser from my home.' Bev balled her fist, trying desperately to suppress the urge to punch him in his smug face. 'There is nothing wrong with Hope's sleeping arrangements. She's safe. She's well looked after. She's *loved*. And most importantly, she's with her mother!'

She'd dropped her voice to an almost-whisper as the toilet flushed. Where the hell was Doc when she needed him? He was lurking somewhere in the suite of offices, but where? Rob was an old school coward who preferred to play the aggressor, hiding behind his solicitor's skirts or else rounding on Bev when she was alone. He'd never dare try this on with Doc present.

'I think you're assaulting me and making your daughter sleep in a dirty and dangerous environment. There's black mould around that window frame.' He pointed to two tiny grey spots on the window's paintwork that could have been attributed to anything.

'Right. I'm calling the police,' Bev said, taking her phone out of her jeans pocket. 'You want a scene? You've got a scene.'

But Rob seemingly wasn't fazed by her threat. He merely stared at her graze, wearing a look of disgust. 'What's that on your forehead?' He opened and closed his mouth wordlessly, clearly ruminating over how best to put her down. 'Did you get that in one of your filthy sex clubs?'

Bev pulled her long dark hair over the car-crash wound. Looked over her shoulder to check that Hope wasn't standing behind her. CBBC had started to chirrup away in the conference room that she and Doc shared as a lounge. Hope was watching the TV, seemingly unaware of her parents' acrimony.

'Don't you moralise in my direction, you hypocrite.' Bev touched her head gingerly. 'I got that on the job, if you must know.'

Rob smirked. Of course Rob smirked. Mr Superior in his New Cathedral Street work clothes, ready for another well-paid day as a marketing director for some Spinningfields company. A career she should, by rights, have still had.

'On the job?' he said. 'So you *did* get it in some seedy swingers club? Like it rough, nowadays?'

'Fuck you.' She tried again in earnest to bundle him out of Hope's room, attempting to wrench his arm uncomfortably behind his back. 'Or I'll be placing a call to my solicitor, telling her you're harassing me. Fancy a restraining order, do you? Bet your new boss will love to see that on your CV. Dickhead.'

'You OK, Bev?' Doc appeared in the doorway, leaning nonchalantly against the architrave. He held his phone up, pointing the camera in the general direction of Bev and Rob. 'Am I filming you defending yourself against a violent attack on your person by an intruder?'

Rob sneered and started to walk to the front door of his own volition, muttering, 'Limp dick,' as he passed her business partner. Finally, he retreated onto the landing, turning on his highly polished heels with folded arms. 'Think you're clever, don't you? Well, you bring nothing but misery to every relationship you ever have, Bev. Just make sure you don't ruin my daughter, won't you?'

'Goodbye, arsehole.'

'And you'll be hearing from my solicitor very soon. Sooner than you think.'

'Yeah, yeah.'

Shutting him out and double-locking the door didn't make her feel any better. She shivered in the narrow hallway, feeling dirty and burdened with a sense of unease. It was the same every time he dropped Hope off. Not even a court order in her favour had put paid to the sense that she was scum, and that deservedly, inevitably, disaster would always be lying in wait for her around every corner.

'Mum-Mum, can I have a snack?' Hope pelted down the hall, grabbing her around the middle. She was almost the same size as Bev now, and exuded a simple goodness that washed the effect of Rob's sullying words away.

'You sure can, Babba. Let's see what's in the kitchen, shall we?' She held Hope's face in her hands, smoothing her dark brown hair from her forehead. Kissed her nose. 'What a girl, eh? Look how big you are! I'm sure you've grown since last Friday.'

'Measure me, Mum-Mum! Go on. I'm the tallest girl in year six. Let's see if I'm as big as you.'

The light in her eleven-year-old's eyes seemed to warm and illuminate the whole dank space. Hope's childish energy infused Bev with optimism. But the edges of her wellbeing started to curl and blacken as her phone rang. She recognised the number as belonging to the man she'd called earlier, leaving a message about his advertisement in the newsagent's window for a cleaner: Anthony Anthony. Answering, she knew was about to play a risky game.

'You called about the job.' Anthony's voice was low and gruff.

The line wasn't the best thanks to a dog – his German Shepherd, presumably – barking relentlessly in the background. Clamping the phone between her jaw and her neck, Bev ushered Hope onto a chair at the little kitchen table, pressed her finger to her pursed lips and slammed some crumpets into the toaster. She held her hand up, fingers splayed, and mouthed, 'five minutes' to her daughter, shoving a tablet under her nose for Minecraft-based company.

'Yes. That's right,' Bev told her caller as she slipped into her empty office, pulling the door to behind her. 'My name's . . . Gail.'

'Have you got previous experience?'

'Oh, yes. Five years. I've got references. I'm working at . . .' She perched on the corner of her desk, mentally nit-combing through her tired memories and imaginings for feasible lies. 'A big house in Wilmslow right now.' She'd pictured Sophie's grand Victorian gentleman's residence in nearby Hale, where she'd spent the first year of divorced life, breathing in mould spores in the damp basement flat.

'Wilmslow? Fucking hellfire. Rubbing shoulders with the hoi-polloi? I can't promise none of that snooty bollocks, here, love. If you're looking for one of them posh coffees in a tall glass on your break, you'll be disappointed.' He chuckled to himself. 'How come you're leaving?'

'It's too far. I need something this side of town.' She was careful to lace her standard northern accent heavily with the flat vowels of north Manchester where it bordered on those little forgotten mill towns in the foothills of the Pennines.

'Mum-Mum. Why are you talking funny?' Hope was standing on the other side of the door, eavesdropping. Shit.

Bev shooed her away frantically, mouthing, *shush*. Praying that her target hadn't picked out her daughter's words above the barking of his own dog.

'I live in . . . er—'

But Anthony seemingly hadn't overheard Hope and wasn't interested in her backstory. 'I'm looking for three hours, four times a week. Cleaning, ironing. All that. It's a tenner an hour, cash in hand,' he said. 'Come to the house and have a look. I need to meet you face-to-face. *If* you get the job, I'll want references. All right?'

58

He'd pronounced, 'all right' as 'a-reet'. His tone came across as no-nonsense but friendly. They agreed to meet the following evening and ended the call.

Ensconced in front of children's TV in the makeshift communal living space, where the collapsible conference table had been propped against the wall, and the office chairs had been stacked in the corner, Bev started to plait Hope's hair while her daughter noisily ate her crumpets. All the while, Bev mulled over the call, deciding that visiting Anthony's house once Hope had gone back to Rob's and under cover of darkness made sense. The last thing she needed was fussy old Jim Higson spotting her and sticking his oar in, inadvertently sabotaging his own investigation.

'What up, man?' Doc asked, puncturing her contemplative bubble. 'Rob's such a . . .' He mimed masturbation as he wandered in, smoking a joint, bringing with him a waft of marijuana-stink.

'No! No! No!' Bev cried, jumping to her feet and prising the joint from between his finger and thumb. She stubbed it out hastily in an empty fruit bowl. 'Not in front of Hope! Are you mental?'

But Hope wasn't fazed in the slightest. 'Doc!' She looked up at him with undisguised glee in her eyes. 'Can we play Fortnite on your Xbox again? *Please*?'

'Xbox is bust, kiddo.' He shrugged. 'You gamed it to death last week. You're a console killer. What can I say?'

Clearly crestfallen, Hope pressed her fingers to her lips. Looking from Bev to Doc for signs of disapproval; blushing. 'Oh no. I'm so—'

But Doc looked over his shoulder as though he were a shoplifter with store detectives on his heels. 'Only kidding.' He pulled two controllers from under his Metallica T-Shirt. Winked. 'Prepare to fight as if your life depended on it.'

'Yay!' Hope immediately abandoned Bev's hairdressing efforts and CBBC in favour of Doc's Xbox. 'You pranked me like a pro!'

'High five?'

The two slapped palms and flung themselves onto the second-hand sofa, leaving Bev wondering at this unconventional alliance of her daughter and her dork of a business partner. Realising she was surplus to requirements, she sat cross-legged by Hope's legs; her thoughts turning to how she might feasibly pull off a stint undercover in a far-flung location when she had no transport. She needed somebody who had a car they hardly ever used. Somebody who might lend it to her for considerably less than the cost of a rental or even in return for her running errands.

'I've got no wheels,' she said. 'Doc! Are you listening to me? I've got no wheels and I need to get up to Little Marshwicke. The insurance are making noises like the Polo's gonna be a write-off.'

Doc tore his gaze from his agile Fortnite avatar, treating her to a yellow-toothed grin. 'Well, that's OK. You'll get a new car, right? Don't they send you a big fat cheque?'

Bev looked up at him. 'It's not as simple as that. Listen, you've got pally with the old bird who runs the charity shop next door, haven't you?'

'Sandra? She's the mutt's nuts!' He looked back at the TV screen, stretching out his long legs – holes in his thick white socks.

Silence abounded but for the intermittent gunshot coming from the game.

'Are you listening to me, James?' Bev said, frustration mounting. 'Or am I talking to myself? Sandra!'

Doc snapped out of his reverie and smiled at her benignly. 'Yeah. I got the Egg Chair of Great Happiness off her. It's mint. We've got a mutually beneficial thing going on, me and San. I took a virus off the shop's wanky old computer and in return, she lets me get first dibs on the shop's coolest vintage homeware.'

'Didn't you say she had gout?'

He nodded. 'Well, lumbago and swollen ankles. Same sort of shiz.'

'And hasn't she got an old Morris Minor van thing parked at the back there?' Bev gestured to the world beyond the barred-up window that the industrial-sized dumpsters shared with the charity shop's loading bay and only off-street parking.

Doc shrugged. 'I dunno. I don't notice things like that. I iz a confirmed pedestrian, innit?' His Buckinghamshire twang morphed momentarily into pure South East London patois.

Bev sighed deeply, rubbing Hope's legging-clad knees. 'Do us a favour. Ask if you can borrow her car in return for doing her shopping or taking her to the podiatrist something.'

'No way,' Doc said, his eyes darting to the screen. Only half listening, by the looks. 'I've got a job to do, remember? Researching Anthony Anthony?'

'Please, Doc. I'll ferry her to wherever she wants as long as she lets me borrow her car until I've either got Higson to cover my expenses or the insurance sorts me out. I'll pay for petrol. I just can't afford what they charge at these car hire places. It's ridiculous. And I'm insured to drive somebody else's car.'

'She'd never let you borrow the Morris.'

'Since when were you and chazza-shop Sandra so close? She might! It's covered in bird poo. She's clearly not using it. I've seen her getting dropped off every morning. Go on, Doc. If we don't do this job, we don't get paid.' She stared at Hope pointedly.

Doc shook his head. 'I'll ask. I can't promise anything.'

The doorbell ringing shrilly interrupted them. Bev felt the blood drain from her lips. She froze with fear momentarily. 'I hope that's not Rob again. What the hell does he want now?'

Hope pushed the tablet into Doc's hands and ran to the front door.

'Wait! Hope! Leave it!' Bev jogged after her only to find her daughter wearing a confused smile as she held the door open to two uniformed behemoths.

'Mum-Mum! There's two policemen here to see you.'

'Beverley Saunders?' the older of the cops asked, the radio on his shoulder hissing and crackling.

'Yes,' Bev said, registering an ominous rumble in her digestive system. Feeling instinctively that something was off. 'What's wrong?'

The second cop was sniffing the air. His pupils dilated with immediate recognition. He'd smelled Doc's weed. 'I think we'd better come in for a chat,' he said. 'Don't you?'

CHAPTER 8
Hope

'Go back in the lounge, love,' Mum said. 'This is grown-ups' stuff.'

Hope looked up at the policemen, thinking they seemed like giants with those tall helmets. Transfixed, she listened to the constant feed of hiss and information that was coming from the walkie-talkies on their shoulders. Why weren't they answering? Maybe the person on the other end wasn't speaking to them. She desperately wanted to know why they'd turned up on Mum-Mum's doorstep.

'But—'

'Hope!'

'Do as your mum says. Be a good girl.' The slightly smaller policeman smiled at her, but like her headmistress, Mrs Stuart, it was a strict smile that wasn't really that friendly at all.

Nodding, Hope reluctantly retreated to the living room, where Doc was throwing his half-smoked cigarette out of the window. He looked pale, as though he was about to faint. Then he slipped silently out of the living room. She could hear him lock himself in the shower room and flush the toilet. He reappeared moments later, even paler than before.

But Hope was only interested in Mum. Was she in trouble? She stood by the doorway, just out of sight and listened . . .

'What's this about?' Mum asked. 'Is it the accident?' Her voice sounded shaky but cheerful, like when you pretended everything was OK, but really, you were scared.

'We're responding to a complaint, Ms Saunders. You've been seen hanging around a private cul-de-sac in Little Marshwicke. One of the residents reported that you'd parked up, obstructing a driveway, and that you were taking photos with a pretty professional-looking camera in the early hours of the morning.'

Hope popped her head beyond the threshold and could see Mum-Mum had her arms folded; chuckling nervously.

'Yes! Yes! Sorry for the confusion. I'm a Private Investigator.' Her mum pointed to the plaque on the hall wall that showed the company's name. 'I bought the company as a going concern off Ronald Braithwaite. He was looking to retire last year, and I . . . You must have heard of Ronald.'

The taller of the policemen nodded. 'He was going for years, was Ronald. Very well respected.'

'Well, anyway. I was watching somebody for a job I've just started. Neighbour dispute, funnily enough. You know what suburbia's like. Fully of nosy so-and-sos and bullies.'

'Have you got a current SIA Licence?'

The colour drained from Mum's face and her voice thinned almost to a whisper as though somebody had stolen her breath. 'Yes. Course I've got one! What do you take me for? Didn't you hear the bit where I said I took over from Ronald?'

'But you're not Ronald.'

Behind her, by the lounge window, Doc whispered, 'Shit', though Hope didn't know why either of them were acting strangely.

'Don't you remember the Fitzwilliam case? The shadow Cabinet Minister?' Mum said. Stronger, this time. 'That was me!'

'Oh, yes. Yep. Right. Now this makes sense. OK,' the smaller of the two said. He was doing that smile again, though Hope thought he looked in pain like Dad did when he said his piles were playing up.

The policemen looked at each other and nodded.

Mum grabbed hold of the edge of the door and started to close it. 'Well, thanks for calling round. I'm sorry your time was wasted. You know what nosy neighbours can be like. Village cul-de-sacs are notorious for it.'

But the taller policeman pushed his hand against the door. 'There's still the issue of the marijuana I can smell, I'm afraid. Do you mind if we come inside?'

Without saying a word, Mum let them in.

'Fuck it!' Doc said, moving quickly from the window to the sofa. He lay down with a cushion beneath his head, closing his eyes.

Hope backed into the room, not really knowing how she should react as the giant policemen walked slowly down the hall, the hiss and chatter of their walkie-talkies growing louder with every step. She opted to perch on the end of the sofa by Doc's feet, putting her thumb in her mouth, even though Mum told her off for that because it would make her teeth crooked and she was far too old to be sucking her thumb.

'Hello there,' the smaller of the policemen said to her as he came into the living room. He crouched down by Hope as though she was a toddler. 'What's your name?'

'Hope Mitchell.'

'This is my lovely daughter,' Mum said, stepping around the policeman to put her hand on Hope's shoulder.

'And how old are you?' the man asked while his taller companion stared at Doc.

'Eleven.'

'And who's this?' He looked at Doc, then. 'Is this Daddy?'

Doc opened his eyes slowly, as though he'd just woken up. 'No. Bev's business associate.' He held out his hand but the policeman didn't shake it.

'Have you been smoking an illegal substance in front of this nice young lady, Mr . . .?' The policeman sniffed the air dramatically.

'No.' Doc didn't give his name. 'But I won't say I haven't used some medicinal product in the last twenty-four hours. For my *unbearable* pain. Are you going to waste police time harassing a man with advanced Multiple Sclerosis? I'm sure the *Manchester Evening News* would love to hear about that.'

'Take no notice of my colleague,' Mum said, giggling and blushing. 'He's really very ill. He only came over to brief me on some admin he's done. It supplements his disability benefit, doesn't it, Colin?'

'Possession of marijuana is an arrestable offence . . . Colin.'

'Are you going to arrest me?' Doc held his skinny arms out, joined at the wrist as though he was inviting the policemen to snap cuffs on him.

'Turn out your pockets, son,' the tallest policeman said.

Doc winced and groaned as he rearranged himself on the sofa trying and failing to tug at the lining of his jeans pockets.

'Get up!'

'I can't. I'm in spasm.' Doc clenched his eyelids shut, breathing quickly as though he was in agony.

'Forget it,' the smaller cop said. He turned to Mum. 'We're sorry to have disturbed you, Ms Saunders. Good luck with your case.'

Mum escorted the policemen to the door. Hope stayed behind on the sofa, her hand clasped to her mouth as Doc winked at her and smiled. She heard Mum saying goodbye and the door clicking closed. Footsteps down the hall.

'You total—!' Mum started to shout at Doc.

'Total what? Don't swear in front of your daughter. It's all cool, man.'

'What's marijuana?' Hope asked.

But Mum was too busy beating Doc around the head with a cushion. 'Tosspot! What made you think you could pass-ag your way out of that, Mr M.S.?'

Doc started to laugh, the colour flooding back into his cheeks. 'It worked, didn't it?' He batted the cushion away playfully and punched a fist in the air. 'And you're not so squeaky clean, Ms I've-Got-A-Current-SIA-Licence. You forgot to tell them you're still using Braithwaite's name and ex-cop's CV to qualify.'

'I started a course! I'll get my accreditation. I've just not had time. I did pay for his business fair and square with the last few quid I had.'

'You could get fined £5,000, liar, liar, pants on fire!'

Hope stifled nervous laughter as Mum grew even redder in the face. 'Shut it, Doc.'

'I can't believe you didn't sort all that out after the Fitzwilliam trial. You're lucky your evidence was still admissible in court. So, before you have a go at me for smoking doobies . . .'

'What are doobies, Mum?' Hope asked.

'Jazz cigarettes, darling. Doc's behaving like an idiot teenage boy. Take no notice. And don't mention *any* of this to your father.'

'Why not?'

Mum smiled then. 'I tell you what. Let's get you a glass of Diet Coke as a special treat. That was mad with the coppers, wasn't it? Come on!'

'Yay! I fupping *love* Coke.'

'Don't say, "fupping", Hope. You know it counts as swearing.'

Sitting in the kitchen with her Coke, which Mum had also warned her not to tell Dad about, Hope pondered the nature of jazz cigarettes while Mum and Doc continued to bicker in the lounge. Eventually, the snarky conversation gave way to relieved-sounding laughter, and Hope was allowed to watch *Hunted* on TV before bedtime.

But the Coke and the police visit and memories of regular arguments between Mum and Dad kept her awake most of the night, so that when Hope went to school the following day, she found herself teetering between feeling slumping-by-the-coat-pegs-droopy-eyelids sleepy and wondering if anything she experienced was real. She had two odd encounters that felt like a dream.

The first involved a supply teacher. Hope didn't quite catch her name. She was tall though. Tall like a wizard or a man. The woman came up to Hope just as she was about to go out into the playground at break time.

'Hello, Hope,' the teacher said. 'Do you have a minute?'

Hope nodded. 'How do you know my name?'

The teacher smiled. 'It's my job to know all the children in this school. I know your mum, too.'

'How?' Hope smiled and yawned.

'Does she drop you at school every morning?' The teacher sat down on the bench beneath the coat pegs, smoothing her skirt. She had big muscly legs like the women in the Olympics. Her flat shoes looked the same size as Doc's.

'No. Only on the days when Dad's— Are you a giant?'

The teacher shook her head and laughed. 'Ha. No. I hear you're a very clever girl. You're the cleverest girl in Chorlton, aren't you?'

'Didsbury.'

'Is that where you live? I bet I can guess your street name.' She held a large hand up and closed her eyes. Her lids were covered in pink eyeshadow. 'Water . . . no. Acacia . . . no.' She looked at Hope. 'Ffffaaaa . . .'

Hope nodded. 'Nearly.'

'Fairy Road? Fenchurch . . . No?'

'Fog Lane.' Hope told her the number and then covered her mouth. Should she have revealed to this teacher where Dad's house was? But then, she was a teacher, so that was OK, right?

'What's your favourite sweets?'

Hope started to sway slightly and stumbled. 'Wispa. Can I go? My friends are waiting for me in the playground.'

The friendly supply teacher waved through the glazed classroom door as Hope joined in the Year 6 fray. Yet, as Olivia Dodds started to bully her, calling her a 'beggar' because she had holes in her non-brand schoolbag, the teacher was nowhere to be found. The only evidence that she and Hope had ever met came in the form of a Wispa bar that appeared in her coat pocket towards the end of the day.

The second strange episode was after the school bell had rung at the end of the day. Struggling to stay awake during after-school club and very tempted to lay her head down on top of the drawing she'd begun for her history homework, Hope caught sight of a man, standing on the other side of the school fence. He was wearing a bright green Puffa jacket, with the hood pulled up so that she couldn't clearly see his face. The man seemed to be staring straight at her.

Hope looked around to check. The other children had all gone home – even Sacha Barnes – as it was Friday. Only Hope was left alone in the classroom with Mrs Murray, who was filing her nails and humming. Dad was late. Typical.

Checking again to see that the man was, in fact, peering in at her and that she hadn't just imagined him, Hope pinched her forearm. It always paid to check you weren't dreaming when you'd been up all night because of Diet Coke.

Nope. He was still there. And though she couldn't see his face clearly from that distance – certainly not his eyes – she shivered. Knew instinctively that he was watching her.

'Mrs Murray?'

'Yes, dear?' Mrs Murray looked at her watch. She sounded tired and disappointed. 'I wonder where your daddy's got to.'

'There's a man outside the playground. I think he's staring in at me. It's weird.'

Mrs Murray frowned, rose from her chair and came out from behind her desk. 'Where? I can't see anyone?'

By the time Mrs Murray peered out of the classroom window, the man in the green Puffa had gone.

CHAPTER 9
Bev

'Is that coppers coming up behind me?' Bev asked, peering through the rear-view mirror at a white car that had a flash of lime green across the bonnet. Was that a light on top that she could see?

In the passenger seat of the old Morris, Doc turned to look behind them. 'Looks like motorway maintenance. What are you worried for, anyway? You're only doing sixty, and you *said* you had insurance to drive someone else's car.'

Bev bit her lip. Her cheeks were suddenly on fire. The wig she'd donned for the interview was itching, itching, itching. 'Er . . .'

She could feel Doc boring into her with his laser-like gaze. 'You're not insured, are you? Jesus! Sandra's going to go ballistic. You're playing fast and loose with her pride and joy, you know.'

'Stop being so judgy! I'm not made of bloody money. I get pretty basic insurance. OK? One step up from third party, fire and theft. Anyway, she won't even know.'

'Oh, cos you're such a careful driver?' He faked a coughing fit. 'I'm taking my life in my hands even getting in a car with you.'

Bev punched out at him, though she didn't dare take her eyes off the pre-rush hour build-up of traffic on the motorway. 'Shut it, you. You're my lookout and my muscle. When you've actually learned to drive, then you can lecture me about my road-safety record.' She massaged her shoulders with her free hand. 'You're making my whiplash flare up.'

Pulling into Little Marshwicke, which looked a picture of Pennine perfection in the late-afternoon sun, Bev steeled herself not to think about being pursued and bullied off the road by the very man who was about to interview her for a job. They turned onto the leafy cul-de-sac and parked two houses down from the Higsons.

'Do I look the part?' she asked, wishing she didn't sound so breathless, thanks to her thunderous heartbeat.

Doc looked her over. 'Your hair looks like shit. How did you find a badly-dyed blonde wig with dark brown roots?'

'PI magic.' She donned a pair of old-fashioned glasses that sported prescription-free lenses.

'Well, I don't know where you got that shade of foundation from, but you look like you've only eaten value sausages your entire life. Your clothes—'

'They're my normal clothes. Watch it!'

Doc grinned. 'You've even got gnarly washerwoman hands like my mum's cleaner. You're spot on.'

'Wait here, out of sight,' Bev said. 'Any trouble, I've got your number at the ready.'

The few metres she had to walk to cross the cul-de-sac felt like half a mile. Would Anthony recognise her as the woman he'd put in a ditch? She glanced down at her hands, fleetingly niggled that Doc should have insulted them. Prick.

The tall gates were locked. She pressed the buzzer on the intercom system, noticing the lens sunk into the steel fascia. Anthony would get a good look at her before she even got over the threshold. She felt exposed.

'Come in!' His voice sounded thin over the intercom, almost drowned out by the barking. 'Calm down, Soprano!'

There was a blur of brown as the front door opened and his giant dog bounded down the drive, flinging itself at the gate in a flurry of fur, teeth and spittle. Anthony followed it.

'Soprano! Get down! Get down, you silly bastard!' The landscaper stuck his fingers in his mouth and whistled, but if that was meant to be a command for the dog to retreat, Soprano hadn't been paying attention in dog-training class. 'Don't worry, love. He's harmless.'

Bev had taken two steps back and was now staring in open-mouthed horror at the German Shepherd's snarling snout as it chewed the gate's bars; her handbag clasped over her chest, as though it might provide a protective barrier against the dog. She barely registered the presence of Jim Higson in the side alley between Anthony's house and the neighbouring property, craning his neck to spy over the fence on his nemesis. 'He doesn't look harmless.'

'Oh, he's a big soft shite. He'll get used to whoever gets the job.' Anthony grabbed his dog by the diamante studded collar and attached a lead. The dog immediately started to frolic around like a giant swing-ball, trying to break free of its bonds. 'Calm down, Soprano! No biccies for bad doggy.' He smacked the dog on the haunches and it finally came to heel, whimpering with its bushy tail between its legs.

'I'm Gail,' Bev said, feeling dread weigh her down as the gates swung inwards and she crossed the threshold. 'I'm here for the interview.'

'I know,' Anthony said, dragging his stubborn dog towards a large kennel that sat on perfectly manicured lawn to the side of the triple garaging block. 'Hang on . . .'

He waved her towards the front door. 'Let me get this soppy bastard tied up and I'll give you the guided tour of Chateau d'Antoine.'

So far, her prospective employer had barely looked at her, but Bev could feel Higson observing everything from his vantage point behind the fence. She noticed that there was a sizeable outbuilding on his side, abutting the boundary. Might that be Higson's piano workshop, she wondered?

Following a cacophony of barking and snarling, there was a further flash of fur. Soprano had escaped his master and had streaked back inside the sprawling house.

'Dog's a fucking nightmare,' Anthony said, finally sticking out his hand in greeting.

Bev shook it, wishing she could beat a retreat to the Morris Minor. But the gate clanged shut. She was trapped. 'It looks . . . healthy.'

'Aye. I should hope so. He costs me a fortune to feed. Fussy little bastard'll only eat best steak.' As they drew level with a pale blue Bentley Continental GT with the number plate, '2ToNE', he came to a standstill and turned to her. 'You're not allergic are you? To dogs.'

'No, no,' Bev said, already feeling her sinuses catch fire, though perhaps that was the wig. It had been a second-hand eBay acquisition, after all.

Inside, Bev couldn't be certain she hadn't entered a Premier League footballer's suburban palace. The white and grey marble floor in the hall gleamed beneath the light cast by a contemporary chandelier that hung in long crystal tracts from a double height ceiling. On closer examination, the grain in the marble wasn't just grey, it glittered! On the walls, a portrait of Anthony hung in a heavy gilt frame.

He posed in regal fashion on a purple and gold throne, wearing a tight T-shirt that showed off the musculature of his upper body and his tattoo sleeve in all its intricate glory. At his feet, Soprano sat – a picture of canine obedience.

She felt a giggle tickling the back of her throat. *Not now, silly cow!*

'Come on through to the kitchen,' Anthony shouted, pushing Soprano into a room on the other side of the grand staircase that rose in the middle of this opulent entrance hall to a galleried landing above.

'Landscaping's lucrative, then?' Bev said quietly, judging his taste in furnishings.

Following him to the back of the house, she found a kitchen that wouldn't be out of place in the palace of Versailles.

'Hand-made, this is,' Anthony said, describing the giant space with an ostentatious sweep of his arm. 'All of it. I've got a mate works for one of them top-end designer companies what the footballers use. He did this for me as a favour. All them scrolly bits are hand carved.'

'Bet they get dusty,' Bev said, eyeing the ornate, neo-classical columns either side of the range cooker. They clearly had no structural function. She turned to the lights. 'Your chandeliers could do with a damp cloth.'

'Aye. Well, that's why I want a cleaner. Mavis, me old cleaner . . . she's retired on me with bad kidneys.' He filled the kettle and flicked it on. 'Brew?' Pulled mugs out of the dishwasher and set them on the side. Gestured she should sit at one of the bar stools at the central island.

Bev nodded and took a seat, watching him prepare tea that looked like stout.

'Go on,' he said, pushing a mug towards her. 'Get your laughing gear round that. That'll put hairs on your chest.' He looked pointedly at her breasts.

Clasping her hand instinctively over her ample bosom, Bev felt herself colouring up. 'Damn it. I already shaved today.' *Jesus, woman! What are you doing? Don't engage in flirtatious banter with him. He's a bully and a psycho, if the Higsons are to be believed. Concentrate on proving that.*

But 2Tone wasn't aware of her internal monologue. He chuckled to himself. 'I like it.' Then, more seriously: 'You don't look like a cleaner to me.'

'Sorry?' Had Bev's disguise already been rumbled?

'Cleaners are usually whippet thin with hands like a navvy.'

Instinctively, she hid her hands beneath the granite worktop, almost glad that this stranger had treated her to a back-handed compliment about her hands, when Doc had poked fun at them. 'I wear rubber gloves and come from a long line of curvaceous women, what can I say?' She wanted to slap Bev the Coquette who kept surfacing beneath Gail, the cleaner's wig. 'Anyway, I've been at this house in Wilmslow for years. It's a big five-bedroomed Victorian place. The woman who owns it is a really fussy type, so everything has to be bang on.' As she spoke, she studied Anthony's face, trying to fathom the man behind the mahogany tan and stubble. On the morning she'd been run off the road by his colleague, he'd been dressed for work in the sort of rough garb she'd expect of a manual worker. Now, he was in designer casual gear and smelled of expensive aftershave. She could imagine him the sort of man who hosted fundraising dinner parties, however nouveau riche the established middle class might consider them. Was Jim Higson merely jealous of his neighbour?

'Do you do ironing?' Anthony asked. He knocked back his tea and set the cup carefully in the sink.

'Of course. I'm a belting ironer. I've been doing it since I was ten! I come from a big family,' she lied. 'Lots of bedding.'

'Catholic?' he asked unexpectedly.

'Yep.'

'Which church do you go to?'

She hadn't been prepared for this. Bev made a mental note not to embellish her story unnecessarily in future. She wracked her brains for a well-known Catholic church in North Manchester but could think of none. 'Lapsed. Too many years of being taught by nuns. You know how it is.'

Her potential employer smirked. 'Oh, aye. Say no more. Listen, I need the number of the Wilmslow woman so I can have a quick natter. All right?' He pushed a notepad towards her and offered her a gold pen.

In answer, Bev pulled an envelope out of her handbag. She offered it to him. 'I've got a written reference right here. If you're happy, I could start tomorrow.'

Anthony waved it away. 'I prefer to do things personal, like.'

She nodded. Slipped the envelope back into her bag, wondering if the landscaper's literacy wasn't up to much or if he was perhaps dyslexic.

'You don't want me talking to your old boss, do you? Are you hiding something?' He cocked his head to the side and grinned at her. Winked. 'Did you get caught nicking?'

'No!' Despite the fact that she was lying through her teeth, being wrongly accused of anything was a trigger, since Rob's sadistic slander had stripped her of everything. 'I most certainly did not. I'm a very honest person. You just sounded keen on the phone and, let's face it, this place is lovely.'

'It's Chateau d'Antoine. Of course it's lovely. Only the best in my house.'

'Yeah, whatever. But it could still do with a good tubbing. When was the last time you had your floor mopped?' *Can it, Bev. Are you trying to self-sabotage this interview, for God's sake?*

He pushed the pad towards her again. 'Do me a solid. I prefer phone calls and face to face than letters. Anyone can write and print out a letter. I like to know who I'm dealing with. I'm good at reading people. Really good.'

He stared into Bev's eyes with an intensity that almost forced her to look away. Could he hear her heart, clanging raggedly inside her? Could he sense her dishonesty? In the other room, she could hear the dog start to bark. Had it sniffed out her façade?

'Hey up, you've set our Soprano off. That dog can smell bullshit a mile off. You're not bullshitting me, are you, Gail?'

Clutching her bag, she stood up, the blood rushing to her head. Taking the job was nothing but an investigative ploy, but if she was to be in this idiot's house for any length of time, she couldn't let him treat her like this.

'Forget it. I'm happy to give you references, but you can't—'

He laughed heartily. All the menace had gone from his voice now. 'Sit down! Sit down! I'm having you on. Sorry, love.'

Bluff it, or you're blown, Bev counselled herself. Willing her hand not to shake, she wrote Doc's number down. 'Here you go. I've got nothing to hide.'

Her business partner had better start practicing his falsetto. She prayed 2Tone wouldn't call Doc before she'd had chance to warn him that a stellar performance was required.

'Come on. Let me give you the guided tour,' Anthony said.

'Shouldn't you do that once you've decided I'm right for the job?'

'See what you're letting yourself in for,' he said, leading the way back into the hall. 'How do you know you can trust me? He-he.'

Was that a smile or a sneer?

He took her behind the grand staircase and opened a door that led down to a dark basement. Switching a light on that didn't make the place any more inviting, he ushered Bev to the top of a steep, narrow staircase. 'After you.'

Bev swallowed hard. 'I don't really like—'

Anthony unexpectedly barked in her face, emulating a rabid dog, setting Soprano off yet again. He guffawed when she winced. 'Are you worried I bite?'

She shook her head. Put her hand in her pocket, wondering if she'd be able to speed-dial Doc.

He placed his hand on the small of her back. 'Go on, then. After you.'

CHAPTER 10

Bev

'I'm sorry,' Bev said, shrinking away from Anthony's touch. 'I'd rather you went first. And I'm not comfortable with . . . you know. Touchy feely . . . or being in enclosed spaces with strange men. You understand, right?'

Screw him. If 'Gail's' prospective employer didn't like it, Bev would revert to trying to photograph any wrongdoing from a distance. And balls to Higson. He might never get the result he wanted, but she was not about to endanger herself with a man who had a reputation as a bully-boy – however spurious. She'd learned her lesson with the Fitzwilliam case, where she'd narrowly escaped being attacked and killed on more than one occasion. And now, the cold sweat that ran down her back, the adrenalin that coursed around her body were both telling her that Anthony's behaviour was off.

'Jesus! I was only going to show you the utility area,' he said, holding his hands up. 'Start at the bottom and work our way up.'

There was an awkward moment where they stood facing one another at the top of the narrow stairs. Standing too close together and almost the same height. So close that Bev could see a fleck of red in his left eye and the beginnings of white cholesterol rings around his dark blue irises. Run for it or play along at great risk?

'Budge over, then,' he finally said, pushing past her and hastening down the steps himself. 'There's a proper laundry down here. I'm telling you, I could set up professional. Come and look. No funny business. I promise. You mustn't worry, love. I'm spoken for.'

He seemed sincere. Tentatively, against her better judgement, Bev climbed down to discover a subterranean network of well-furnished, well-lit rooms, including a home cinema, games room – complete with full-sized snooker table and bar – a pump room where the filtration equipment for his swimming pool was housed, and finally, an impeccably well-equipped utility room with an industrial sized top-loading washing machine, together with a giant tumble dryer. None of it impressed Bev, but she realised her alter-ego, Gail, would love it.

'Have you robbed a laundrette?' She grinned. Ran a hand over the washing machine, clicking her tongue against the roof of her mouth. 'This is state of the art gear.'

'Told you it was like professional. Hey! Nothing but the best in my house. I graft too hard to settle for shite what'll break after five minutes.'

'Do you open up the tumble dryer and find a meth lab underneath it?' she said, nervously cackling in a way she imagined Gail might do.

He looked momentarily puzzled. Frowning. His body-language stiffened suddenly. 'What do you mean? Is that some money-laundering joke? I'm straight as a die, me.' He poked his thumb into his chest for emphasis.

'No, no, no! I wasn't having a pop at you. It's *Breaking Bad*, isn't it?' she explained. 'The telly series about the . . . You not seen it?'

He shook his head. The frown gave way to visible relief. 'I don't get to watch much telly. I like old war films and that.' He sniffed and turned back to the staircase. 'Come on, then. I'll show you upstairs.'

The rest of the interview passed without incident, but Bev was relieved to climb back into the Morris.

Her hands shook violently as she tried to get the key into the ignition. Her clutch leg was bouncing involuntarily at such speed that she stalled three times before she managed to get the engine running.

'Keep your head down. I don't want anybody to see you,' she told Doc in the passenger seat. She waved to Anthony who was standing in a bedroom window, smiling at her.

In the neighbouring house, Penny Higson looked out from her living room window as she cleaned the glass with a duster, perhaps unaware that her husband, Jim, was once again craning his neck to see what was going on in the otherwise dead cul-de-sac.

'Let's get the hell out of here,' she said, kangarooing to the junction. 'This place is like Village of the bloody Damned.'

'Well, what did you make of him?' Doc asked, closing the lid to his laptop.

Out of the corner of her eye, Bev could see that the complexion of her business partner had paled to a sickly off-green. 'Don't puke in Sandra's car.'

'You drive like an animal,' he said, wiping the condensation from the windscreen with his sleeve.

Bev pulled off the wig and was suddenly no longer downtrodden domestic goddess, Gail. She scratched at her hot sweaty scalp. 'That's going to do my head in if he gives me the job. I hate wigs!'

'Well? Is he the ogre Higson's making out?' Doc started breathing in through his nose and out through his mouth dramatically, presumably trying to quell his nausea.

'The jury's out, for now. He just seems like a harmless knob.' Bev replayed all that had come to pass in the landscaper's house, opting to head uphill for the M62 rather than face the hairpin bends that led in winding fashion down to the ring road encompassing Manchester. Doc didn't look like he could cope with the shorter route. 'He has no control over his arsehole of a dog. He's a *terrible* show-off with *shocking* taste but . . . I'm guessing he's come from nothing and has made every penny through hard work. He's allowed to show off! I reckon he's maybe dyslexic. Thinking about it, the only real reason I got freaked out in there was down to the stuff the Higsons accused him of . . . oh, and his workmate running me off the road, which I can hardly blame Anthony for. Maybe the twat driving the van would have tailgated me anyway, even if he'd been driving alone.' She shrugged. '2Tone's a loudmouth, for sure. I don't know. Maybe he's a bit deaf!' She barely registered the glorious undulating countryside spread out before them and lit by an early sunset as she descended from the moors towards the grey urban sprawl of north Manchester; wind turbines turning slowly on the distant horizon beyond Bury like the grinding wheels of divine justice. 'I won't get the measure of him properly until I can somehow get on the inside. Just brace yourself to be Shirley Dawson from Wilmslow. OK?'

Doc belched quietly. 'I get all the plum jobs.'

'Stop whingeing. At least nobody's asking you to scrub toilets.'

'Nobody's asking you!' He opened his laptop lid, then shut it immediately, clutching at his stomach.

'If you're going to do a job, do it properly, Doc. Remember what I've got riding on making this business work. What did you find out about 2Tone's financial affairs, then? Did you get in?'

Nodding very slowly, Doc finally treated her to a weak smile. He stretched his long stonewashed denim-clad legs into the passenger footwell of the car. 'Course I did! I'm a pro. And 2Tone's got absolutely sod all in terms of cyber security know-how. He had all his passwords and pins for banking saved in a Word document with no password or pin! Dimwit.'

'And?' Bev's pulse was finally calming now that she saw signs for the Trafford Centre and the 50 mile-per-hour speed limit came into force by the Prestwich turn-off. Almost home.

'He's clean as a whistle, superficially. I found a PDF of his latest company accounts and VAT returns. He pays his tax. No overdraft. No mortgage. I checked Companies House. His business has hardly any assets listed – a few grand. That's it. I'll guess that's machinery and vehicles. But that's not unusual for a landscaping company.'

'How would you know? Since when were you an expert on all things landscaping?'

Doc grinned. 'Are you forgetting my horticultural pedigree, Beverley?'

Bev snorted with derisory laughter. 'What? A weed farm in your loft?'

'There's nothing I don't know about cultivating exotic crops in a hothouse environment.'

'You're full of shit.'

'Look, his accounts compare to similar businesses in the North West. He's clearly loaded. I'll bet he's got all kinds of cash-in-hand fiddles going, but that's why you're trying to get this job, isn't it?'

At that point, Doc's phone rang, blasting the fuggy interior of the old Morris with an ear-splitting snippet of Iron Maiden.

Bev glanced over at his phone's display as Doc held the device away from his body like it was radioactive. 'It's him,' she said, feeling excitement and dread churning in her gut. 'You're Shirley. Don't screw it up.'

Doc pressed the green button. 'Speaking.' He spoke in a soft falsetto.

Not daring to look at him, Bev imagined she were a stranger on the other end. Might Doc be sufficiently convincing?

'Yes. That's right. Gail. Oh, she's such a good worker. I'm absolutely gutted that she's off to pastures new.'

He sounded like a heavy smoker with a slightly deeper voice, but to the uninitiated, he was definitely a middle-aged woman. Bev treated herself to a relieved smile, though her face was so tense, she was surprised her skin didn't crack.

'Honest as the day is long. Yes. A little belter. You should see the elbow grease she uses on my silverware. Her ironing's spot on too.'

Doc knew she hated ironing. And she'd never polished so much as a candlestick in her life. Bastard.

When he ended the call, she reached over and squeezed his arm. 'Wow. What a bloody performance, our Shirley. You even got the accent spot on. Just enough posh. Just enough northern!'

Doc placed a warm clammy hand on top of hers. 'He sounded satisfied.'

Bev withdrew her hand quickly, slamming it back onto the old wooden steering wheel. 'Yeah well. We'll see.'

CHAPTER 11
Bev

Three days later, Bev had still not heard from Anthony about the job. She was going to have to reconsider how to gather intelligence on her target. As she buttered toast for Hope's breakfast, she rehearsed what she might say to Jim Higson at their first catch-up meeting regarding her progress.

Well, Mr Higson. I've managed to get a lot of photographic evidence of Anthony in a beanie hat before sunrise. And I have anecdotal proof that his dog is psychotic and that Anthony prefers women who pump iron.

Hardly impressive. Maybe Doc was right. Perhaps she'd been wrong to take on this job, after all.

'Mum-Mum,' Hope said, flinging her arms around Bev's waist. 'You're putting too much Marmite on the toast. I don't like it when it's that thick!'

Bev closed her eyes and shook her head. 'Sorry, love. You're right. I'm in another world.' She kissed her daughter's hair, drinking in the scent of her coconut shampoo. 'You get sat down and drink your tea. I'll sort this out.' She started to scrape the Marmite off the offending piece of toast, absently smearing the excess onto a second slice.

Once Hope was satisfied and tucking into her breakfast, Bev made a tuna and mayonnaise sandwich and put it together with some dried fruit and crackers into Hope's rucksack, making a mental note to stitch up the two large holes that had appeared at the bottom.

'You're carrying way too much crap in this bag, young lady,' she said, leafing through the contents. 'It's bad for your posture to be carting this much weight around. No wonder there's holes.' She was just about to zip the bag back up when she felt something hard and silky. She pulled it into view from beneath an overstuffed pencil case. 'A four pack of Wispas? Who gave you this?'

Hope shrugged, nonchalantly chewing away. 'Teacher,' she said.

'For good classwork? They shouldn't be rewarding that with sugary rubbish. It's bad for your teeth. And you've got lovely pegs. Which teacher was it? I think I need to have a word.'

'It's this supply teacher, and she says she knows—'

'Don't talk with your mouth full,' Bev said, holding up her hand and wrinkling her nose. 'I don't need to see your chewed up toast, thanks. It's like dirty old sheets going round in a washing machine . . .'

Bev's mind was whirring like an overtaxed fan inside an old laptop. She was so beset by mothering and professional concerns that she jumped when Gail's burner finally rang. Jogging to her empty office, she answered the call just before it went to voicemail.

'Oh, is Gail there?' Anthony Anthony, of course, sounding decidedly serious, bordering on stern.

'Hiya. It is Gail. Speaking.' Bev bit her lip, feeling like she was on the cusp of something ill-advised.

'Good. Listen, you and me . . . we really need to have a little chat.'

Shit. This sounded bad. Was it possible that her target had uncovered something damning about the fictitious cleaner, Gail, over the course of the last two days? Had Mrs Nosy Slippers, the neighbour, shared information about a woman in a VW Polo who had been taking photos of his house? Perhaps he'd put two and two together . . .

Bev chuckled nervously. 'You make it sound like I'm in trouble.'

'Oh, you are, you cheeky bastard.'

No, no, no! Bev thought. I've blown my cover and killed the case before it even started. I'm jinxed.

'Only joking!' he said brightly. 'You've got the job.'

Feeling her knees on the brink of giving way, Bev exhaled deeply. 'When I didn't hear from you, I—'

'Yeah. Sorry I didn't get back to you. I got busy with work, like. Anyway, when can you start?'

Bev pressed her hand to her chest. Was she ready to potentially walk into the lion's den? 'Let me check my calendar and I'll give you a tinkle back. All right?'

'Aye. In a bit.' He hung up.

Holding the phone with a shaking hand, Bev padded to the front door as the post was being pushed through the letterbox. There on the mat she spied a brown envelope and a white envelope. She picked them up. They were both addressed to her. One from the local council and the other showing the branding of Rob's solicitor in the corner. Neither could conceivably contain good news.

Silently now, but for the thudding of her heartbeat and the rush of blood in her ears, she made her way back to the kitchen and set her post down onto the worktop. Filled the kettle and studied the offending envelopes from a safe distance. 'Go and brush your teeth when you've finished brekky,' she told Hope.

Hope rose from the little table, hugged her and skipped off to the shower room, leaving Bev alone with the dreaded post.

She opted to open Rob's solicitor's letter with trembling fingers. 'What the hell does he want now?' Unfolded the crisp legal letterhead. Scanned the text.

> . . . *It has come to our attention that Hope's living accommodation at the offices of your business, 'Beverley Saunders, Private Investigations' are inadequate and unsafe for a child . . . furthermore, the nature of your work with its unsociable hours and the risk to which you are personally exposed is considered inappropriate for . . .*

'Not again. He's trying it on *again*. Petty, petty bastard won't just lay down and die.'

But there was nobody there to sympathise. Doc was presumably still asleep in his own office after a late night spent trawling for evidence of misdeeds through Anthony Anthony's email correspondence with his business contacts and clients.

Bev wondered then if this unpredictable career path she'd chosen would stand in the way of her obtaining full custody of her daughter. She *was* constantly risking her safety. She *did* sit on overnighters, watching her persons of interest. Was Anthony Anthony any different? Was it not feasible that, if the man was ogre enough to drive his neighbours to pay a professional to dig up dirt, where superficially he seemed made from Teflon, he was dangerous?

'I'm throwing in the towel on the Anthony case.' She said it out loud, as though that would make her decision more legitimate and final.

Resolute, she thumbed out a text on Gail's burner phone.

Something come up. Not able to take cleaning job after all. Soz. Gail.

Then, feeling the lino beneath her sucking her down, down, down along with her sinking mood, she opened the dreaded brown envelope. It was a council tax bill. A massive overdue council tax bill. And she had no way of paying it.

Kicking the kitchen cupboard door in frustration and wiping angry tears from her cheeks, she thumbed out another text to Anthony.

Forget last text. Kid sister messing about with phone. Am fine to start Wednesday. Gail.

She may be walking into the lion's den, but what choice did she have?

CHAPTER 12
Bev

'Here's the keys,' her new employer said, thrusting an unsavoury-looking rabbit's foot keyring towards her, containing at least seven keys.

Anthony Anthony looked harassed at 6.15 a.m. Barely making eye contact with Bev, he scratched beneath his black beanie with a rough finger. Jumped when the idiot who had forced her into the ditch honked his horn.

'Ta,' Bev said, clutching her bucket. She noticed the curtains at the Higsons' twitching. Prayed they wouldn't recognise her. At least the Morris Minor couldn't be traced to her. She wouldn't put it past Jim Higson to ask her to look into who owned it. 'Anything in particular you want doing today?'

'I've left a list in the kitchen,' Anthony said, gesturing to his colleague that he was on his way. 'Listen.' He finally met her gaze. 'How do you fancy earning a bit extra?'

Bev frowned, searching the landscaper's expression for clues as to what was coming next. 'What do you mean?'

'I've got a fundraiser on Saturday. Dinner for twenty. I need a waitress. Wondered if you fancied giving it a go. The agency I normally use buggered up my booking, so I'm up shit creek. It's just wandering round, topping up drinks and dishing out the grub and that. I'll pay you time and half, seeing it's short notice.'

'I'll have to get a babysitter. That costs,' Bev said, making a swift mental calculation and realising that she stood the chance of earning enough to buy almost thirty minutes of her family solicitor's time or a chunk of her council tax bill. Perhaps she was in the wrong line of work. 'Make it double and you've got a deal.'

'Hurry up, you wanker!' came a gruff voice from the driver's side of the Mercedes Sprinter van.

Beneath the yellow glow of the streetlight outside Anthony's house, Bev got a glimpse for the first time of the oaf that had nearly caused her death. He was a stockily built man in his forties, maybe, who looked like he had rolled straight out of a nightclub and into the van. Unshaven, with a broken nose – he put her in mind of the cartoon character, Desperate Dan. Like Anthony, he wore a beanie, except his was a Manchester City one, judging by the badge and the colours. The temptation to march back down the drive and punch him on his square jaw was strong. She was aware of a rush of adrenaline coursing around her body. Gripping her bucket full of cleaning products, she hoped that Anthony wouldn't see her hands shaking.

He was too busy with his compatriot. 'Shut your gob, you fat bastard. I'm coming.' Under his breath he muttered, 'Dickhead.' Turned to Bev and smiled. 'Double. Aye. All right. Make sure you get my best shirts all nice and starched like in the dry cleaners. My beds all want changing. I've put bedding out. There's biscuits in a tin on the side. Help yourself.'

Turning his back on her, he marched to the waiting van so quickly that Bev had no time to ask him what his arrangements with the dog were. Even if she shouted after him, he wouldn't hear her. He was too engrossed in a loud exchange of manly insults with Desperate Dan. Then, with a slam of the passenger door and a rev of the engine, they were gone.

Bev could feel Jim Higson's eyes on her. Sure enough, the moment the Sprinter had left the cul-de-sac, the side-door to the Higsons' house opened and Bev could make out the slightly hunched silhouette of her latest client. Pulling the fringe of her wig down as low as possible over her face, she fumbled with the key in the lock of Anthony's front door, desperate to get inside fast.

'Excuse me!' Higson was already standing by the six foot fence, strangely a full head and shoulders taller than it. Was he perched on a box or a planter? 'You there! Hello!'

Finally, Bev opened the door, hastened inside and slammed it behind her. The last thing she needed was Jim Higson blowing her cover and ruining his own job.

Her relief was fleeting. The cacophony of barking reminded her that there were worse things than interfering middle-aged neighbours. There was Soprano. The dog bounded into view – a blur of fur and barred teeth.

'Sit!' Bev bellowed, praying the dog would somehow remember she'd been in the house before at the invitation of its owner. She flattened herself against the door, barely aware of the letterbox cover biting into her back.

Soprano leaped up at her, pressing its paws into her shoulders – adult human height on its hind legs. Bev clenched her eyes shut against the deafening barking. Opened her left eye a crack to spy a salivating maw full of fangs and blackened gums. Waiting for the crazed hound to bite her, every terrifying childhood memory of being attacked by the neighbour's dog flooded back: five-year-old Bev, standing in the back yard of the red brick two-up, two-down she'd called home. Her mother had been too pissed to intervene. She'd just watched the spectacle from the safety of the back room, shouting advice through the window as she daubed at her canvas and chugged a triple V&T.

Drinking in the acrid pong of Soprano's doggy breath, Bev searched her memory frantically for pearls of wisdom that might calm the dog down. Should she stick her finger up its rectum? No. That was when a pit bull's jaws locked on and wouldn't let go. Could she punch the giant German Shepherd or otherwise clock it over the head with her cleaning bucket? Possibly. Then, she remembered Anthony's words and the timbre of his voice in that rolling Pennine accent.

'Get down, you silly bastard!'

Almost as if the dog had been caught by surprise, it stopped barking at the sound of its owner's words coming out of a stranger's mouth.

'Get down, you soppy shite!' Bev yelled again in a baritone, advancing into the dog's space and pushing at its paws. Her heart thundered in her chest almost to breaking point, but finally, Soprano whimpered and retreated to the dining room doorway, cowering with its tail between its legs. Growling intermittently, though there was no real menace there.

Finally, Bev was left to explore the house unencumbered. The place was already tidy. Only the dust and dog hair bore testament to weeks without a cleaner, and dealing with dust and dog hair wasn't Bev's strong point. She made straight for the fifth bedroom, which doubled as Anthony's office. Found nothing apart from half-empty, unlocked filing cabinets full of divorce paperwork and the odd bank statement. If Anthony had dirt to hide, he wasn't hiding it in his office. The file that contained his divorce court order revealed that his wife had kicked him out for infidelity some seven years earlier. He had kept the family home but had given her a portfolio containing three semi-detached houses that he had seemingly built and which he'd rented out.

'So you don't just make people's gardens pretty, do you, 2Tone?' Bev said, kneeling on the springy carpet, rifling through the bottom drawer full of photographs of the ex-Mrs Anthony. Many were still in their frames. Mrs Anthony, flashing her gym-honed guns in her sequinned skin-tight wedding dress, looking like Jodie Marsh had morphed with Katie Price in some warped cosmetic surgeon's experiment. Mr and Mrs Anthony, posing with flutes of champagne in some palm-tree-studded resort. Blue skies, dazzling white smiles. Bev was sure if she sniffed the photos, she'd smell freshly minted new money.

'What a pair! Talk about plastic bloody fantastic.'

Bev's legs, folded beneath her, had gone dead. She stood up, propping herself on the corner of the filing cabinet, waiting for the inevitable pins and needles as the blood returned to her bottom half. She needed a break.

Walking to the window of the office, she looked out at the side garden and just beyond the tall fence that demarcated the border between Anthony's and Higson's land. There was Jim Higson, standing on an uppermost rung of a ladder leaned against his wooden workshop. On the roof of the workshop, which was covered in thick, florid green moss, he'd placed a black plastic gardening trug. He wore gardening gloves on his hands. Clearly, Higson wanted any casual observer to think he was engaged in a simple act of property maintenance. But it seemed to be a ruse. Higson only had eyes for Anthony's house. Squinting, he seemed to be peering in through the kitchen window below.

'Nosy old bastard's trying to get a good look at me, I'll bet,' Bev muttered, backing away from the window as Higson shifted his attentions to Anthony's first floor.

*

Anthony's house was labyrinthine in layout, with its numerous reception rooms and vast bedrooms, opening into large en suites and smaller dressing rooms – reminiscent of a Russian doll that revealed its ever-shrinking doppelgangers with a twist of its wooden belly.

It was time for Gail, the cleaner, to do a little cleaning. Dragging the vacuum and a stack of clean bedlinen from one cluster of tastelessly appointed accommodation to another, Bev understood why Anthony wanted a cleaner's services four times per week. Though it had sounded like overkill, with her non-existent domestic prowess, it might not prove enough. She could spend an entire day just changing beds.

By the time she'd dusted all the furniture badly and rifled fruitlessly through the almost empty drawers, it had already got to 11.00 a.m.

'He's going to sack me when he sees how little I've done,' she said, starting to strip the bedding from the master bed.

Wondering what had come to pass in each of the beds, she had to face carrying the dirty laundry down to the giant, creepy basement that whirred and whined with the pool heating and filtration mechanism.

Once she'd loaded the industrial-sized washing machine and set a hot wash, Bev gravitated back up to Anthony's office and the filing cabinet full of photos of his past. Within moments, she was utterly engrossed again, studying the faces in the wedding group shots with friends and family, wondering what their stories were.

The knock on the front door made her jump.

It was insistent, accompanied by several rings on the doorbell. Bing bong, bing bong, bing bong. Thump, thump, thump.

'Shitting Nora,' she said, hastily shoving the photos away. 'He's back.'

Advancing to the window, she tried to see who was at the front door. No sign of Anthony. Though it then occurred to her that he would simply have let himself in with his own key.

Standing on the galleried landing, she watched the dog barking and snarling in a frenzy, hurling itself against the front door. She quietly descended the stairs in search of a better vantage point. Sneaking on her hands and knees, lest the visitor see her, she crossed the hall. Soprano was no longer interested in her. He only had saliva and doggy ill-intent for the lunatic who was close to hammering down the door.

Bev slapped her hand to her mouth when she peered through the dining room window and saw that Jim Higson was standing on the doorstep. He couldn't possibly know that the woman in the terrible blonde wig, carrying a Vileda bucket full of cleaning products was her. Could he?

'What a pain in the arse,' she whispered under her breath.

Higson looked her way. She ducked below the sill, her heart pounding. Suddenly, Soprano decided that that was the moment at which to launch a fresh attack on her. With a salivating dog pawing at her and Higson peering through the window only feet above, Bev wished Doc was on hand to come to her aid. Why the hell had she thought going undercover was a good idea? Had she learned nothing from her last case?

'I can see you, you know,' Higson shouted through the glass. 'Come to the door! I want a word.'

CHAPTER 13
Bev

'What's with all the cloak and dagger?' Jim Higson asked, sitting down at the sticky table in the pub in Milnrow. 'Why did we have to meet here? Why couldn't you have come to my house?' He sipped from his pint of ale, leaving a thin moustache of foam on his upper lip. Sat bolt upright in his chair, as though whatever was left of his musculature was supported by a broom handle, shoved right up his rectum.

Bev ran a finger around the rim of her lime and soda. Wondering why her new client had called an, 'emergency task meeting', as he'd referred to it on the phone. She'd successfully waited it out beneath Anthony's dining room window when he'd been peering in. He'd shouted through the glass that he could see her, but had he merely been bluffing in a bid to get the mysterious new cleaner to reveal herself? Or did he know that his own Private Investigator was, in fact, Gail, the well-scrubbed scrubber in a badly bleached wig? Perhaps he was about to sack her for some petty reason. Bev had him pegged as the sort of man who found fault with everything – even his own choices.

'I'm in the middle of covert operations,' Bev said. 'Surveillance and background research. That's what you're paying me for.'

'I've not noticed you on the cul-de-sac.'

'Good. That means I'm doing my job properly. Listen, the last thing I need is our person of interest seeing my car outside your house and realising what you're up to.' The tangle of anxiety in her gut was telling her that she needed to put herself in a position of strength. She pulled the cowl of her old funnel-necked jumper up to her chin. 'You don't want to get done for harassment, do you?'

Jim pressed his lips together. 'Couldn't you have picked somewhere more upmarket?' he asked, sneering slightly at the swirling carpet.

'Does it matter?' Bev started to breathe more easily. Maybe the gut-wrenching tension was the generalised guilt she carried with her at all times like an EpiPen or a rape alarm. Maybe it was a hangover from Rob's crappy solicitor's letter. It was clear Higson wasn't about to confront her about going undercover as Anthony's cleaner. 'OK, Jim. We're here now. What was so urgent that we couldn't talk over the phone? How can I help?'

Her client straightened his slacks with precise pianist's fingers. 'I wanted a face-to-face update. I wanted to know what you've got on Anthony.'

'It's only been a week.'

'My situation is desperate. He's got one of those fund-raising dos tomorrow night.'

'How do you know?'

He looked around the empty pub as if assessing the possibility of the bar staff or another customer being spies. Dropped his voice to a near-whisper. 'I saw the vintners delivering booze. It's the same every time. The booze gets dropped on a Thursday. Means there's one of his blasted parties coming on the Saturday. We told you about them, didn't we?' He squeezed his eyes shut momentarily and breathed in sharply. 'They're intolerable.'

Bev nodded. 'I'll be keeping tabs on him, Jim. Don't you worry. If there's incriminating dirt to be found, I'll find it. My digital-intelligence partner hasn't uncovered any wrongdoing yet. His business accounts are in order. He seems reasonably well-regarded in the local community.'

Jim's craggy brow furrowed. His shoulders drooped. He cocked his head and when the angle of the light changed, the dark circles beneath his eyes were accentuated. 'Smoke and mirrors,' he said. 'They don't know the half of it. See a bear in his own den before you judge him.'

'We're still getting a feel for him,' Bev said. She sipped her lime and soda, wishing she had a bone to throw this hangdog man. 'You need concrete evidence of anti-social or illegal behaviour to take to the police or something that will stand up in a civil case.'

He nodded enthusiastically, suddenly perking up.

'Well, *you* haven't been able to pin anything on him in a decade and you live next door to him, so . . . Bear with me. These things can take a little time. If people have dark secrets, they usually take the trouble to make sure they're well-hidden. Let's see what Saturday brings. I'm a professional, Jim.' She pictured him, staring in through 2Tone's dining-room window; refusing to take no for an answer. 'Take a step back. Leave it to me.'

CHAPTER 14
Bev

The prospect of waitressing after hours at Chateau d'Antoine was both nerve-wracking and exhilarating. 2Tone had since texted her with the waitress' dress code for the evening.

Ware summat shrot n blak

Bev would be forced to wear the itching wig and glasses if she was to keep up the façade that she was Gail, but the demand for a little black number meant that her downtrodden alter-ego was due a makeover.

With her newly red-raw cleaner's hands, Bev fixed herself a single G & T and started the transformation.

Her clothes rack, concealed in the store cupboard along with her origami hoard, had little hanging from it. She picked out the only little black number she owned. Far lower cut than was appropriate for a professional waitress, this is what Bev had worn to the XS club after she and Rob had split.

Holding her stomach in, she tried to tug it up over her hips and bottom.

'Jesus!' she muttered, glancing in the mirror at the roll of flesh that sat on top of the bagel of unyielding material. 'This is a damn sight easier to peel off than pull on.'

At least, if she continued to clean Anthony Anthony's house for another few weeks, she might lose some of the weight she'd gained, post-divorce. Finally, after almost wrenching her arm out of its socket, she pulled the mini velvet number over her large bosom.

'What the hell do I look like? What am I doing?'

She was tempted to ask Doc if her bum looked big in the dress, but checking her reflection in the cheap full-length mirror she'd pilfered from Sophie's garage when she'd been living in her basement flat, she already knew the answer.

With her make-up subtly applied and the wig in place, Bev regarded herself as Gail.

'Better.'

From the neck up, she looked demure and at least twice as attractive as she had with a well-scrubbed face. From the neck down, she looked like an overweight working girl who'd drawn the short straw in a shoplifting spree in Primark. It would have to do.

The slimline tonic from her gin mingled with the butterflies in her stomach as she drove into the Pennines behind the wheel of Sandra's old car – flats on her feet; stripper platform heels in her holdall.

When Anthony answered the door, he looked more like the photos she'd seen of him in the local paper – dressed in an expensive-looking T and jeans, with those sleeves of tattoos on show like exotic living exhibits in a pop-up gallery. Peonies, cranes and . . . Soprano. It was the strangest ink she'd ever seen. But he wasn't aware of her judgemental gaze. He seemed distracted.

'Good. You're on time. Did you park on the other side of the cul-de-sac? Good. Fuck the neighbours. I need the space for my mates. Come in. Let me show you what's what.'

He ushered her through to the kitchen. The work surfaces were bedecked with silver catering trays of food, covered in cling film.

'Right. There's canapes.' He pronounced the word as can-apes instead of can-a-pays. It was hard to glean from the rapid-fire of his instructions if he'd done that knowingly or not. 'So, don't take the covers off those 'til people are here and mingling. Right? Get 'em leathered on some Tattinger.' He waved his hand in the direction of cases of Tattinger champagne that were stacked high in the corner. 'Then give 'em the canapes. Over there . . .' He pointed to the worktops closest to his range cooker, sandwiched between those neo-classical pilasters. '. . . That's the main meal what wants heating through. Coq au thingy. I can't remember. Summat involving cock. Ha ha. The caterers have done everything, and I mean everything. No expense spared. This is a five-course dinner for twenty of my mates and they've all got deep pockets and long arms. They've forked out £300 a head to sit at my table before they've even walked through the door, so it has to be reet. It's all about raising money for them kids.' He was blinking hard and barely pausing for breath. Clearly amped over the impending arrival of his guests. 'Oh, and you did a good job on getting the place straight, so ta. But your ironing's a bit shit. Try to—'

The doorbell chimed, mercifully interrupting her employer's gift of ironing wisdom to the domestically incompetent. Bev could hear Soprano barking in his kennel, stationed in the front garden. *I bet Jim Higson's loving that noise,* she mused.

As Anthony greeted his guests, she took out the first bottle of champagne. It was already cold. Never a dab hand with fizz, even during her marketing years in London, where she'd cracked open many a bottle of prosecco to celebrate the successful launch of one of BelNutrive's latest cod-science health products, she almost ripped her fingertips off as she popped the cork.

From the kitchen, she could hear gruff voices.

'Come here, you luscious little bastard. If I wasn't straight, I'd be having you right up the arse.'

'Dan the man. I hope your lovely missus here has brought her spare pair of travel-balls, cos I'm gonna grab you by the knackers later and squeeze you dry in the name of charity, you tight bastard.'

Bev timorously stepped into the hall to see Anthony in an embrace with a man almost a foot taller than him.

'Get a drink down you, Danny Boy.'

Anthony thrust empty champagne flutes, which were standing to attention on the console table in the hall, into his first guests' hands. Bev charged the glasses with Tattinger, smiling coyly when Dan did a double take of her chest, clearly to his wife's chagrin. Irritated that she had made such an error with the stupid tight dress, Bev momentarily ducked into the kitchen and flung a large linen napkin over her shoulder, partially obscuring her eye-popping décolletage.

Once people's glasses were filled, Bev stepped back to accommodate and observe the rapid influx of guests into the hall. Her interest was piqued by a tall, arresting-looking man with a craggy face and shaven head, who disappeared quickly off into the kitchen. She felt an unexpected thrill of sexual anticipation. *Concentrate, you unprofessional berk!*

Under close inspection, Bev assessed that Anthony's guests were almost exclusively working class made good. The women looked at least ten years younger than the men and Instagram-ready – complete with long red talons, boob jobs and collagen lip implants or whatever it was they did to themselves to get that ludicrous trout-pout. Apart from a brassy redhead whom she complimented on her stiletto shoes, they were almost exclusively blonde, their cheeks daubed with the telltale shades-of-mahogany-and-white stripes from a Kardashian-style contouring kit. Their wardrobes looked to be an unsubtle blend of Michael Kors and New Look, because some habits clearly died hard. The men were almost all balding with shaved heads and dressed in designer jeans and clinging Ts, like Anthony. Bev tried to eavesdrop on their conversation.

'Yeah, well my Tesla's being delivered next week.'

'A fucking Tesla, you big poof? You wanna get yourself an Overfinch like mine. Hey, did I tell you about this new job I landed last week? £2 million house in Bowdon for some Indian doctor. He bought the plot for half a mil. I made my own bloody price up, didn't I?'

'Jesus. Hey. You think that's good, Frank landed this job . . .'

The men – mainly working in the trades – were all about making money hand over fist from their middle-class clients. Given her own father had been a master tiler, knowing the disdain with which professionals generally regarded tradesmen, it made Bev smile to hear them talk about doctors and solicitors as if they'd been born stupid.

The women looked ladies of leisure whom Bev imagined spent their days in velour tracksuits or onesies with rollers in their hair and Uggs on their feet, toting giant handbags around Harvey Nicks whilst they dragged their work-worn Mams around clothes carousels that contained overpriced, unbecoming pieces the older women wouldn't let the dog sleep on. Manchester's shopping centre was full of such spectacles on any given day. And now, both genders had met in the grand marble entrance hall of Chateau d'Antoine, beneath the crystal chandelier that would have made the lighting in Buckingham Palace look decidedly B&Q. The women spoke to the women. The men exchanged raucous banter with the men. It was deafening. But amid the mayhem, one man sought out Bev and appeared at her side.

'Hello. My name's Archie,' he said. 'I'm Tony's right-hand man.'

It was the craggy-faced, tall man who had caught her eye earlier. Inspecting her new companion, Bev privately decided that with his broken nose and rugged features, he was ugly-hot. He had little in the way of hair, but beneath his tight top, she made out a well-honed torso. It took her only moments to check out his shapely and muscled lower portions that bulged in all the right places.

'I'm Gail,' she said. 'Top up?' She thrust the bottle towards his glass. Knew it was a mistake to speak to anyone there, let alone to allow one of 2Tone's workforce to chat her up. At least this wasn't the chump in the Sprinter who had run her off the road. Or perhaps it was, and he merely scrubbed up exceedingly well. She treated him to a dazzling smile, trying to encourage him to smile back and show his teeth. Sprinter Chump had had a mouth full of stumps like an extra from *Deliverance*. Or had he? It had been hard to tell in the pre-dawn darkness.

Archie's teeth were mediocre but stump-free. 'You're not his usual waitress. I hope he's paying you extra for coming in that dress. I wouldn't mind making you come in that dress.' He winked. 'You're good at popping corks.' He inclined his head towards the bottle but Bev could see he was looking at her rebellious, erect nipples, poking through her bra and the velvety fabric of her dress.

Bev looked down at the bottle of champagne, but now it felt like a cheap innuendo. 'I'm not the kind of girl to pop her cork so easily,' she found herself saying, despite her best efforts to walk away. She ran the tip of her tongue

106

coquettishly over her bottom lip. Pulled her glasses to the end of her nose and peered over the top like a suggestive school ma'am. It had been months since she'd last got laid. Living with Doc and having Hope stay over regularly had put paid to any sexual adventures. She suddenly felt the pressing need to scratch that itch. 'And you've got to be careful. If this stuff gets too warm or there's friction, it explodes everywhere.' *Shit. Just shut your mouth, you idiot! This is not a club!*

The loud tinkle of a fork being rapped against the side of a champagne flute mercifully disrupted the electricity between them. 2Tone was standing on the third step of the grand staircase, clearing his throat.

'Ladies and gents, let's move this into the billiards room, where you'll be served canapes and all that fancy posh shite.'

Bev made her excuses and repaired to the kitchen. The can-apes weren't going to serve themselves. She slammed the trays of ready-prepped dinner into the range's double ovens, praying she wouldn't burn them to a crisp. Fish fingers and chips and other 'brown food' had always been the extent of her culinary capabilities. Rob had been the one to cook when they'd entertained, skilled as the loathsome bastard was in preparing dishes from the four corners of the earth. Hardly surprising that she was a rotten cook, given the useless cow of a mother she'd had. It was amazing she'd ever reached adulthood, she reflected. Findus crispy pancakes and Fray Bentos pies.

'Do you need a hand with that?'

She turned round to find the owner of the man's voice – Archie. Under the bright light of the kitchen, she could see he was anything but a refined-looking man. His skin was ruddy and prematurely lined with large open pores like a man who spent all day in the elements. Perhaps he *had* rear-ended her into a ditch. But Bev imagined that body beneath the clothes again.

'If you like. Depends how good you are with your hands,' she said, turning around abruptly and grinning.

Was he watching her in the reflection of the shining tiled splashback? She could see him drawing close behind her; felt the heat of his body, pressed against hers now. He reached around to the worktop and snatched up a silver platter of tiny deep-fried eats. Backed away and was gone.

'Tease!' Bev said, raising an eyebrow.

Fleetingly, she wondered if this man genuinely found her attractive or did he merely take it for granted that making sexual advances towards the lowly paid help was acceptable sport? Admittedly, she had clearly been flirting with him. As Bev, at a party where they had been on an equal footing as guests, it would have been easy to close him down, had she wanted to – she was no stranger to pushing men away politely but firmly when they weren't her type. But how much control over this kind of situation might a woman like Gail have in the real world? Very little. Archie was out of line; this was no place to pick someone up; Bev needed to keep a professional distance from Anthony's guests.

Steeling herself to focus on the task or waitressing, she served the rest of the dinner, giving Archie barely a sideways glance until late in the evening.

By eleven, the guests were drunk and dinner table small talk had given way to yelling and guffawing. Anthony cranked up his state-of-the-art sound system and the entire house shook with R&B and rap music. Outside, the kidney-shaped pool was invitingly spotlit. The water was the colour of the poolside in Mediterranean resorts on hot summer's evenings. It steamed gently, thanks to the heating system. It wasn't long before the guests were disappearing into a bedroom upstairs to discard their clothing, returning to the patio wearing swim-gear. They had clearly been given a mandate to revel to the best of their abilities, and revel they did, bombing into the perfect azure blue until the surrounding area was drenched.

'Let's get the fucking quad bike out, boys!' Anthony bellowed, sprinting through the house, wearing only dripping swim shorts.

He burst through the front door into his garden. Moments later, there was the sound of one of the garage doors squeaking as it lifted on its automated mechanism. Then, the growl and phut, phut, phut of the quad bike's engine. He reappeared in the back garden, revving the bike repeatedly, pausing only to allow two other men, including Archie, to clamber on the back.

From the relative sanctuary of the kitchen, Bev observed this show of mindless, macho hedonism.

'Thoughtless bastards,' she muttered.

Washing a thick slick of brown lipstick off a used champagne flute, she pondered how badly the terrible din from the shouting in the pool and the quad bike's engine might be for neighbouring properties.

As if the neighbours had sensed that someone sympathetic to their plight was in their midst, Bev's train of thought was interrupted by hammering at the front door and the sound of raised voices.

She crept to the threshold of the kitchen and peeked around the door to see Jim Higson standing on the doorstep with a coat over what appeared to be pyjamas and slippers. Drained of any colour, he was balling his fists and visibly shaking.

'I demand that Anthony comes to the door!' he yelled.

One of Anthony's drunken guests threw his head back and laughed. 'Get to fuck, you interfering old cunt. We've heard all about you. You're nowt but a bully.' He made to slam the door in Higson's face, but Higson pushed against it.

'Woah! Woah!' came Anthony's voice from the back of the house. 'Hang on, Matty. Let me deal with this wanker.'

Not wanting to be spotted, Bev shrank a little further back into the kitchen until Anthony had padded past her, naked but for his swim shorts and dripping with pool water. For a small man, he seemed to fill the doorway of his grand entrance.

'Turn that dratted music down, Anthony!' Higson was trying to shout but his voice had a reediness to it, now. He took a step backwards as Anthony encroached on his personal space with shoulders wide and chest puffed out.

'Get off my property, Jim. You're trespassing.'

'You're . . . you're . . . noise pollution!' was all Higson could manage. 'It's 2.00 a.m., for heaven's sake! Have you got no consideration for your neighbours?'

Anthony grabbed his door frame on high and leaned against it territorially. 'You got a problem? Call the police. I'm within my rights.'

'I'm keeping a diary!' Higson held his phone up and snapped a photo of Anthony. 'The council's going to hear about this debauchery. It's like Sodom and Gomorrah.'

'What I do on my land is my business,' Anthony said, wrenching Higson's phone out of his hand.

'That's assault!'

'Assault?' The landscaper raised his voice, sounding not unlike his snarling, barking German Shepherd. 'I'll give you fucking assault. I'll jam this phone right up your tight arse if you don't get down my path and leave me alone. I'm sick of you spying on me and grassing every time I fart.' He poked Jim in the shoulder and punched the phone into the piano tuner's belly. 'Take your pictures and keep your diary. I'm not frightened of you. And I've got thirty witnesses in here'll say you're trespassing and harassing me.'

'Harassing—?' Higson was rubbing his stomach. The quizzical look on his face said he didn't understand how he'd come to complain about the bad guy and yet suddenly, he'd become the pariah of the cul-de-sac himself.

'That's right. Now, sling your hook before I feed you to my dog, you old pain in the arse.' Anthony slammed the door in his face, then.

Biting her lip and retreating to the relative calm of the utility room, Bev breathed in and out slowly until her pounding heartbeat calmed. What had she witnessed exactly? It had felt like violence, but who was the perpetrator? Anthony was a clever manipulator, she decided.

Needing to see how bad the noise was for the Higsons, Bev slipped out of the side door and made her way over to the adjoining fence. Despite his bedtime attire, the lights were on in Higson's large wooden workshop, but she could see little else beyond a glow over the fence. There was a strong chemical stink coming from there.

Hoisting her dress above her hips, praying nobody would spot her with her knickers on show in the half-light cast from the kitchen, she clambered onto the large stump of an old tree trunk to get a better look at what else was going on at this hour in the sleepless world of Jim Higson.

Tottering in her heels on the uneven trunk, she tried to pull herself up against the fence post. She was just about to peer over the top into the workshop window, when a gruff voice punctuated the thrum and chatter of Anthony's party.

'What the hell do you think you're doing?'

Bev breathed in sharply; started to turn around; felt her footing slip . . .

111

CHAPTER 15
Bev

'Mind my hair. I don't like it being touched,' Bev said, pushing Archie's persistent hands down. She wanted to shuffle up on the back seat of the cab to save herself from being unwigged, but there was nowhere to go.

'Why? Is your hair playing hard to get?' Seemingly unperturbed by the fact that they weren't alone, Archie forced his tongue between Bev's lips, exploring her mouth. His fingers slid from the wig to her left breast.

Bev caught a glimpse of the Uber driver's scowl in his rear-view mirror. She broke away from her conquest, panting. 'Save it 'til we get to yours, eh?'

This journey to his house felt fraught with danger. The adrenaline was still coursing through her body after he'd confronted her by the Higsons' fence. With her dress hitched up around her hips and her knickers on show, Bev had never felt so vulnerable. She'd been caught snooping in the dark by Anthony Anthony's already amorous right-hand man. There had been nobody but her client within earshot, and even then, at that moment, Higson had started to play whatever piano he'd been working on in his work-shop. Archie had lunged at her in an advance that might have felt like a borderline sex attack had Bev not been utterly excited by the prospect of an opportunistic lay after her prolonged sexual drought with a craggy-faced man she found strangely attractive.

They had kissed – she, pressed up against the fence, praying her wig wouldn't come off in his hands as she pulled down his swim shorts to see if *all* of his muscles were perfectly developed; he, trying to yank her pants down further to cop a good feel.

'Jesus, you're hung like a donkey,' she'd said, massaging the foreman's erect cock. Already able to anticipate how he'd feel inside her. Real flesh instead of the latex of her vibrator.

'They don't call me Eeyore for nothing. Come here! You've got magic tits.' He buried his face in her cleavage.

Though he lacked finesse in his seductive talk, Bev was willing to see how he might compensate for that in other ways. But when he tried to lift her in a bid to take her against the fence, she had a sudden and overwhelming feeling that they were being observed or overheard by a third party. Nobody else seemed to be with them in the garden. She'd have seen them approach. Was one of Anthony's other guests watching from above? Bev looked up at the windows that faced onto this side elevation. No sign of a voyeur.

'Not here,' Then, she'd remembered she shared a ramshackle suite of offices with Doc, a good 40 minute drive away. 'Take me to your place.'

'My shorts are wet,' Archie had said.

'You'll be wet enough when I've finished with you,' she'd whispered.

As she'd yanked down her dress, waiting for Archie to return in his dry clothes, she'd wondered if Higson had been standing outside his workshop, eavesdropping on the tryst. Could she hear him heavy-breathing on the other side of the fence or was her imagination privately fired by the thought of a little voyeurism?

Now, they were bumping down a single-track country road in near total darkness in an old Toyota Previa that was rapidly filling with Archie's alcoholic breath. Bev felt sorry for the cab driver.

Archie's house was a stone-built semi – unremarkable in the moonlight. With the taxi gone, Bev realised for the first time what a risk she was taking, going home with a total stranger who lived in the middle of nowhere. She'd never agreed to a one-night stand in such a remote location before.

'You could strangle the life out of me, bury me in your back garden and nobody would be any the wiser,' she said, unbuttoning his shirt in the middle of a living room that was bachelor-bland and smelled of dust.

'You're all right, love,' Archie said. 'Dead birds aren't my thing. I like 'em warm and bouncy, just like you. And that hair . . .' He reached out to touch her badly bleached wig.

Bev yanked her head backwards beyond his reach. 'Not the hair. That's the deal. Touch it and I call a cab now.'

'I like a woman who gives me the runaround,' he said, lifting her dress off. Removing her underwear. 'Ooh, you've not got matching collar and cuffs, then. I've not seen a bird with old-fashioned muff hair in years. I like it.'

'It's not called pussy for nothing.'

Naked, Bev felt overweight, lumpy in the wrong places and freakishly big-chested. Gail, however, was allowed to be buxom and desirable. Taking down Archie's trousers, she pushed him to the floor, tore open his shirt and proceeded to rub herself along his semi-naked body. All of Bev's anxieties and guilt ebbed away as she slid him inside her . . .

'That didn't last very long,' she said, three minutes later. Lucid once again and already calculating what could be gained from this one-night stand. Saving the price of a taxi all the way from Little Marshwicke to Altrincham and gathering intel on Anthony would be bounty enough. 'Can I kip over?'

Lying in a bed that smelled like the sheets hadn't been changed in a good couple of weeks, Bev shared a cigarette and studied the weather-beaten face of her new lover.

'What do you do for Tony, then?' she asked.

'I go from site to site, don't I? Checking the lads are doing what they're supposed to. I'm a joiner by trade, so he has me overseeing a lot of the decking and anything with railway sleepers. You know?'

Bev didn't know. 'Oh yeah. What's Tony like to work for, then? How long have you been with him?'

Archie caressed her shoulder with thick, dry fingers. The skin was red. His nails were cracked and malformed in places where he'd been injured. These were a manual workers' hands. The polar opposite to Doc's, which were soft like a woman's and slender. 'All my life,' he said. 'Tony's my brother.'

'You what?' Bev felt the blood drain from her cheeks. Her lips prickled with anxiety. 'You never said!' Damn it. The last thing she'd wanted to do was get involved with someone so close to her target. How had she not seen the connection? And yet, the two men looked nothing alike.

Archie was grinning at her. 'Have I had chance? We've not exactly done much talking! Anyway, he's me half-brother. Different dad.'

Forcing a smile, Bev noticed a scar that ran along his square jawline for the first time. A secondary one, where his ear met his cheekbone, that looked as though his ear had been detached and hastily stitched back on. Fighting? Accident in the workplace?

Clearly, he'd caught her looking at the scars. 'Wondering how I got them? Our Tony's a belting lad, but he always was a show-off and a dickhead. I had to smooth things over when he'd opened his gob to someone, didn't I? Anyway, this one night, we're in a nightclub on Oldham Road, and Tony starts getting frisky with someone's girl. We ends up in a fight with these two brick shithouses from Warrington. One of them pulls a knife and says he's going to cut Tony's knackers off. I tried to calm things down like the UN. I put myself in the way.'

'You've got a peace-keeping head?'

He chuckled. 'You could say that. They managed to sew my ear back on, thankfully. And Tony owes me for life.'

'So, you've always worked for him? Brothers but not business partners?'

'I wouldn't want that kind of responsibility. It's not my thing. He's a couple of years older than me and much uglier! I did the same sort of apprenticeship as what he done, but I never wanted to run a company. I'm good with my hands.' He smoothed his hand over her hips. The callouses scratched at her skin. 'But I'm terrible with numbers. He's good at numbers but can't read. We make a good team, but I'm happy with my lot. I don't want to be a big boss.'

'Just a medium-sized one?'

'Yeah. You'll be all right working for our kid, though. He's smashing. I don't know anyone who doesn't like him.'

'I bet he's popular with the ladies. I thought he said he had a girlfriend. Wasn't she there?'

'Ah, Tony's mystery bird! Well, he says he's going out with a teacher. PE teacher, I think he said. But he's full of shit.'

'It was quite some party he threw tonight.'

'Oh aye. He's very generous. Very charity-minded with them lads in Full Marks. He knows how easy it is to get into mischief and get labelled a wrong'un. He likes to put a bit back, you know?'

Yawning, Bev wondered how much Archie might know about his brother's relationship with the Higsons. 'Bet he pisses his next door neighbours off.'

Archie laughed and turned the bedside lamp off. 'He's a fucking nutter, that old wanker next door to him. Proper mental stalker-type. He's had it in for Tony since he moved in. Tone takes no notice. I'd have buried the old bastard in the foundations of a building site by now.'

'Along with all Tony's other victims. Ha ha.' Bev stared blankly into the dark, wondering if she would elicit a revealing response.

'I know where all the bodies are buried, me! You don't get to be as successful a developer as Tony without ruffling a few feathers.'

He fell silent, then. Bev opted not to risk drawing attention to herself by probing further. There was no light pollution this far from the city at all. The dense blackness felt like Kryptonite, draining her of her power.

As she started to drift off, a pang of homesickness for her daughter and Doc and their little office pulled her back to wakefulness like a sudden hiccup interrupting steady, deep breathing. 'I thought Tony specialised in landscaping.'

117

CHAPTER 16

Bev

'I hate to say it, but I think you were right,' Bev told Doc, who was busy drying a mug that still looked dirty.

'What do you mean? That you shouldn't have gone undercover? Well, I'm glad you've finally seen sense. I really don't think you should. You're putting yourself at risk. Again. Where were you last night?'

'Out.' Bev held her dressing gown tightly shut and stared at her toenails which still bore dwindling red nail varnish from two months earlier. She felt heat creep into her cheeks. 'I crashed at one of Anthony's guests' place. It was late. I couldn't face the journey home in the pitch black.'

'Oh really?' The sarcasm dripped thickly from his tongue. 'A guest?'

She could feel Doc's accusatory eyes on her but refused to meet his gaze. He was neither her parent nor her lover. She owed him no explanation. Let him think what the hell he liked.

'Yes. Bloody really. A guest. Turned out to be 2Tone's half-brother. Anyway, I didn't mean you were right about me not taking the cleaning job. I've got everything under control, there. Gail's earning cash that I wouldn't other-wise get, as well as Anthony Anthony's trust. I wish I was more like her, if the truth be told. Life would be a damn

118

sight more straightforward if all I had to worry about was keeping Chateau d'Antoine clean. I think I'm even getting the hang of ironing.'

Bev scratched at her scalp, unable to rid herself of the itchy, clammy feel of the wig she'd been forced to sleep in. She grimaced at the thought of Archie's dried-in sweat that still clung to her body thanks to her having left Little Marshwicke at first light, while he'd still been deep asleep, snoring like a pneumatic drill. Her journey home had been epic, involving walking in her bare feet at least a mile back to Anthony's, where she'd retrieved the Morris and had carefully driven back to Altrincham on the empty early morning motorways.

She'd dragged the wig off and had flung it onto the passenger seat of the Morris as soon as she'd started her descent on the M62 back towards Manchester. Now, it sat atop her row of filing cabinets like bad taxidermy; her dress lying crumpled in a heap beneath her desk. She desperately needed to erase the after-effects of the last twelve hours.

The shower beckoned. She needed to stopper the spectre of Doc's bad feeling back in the bottle like some wayward genie.

'This case,' she said. 'That's what you were right about. It *is* trouble.'

'Drop it then,' Doc said, artlessly spooning sugar all over the worktop as opposed to into the cup.

'How can I?'

'Easy. Just walk away. We can pick up another infidelity case or insurance fraud, maybe. Didn't you get a call off some poxy little specialist insurer who thought one of his claimants was fiddling injury?'

'Yeah,' Bev said, stretching her arms in front of her in a bid to loosen her aching back. 'Except I've committed now and I've racked up expenses. I don't think it would be financially sensible or professional to walk away. But I *do* reckon we've got a potential problem with our paying client.'

'What do you mean?'

'Jim Higson. There's something not right with him, and we need to find out what.'

She related the almost farcical episodes of Jim Higson standing on a ladder at the boundary, gawping into Chateau d'Antoine to get a closer look at her and then shouting at her through the dining room window so that she'd been forced to crawl away, commando-style, dragging an amorous Soprano with her.

'I could have mentioned the Gail business at the briefing session, I suppose. Or I could just have gone to the door and told him to bugger off back to his own property before he blew my cover. But I don't know . . .' She looked down at her newly work-worn hands – bright red, thanks to her having washed them too enthusiastically in scalding water after her liaison with Archie. 'I think Higson's hatred of Anthony is obsessive. OK, 2Tone is an irritating twat with his dog and his loud voice and show-off chateau of shite. His half-brother was making noises like he got into trouble with the law when he was a kid. But I think there's more to their relationship than a neighbour dispute, starring Higson, the victim and 2Tone, the bully. I get a whiff of stalker from Higson. I think it's only doing due diligence to get the measure of the man who's paying us to get dirt on the gobshite clown he hates with an unnatural passion.'

Doc stirred the instant coffee he'd made with such vigour that it splashed onto the worktop – not that he seemed to notice. He pushed it towards Bev wearing a weak smile. 'You look like you need this.'

'Ta.'

They both took a seat at the small kitchen table. Bev put her stockinged feet up on Doc's bony knees and started to think aloud. 'What's the score with Higson's workshop? That's what I want to know. It's directly abutting Anthony's land, isn't it? Seems like a poorly thought-out position to build your main workplace when you hate your neighbour that much. But then, he uses a lot of smelly chemicals. Maybe he just wanted to do his dirty work away from the house. How about you check out the local planning portal? See if Anthony's ever tried to extend closer to the Higsons'. Maybe an attempt to encroach on Higson's workspace was the final straw.'

Realising by the blush in her normally pallid business partner's cheeks that putting her feet up on Doc was a mistake, Bev beat a retreat to the shower. She stood under the steaming jet for ten minutes, allowing the hot water to ease the tense muscles she'd sustained during her athletic one-night stand. Mulling over whether she was actually cut out for PI work, given she couldn't just stick to the paid brief, she fantasised that instead she could perhaps join the police as a mature trainee, kicking the ass of Detectives Curtis and Owen. Doc's voice on the other side of the door jolted her back into humdrum reality.

She turned the shower off and wrapped herself in her towel, suddenly feeling vulnerable.

'What? Can it wait 'til I'm out, for God's sake?'

'Higson's got a *massive* axe to grind.' Doc sounded like an exuberant boy who had logged onto his parents' computer and discovered the joys of Internet porn for the first time.

Bev threw the shower-room door open, stepping out into the freezing cold in a cloud of clammy steam. 'Like what?'

Doc looked everywhere but at her towel-clad body. Blushing again. 'He applied for planning permission two years ago.'

'Higson or Anthony?'

'Higson. Listen. He wanted to build a massive new workshop right next to the boundary with Anthony. Much bigger than what he's already got. Pretty much the size of your average bungalow.'

Bev padded through to her office-cum-bedroom. Doc followed close behind her, putting her in mind of Anthony's German shepherd. 'And?'

'He was turned down. Twice. He applied a third time and then withdrew the application. Nothing after that.'

'Could be for all sorts of reasons.'

'My guess is Anthony objected and put the kibosh on Higson's grand plans,' Doc said, scratching his nose, looking at his white-socked feet, now. 'The online info said there was one objection. Just one!'

'Can you get into the system and access any letter that was sent? Must have been a bloody powerful objection if his plans were thrown out on the basis of it. Twice!'

'If it was Anthony, what's the bet he's got someone on the planning committee in his back pocket?'

'Mr Rotary?' Bev said, disappearing into her store cupboard to get dressed. 'I wouldn't be surprised.' Closing the door, she pulled on the previous morning's jeans and bra. Sniffed the armpits of the top. It almost had another day in it. She pulled it on and re-emerged, glad the scent of Archie was gone. 'And I'm guessing Higson went ballistic, given the hypocrisy of 2Tone complaining – assuming we're right. He got a whole bloody cul-de-sac of houses approved! And yet the council says no to one single-storey workshop? It's not like the plots are tiny. They're at least half an acre each. The noise from Anthony's party wasn't half as bad as I expected when I stood against the fence that borders Higson's land.'

Doc perched on the edge of Bev's desk, though her laptop was still open. She prayed the screensaver had kicked in, obscuring the porn she'd been enjoying on return from her Pennine adventure. Last night's encounter had only served to fire up her unruly sexual mojo after its prolonged dormant spell.

She snapped the lid of her laptop shut.

'Do us a favour, Doc. When Higson and his missus go out to tune pianos or whatever the hell it is that they do, how do you fancy having a snoop around his workshop? Find out a bit more about him. Something doesn't sit well with me and I can't quite put my finger on it. And I need to do more digging where Anthony's concerned. Archie said—'

'Archie, is it? Who's Archie, then?' Doc leaned forward, pursing his lips with his head cocked to the side. Eyes narrowed.

Shit, Bev! Think before you speak, dammit! 'Nobody.'

'Nobody? Sounds like somebody to me.'

Bev pushed the mug of coffee he'd made her away. 'Archie's Anthony's half-brother I told you about. He's his foreman, too. I got talking to him while I was wait-ressing at the party, if you must know. And let's get this straight. Who I talk to and where I go after dark and where I spend the night when Hope's not here has got fuck all to do with you. OK? You don't own me. We're business partners.'

'And friends. We're friends. Or do you only connect on a superficial level with people you've got use for?' Doc's voice cracked. His nostrils flared. He laced his fingers tightly together and crossed his legs.

'Of course we're friends.' Bev reached out to take his hand, then thought better of it.

'Well, friends are allowed to be concerned for each other's well-being. Right? That's all. It's obvious you spent the night with this Archie. . .'

'Fuck off, Doc!' Bev said, standing abruptly and wishing there was somewhere in the suite of offices she could retreat to in order to be genuinely alone. Closing her door didn't count. 'Just look into Jim Higson. OK? Higson. Not me!'

CHAPTER 17
Doc

Slumped in the Morris Minor Traveller, praying he wouldn't be questioned by some prying neighbour, Doc watched Bev disappear into Anthony's ridiculous sprawling pile, carrying her cleaning bucket and wearing a bobble hat on top of her trashy wig, as if an extra knitted layer of camouflage would perfect her disguise.

'You need your head testing,' he told himself.

He reached into his anorak pocket and thumbed the tiny Lego Darth Vader figurine that he'd been carrying with him since the age of ten. Would the talisman, worn brittle with regular rubbing, protect him on his mission?

Watching Bev flit past the window on the landing, carrying a hoover, he sighed. One day . . . Had she not put her feet up on him, implying a degree of easy intimacy between them? Did that count for nothing?

Knowing he had to prove himself an equal to Archie, the almost certainly muscle-bound meathead, who was apparently so many leagues above him on the Fuckable Index, he slid off his anorak, revealing the overalls he'd bought from charity-shop Sandra. He was ready. All he needed was for the Higsons to go out.

Twenty minutes later, he watched as Penny Higson gave a cheery wave to her husband, leaving him on the doorstep.

She marched smartly to her Mazda two-seater. She wore a lilac wool coat over a pleated skirt. Doc was no fashion expert, but even he could see that this was a woman who dressed well beyond her years. Maybe it was down to being married to a man so very much older than her.

She drove purposefully away without a backwards glance. Only Jim Higson was now left.

'Come on, you old fart. You have to leave the house at some point!'

If he ever emerged, would he take the van with the *Higson's Pianos* livery on the side or the old X-type Jag? Higson looked like the kind of guy who wore part-leather driving gloves, Doc mused. Reminded him of his own old man.

A smart rap on the passenger side window made Doc jump.

'Excuse me.'

Who was the red-faced old bird in the kilt, socks and slippers? She was carrying something under her arm like a sheaf of newspapers. What was it? A dog! It was a damned dog. This was surely the lunatic Bev had mentioned who had reported her to the police for loitering. Doc wound down the window.

'Why are you parked here?' the woman demanded. The white furball tucked under her arm yapped, as if echoing its owner's sentiment. 'What's your business?'

Doc felt light-headed. His fingertips started to tingle. Confrontation was something he didn't do and he was no good at delivering the sort of consummate performance that came so naturally to Bev.

'I'm waiting,' he said. 'For my colleague.' Stick close to the truth. Surely that wouldn't let him down. 'What's it got to do with you?'

The dog started to growl at him through bared, tiny teeth.

'This is a Neighbourhood Watch area,' the woman said, her fleece-clad bosom heaving as she spoke as though an adrenaline tap had been switched on within her and the hormone was now flooding her flabby, varicose-veined old body. 'And I'm the regional co-ordinator.' Perhaps this was the only thing of note that might happen to this interfering old battleaxe all day . . . maybe even all week. But Doc was in no mood for drawing attention to himself. Bev had given him specific orders to keep a low profile.

'I'm doing pest removal. Don't come closer, Mrs, I'm full of toxic chemicals.' Doc wound the window back up, fast.

The red-faced neighbour stood for several agonising moments, shaking indignantly at the car and the side of Doc's face, muttering inaudibly to her dog. She took a mobile phone out of her fleece pocket with her free hand. Stood in front of Sandra's Morris Minor, taking photographs.

As Doc spotted Jim Higson emerging from his front door, carrying a tool box and making for the van, it was apparent he had a decision to make – stay put, or somehow give the cul-de-sac's slipper-wearing super sleuth the slip. Damn it.

He turned away from the neighbour, pretending to search for something in the car's glove box. Surreptitiously watched Higson drive off. Mrs Nosy Slippers said something to him through the windscreen. Then she trudged back up her drive, carrying her dog, tartan kilt-covered big bottom swinging behind her as if it had a life of its own. She had the air of a woman who was about to write a strongly worded letter of complaint to the council or, most likely, to call the police. Doc was briefly alone. If he was ever to prove to Bev that he was as capable as the likes of Archie, this was his perfect window of opportunity.

Slipping stealthily from the car, Doc sidled up to Higson's open driveway. The rusting cast-iron gates looked like they hadn't been shut for a while, giving the place an entirely different feel from Chateau d'Antoine, with its shining railings and CCTV. Doc looked around. Nobody was watching the Higsons' apart from Bev, who glanced out of a bedroom window, treated him to a meaningful wink and then retreated from view.

With the blood rushing in his ears, Doc engaged in the sort of trespass he wasn't used to. No click of a mouse was involved. There was no firewall to conquer or password to decipher. He slid around to the back of the house, peering in through the windows, wondering how the hell he might break and enter with no tool to hand and without setting off the alarm.

He froze at the sound of a door opening on the other side of the tall, larch-lap fence.

'Doc! Are you there? Doc!' It was Bev.

He couldn't see her, but he guessed she was standing right behind the fencing panel closest to him.

'Yeah. What?'

'When you're inside, see if Higson's got an office or a filing cabinet tucked away somewhere.'

Doc stood with his cheek almost pressed to the wooden panel, touching the place where he imagined her crouching on the other side. 'I can't do it, Bev,' he whispered, aware that he desperately needed the toilet. 'This isn't hacking. This is next-level burglary shit.'

'Oh, for God's sake!'

'They've got an alarm.' Doc looked up at the faded logo on the ageing metal box on the side of the house.

'It's old. You can see it's knackered! I'm not sure they even set it. There's no sound of bells or beeping when they go out. You get a countdown with those things. I'm sure you'll be fine.'

'You're so sure, you bloody well do it, then!' Doc felt queasy. He grabbed at his stomach as he imagined forcing a door. 'I've got a criminal record, man. If I get caught . . . I'm totally going away.'

Behind the fence, Bev tutted. 'Well, at least try the workshop. Don't let me down.'

What option did Doc have? He couldn't disappoint Bev.

Skulking over to the large, wooden outbuilding, he could see that the place had seen better days, covered as the roof was in thick florid green moss and judging by the haze of cobwebs strung around the tops of the walls, where they met the roof's overhang. It was as though a Hollywood set designer had dressed the place for a Halloween slasher movie.

Doc surveyed the security arrangements – they consisted solely of an old, rusted combination lock. Now, here was something he could work with. His nimble fingers spun the numbered barrels round, testing scores of feasible combinations. Naturally, he'd already memorised the Higsons' birthdays and anniversaries of note. People were predictable whilst believing themselves to be enigmatic and cunning.

'Gotcha!'

The month and year of the Higsons' eldest son's birth date – 691. Doc smiled and wistfully wished that Bev had witnessed how he'd cracked the simple lock like a ninja.

Inside, the workshop was surprisingly roomy; its walls distempered white. It smelled strongly of chemicals with an undertone of earth and rotting wood. Doc shivered at the sudden drop in temperature. It was colder in here than outside. He wished he'd not left his anorak in the Morris. Feeling his nose tickle at the pungent smells, he failed to stifle a sneeze.

In the middle of the floor stood the stripped-down shell of a piano. Doc whistled softly, recognising it to be a giant like the concert grand he'd seen his mother play on occasion at the local AmDram production of *Les Misérables* in Chalfont St Terminally Dull. Lining the walls of the workshop on one side were tables containing all manner of piano paraphernalia – coils of rusting strings, old ivory and ebony keys that looked like lonely chunks of driftwood, cut loose from a raft. An entire dog-eared keyboard in a state of mid-repair. On the other side stood two old uprights that looked like they had been hollowed out by a musical taxidermist, leaving only the shell. Nothing untoward to the untrained eye. Except, as Doc turned to beat a retreat to the Morris, a pair of black parallel lines caught his eye beneath the piano carcass. The find was partially obscured by industrial-sized tubs of paint- and varnish-stripping Nitro Mors standing in a neat row. What did the lines belong to? A trapdoor?

Doc felt a cold sweat break out on his upper lip and between his shoulder blades. Dropping to his knees, he crawled behind the canisters of chemicals. Stretching out, he traced his fingers along the black lines. Grooves in the scuffed, painted concrete floor. It was indeed a trapdoor and he discovered a neat, recessed brass handle.

He was just about to lift the door to see what lay beneath when he heard the diesel rumble of an engine and the crunch of gravel on the Higson's drive. No way was it Penny's Mazda.

'Shit!' Doc said, trying to stand in haste and succeeding only in cracking his head hard on the unforgiving underside of the concert grand. He felt warm liquid as he touched the wound.

Hastening to the dirty single pane that faced onto the front garden, paying no heed to the two perfect red drops of blood he'd left behind on the white floor, Doc spied their client climbing out of his van.

'No, no, no!' he said beneath his breath.

Should he hide? He was thin enough to wedge himself easily behind one of the uprights. But if he opted to do that, Higson would see the combination padlock, dangling open on its hook.

Doc could hear Higson's footsteps crunching along the driveway as he made straight for the workshop door. Closer, closer . . .

CHAPTER 18

Mrs Nosy Slippers

Marjorie Wilson was busy uploading the photos she'd taken of the unfamiliar half-timbered Morris Minor Traveller to her computer when the doorbell chimed. Her westie terrier yapped and pricked up its ears.

'Not now! Sit down, Mr Mimsy. *Sit!*'

At first, she ignored the bell. It was probably a cold-caller, ignoring her specific instructions on the laminated sign that she'd posted in her porch that neither cold-callers nor junk mail were welcome, and door-to-door hawkers could go and boil their heads.

Yes, the burgundy Morris Minor Traveller was a car of interest in Marjorie Wilson's almost-semi-professional opinion. She liked to keep a log of this sort of irregularity on the cul-de-sac. It was her responsibility as Area Co-ordinator of the local Neighbourhood Watch and she took her duties very very seriously. She certainly didn't like to be interrupted. Keeping accurate, nay, meticulous diaries and records of the movements of both visitors and residents, whilst they were fresh in her mind, was absolutely essential. Everybody knew cul-de-sacs were particularly vulnerable to burglary and trespass because of their being no through roads with fewer potential witnesses to illegal goings-on. And she, as an elderly single woman, was more vulnerable than most, despite living with Mr Mimsy.

The doorbell rang again. Mr Mimsy streaked out of the kitchen, yapping at the front door.

'Oh, who could this be, Mimsy Moo-Moo?' she muttered, grunting as she prised herself out of her typing chair and slid her leather mules back on. Her feet were so hot and swollen that it was a struggle.

Yet again, the bell sounded. She could feel her blood pressure rising. The GP had warned her about getting irate and cutting back on pork pie and anything salty, but Marjorie was a mistress of her own destiny and queen of her own castle and *didn't* like being told how to live her life by some feckless boy in a white coat. She had clothes in her wardrobe older than that GP! She'd spent her entire professional life teaching geography to his ilk. What did an upstart like that know?

There was a knock at the door now. Mr Mimsy leaped up at the letter box, apoplectic with territorial rage or curiosity or whatever got a dog hot under the collar when a stranger came to the door.

'Being hounded in our own home, Mimsy. What a liberty! I'm coming, for heaven's sake. I bet this is some delivery man for that dreadful little thug, Anthony.'

The thought suddenly occurred to her that this might be the long-haired oik she'd confronted in the errant Morris Minor. She grabbed her golfing umbrella from the Chinoiserie umbrella stand by the front door. Any trouble and Marjorie Wilson would be ready. She'd had a brief spell teaching in Tanzania after all, and greasy-haired ne'er do wells didn't frighten her!

When she picked up Mr Mimsy and opened the door, she was perplexed by the figure standing on her doorstep.

133

'Delivery for Marge Wilson?'

It was a young post-girl wearing the livery of an international courier company and she was smiling at her. Smiling, like she'd come to inform her of a win on the Premium Bonds. In her hands, the girl held a box wrapped in brown paper.

'It's Miss Wilson to you, my dear, and I'm not expecting a parcel.' Mimsy barked in agreement.

'Well, you've got one, Marge.' She pushed it into her hands. 'Cute dog!' Started to make her way back down the driveway.

'Wait! Don't you want a signature?'

The girl didn't even look back. She merely waved and kept going. Where was her van?

Marjorie Wilson stood on her tiptoes, trying to see where the van was, but the curiosity of what the package contained bit deeply. She took it inside, kicking the door shut behind her. Mr Mimsy leaped and yapped at her heels.

The last time she'd had an unsolicited delivery, that disrespectful little runt, Anthony, had sent her faecal matter. A canine stool! Or perhaps human faeces. Marjorie Wilson wouldn't have put *that* past the lout. And it had been all because she'd complained informally to the Dog Warden and the RSPCA about the infernal din coming from that poor feral beast he called a pet – Anthony's failure to train the German Shepherd was tantamount to abuse. Yet, he'd responded with hate mail of the foulest variety. She'd called the police about the stinking Jiffy bag of dirt and Anthony had been forced to apologise, with Jim Higson acting as witness. At least Higson was a reliable friend and ally.

'Maybe it'll be something nice.'

Marjorie Wilson opted to look on the bright side. It had been her birthday last week. Perhaps the local members of the Neighbourhood Watch had clubbed together to buy her a belated gift. She looked at her pinboard which held photographs of each and every member, together with the notes she'd compiled about them – all the secrets they wouldn't want her to know and hadn't realised she'd discovered. It was important to have a thorough understanding of who she was dealing with, after all. She doubted they'd think she'd been spying on them. She had everyone's best interests at heart.

Setting the package on the kitchen table and ripping the paper from it, Marjorie Wilson realised her heartbeat was running a little too fast and her chest felt as though she was lying beneath a blanket of heavy masonry. Mr Mimsy pawed at her calves and yapped enthusiastically.

'Calm down, Mimsy Moo!'

What a delightful surprise to find there was a box within the box from a well-known local patisserie. It had been wrapped artistically with purple ribbon. Marjorie Wilson beamed. She was appreciated after all!

'They love me,' she whispered, pulling the little gift card from its envelope.

Dear Miss Wilson,
Belatedly many happy returns. Here is a token of our gratitude for your work.
Best wishes,
Little Marshwicke N.W. Committee

'How did they know I love a nice slab of cake with a mug of tea?' she said, admiring the pale blue icing.

Retrieving a knife from her kitchen drawer, she couldn't wait to cut a slice to see what sort of cake it was.

'Battenberg! Oh, Lady Luck is on your side today, Madam. Look at this, Mimsy Moo-Moo! My word. What a beauty. Soft as a cloud and smells like heaven.'

She saluted the faces staring down at her from her pinboard and put the kettle on. Some minutes later, she was sitting at the table with her special Queen's Silver Jubilee mug of steaming strong tea, salivating at the thought of the first bite.

'Happy birthday, me.'

The Battenberg was delicious though she privately admitted that the icing had a strange aftertaste to it. Bitter. Though never much of a home-baker herself, it wasn't as good as some of the home-made cakes she'd sampled from her friends at the WI. Still, on the whole, it was a good 8/10. One slice, of course, was not going to be enough. No. It had been many moons since anybody had sent her a gift – let alone a delicious cake from an expensive patisserie.

She helped herself to a second slice, savouring the sugary, marzipan flavours and ignoring the slightly disappointing bitterness. Put a small sliver into Mr Mimsy's dog bowl, which he gobbled hungrily. Her stomach was starting to feel a little off, however. But the cake was so moreish. As she swallowed the last mouthful of her final pink square, her stomach protested audibly and she was forced to abandon her tea party in favour of a trip to the little girl's room.

Marjorie Wilson breathed her last, enthroned on her quality British-manufactured Armitage Shanks WC. Her penultimate thought was one of desperate sadness for Mr Mimsy, who would surely succumb to the poisonous cake. Her final thought, however, was not expended on wondering who might have poisoned them both, but on how embarrassing it would be that the members of the Neighbourhood Watch would find a formidable pillar of the community such as herself so indisposed in death, with her kilt hitched high around her spreading thighs and with her fourth best pair of big knickers around her ankles.

CHAPTER 19
Mihal

'You call for a cab, mate?' the black man behind the wheel of the old Audi asked. 'You Clive?'

Mihal shook his head. 'No, sorry. Not me. Not unless you want to give a free man a free ride.'

The cabbie rolled up his window, tutting.

Mihal merely smiled wryly. Shoved his hands into his empty pockets. The filthy clothes he had been wearing when he'd been arrested on the night of Bogdan's death were rotting rags in some landfill by now. The cheap, ill-fitting grey suit he wore today was the garb his defence had bought for him for the trial. Apart from the hand-me-down old parka and the pinching shoes he'd been given by a refugees' charity, he had nothing of any value in the world apart from the travel warrant in his pocket – a freebie ticket to anywhere in the British Isles that he was reluctant to use, since his intended destination would be instantly trackable by the authorities. He also had his newly-reissued passport. A replacement for the one that bastard had taken from him. But some things could never be replaced.

Standing outside Wandsworth prison, Mihal drank in the scent of freedom. The lungful, thick with diesel particles from the cab and rain on the wind smelled no better than the foetid air inside the prison. Instead of the lightness he should have had in his heart on the day of his release, he felt leaden and weighted down by the journey that lay ahead of him.

He began the walk.

'Please can you spare some money? I need to get to Victoria. My brother is missing and I must travel to find him. Madam! I will carry your shopping upstairs. Please can you give me one pound?'

Taking a detour through the brightly-lit, alien world of Wandsworth shopping centre, where well-heeled workers and Puffa-clad local youths scurried or ambled past temples to consumerism with money in their pockets; passing some flats where the lifts were fortuitously broken, Mihal tried his luck to raise tube fare to the coach station.

He could have picked a few pockets – in theory, it would have been easier. But London had eyes everywhere . . . as long as there was something of monetary value to protect. CCTV on the lampposts. Ever-watching orbs in the shops. Omniscient black domes outside the flats which might once have been council-owned but were now mainly private. No. Mihal had no intention of getting his collar felt for stealing on his first day out. He had work to do.

His impressive English skills and impeccable politesse garnered him more than ten pounds within only a couple of hours. Enough to buy a cheap loaf and a bottle of water. Enough to get to Victoria.

'How much is a ticket to Manchester, please?' he asked the sullen-faced man behind the Perspex at the Victoria ticket counter. The sheer size of the station and the hustle and bustle of thousands of people scurrying behind him in all directions, unregimented, was making him feel light-headed. Sweat was already pouring down the insides of his polyester shirt.

Too much for a walk-on fare. He hadn't qualified for the paltry £46 discharge grant. Staying in London to beg for the amount of money he'd need would mean sleeping rough for too many nights. Only one night on the street would inevitably mean getting his passport stolen, getting beaten up, getting arrested for some petty misdemeanour he'd have to commit just to stay alive. He had neither a sleeping bag, a robust cardboard box, nor an established safe corner of the city in which to bed down. And in any case, the coaches were all booked solid for days in advance. He might have known. Perhaps his destiny was not to travel north to seek revenge. Except Mihal didn't believe in destiny and the next coach to Manchester left in less than thirty minutes . . .

Locating the Manchester-bound National Express, he waited until the steward in charge of the luggage was distracted by five Asian pensioners, each pushing a trolley piled high with oversized, overstuffed tartan plastic laundry bags.

'I'm sorry, madam. I'm afraid the answer is no. You've all exceeded the luggage allowance. If you want to pay for excess baggage, you—'

'The man said it was OK when we bought the tickets.'

'No. No he didn't, because our rules state—'

The din, presumably of horrified protest in Punjabi or Urdu or whatever they were speaking, was enough of a distraction for Mihal to open the rear baggage compartment.

'You have to pay online . . .' The steward was shouting slowly as though the capable pensioners were both deaf and remedial.

Mihal pulled out a large green suitcase, setting it upright by the kerb and wedging it at an angle that would screen him from view. Saying a silent prayer that his escape from

London would be unhampered, he snuck behind the case, jostling the rest of the baggage aside to make room for a slender man. It reeked of diesel this far back in the baggage hold. The engine was just beyond the metal partition at his feet, after all. It was likely he'd feel sick all the way north and the chance of cases sliding whilst in transit and hitting him on the head was high. But he needed to return to where it had all begun. He needed to find out what had become of his younger brother, Constantin; he needed to avenge Bogdan's death.

'What's this doing out?' The steward's voice was audible from where Mihal was concealed. He could just see the man's rotund belly, clad in the National Express uniform. 'I thought I'd locked this.' He was muttering. Grunting as he lifted the green case back into the hold.

Had he seen Mihal? The steward started to shunt baggage around to accommodate the green case, shoving a hard guitar case painfully into Mihal's exposed groin.

Hold your breath. Count to ten. Don't make a sound.

Clenching his eyes shut and his teeth together, Mihal finally exhaled when the rear compartment door was shut. The engine started up, vibrating throughout the freezing cold luggage hold. The doors further forward were shut, one after the other. Finally, he heard the pneumatic hiss of the door to the coach being closed. The giant vehicle rocked back and forth as the handbrake was released and they pulled away.

He'd made it on board. Now, he had an hour or more before their first stop during which he could plan his next steps. Over the course of his prison sentence he'd curated any information he could about The Bastard who had bought the three of them as slaves from their trafficker, put them to work on unsafe building sites and got them hooked on the Thai Dragon's deadly brand of Spice. Mihal had worked out from the hearsay of other trafficked men in prison, as well as Internet research, whenever he'd been able to lay hands on an illicit mobile with Wi-Fi connectivity, that The Bastard was still living high off the hog in some mansion near Manchester. His first priority was to track him down and torture news of Constantin from him.

'And then I will cut out The Bastard's heart for what he did to us,' he whispered to the darkness.

The coach started to slow and veered left. They were pulling off. How long had he been in the baggage hold? Even if he'd had a phone or a watch with which to check the time, he wouldn't have been able to reach either in that cramped space.

There was a squeal of brakes and the smell of hot rubber, intermingled with the diesel. Mihal was only a breath away from vomiting up what was left of the bread he'd eaten that morning in Wandsworth shopping centre. He needed fresh air. While the passengers were visiting the toilet and having a smoke would be his best chance of sneaking aboard without the driver realising he had a stowaway.

'Oh, for Christ's sake, Dave! Just get the bloody pushchair out of the hold! I'm not carrying him. Where's the change-bag?' A woman's voice right next to the hold door told a tale of blind panic and frustration. Her child's fretful whining rendered her almost inaudible. Almost.

'I thought you had it.'

'No! I thought you had it. Jesus. It must have gone in with the pushchair. Get them out! Get them both out! Come on!'

The sound of the child squalling cut through the thrum of the idling engine, amplified five-fold when the engine abruptly cut out and harsh daylight flooded the darkness of the baggage hold.

'There it is!' the child's mother yelled. 'At the back.'

Through the small gap between the suitcases, Mihal could see them – two sets of legs. One big. One small. The father of the child – presumably – started to play Tetris with the baggage, manoeuvring the pieces so that the pushchair became accessible. Mihal suddenly found he was able to move his legs. Then, the giant case that blocked him in was shunted down the hold freeing his upper body.

The father bent down and leaned into the hold to retrieve the pushchair. Mihal was exposed. He held his breath. If the man looked in the right direction, he'd see the stowaway and the alarm would be inevitably raised.

Mihal felt his leg encased in a firm grip. The man yanked at him. Pushed his unyielding leg back. Grabbed something adjacent and pulled it free. The change-bag.

'Here we go. Found it!'

Exhaling slowly, Mihal realised he'd had a near miss.

When the couple had left, wheeling their infant son in his stroller, Mihal hastily wriggled out of the hold. While the driver was distracted, sharing tales of footballing triumph and woe with a Manchester City fan, he crept on board. There was not a soul to be seen apart from a sleeping fat woman, halfway down. Making straight for the toilet, which bore the handwritten sign, 'OUT OF ORDER', he concealed himself inside the stinking, cramped space and locked the door. It was hardly better than the luggage hold, but at least he could put the lid down over the blocked mess in the bowl and sit for the rest of the way, undisturbed but for the inevitable frequent attempts at the handle, when passengers failed to read the sign.

A while later, Mihal woke, stiff-necked and cold. The coach had shuddered to a halt. Unlocking the door and opening it a fraction, he waited for the chaos of people getting out of their seats and retrieving their hand baggage from the overhead racks before slipping out of the cubicle. Several travellers grimaced at the smell that wafted out with him, but that seemed to make them all the keener to turn away from the dishevelled man who hadn't boarded the coach with them in the first place.

He alighted at Manchester's Chorlton Street Bus Station, corralled by the other passengers towards four uniformed policemen who were staring straight at him. One spoke into his radio; another started to walk briskly towards him.

'Excuse me, Sir!'

How the hell had they known? Had the couple with the child spotted him and reported him to the driver? Had the driver seen him crawl from the baggage hold in his wing mirror? Damn it!

Mihal held his breath, almost rooted to the spot with fear. Why the hell hadn't he used his travel warrant? Half a day out of prison and already, he was going to be arrested and thrown back inside. Maybe this time, he'd get put on the first coach back to Romania.

But the policeman walked straight past him, making instead for a youth who wore a hoodie and was hanging around the group of Asian pensioners who had got on at Victoria. A pickpocket.

Realising he was in the clear, Mihal followed the stream of coach passengers who were hastening away towards Piccadilly Gardens. He kept his head down as he moved past the neon-lit, faded Victorian splendour of the Britannia hotel. Across the road, he glimpsed men staggering aimlessly outside a shop proclaiming to be *the* place for Manchester souvenirs, situated under the canopy of a huge 1960s concrete Piccadilly Plaza complex. Mihal recognised the men immediately by their filthy clothes and tottering demeanour as being Spice-afflicted. Manchester's tax-paying citizens, going about their daily business, were giving them a wide berth but otherwise acting as though they were invisible. Though he felt the tug of the drug, he reminded himself of the mission in hand.

Mihal needed to seek refuge among other Romanians who had come to Manchester, either by choice or by force. He needed to make his way into the foothills of the Pennines to Oldham. And he knew just the man who might give him shelter.

Revenge was almost within his grasp.

CHAPTER 20

Bev

'Not tonight, Joseph. I'm washing my hair,' Bev said, clutching her phone to her ear with a rubber-glove-clad hand. Archie had caught her on her knees. But her prone position and rubber garb was anything but sexy as she stared into the bowl of Anthony's downstairs loo with the smell of Harpic Limescale Remover stinging the backs of her nostrils.

'What are you on about? My name's not Joseph.'

Bev sighed. 'Not tonight, Josephine? You know? It's a play on—'

'Are you calling me a poof?'

'Jesus! Forget it. Look, Archie, it's nice of you to want to take me out, but I've got a lot of commitments at the moment.'

It was the third time 2Tone's right-hand man had called her that morning. The first couple of calls, she'd sent straight to voicemail, wondering if it was wise to venture beyond a one-night stand with her target's brother. But when Archie called for a third time, the memory of their energetic sex session sharpened in her mind and she decided to allow herself the cheap thrill of being chased.

'What's a woman like you got on that can't be taken off, eh? I want to suck on those luscious big titties of yours. Come on. Come out for a drink with me and then we can go back to mine and shag 'til my walls start shaking.'

145

He pinged her a dick pic that was both revolting, since he'd taken it in a builder's portaloo and arousing, since he really did have a photogenic penis. It was no use. For all Archie had zero finesse as a seducer, the very suggestion of sex was enough to distract Bev from cleaning and her intended goal of returning to the office to see what else Doc had dug up on Higson. Now, she was thinking about action of an entirely different variety – the kind that would dull her fear. Pulling off her rubber glove with her teeth, she shoved her hand into her jeans and started to pleasure herself.

'I'm all sweaty. I haven't showered.'

'Neither have I. Anyway, I want to smell you as nature intended. I like a dirty woman.'

'You've got me going, now! Pick me up from Anthony's?' She bit her lip, imagining the muscular builder entering her from behind as she leaned on the toilet. *Terrible, Bev. You have no self-control! You don't deserve anything wholesome in your life – especially not full custody of your daughter.*

She withdrew her hand from her pants, feeling suddenly guilty and weak. But by the time she'd opened her mouth to register her change of heart, it was too late.

'Good girl. I'll get off work early. I'll be round in a bit.'

She'd committed to another encounter. She might as well enjoy it. It's not like she'd be able to do this sort of thing once Hope was living with her full-time.

Rifling through the chest of drawers in Anthony's master bedroom, Bev found some make-up at the back of the sex toys and fluffy handcuffs. Leftovers either from 2Tone's on-off girlfriend or some fundraising dinner attendee who had won herself a slice of muscle-bound small man in the charity auction.

Giving the Yves Saint Laurent eyeshadow and Guerlain lipstick a sniff to see that they weren't entirely antiquated and rancid, she deemed the make-up useable. Within five minutes, she'd made a fair fist of glamourising plain old Gail the cleaner. Her skinny jeans, now knackered at the knees and bleach-stained, were a better fit at least. Manual labour had its benefits. There was nothing to be done with the wig, however. Any attempts to style the tresses of poorly bleached hair would reveal her artifice. She unbuttoned her cheap blouse to show off some cleavage. Job done. It wasn't like she planned to be in her work clothes for very long.

She texted Doc.

> Change of plan. Won't b home til much later. Going on date
> with Archie. Will see what info I can get. Don't wait up.

Surprisingly, Archie arrived in a souped-up red C Class Mercedes with tinted windows and pimped-up black alloys. He'd definitely showered and was dressed smartly in chinos and a Ralph Lauren polo shirt as opposed to the landscaper's garb she'd imagined him in. Bev felt underdressed and dowdy, but the foreman only had eyes for her chest.

'Gorgeous Gail. Let's go afternoon-drinking and then I'll give you one on my lounge rug in front of the fire. What do you say?'

'One step at a time, Archibald.' Bev winked.

Leaving the Morris behind, she climbed into the Mercedes, anticipating being taken to some stylish wine bar. Surely a well-heeled Pennine enclave like Little Marshwicke would have one establishment where she'd be able to get a decent glass of Malbec or a nice gin.

When her phone rang and she saw from the screen that Doc was calling, she ignored it. He was almost certainly going to whinge at her for standing him up. Well, he could wait. If it was urgent, he'd surely text.

'Here we are,' Archie said, pulling up in the customer car park of a down-at-heel looking pub that looked like a favourite destination of families wanting a cheap Sunday lunch (the sign outside said the carvery was only £6 per head) and an obvious choice for those wanting to watch the big match on a fittingly big screen (The Bricklayer's Arms boasted Sky Sports).

'Oh,' Bev said.

'Don't worry. They have wine on tap for lasses.'

Inside, the place smelled of vinegar, stale lager and lard. Archie ordered a pint of Stella Artois.

'I love this place, me. They still serve "Wife-Beater"!' he said, winking.

'Eh?'

'Few pints of this and I'll be going home to give my Mrs a good pasting.' He started laughing at the shockingly poor-taste joke.

Bev swallowed hard. 'Is that why you're divorced?'

'Yeah,' he said. Then he nudged her hard and put his arm around her. 'Only joking. Course not. I'm divorced because my ex ran off with her childhood sweetheart. A fucking Paki, of all things. Said she didn't fancy me once I'd lost my hair.' He rubbed his shining pate. 'Fat cow must have been bleeding mad to leave me for him. Solar panels for a sex machine, this.' Then he grabbed his crotch. 'I reckon I've got a bit of black in me, and all. I'm surprised my kids didn't come out brown.'

Feeling her stomach contract, she was just about to challenge his mind-boggling racism when the barman cleared his throat.

'What can I do you for, love?'

148

'Do you have Hendriks and Fever-Tree?' she asked, already knowing the answer. If they dispensed cooking wine on tap, there wasn't a hope in hell's chance that they'd have her tipple of choice. Perhaps she should just call a cab and go. The last thing she wanted to do was waste an evening, listening to the racist bilge that came out of this uncouth man's mouth. Any attempt to school him in common human decency would be a waste of time. Racism became entrenched in Archie's type. They'd grown up with it and it was almost certainly reinforced on the job. Once again, Bev had chosen badly. Was she doomed to attract the worst of men?

'Yes,' the barman said, unexpectedly. 'Slimline or normal tonic?' He grabbed a black Hendriks bottle from a shelf on the other side of the bar, returning with a large goldfish bowl of a glass full of ice. 'Lemon or lime? Sorry. We've not got cucumber. It went slimy.'

'Full-fat with lime, please,' Bev said, feeling her resolve weakening. 'And make it a double.' She'd just have the one. Her phone was being called yet again by an insistent Doc. She sent it to voicemail and switched it to vibrate. If she went straight back right now, he would know she'd crashed and burned with another man she was sublimely ill-suited to. She'd also miss the chance of finding anything more out about 2Tone.

'Who's this mystery woman Anthony's got an on-off thing with then?' she asked, now unable to look Archie the Racist Landscaper in the eye.

'I haven't met her,' he said. His right eye twitched. It was clear he was lying.

Bev pondered what Archie might be hiding and why. She took a deep slug of the gin and tonic, instantly feeling the relaxing effects thanks to not having eaten since the frozen pizza Doc had rustled up the previous evening. 'Is she a weightlifter?'

'How do you know our kid's got a thing for weight-lifters?' he asked, pawing at her knee and pushing his face close to hers, almost confrontationally. 'Eh? Have you been rooting through his raz-mags or have you seen his browsing history?' He started to guffaw with laughter.

Damn it! Bev had slipped up badly. 'The night of the party. I heard him saying it to one of the other guests. He was talking about Jodie Marsh and how he had a thing for muscles on women.'

Archie nodded. He seemed to buy it. 'His ex-Mrs were a right weighty piece, you see. Tony always loved a lass with a big fat arse. Anyway, she starts going to the local gym and gets into bodybuilding in a big way and Tony gets a taste for it. You know? Next minute, he's dipping his wick all over town with any muscly bird he can get a grip of. We were doing a renovation project on a gym near Bacup. By Christ! He were like a kid in a fucking sweet shop, knee-deep in all these weightlifters.'

'So, he still fancies muscle-bound women, even though his ex was one? Does he hold a candle for her?'

'Nah.' Archie drained his pint. 'She fucked off with the gym instructor. It were another woman, wasn't it? Left our Tony-boy with an itch he couldn't scratch no more. And his mystery bird . . . well, I think she's a PE teacher or summat.'

'A teacher? Really?'

'Aye. I'm sure he said she were the football coach for the local Duke of Edinburgh's. Proper sporty like.'

Maybe he wasn't lying after all. 'Why's he keep her a secret, then? Is she married?'

'She's a lezzer, but her girlfriend doesn't know she still likes a bit of hot sausage.'

Bev almost spat out what was left of her gin. She gestured to the barman to pour her out another. 'I can't tell what's truth coming out of your mouth and what's bullshit, Archibald.'

'Less of the bald.'

He started to caress the inside of her thigh, which was within easy reach, perched as they were on bar stools. Given they were the only clientele in the pub apart from two old men sipping bitter and playing dominos in the far corner, she didn't push him away. Her phone vibrated on top of the bar. A quick glance at the screen told her it was an email from Rob. She'd responded to the threatening letter from his solicitor with one from her own, outlining a reasonable demand that she should have made as soon as they'd split. It had clearly more than rattled his cage.

Dear utter bitch,
You can piss off if you think I'm going to sell the house and give you a share of the equity so you can shack up with that hippy and steal my daughter off me.
See you in court!
Rob

Even the warm glow of the alcohol in Bev's belly couldn't help dispel the icy-cold dread that spread like frostbite inside her. No matter how hard she worked and how she tried to be the best mother she could possibly be, enduring Rob like a chronic illness – keeping the peace and tolerating his crap for Hope's sake, so that her daughter could maintain a relationship with the man she thought was her father – she was still losing the war. She was losing at life; a failure. She'd abstained from sex with strangers at swingers' parties and sex clubs. She'd eschewed her origami habit almost entirely (but for the koi carp she was making for Hope's birthday). Bev was doing everything by the book and yet here she was, still a victim. Unable to get her own money out of Rob's indulgent Didsbury pad to fund a proper home of her own without a costly legal battle. The bastard simply wouldn't give an inch.

'Is it any wonder I get too involved in work?' she said, pushing the phone away.

'What did you say?' Archie asked, frowning quizzically.

'Nothing,' she said. 'Just hassle with . . . It doesn't matter.'

She downed her drink in one. Took her unpleasant but available new lover by the hand. 'Your car in that car park. Right now. Fuck the pain away, Archie. Help me to forget, just for five minutes.'

Her phone made a gong noise at that moment, telling her that Doc had sent a text. Perhaps it was something urgent. But Bev was distracted by the joyful glint in the foreman's eyes.

Archie looked deep into the chasm of her cleavage. 'With tits like that, Gail, love, I'm not sure I'll even make it to five. Good job I've got fat fingers.'

CHAPTER 21
Dotty Grimshaw

'Coming!' Dotty Grimshaw shouted through the living room window of her dormer bungalow, flustered and slightly panicking that she was running late. 'Hang on!' If only she hadn't slept through her alarm.

The doorbell rang again. Penny clearly hadn't heard her. As Dotty pulled on her best cardigan, she glanced outside to see her neighbour, clutching three large plastic boxes full of croissants, looking bedraggled in a damp raincoat. Little Marshwicke was in an early morning cloud.

'Oh, dear.' She rapped on the glass.

Penny met her gaze and smiled.

'Two minutes,' Dotty mouthed. She barrelled into the kitchen and collected the large dispensing Thermos full of coffee that had been her responsibility to prepare. 'Come on, Dotty! Get a shift on. You can't keep everybody waiting.'

Finally, she slid on her coat and stuffed her bunioned feet into her Clarks shoes and was ready. She opened the door to Penny. 'Morning, Penny, love. Sorry I'm still faffing around. I'm such an old fusspot, aren't I?' She slammed the door and put the mortice lock on. Yawned. 'We're late, aren't we? Marjorie hates it when anyone's late.'

Penny started to walk slowly down the path. 'Just because Marjorie's up with the larks every morning doesn't mean the rest of the Neighbourhood Watch committee has to march to her tune. If she insists on calling a breakfast meeting, she's got to cut us some slack on punctuality. Especially if we're lumbered with bringing the breakfast.'

Dotty nodded but still looked over at Marjorie's neat house with its perfectly groomed and regimented herbaceous borders with a degree of trepidation. Marjorie Wilson was the sort of woman who didn't tolerate fools gladly, which meant she was both intimidating to an introvert like Dotty, but admittedly a woman you wanted on your side when the chips were down. And the chips were decidedly on the floor. 'I'm glad we're having an, "emergency summit". I can't say this feels very urgent, mind. Four days after all the aggro is like four days too late, if you ask me. Say we decide to involve the authorities now . . . They'd just laugh.'

'Not everyone could just drop their plans and meet on Sunday, like she wanted. All Marjorie needs to worry about is feeding and walking Mr Mimsy. The rest of us have got family and jobs.'

They'd crossed the cul-de-sac. There was no sign of the others, yet. No Marjorie in sight, either. 'I'm surprised she's not standing at the door with her arms folded, looking at her watch,' Dotty muttered. She yawned again. 'I can't see that this will change anything. What can *we* do about those dratted parties? I'll tell you what. Nowt.'

Balancing the pastries under her left arm, Penny pressed Marjorie's doorbell. 'Keep your pecker up, Dotty. Think positive. Anthony Anthony's only human. He's bound to have a weak spot, and we'll find it and take him down to China Town.'

'I blummin' well hope so, Penny.' Dotty yawned again. 'I'm perpetually shattered. I can't go on like this, being kept awake 'til all hours.'

Heavy rain came down then in a sudden shower.

154

'Come on, Marjorie!' Penny shouted through the letterbox. 'The croissants are getting soggy.'

But there was no answer.

'Funny,' Dotty said, dragging the Thermos over to the window of the dining room that Marjorie used as her 'head office' and cul-de-sac lookout post.

The nerve centre of the Neighbourhood Watch was empty. No sign of Marjorie at her desk, though Dotty did spot something on the carpet that she couldn't initially make visual sense of. It was a heap of rags in a puddle of orange and brown. There was a dark shroud over the object that seemed to move. Whatever it was, it made her shiver involuntarily. Then, she realised what she saw. 'Ooh, I say. Mr Mimsy's on the floor. Look, Penny! He doesn't look well. What's that muck on him?'

Penny approached and peered in over Dotty's shoulder. 'He looks . . .' She knocked smartly on the window. The dog didn't move but the dark, wriggling shroud lifted from its body, hanging overhead like a raincloud. 'Dotty, I think he's dead.'

Dotty dropped the Thermos and clasped her hand to her mouth. Gagged as the disturbed bluebottles started to pelt against the window. 'Call her.'

Still juggling the croissants, Penny took out her phone and dialled Marjorie. She looked at Dotty with a concerned expression and shook her head. 'Haven't you got a key?'

Nodding, Dotty took her purse out of the shoulder bag she'd hastily slung across her coat. From inside a zipped pocket, she retrieved Marjorie's spare key, labelled in the geography teacher's neat hand on a blue tag attached with string. Dotty looked down at the shining piece of metal, momentarily mesmerised; guilty that she was about to trespass; breathless with fear at what they might find.

Her hand shook as she opened the front door. A sickly sweet smell of decay hit her immediately. She covered her nose with her scarf and glanced through the doorway to the office. Squeezed her eyes shut at the sight of poor Mr Mimsy. Headed to the kitchen, where only the remnants of a boxed Battenberg cake attested to the house's owner having sat at the table, perhaps some days ago, now, given the cake was fly-infested. Except the flies were all dead.

'That ungodly pong is stronger at the front of the house,' Dotty walked back out to the hall. 'Do you think maybe she's collapsed?'

'Marjorie!' Penny shouted, grabbing the newel post of the stairs and glancing upwards.

She climbed to the first floor, opening each of the bedroom doors in turn. Checking the bathroom. Dotty waited below, breathing through her mouth and clutching her hand to her chest. Gripped by a bad, bad feeling.

'No sign,' Penny said, descending with a shrug. She dialled her number again.

The ringtone of Marjorie's phone trilled dully through the house.

'It's coming from the downstairs loo,' Dotty said.

Gingerly, Dotty pushed the door inwards. A swarm of flies buzzed out towards her, hitting her in the face so that she was forced to close her eyes tightly. The sickly stench of death was overwhelming.

'Oh dear,' Penny said. 'Oh no.'

Dotty opened her eyes again and was greeted by the sorry sight of Marjorie Wilson, grey-faced and slumped against the toilet wall with her kilt hitched around her middle and her knickers around her ankles.

'She's dead! Oh my God, she's dead, Penny. Her and Mr Mimsy. Call someone. Quick! Call the police!'

CHAPTER 22

Bev

'Aye-aye! What's going on here?' Bev said, manoeuvring the Morris out of the way of a police car that appeared close behind her in the rear-view mirror, flashing its blue lights. It pulled past her in the entrance to the Little Marshwicke cul-de-sac to join a fleet of other police vehicles and an ambulance. They formed a veritable roadblock – a glare of lights and neon colour – in the middle of the small development.

'Bloody hell.' Sitting in the passenger scat, Doc craned his head to spy on the drama that was apparently unfolding outside the house diagonally opposite Anthony Anthony's and Jim Higson's places. 'Seems there's something wrong with Mrs Nosy Slippers.'

Bev mounted the kerb outside Anthony's and switched off her engine. She parted the poorly bleached locks of her wig to see two women and a man getting out of a smaller van which had parked at an awkward angle. They were dressed in white protective suits, complete with elasticated hoods. 'Can you see what it says on the side of that one? I can't make it out from here.'

She noted the Adam's apple bounce in Doc's throat. His voice cracked as he spoke. 'Crime Scene Investigation, I think. Shit. And there's an ambo. Do you think . . .?'

'Maybe there was a break-in and Nosy Slippers got bonked on the head. Anything could have happened.'

A young-looking uniformed officer started to unravel blue and white police tape across the driveway, tying it to the gate posts. There was a small crowd of cul-de-sac residents assembling by Nosy Slippers' garden wall, clearly trying to elicit information from the uniform. One of the women was sobbing into a handkerchief with a large Thermos at her feet.

Bev watched Penny Higson put an arm around the weeping woman. 'Do you think she found her? The one who's crying.'

'Looks that way, doesn't it?' Doc said. 'Seems to me, this has just kicked off in the last half an hour. I wonder if she's already in the ambulance?'

Just as he pondered this aloud, his answer came in the form of two men exiting the house, wearing the green uniform of ambulance drivers – one carrying a heavy-looking paramedic's bag over his shoulder. They marched along the drive looking sombre. There was a brief exchange with two men wearing suits and raincoats.

'Detectives,' Bev said. 'You can practically smell them from here. This looks very rum indeed.'

The ambulance men got into the ambulance and performed a three-point turn. No sirens. No flashing lights. At that moment, another van bounced onto the cul-de-sac.

'Oh, here we go,' Bev said. 'This is not good. Not good at all.'

It was a coroner's van, replacing the ambulance in the mêlée of Little Marshwicke interlopers. A stern-looking woman wearing a white jumpsuit emerged from the house, approached the van and said something to the drivers. Moments later, they pulled an empty gurney from the back of the van and wheeled it up to the front door.

Beside her, Doc paled visibly, wiping his mouth with shaking fingers. He dropped his hand onto hers and squeezed her forearm. 'Shall we go? We should go. Nosy Slippers must have been iced. I've not got the stomach to see a dead body and I'll bet the feds will want to question everyone. The last thing I need is the long arm of the law lifting me for murder because Nosy Slippers carked it; I've got a record.'

'Don't talk shit, for Christ's sake!' Bev said, feeling her breakfast, which had been sitting at the bottom of her stomach like a lead weight for the last hour, start to head north to her gullet. She was cold, all of a sudden. Shivering, in fact. *Pull yourself together woman*, she counselled herself. *See this as an opportunity, not a threat.*

'Oh my God!' Doc said. 'Nosy Slippers took photos of me in the Morris. The cops will find it when they examine her phone and they'll see I've got a motive! Fucking hell, man. This shit's unreal. I'm outa here.'

But Bev was watching Jim and Penny Higson as they broke away from the gaggle of rubber-necking neighbours and retreated to their own drive. Red-eyed, as though they too had been weeping, they climbed into Penny's Mazda and sped off.

'Hold your horses,' she told Doc, swallowing down her fear and half-digested scrambled eggs. 'This is the perfect opportunity to slip into Higson's workshop when he's not around.'

Doc looked at her askance. 'You're joking. With half of the Pennine police force standing thirty feet away? Bollocks to that!'

'No! Think it through.' Bev wiped the fogged windscreen with her sleeve. 'They're all busy attending to Dead Nosy Slippers.' She pointed to the garden which had been cordoned off with fluttering police tape, now. It was empty but for two uniforms who were still chatting to the neighbours. The detectives, forensics team and coroner's people had all disappeared inside. Furthermore, it had just begun to spit with rain again. 'An anonymous-looking man in overalls hanging around on a morning when the place is crawling with strange faces? You'd totally be hiding in plain sight.'

But her partner shook his head virulently. 'Too risky. I managed to get out of there by the skin of my teeth when Higson came back the other day. I mean, literally, with a second to spare, yeah? And if he'd memorised how he'd left the combination on that lock, he'd have known someone had been tampering with it. What's to say he's not clocked the Morris, put two and two together and he'll be back here in five minutes to catch me in the act?'

Bev resolutely took the Morris keys out of the ignition. 'Come on.'

'God knows he's got form for being a watchful motherfucker, that Higson. I bet he's rumbled who you are, for a start.'

'You're catastrophising. Pack it in.' Bev climbed out of the Morris and retrieved her cleaning materials in the Vileda bucket from the boot. Nobody had eyes for Anthony Anthony's cleaner this morning. They were rapidly making for their own front doors as the icy Pennine rain started to fall in earnest. Pretty soon, the detectives would start door-to-door enquiries. Now was the time for a spot of unsanctioned snooping.

With drooping shoulders, Doc got out of the car too. He still looked as though he was about to vomit.

'Get your toolbox,' she said, handing him the old kit she'd bought him as a prop. 'You can deck over Anthony's fence in the back garden. There's a panel that Soprano flung himself against and loosened.'

'Soprano? The hell hound?'

'He's soft as shite,' Bev said, winking.

Thankful that Anthony had had the forethought to leave the dog inside, instead of haring through the gardens, barking and growling at every passing bird and foraging squirrel, Bev shooed Doc around to the back while she unlocked the front door.

Soprano leaped on her the moment she opened up, licking her wig and wagging his tail. She stumbled backwards with the force, relieved that the dog had warmed to her so quickly. Inside, the place was pristine and silent. No trace of the raucous party at the weekend, thanks to her domestic ministrations. The memory of meeting Archie floated to the forefront of her mind and she felt a twinge of recognition in her knickers. Archie, who was keen to see her again and had inundated her WhatsApp account with semi-literate sexts and dick pics, could wait.

Moving through to the kitchen, she opened the side door and stepped back outside, beckoning Doc to follow her. Together, they trudged in silence to the loose fence panel. But Doc seemed hesitant.

'I'll come with you and keep a lookout,' she said, shoving the panel aside to reveal a gap large enough to take a man. 'Will that make you happy?'

Doc nodded. 'You owe me.'

'Shut up, you big banana.'

Peering past the large wooden workshop, there was no sign of Penny's Mazda having reappeared on the drive. They crept up to the door. Rainwater streamed from the roof onto them both as Doc spun the combination lock's wheels to show the correct numbers.

'My God!' Bev said, shaking her head and grinning. 'I don't know how the hell you work stuff like that out.'

Tapping his nose, Doc pushed the door open. 'Dork magic.'

'We'll have to dry our wet footsteps on the way out in case he does come back soon,' Bev said, looking at the smooth surface of the painted concrete. 'Or take your shoes off.'

'Oh yeah,' Doc said, looking at the pair of wet size ten footprints his trainers had already left. 'I don't know how the hell you work stuff like that out!'

Bev tapped her nose. 'PI magic. That's why we're a dream team. Right, where's this trapdoor?'

With one eye on the window in case unexpected company arrived, Bev watched Doc sink to his knees and push the heavy canisters of Nitro Mors and other French polishing chemicals aside to reveal the outline of a trapdoor. Painted the same colour as the concrete, directly beneath the half-restored grand piano, it was easy to miss.

Bev sneezed. 'It's an old inspection pit,' she said, drawing closer. 'This place must have been built originally as a garage, and then Higson started using it as his piano workshop. I think this is a wild goose chase, Doccington.'

'Only one way to find out.' Doc said, lifting the brass ring that served as a handle.

Kneeling beneath the piano together, all thoughts of the Higsons' possible return were gone from Bev's mind. She had eyes only for the inspection pit and was so absorbed by imaginings of what might lie beneath that the arrival in the workshop of a third party took her by surprise. She leaped up and hit her head on the unforgiving underside of the grand, just as Doc had done the previous day.

'Soprano!'

There was a volley of frenzied barks as Anthony's German Shepherd made neither for Doc nor for the pit but for Higson's own toolbox that sat on a worktop beneath the window. The dog leaped up and started to gnaw at the toolbox's handle, pulling it towards the edge.

'Quick!' Doc said, scrambling backwards from beneath the piano. 'Grab the dog before it pulls the whole lot off the side.'

Too late. With a yelp from Soprano, the contents of Higson's toolbox clattered to the floor, scattering in all directions.

'Shit!' Bev said. She grabbed the dog by his collar, patting him gingerly on the head until he stopped whimper-growling at the piano tuner's tools and the box that was now lying on its side. 'I left 2Tone's kitchen door open, didn't I? Now, who's the silly soft bastard?' The dog wagged its tail and licked her knee. Barked. 'Sit! And be quiet or no Bonio for you, pal.'

'Wow. Bev! Bev! Cop a load of this!'

Bev turned back to Doc. He was sitting cross-legged on the floor by the worktop with Higson's toolbox on his lap. Empty, but for several green egg shapes that had been securely wedged in the bottom. Doc plucked one out and held it up between his fingers. It shone, as though it were wrapped in cling film.

'Is that weed?' Bev asked, leaning in for a better look.

Doc narrowed his eyes. Set the egg on the floor and unwrapped it. He shook his head as he poked a finger through the dried plant matter. 'It looks a bit like dope but it's not.' Taking a pinch, he bought it up to his nose and sniffed. 'Nope. Doesn't smell right. I know my Mary Jane well enough to know this ain't it.'

He pocketed just enough to take back to the office for closer inspection. Rewrapped the egg, setting it back in the bottom of the tool box. Then, he crawled back towards the trapdoor.

'Well, I wonder . . .' he said, yanking the door up with determination.

Still gripping the wayward Soprano by his collar, Bev approached the deep inspection pit, dropped to her knees and peered in at the strange array of equipment that was stored there. It held agricultural-standard spraying equipment, sacks of oregano and one extremely large, white sack with red Chinese writing on the side.

'I'm not sure exactly what this is,' Doc said, taking out his phone and taking photos of the eclectic collection of kit. 'But I'd say old Jim Higson is Little Marshwicke's answer to Walter White.'

'Higson?!' Bev said, open-mouthed at the odd scene they had uncovered. 'This isn't *Breaking Bad*, Doc. This is Barking fucking Mad.'

CHAPTER 23
Doc

'Hey, man. Any ideas where I can get hold of The Poison Dwarf?' Doc asked the attractive goth girl with the asymmetrical fringe and lip piercings. Blushing, he smiled his best smile towards her flat white, noticing in his peripheral vision that the girl was balking at this show of teeth.

'Er, no? Sorry. Never heard of him.' She treated her androgynous-looking companion to a meaningful, who-the-fuck-is-this-weirdo side-eye.

Realising how out of place he must look in the overalls he'd donned as his Little Marshwicke disguise, Doc scanned the rest of the unfamiliar faces in Whalley Range's most popular co-op café. This place had been his hang-out of choice when he'd first moved to Manchester. He'd been far younger then and, his dorky rocker status notwithstanding, had insinuated himself into the area's hipster milieu with relative ease. Being able to grow weed had proven to be his social green card, admitting him entry to just about everywhere. Now, the place that had once felt like a second home was *Under New Management*, according to the chalkboard sign outside. It was still freezing cold at the front, boiling hot at the back and full of students enjoying the free Wi-Fi and unlimited Fairtrade organic coffee refills, but today, Doc felt like he was an old crock out of his depth, encroaching on alien territory that belonged to the young.

He asked several other customers. All of them shook their heads or shrugged at the mention of The Poison Dwarf. Was his former ally and the area's most affable drug dealer even still alive?

Disoriented by being on turf that no longer felt familiar and still shaken by all that had come to pass that morning, Doc wandered through to the Chorlton borders in search of a bus home. The sudden onset of a downpour caused the rain-spattered lenses of his glass to fog. Shivering without his anorak and with his stomach rumbling, when he spotted a Jamaican café sandwiched between a pharmacy and an afro hairdressers in a run-down strip of shops, he decided a nice hot patty might be just the thing to thaw him out.

'God, I hope I've got enough cash,' he muttered, pulling a fistful of change from the pocket of his overalls.

He was still thumbing through the coins as he joined the queue, not paying attention to his surrounds or realising that there was soon wide open space between him and the guy in front, thanks to a gaggle of teenaged girls being served together.

'Move along, young man.' An old lady nudged him into action.

Finally, Doc looked up. At an eye-watering six feet six in height, coupled with the fact that he was the only middle-aged white Rasta leaning up against the counter in a restaurant otherwise filled with black old folks and young mums with babies in prams, the Poison Dwarf stood out immediately.

Doc wiped his damp glasses, not quite believing the serendipity of the encounter.

'Jesus! Poison Dwarf! Just the man,' he said, forgoing his place in the queue to engage in a complicated handshake full of fist-bumps and back-slaps with his former ally, as though the two of them were thirteen-year-olds.

'Doctor Doc, he be all brains and no cock! Greetings, man. Long time, no see. What gives?' As ever, Poison's eyes were bleary with watery pupils that looked as though they'd been diluted with a dropper full of liquid cannabis.

Doc noticed the eye-rolling of the other diners, who clearly thought he and this dreadlocked white man in their midst were a pair of pricks of the highest order.

'Not here,' he said. 'I need your professional opinion on something.'

As The Poison Dwarf led him deep into a small 1960s estate, he regaled Doc with tall tales of an exotic, globe-trotting semi-retirement from drug-dealing.

'So, you wouldn't believe how international my operation is now, Doctor Doc, man.' Poison did a complicated thing with his fingers that made his joints crack audibly, like an arthritic Ali G. 'Me got a woman in Paris. Me got women in Kingston – all beautiful girls.'

'Kingston, Jamaica?'

'Nah, man. Surrey, innit? And naturally, me got the good loving of an African Queen.'

'Cool. Whereabouts in Africa is she from?' Doc asked, wondering where the hell Poison was taking him.

'Actually, she be from Moss Side. But she's well . . . African on her grandad's side, even though her fam be from Droylsden originally.'

'Are you still dealing?'

They slipped inside the unlocked bin store at the foot of block of council flats.

'Odds and sods. You know. A bit of this and that. Why?'

Doc produced the herbal bounty, wrapped in cling film. 'What do you think this is?' he asked.

Poison opened the tightly packaged bounty and had had a good sniff of the contents. 'Me don't even need to be tasting this, man,' he said in his cod-Jamaican accent. A look of disgust flitted across his anaemic-looking, ageing face. 'This be Spice. Aye. Spice is nice, but not for brothers with their heads screwed on, do you feel me? Manchester be full of it. This be ungodly shit what's getting into prisons and on da street. Where did you get this? You've got quite a few quid's worth here, Doctor.'

'It's a long story,' Doc said, feeling flushed warm with the knowledge that his hunch had been correct. Not even the Jamaican patty and a can of Ting could have brought the mornings detecting to as satisfactory a conclusion.

'You're not moving from the honourable cultivation of Jah's most blessed leaf, are you?' Poison asked, scratching at his dreads. Squeezing the Spice in his other palm like a stress ball. 'It be bad karma to peddle this crap.'

Doc shook his head, holding out his hand for the wrap. He knew Poison well enough to guess that for all the dealer was bad-mouthing Spice, he'd pocket it and sell it on, given half a chance. A white man with blond dreads who called himself The Poison Dwarf and who professed to be a bona-fide Rastafarian from the mean streets of Moss Side, though he was really a lapsed Catholic called Kevin from a well-to-do family in Worsley, was hardly trustworthy. But Doc had gathered the information he'd needed.

'You ever hear of a dealer called Higson?' he asked, just as he was about to leave the cover of the bin store.

Poison shook his head. 'Nah, man. Biggest dealer in da North West of this junk be Thai Dragon, yeah? Dat cat's name be legend.'

'Do you know him personally?'

Closing his eyes and frowning, Poison sucked his teeth. 'Me not be running in dem circles with ex-cons flogging bad karma pharma dat make a man into a zombie. Dem be life-threatening motherfuckers, and me don't want no stress. I is a lover not a fighter. You feel me?'

Leaving The Poison Dwarf to the glamour of a semi-retirement that fictitiously spanned continents, Doc returned home on the bus, wondering if Jim Higson had a criminal record. Was it even feasible that such a square should be a manufacturer of the drug that had renewed Manchester's notoriety, post-rave era?

He grabbed a microwave burger and a can of Fanta and holed himself up in his office-cum-bedroom, plugging Jim Higson and Spice into his various search engines – on both the vanilla- and dark-nets. Hours later, Doc knew almost everything there was to know about domestic Spice production and its move from the legal high shops, approximately three years earlier, to the black market. He'd discovered how its use and the ensuing life-threatening damage to health had become epidemic in prisons and among the homeless communities. He'd read how it had spread countrywide, though Manchester's Piccadilly Gardens seemed to be the epicentre of the 'Zombie Apocalypse'. Finally, as he belched loudly to mark the final swig of his drink, he'd read in several local papers that Spice wasn't just a problem among vulnerable adults.

ZOMBIE DRUG FOUND IN REGION'S SCHOOLS

Police have issued a request that all teachers and parents be on alert, after the notorious drug, Spice has been found in several schools. After Head Teachers reported to GMP that a number of pupils from years 10 to 13 had been found in a state of heightened agitation and clearly intoxicated by an unidentified illegal substance, investigation revealed the children were high on Spice.

'They were tottering round like zombies,' a Head Teacher from a Longsight secondary school reported. 'It was frightening to watch – not just for the younger pupils but for the teachers too. One boy collapsed and two others became aggressive.'

'It's a scourge!' said the Chair of the PTA at a well-regarded school in Denton. 'We don't know how it's getting into school but the dealers need burning.'

At the end of the article was a hotline number. Doc made a note of the schools involved and spent a good twenty minutes drumming on his notepad with his biro.

'Higson's a piano technician,' he said, biting his pen. 'And every school has at least one piano in the hall for assembly. So, what if he goes into schools to tune pianos? Bingo!'

With his brain running at double speed thanks to the sugar and e-numbers in his lunch, Doc tried to hack Jim Higson's Outlook in the hope that he'd find a work diary online. To no avail. It seemed Higson was old skool in his record-keeping. Instead, Doc was forced to hack into the e-calendars of each affected school. He'd munched his way through two bags of Quavers, a Mars Bar and a sweet-and-sour Pot Noodle before he'd ascertained that each school had indeed had multiple visits, listed as *Higson: piano*.

At that point, he started calling Bev, only to get a text in response about a date with that brainless hump, Archie. Now, he was spinning in his typing chair, trying to control the frustration and hurt that mushroomed inside him along with the wind, caused by the pop.

'Why?' He shook his head, willing the tears to recede behind his tired eyes. 'Why does she keep getting involved with these . . . these morons?' he asked the ghoulish character, Eddie, in his iconic Iron Maiden poster for 'Aces High'. He felt just as trapped as Eddie was inside his claustrophobic bomber's cockpit. 'I don't understand why she can't just be content with the set-up she's got: a lovely daughter; a great job; me, her and Hope . . . we make a damned good team. But all she can see is some dick called Archibald who doesn't know anything beyond laying driveways and Little fucking Marshwicke with its country bullshit and its nosy dead neighbours.'

Doc's focus moved onto the super-rare, super-valuable Darth Maul Lego bust that Bev had bought him as a bribe for helping her in the previous job. At the time, he had taken it as an indication that she might love him, since when the hell did anyone willingly part with upwards of £500 for a Lego kit, unless they were either addicted, as he was, or in love with the recipient? You bought carefully thought-out gifts for the person you cared most for, didn't you?

'What a load of bullshit. Fuck you, Bev!'

Doc lifted the Darth Maul bust from its pride of place inside his display cabinet. He held it aloft and brought it smashing down on the floor. The bust that had taken him hours and hours to assemble scattered like red and black plastic rain on the hard tiled floor of his office.

The moment the skittering pieces came to a standstill, some reaching as far as the door and the cupboard in which he got stoned, he regretted his actions.

'You thick, arrogant, meathead. What have you done? You've fucked Darth Maul. No! No! You're no better than the macho wankers she shags. Be better than this, you loser!' With shaking hands, he started to sweep the scattered pieces into a heap. Where had he put the instructions? Did he even need them? Doc was a Lego-master. Surely this could be fixed before Bev got back.

As he sat cross-legged in his office, carefully reassembling the bust, heaving occasionally as post-tantrum hiccups took hold, Doc started to wonder if Jim Higson's nefarious deeds hadn't been discovered by Anthony. Perhaps Higson had hired Bev to find dirt on his wide-boy neighbour that would discredit him – a pre-emptive measure to counter anything Anthony might tell the police.

'And what if . . .' Doc mused aloud, snapping the Lego pieces together with practiced fingers. 'What if Mrs Nosy Slippers was also onto Higson, and her pally-wally piano-tuning neighbour murdered her under everyone's noses?'

It occurred to him that if Nosy Slippers had been so easily dispatched, Bev was playing a very dangerous game. If Higson realised she was snooping into her client and working next door incognito with an unfettered view of the Higson family home, might he not also go after Bev?

With a thudding heart, Doc called Bev's phone to warn her.

This time, it was picked up. Except the voice on the end wasn't Bev's. It belonged to a man . . .

CHAPTER 24
Mihal

'Give me the three pound-fifty wash,' the man in the Audi said – no hint of warmth or even basic common decency in his glum, whey-like face.

'It's five pounds for big cars, sir.' Mihal said, armed with the pre-wash spray gun. It was only 10.00 a.m. and already he was soaked through to the skin; quaking with cold, despite two hours of hard physical labour. With frostbite threatening the purple tips of his fingers poking through the soap-soaked fingerless gloves, he wasn't entirely sure he wouldn't sooner still be in prison. At least he'd been warm and dry inside. 'It's very dirty.'

The Audi driver put the full lock on his steering wheel and revved the engine. 'Three-fifty or I'll go elsewhere.'

Mihal sighed. His risible cut from washing £40,000's worth of car would be mere pennies now. He nodded, beckoning the entitled prick forwards. Started to spray the car's cordite- and mud-encrusted bodywork, pausing only when the driver shouted at him through the closed window.

'Make sure you get the alloys gleaming.'

Nodding, he fantasised about spraying the man in his piggy eyes with the same toxic chemicals he'd been breathing in for over a week. Instead, he continued to spray as if his life depended on it, pausing only to cough violently and spit the green phlegm onto the ground beyond the corrugated carwash shack.

'You'll have to work faster than that, Mihal,' his compatriot, Stefan, shouted in their native Romanian. 'Look at the queue! The boss will do his nut if they start turning around and going down the road to Sudz.'

Mihal's back twinged painfully. He swallowed the bitter words forming on his tongue and forced his freezing face to hide any discomfort or resentment he might feel that the boss was warm in his hut with the Dyson heater on, swigging Russian tea that was heavily laced with vodka. 'I'm going as fast as I can,' he said, setting the heavy canister down and hooking the spray on the scaffold that held the shack together.

He waved the Audi driver forwards by two metres. Sprayed the car with a jet of thick soapy foam until he could no longer see the disdain in the man's face. The car stereo was on, its bass thump-thumping at such volume that even in the open, Mihal could feel the vibrations in his empty, growling gut.

'I don't know how you do this, day in, day out, Stefan,' he said as Stefan started to paint the oily shine onto the tyres of a freshly valeted BMW.

'You'll get used to it, my friend. It's better than nothing. It's a start. Look at how much money Alexandru has made since he came to England. He's sitting on a fortune.'

'He's sitting on his fat arse while we all get rheumatic and spoken to like dirt,' Mihal said, pausing briefly to allow the blood to flow back into his cramped arm. Surely it was time for a break.

Stefan lifted his top and slapped his six pack. 'Yes, but the girls love *this*, not Alexandru's fat arse. Working here gives you the body of a god. I don't feel the pain when

174

I've got some nice little blonde with big tits, bouncing up and down on me. Not all stiff muscles are bad.' He laughed heartily at his own joke, abruptly falling silent when Alexandru appeared at the window of his hut, mouthing that he should get on with his work and shut the hell up.

With his right hand that was almost frozen into a claw, Mihal plucked the fat sponge from the bucket of water that had been hot and clean half an hour ago but was now freezing cold, swimming with grit and detergent. This was a grim way to get closer to The Bastard, but tapping into the network of Romanians living in the area had afforded him a roof over his head, some money in his pocket and an opportunity to gather information and lay hands on a weapon.

As the sun started to go down, Mihal's shift finally came to an end. He joined the other guys, lining up outside the hut to get their pay.

'I'm so cold,' he said. 'I can't wait to get back to the house and get warm and dry.'

Stefan grinned a rotten-toothed grin. 'Get some drink inside you. That will warm you up. Florin's making *sarmale* for dinner.'

'He can't cook,' Mihal said, his stomach rumbling at the thought of the traditional Romanian cabbage rolls his mother used to make. Now *they* had been something else.

'Better than prison food, though, right?'

Taking his meagre handout from Alexandru, Mihal hitched a ride with the others back to the house. The tiny Rochdale two-up-two-down stank of cabbage and burnt fried food the moment they walked through the door – a smell that seemed to have permeated the very walls. Ten of them piled in. The TV went on immediately and out came the vodka and cigarettes.

'I'm first in the shower,' Stefan said, sprinting up the creaking stairs before anybody could contest his claim to the limited hot water that the clapped-out old immersion heater could supply.

Repairing to the smaller of the bedrooms that he shared with three others, Mihal took his spare jeans off the radiator. They were still damp from the day before.

'Jesus, why's the heating never on?' he said to Nicolai, a lad of eighteen from a tiny village at the northernmost tip of Romania, who had arrived at the house only a fortnight before Mihal.

Nicolai stood in his grubby pants, unfurling a dry jumper over his thin torso, still bright red from the cold of spending ten hours jet-washing cars at the end of Alexandru's makeshift valeting production line. He shivered and shrugged, his breath steaming on the air. 'Stefan said the boiler broke months ago. The boss won't get it fixed.' He pulled on a pair of jogging bottoms. 'When I've saved enough money, I'm out of here. In fact, some guy came round just before you joined us, offering me work on a building site. Better paid.'

This was exactly the opportunity Mihal had been waiting for. A way back into the hidden world of trafficked labour, where he could enter unseen and with the element of surprise on his side. He felt his lips prickle. 'A building site? What did he look like?'

Narrowing his eyes, the lad seemed to be thinking about it. 'I don't remember. Forget it.'

'Hey, come on,' Mihal said, grabbing his forearm. 'Tell me more. What did the guy you spoke to look like? Was he English? White? Black? From round here? Was he bald?'

Nicolai shook him off and backed away. 'Why the hell should I tell you? So you can snatch the job from under my nose?'

'Don't be fucking stupid. Was he short? Tall? Tattoos?'

But he merely turned away and started to rummage among his things on his grubby bare mattress. Mihal could sense the opportunity for revenge slipping away from him. Impulsively, he lunged at Nicolai, pinning him by his upper arms; throwing him against the wall where he pressed his elbow to the lad's windpipe.

'Tell me!'

Nicolai's eyes were wide with fear, his face reddening. 'OK!'

Releasing the pressure on his throat, though he still had him pinioned to the wall, Mihal nodded. Spoke calmly. 'Describe him.'

'He just looked like a builder. You know?' The lad's voice was hoarse, now. He was visibly sweating. 'His top was covered in plaster. Beenie hat on. He rolled up in a black Mercedes Sprinter. He didn't get out. Just talked to me through the window at the end as he was paying.'

'Did he speak to any of the others?'

Nicolai shook his head. Smiled weakly. 'Only me. He said he'd been watching me while he was waiting in line and was impressed by my hard work.'

'Have you told the others this? Does Alexandru know?'

'No way! Alexandru was out, probably gambling the previous day's take on the horses. And the guy said to keep it to myself cos he wasn't interested in the others.'

Mihal loosened his grip on Nicolai. Patted the boy on the shoulder as if he'd passed a test with merit. Rubbed the stubble on his chin. 'Look, if this guy comes round again, point him out to me.'

Nicolai looked put out as though Mihal were some interfering, domineering father figure, denigrating his modest achievements. 'So you *do* want to muscle in on the opportunity?'

Chuckling mirthlessly, he shook his head. 'Anything but. This guy you've described? If it's the man I think it is, he works for a trafficker and he's a brutal son of a bitch. You think you've got it bad with Alexandru? That's nothing. For years, I lived in a one-man tent with my two brothers until one of the other trafficked guys got high and slashed it to pieces. They took my passport. We worked from sunup to sundown for nothing. They got us so hooked on Spice, they didn't even bother guarding us in the end, because they knew if we left the site, we'd be back for our fix. You understand?' Tears welled in his eyes. 'We took poison to get through it. But it killed my brother, Bogdan. And Constantin, too, probably. Maybe I'll never even find his grave.'

Seeing the confusion in Nicolai's glassy eyes, he shuffled away from him, took the pile of clothes off the only chair in the room and sat down. 'I'm sorry. But just be careful. If an offer sounds too good to be true, it's usually because it is. Us Romanians . . . the English treat us like the dregs of Europe. The newspapers are full of what benefit scroungers we are. They think we're the same as the thieving Roma in the tube stations of London. So, good fortune is never going to come easily in this country. Not without breaking the law. And believe me, as a Romanian, you're a million times more likely to end up behind bars than a Brit.'

He fell silent as one of the other men burst into the room, oblivious to the conversation that had been taking place. Locking eyes with the young lad whose wind-burnt face looked suddenly years older, his features seemingly sagging as if they'd become leaden with disappointment, Mihal winked and pressed his fingers to his chapped lips. 'Tell me, next time you see him.'

*

Mihal didn't have long to wait before a black Mercedes Sprinter bounced onto the car-wash forecourt, pulling up aggressively just short of the bumper of the car in front. Even before he could see the driver clearly, Mihal sensed the hairs on his arms rise from more than just cold. His gut tightened. His gullet felt restricted.

Trying to catch Nicolai's eye, he continued to spray the red Volkswagen at the front of the queue. Was the kid even paying attention? He gave a short, sharp wolf whistle that had the other men glancing over to see what was going on.

Finally, Nicolai snapped out of his reverie, pausing the flow of the jet-wash gun to see who wanted him.

'Two cars back. Is that him?' Mihal shouted over in their native tongue. 'Act natural. Don't stare.'

Nicolai switched the water back on, only stealing a momentary glance towards the Sprinter. Keeping the levity in his voice as if he were telling a joke. 'Yes. That's the one. Same guy. Definitely. No hat today, though.'

Surreptitiously, Mihal worked his way around the front of the Volkswagen so he could get a good look at the man behind the steering wheel. He was balder than he'd been three years ago. In fact, he'd shaved off what was left of his hair, save for the ghost of a day's stubble. But Mihal recognised that weather-beaten face, the broken nose and those hard blue eyes of the foreman that had kept watch over him and his brothers like a concentration camp Kommandant.

Setting down the sloshing canister of pre-cleaner and dropping his spray, he calmly put on his hood, put his head down and walked briskly over to Nicolai.

'Run,' he said. 'If you've got sense, you'll run. Or hide. But whatever you do, get as far away from that man as you can.'

179

'What?' Nicolai said, frowning quizzically. 'Why?'

'He's dangerous and he's evil. You can turn him down maybe once or twice . . .' He started to walk backwards towards the exit. 'But soon, he'll take you by force. He'll drag you in the back of that van and your life will be over. You'll be a slave.'

'Where are you going?' the lad asked, blanching.

'I need to go shopping.'

By the time the Mancunian twilight had started to bring the young thugs in hoodies onto the street like cockroaches on the hunt for rich nocturnal pickings, Mihal had made his way back to East Manchester. Combing through memories of the last six years which were entangled with fear, desperation and loss, he made his way in a daze back to the kebab, pizza and curry shop where a small group of Romanians hung out after work, vaping until the place was filled with a cloud of cranberry-flavoured smoke. Drinking strong coffee.

'You're back?' Dumitru Popescu said.

The chatter fell silent and the elderly Romanian held his arms out for an embrace. He was sitting at the head of one of the café's tables like a king in cheap knitwear, surrounded by six other men. This was his dominion where he ruled the community of recent immigrants, doling out advice and making connections. He'd lined Mihal up with the car-wash job, though it had felt more like exploitation than paid work. But still. It had been semi-legit. Maybe he'd help him a second time.

Mihal embraced him and kissed his cheeks as if he were an uncle. Took a seat by his side when one of the other men moved up at the elder's insistence.

'You look thin,' Popescu said. 'After only two weeks, I see Alexandru has trained the fat off you like an athlete.'

'I had to leave,' Mihal said, registering the disapproval in the hard set of the old man's features. 'It's time to move on. I have business to attend to.'

'What did Alexandru say?'

'I haven't told him.'

'You left without giving notice?' The old man never took his eyes from Mihal. He was clearly appraising him with sharp eyes and a downturned mouth. 'You've embarrassed me. I recommended you to Alexandru and you've let him down and betrayed my trust.' There was a sharp edge to Popescu's words, though he kept his voice low.

Mihal folded his arms. He'd had years of taking shit off people. He hadn't got rid of The Bastard only to allow himself to be saddled with a new master. 'I need a gun. I have money. And I need somewhere to stay tonight. Just a gun and a bed for one night, and then I'll be on my way.'

The other men started to laugh as if he'd requested the keys to the Oval Office in the White House along with the codes for nuclear detonation.

'You've already overstayed your welcome,' Popescu said, dragging hard on his e-cigarette. Blasting a stream of fruity smoke towards Mihal through hairy nostrils. 'And I don't know anything about no guns.'

'I don't believe you.'

Popescu's men suddenly bristled visibly with aggression. They rounded on Mihal, pushing him in the back and the chest. 'Fag. Did you play the girl in prison? Fucking homo.'

Feeling that the situation had turned against him irrevocably, Mihal started to back away with his hands held high. Fuck these stubborn sons of bitches. He had the number plate of the man who was the key to finding The Bastard. He could smell blood in his nostrils. And in a city full of illegal weaponry, Mihal knew it wouldn't take long to source the hardware he needed at a price he was willing to pay.

'Wait!'

Mihal had walked maybe ten metres along the run-down high street before one of the men from the kebab place came after him. 'What? Have you come to pour more scorn on me?'

The guy shook his head and pressed a piece of paper into Mihal's hand. 'There's an address,' he said. 'A squat. It's pretty ropey but it's somewhere to lay your head. There are a couple of Bulgarians dossing there, but the rest are junkies. Just stick with the Bulgarians. They're OK. Tell them Iulian sent you.'

'Why are you doing this?' Mihal asked.

His new-found supporter shrugged and treated him to a melancholy smile. 'Popescu told me your story. About your brothers. My fourteen-year-old sister has been trafficked. We thought she was coming over here to be a hairdresser . . .'

'Have you found her?' Mihal asked.

Looking at the pure white trainers on his feet, Iulian pursed his lips. Met Mihal's gaze anew. 'Not yet. But I will. And when I do, I'll kill the bastard that took her.' He raised an eyebrow. 'I get you, man. That's just what I'm trying to say.' He looked over his shoulder to check that they weren't being watched or overheard. 'I can see you're angry and hurting and I totally understand. I also know where you can get that gun. I'll be in touch.'

Arriving at the address he'd been given, Mihal found an old Victorian three-storey house. Once upon a time, he imagined it had been a grand family home – perhaps belonging to a doctor. Now, filthy blackened net curtains billowed through a large hole in the glass of one of the bedroom

182

windows. The door was open, though it was anything but inviting. In the small front garden lay a man who appeared to all intents and purposes to be dead, were it not for his breath fogging the cold air. His head lay in a puddle of his own vomit. With a sinking heart, Mihal realised the sort of drug that was being taken inside.

'Spice?' one of the junkies said inside, assembling a simple glass bong in readiness. 'Yeah, I fucking love it, me.' He scratched at his tattooed neck which bore the crest of Manchester City Football Club. 'Better than all the strong lager and superskunk and what have you. It's the bomb, man. It helps me to forget.'

He was schooling some woman who sat beside him on a filthy mattress, swigging from a bottle of cheap whisky. Dressed in yellowed skin-tight jeans and a stained top, she looked in her fifties but could have been in her thirties. As the junkie lit up, she watched him take his first hit with hunger in her eyes.

'I wanna get mashed up, me,' the woman said. 'Give us a go.'

Her compatriot fell backwards onto the mattress, staring at the corner of the ceiling as though the mysteries of life were inscribed there among the cobwebs.

She prised the bong from his fingers; noticed Mihal watching her. 'What you looking at? You want a bit?'

For the first time in years, Mihal felt the pull of the drug that had killed at least one brother and ruined his own life. He remembered the feeling of agitated invincibility followed by oblivion. Spice had filled the emptiness inside him at a time in his life when he'd felt utterly hollowed out. And as the sun went down on East Manchester, alone in a squat with the smell of foetid unwashed bodies, vomit and sex all around him, Mihal was feeling emptier than ever.

'Where did you get this?' he asked in English. 'Who sold you the Spice?'

The junkie on the mattress coughed and shuffled up against the wall, snatching the apparatus back from the woman. Inhaling deeply. 'Thai Dragon,' he said.

The need to get high was swilled cleanly from Mihal's weakening mind at the mention of the name. He was suddenly alert. 'Did you buy it direct?'

Chuckling, the junkie shook his head. 'Could have, like. I got connections, me. But, no. I got it from a mate.'

'Do you know where the Thai Dragon is?'

The junkie opened one eye. 'Manchester, man!'

'Who's your connection? Does he deal for the Thai Dragon?'

'You're asking a lot of questions,' the woman said. 'Who are you? Some undercover copper?'

Suddenly, the woman scrambled to her feet, regarding Mihal as though he was the proverbial cuckoo in the nest. Without warning, she brandished the whisky bottle like a cosh. Smashed it against the wall, coming at Mihal fast with the jagged edges trained on his throat.

A sharp sting as the glass punctured his skin gave way to the tickle of hot, wet blood flowing down his neck. Grabbing the woman's skinny arms, he tried to push her away but she had insane whisky-fuelled strength. Was he destined to die in this squalid hovel, thousands of miles from home and all alone?

'2Tone,' the male junkie said, blithely indifferent to the attempt that was being made on Mihal's life. 'My man, 2Tone lines me up with the Thai Dragon's best shit. Told you I . . .'

But Mihal had sunk to the floor. He failed to hear the rest of the junkie's told-you-so revelation as consciousness seeped from him, along with his life's blood.

CHAPTER 25
Doc

He felt her presence before he even woke. Smelled her deodorant — more pungent than usual, as though she'd deliberately sprayed too much to mask another smell. Saw her standing there in his mind's eye, clad in a low-cut dress with a hem that barely grazed her thighs. High heels. Make-up on. She was Bev the seductress, though his eyes were shut and she was only a sleepy mirage.

'Doc.' Bev's voice. 'Doc.'

But Bev really *was* standing there. He felt her hand on his arm. Slowly, his eyes opened and he realised he was freezing cold and stiff.

'What the hell are you doing in the egg chair? Go to bed.' There she was in the flesh, clad not in a revealing dress but in jeans. Still showing a lot of cleavage, though. She looked like she'd spent the night uncomfortably in a strange bed. Eye make-up, which she hadn't gone out in, was smudged around her eyes. Her hair was dishevelled and flat; the crappy wig and fake glasses in her hand.

'What time is it?' Checking his watch, Doc balked. 'Four? Four in the bloody morning?'

'Have you slept in the chair?' Bev asked, rubbing her arms and making for the radiator which she felt for warmth. 'Jesus, it's arctic in here. Want a brew?'

Feeling wakefulness flood back into his leaden limbs, Doc remembered. He hoisted himself out of the egg chair, unable to stem the tide of pointed words that gushed from his dry, dry mouth. 'Who was it that answered your phone? Was it him? Your new boyfriend? I've been worried sick, you know. I called you a thousand times and couldn't get hold of you.'

'I was out,' Bev said, walking out of his room. Returning, wearing a thick cardigan. 'I am allowed to go on dates, you know. I am a sodding grown-up.'

'When *that man* answered, I thought—'

'You thought what? What exactly did you think about *that man*?' Her hands were on her hips, now. Her stance was one that spelled, 'Fuck off, Doc!' very clearly indeed.

Feeling pressure on his bladder and realising he'd drunk almost a party-sized bottle of Dandelion and Burdock before falling asleep, Doc pushed past Bev. A churlish retort was trying to punch and bite its way out of his tight-lipped mouth, but he was trying desperately to be mature about his flatmate's propensity to take off for extended periods of time with halfwits and oafs.

'What happened to Darth Maul?' Bev asked, pointing to the part-assembled Lego bust on his desk.

'What do you care?'

Locking the bathroom door, he could barely pee with tension. He needed to tell her about Higson's school visits coinciding with Spice being found in the possession of students. He needed to behave like a damned grown-up and focus on the job, but all he wanted to do was burst through the door and tell her, in no uncertain terms that . . .

'You're dating a moron!'

Doc held his hand to his mouth, wishing he could push the statement back in.

Bev poked her head out of the kitchenette doorway, the sound of a boiling kettle in the background. 'What did you just say?'

I waited up all night for you to come home because I was worried. I give a massive shit about your well-being Bev, and I don't want to see you come to harm or get hurt in any way when there's a potential murderer on the loose. Those were the words he wanted to say. Instead, he stood in the hallway and blurted out, 'He's a moron, and you're playing with fire, getting involved with scum like that. Especially when someone's going round, killing off anyone who sticks their beak in where it's not wanted.'

Scratching at her scalp with one hand, clutching the tea caddy in the other, Bev faced Doc down in the narrow hallway as though they were in a cowboy-style shoot-out. 'Do me a favour, Doc. Next time, don't wait up. I'm thirty, not thirteen. The man I was with, for your information, is called Archie, and I'll be the judge of whether he's a scumbag, a moron, a murderer or all three. Who knows? Maybe he's Mr Right. You've never even met him. OK?'

'He sounds rough as arseholes.'

Bev's eye started to twitch. She held the tea caddy against her chest like a shield. 'Well, rough he may be, but at least his flies are done up in public and he flushes the chain, so think on!'

'Flushing a wee is environmentally unfriendly.'

Turning around to yank up his zip, feeling his cheeks sting with embarrassment, Doc wondered why she was being so obtuse. She'd couldn't possibly have developed feelings for a man she had zilch in common with after only a couple of hook-ups. But the moment Doc challenged her about him, she came out of her corner fighting. Perhaps he'd hit a raw nerve. Dare he push harder to see what lay at the root of her belligerence?

'Do you think it's wise or professional to be shagging someone connected to the case?'

'He's not!'

'You said he was Anthony's half-brother *and* his foreman. So, he's very connected. And if 2Tone is as dirty as the Higsons insist, he might also be involved in illegal shit. What if he's a murderer, Bev?'

'Never mind Archie! What if our client is the bloody murderer? Jim Higson could be taking out anyone in his path with poison cake. That's starting to sound pretty likely, now we know he's got a secret drugs factory under a grand piano. Who knows? Maybe Nosy Slippers found out and threatened to unmask him? This case defies logic. At the moment, nothing would surprise me.'

'But exactly how much do you know about your new fuck-buddy? Why are you so quick to turn a blind eye to 2Tone and his bully-boy crap all of a sudden? Because there's a conflict of interest, that's why, and you're not seeing straight!'

'Shut up! Stop mansplaining my own job to me.'

'It's not inconceivable that *Anthony* might have paid his half-brother to bump off Mrs Nosy Slippers. Maybe you've been rumbled and this dickhead you're shagging is planning to bump you off too.'

'Billy bullshit! I'm going for a kip. Maybe you should too. You're not making any sense.'

Retreating to his own room, Doc slammed the door shut and flung himself, still fully clothed, onto the bed. As he drifted off, he was certain he could hear Bev sobbing beyond the walls. He realised he hadn't told Bev any of what he'd discovered – online or in meatspace – since he'd met with The Poison Dwarf. It could wait . . .

*

Three hours later, they were driving up the steep incline of the M62 eastbound with nothing but silence and the hee-haw of the Morris's wipers between them. Both yawning in some sort of relay race of the perpetually exhausted, since Bev had woken only an hour later at 5.00 a.m. to tidy up in preparation for Hope's visit, that evening.

As the little car put-putted along in the slow lane behind a heavy goods vehicle, climbing up, up, up into the low-hanging cloud, Doc agonised about all the things he wanted to say; all the things he knew he should tell her. He looked out at the bleak grey-green moors and shivered at the terrible secrets they held, enshrouded in mist as much as mystery. He felt just as empty and desolate and full of subterfuge.

'I don't know why you're coming,' Bev said, finally breaking the silence. 'You should have grabbed a lie-in. You don't need to chaperone me, for God's sake.'

'Well, maybe I'm going to do a spot of investigation on my own.' In a bid to conceal what his real intentions were, now Doc finally told Bev about the school-based discoveries of Spice abuse and Higson's apparent status as a dealer to the under-18s of the Northwest region.

'Wow.' Bev raised her eyebrows when he had finished, shooting him a sideways glance. 'Just, wow. How the hell have we managed to pick up another case that's more trouble than it's worth?'

'I'd love to say I told you so.' Doc grinned and winked, feeling his insides thaw for the first time since they'd raided Higson's workshop together. He nudged her lightly.

She stiffened in the driving seat, gripping the steering wheel with white knuckles. 'Well, don't then.' Bev sprinkled early morning frost over his burgeoning warmth. 'There's no winning here if Higson turns out to be a criminal mastermind with blood on his hands.' Closing her eyes momentarily so that the Morris almost swerved into the middle lane, she shook her head. 'It doesn't bear thinking about. If he ends up in clink, we've wasted weeks of work and we won't get a single penny for our efforts. I've got too much riding on this, Doc. I need that pay cheque.'

Stop boning 2Tone's brother, then, Doc thought privately. 'Let's focus on finding out the truth, Bev.' He picked at the thick fabric of his navy workmen's overalls, twisting the grain beneath his fingers as he fought the urge to tell Bev how the bad feeling inside him was slowly mushrooming as the case evolved. 'But safety first, right? Anyone gets shirty with you and I'm not there, you call me. And if you can't get to me, call the cops. Maybe you should think about telling . . . Curtis and Owen, isn't it? The twatty detectives you love to hate.'

'We'll see,' Bev said, pulling into the slip road for the turn-off that headed back down from the tops to the Pennine wilds of Little Marshwicke. 'If Curtis and Owen get proof of Higson's little Spice lab, we definitely won't get paid.'

Doc thought about the Coroner's people who had wheeled Nosy Slippers out in a body bag on a gurney to a waiting, windowless van. A sweat broke out beneath his overalls, cocooning him in cold fear. He reached over and gripped Bev's forearm as she dropped down to third. 'Fuck it, Bev. Can't we just ditch this job and forget we ever took it on?'

'It's nothing we can't handle,' Bev said. The set of her jaw said she wouldn't countenance dissent or surrender. 'A couple more days and we'll know where the land lies. OK?'

Nodding, Doc felt the piece of paper in his overalls chest pocket, containing an address that Bev had no idea he'd pilfered from her phone when she'd been tidying up for Hope's visit.

Higson was the ideal excuse for slipping away once Bev was busy about Anthony Anthony's ironing.

'I'm just going to have a root around the cul-de-sac and then go and ask a few questions in the village,' he told her, being non-committal about how long he'd be gone. 'You have another go through 2Tone's drawers. I'll bring you something nice back from the bakery.'

Bev was clearly too distracted by that dumb bear of a dog, Soprano, jumping up on her – tail wagging, tongue lolling and with its deafening bark – to register any protest at being left alone.

Doc had work to do.

It was still early. On the main road, Doc ordered an Uber to take him straight to the home address of Bev's new lover. He sat two doors down in the cab with the engine idling. A black Mercedes Sprinter was parked in a communal bay, not far from the house. Had Bev ever wondered if Archie had been the one to knock her into the ditch? Was it possible she knew and was suffering some sort of Stockholm Syndrome that left her libidinally tied to her own abuser?

Making a note of the Sprinter's number plate, it didn't take him long to ascertain on his phone that it was indeed registered to an Archibald Peabody. Was 2Tone's half-brother home? The house seemed entirely in darkness, though the sun hadn't yet risen in earnest.

'Keep the engine running,' Doc said. 'Don't worry. I'm good for the payment.'

The cab driver eyed him through the rear-view mirror, speaking with the trace of a Polish accent and a hint of ridicule. 'I already have your credit card details, Mister. I'm not worried. Take all day!'

Creeping around to the back of Archie's house, Doc peered through the patio doors at the neat living room, trying his hardest not to imagine Bev cavorting with Archie on the hearthrug. Clearly nobody was home. And if this prick hadn't taken his van to work, how would Doc possibly find him when he could be anywhere from West Yorkshire to North Cheshire and beyond?

'Anthony!' Doc said under his breath.

Returning to the taxi, Doc brought up the tracker he'd had Bev install on the landscaper's phone at the party. Morally wrong it may have been, but right now, Doc didn't care. Archibald Peabody was a threat to the good thing that he, Bev and Hope had going, and he was determined to dig up anything that would sway her from spending time with him. It stood to reason that if Archie was also that idiot, 2Tone's right-hand man, they might feasibly be together on a job.

He couldn't get a precise reading, but the pings coming down from the masts were enough to allow Doc to triangulate the location of Anthony's phone. A wild goose chase this may turn out to be, but right now, the quarry he sought was potentially a twenty-minute cab ride away in Whitefield, North Manchester.

'Pull over here, please,' Doc told the cab driver.

The tracker had led to a leafy estate of uninspiring 1970s houses, some of which had been renovated in a contemporary style to make them seem more architecturally exciting than they were. Navigating steep humps in the road that had made Doc feel car sick, they'd passed a school on the left with nothing but expanses of green playing fields and the manicured suggestion of a golf course beyond. Now, they had pulled in halfway down a long road. Judging by the BMW 4x4s and Jeeps that still graced the well-tended frontages during the working day, it was precisely the sort of aspirational middle-class area where Anthony Anthony and his employees might be working.

'Do you want me to wait?' the cabbie asked.

'No. No thanks. You can go now. I'll call another when I need one.' Doc picked up his toolbox prop and opened the rear door. 'I might be doing this for the next few days.'

'It's not gonna be cheap, all that travelling around.' The driver craned his neck to make eye contact with Doc.

'Maybe.' Doc averted his gaze, feeling his cheeks ignite as though the stranger somehow knew what he was doing and why. 'Some things are worth spending money on.'

It took him less than five minutes of walking before he spotted a Transit van, parked outside a large detached house that appeared to have been recently extended and renovated, judging by the crisp render and grey windows. The livery on the van's side said it belonged to A.A. Developments. In front of it was parked a flatbed truck that held a bright orange mini-digger.

Hello, 2 Tone. Doc could already feel his heart accelerate from a steady beat to drumming a tattoo that would whip a Metallica fan into a head-banging frenzy. With no plan beyond turning up and seeing whatever there was to see, Doc remembered he was no hero, and that if it came to a confrontation with a gang of harassed manual workers, Doc would lose spectacularly. What the hell was he doing?

Stop being a wimp. Be a fucking Action Man for once, you wanky keyboard warrior.

He heard Anthony before he saw him, cracking some bawdy joke and laughing at his own wit or perhaps just the boyish delight at shouting the word, 'Tits!'

As Doc ambled past the van, carrying his toolkit, the house and its driveway came into view. What unfolded was a strange scene.

Anthony was standing on the curtilage, miming jiggling breasts on his own chest, clearly engaged in sexist banter with a tall, muscular bald man who had a face like a weather-beaten testicle. Archie, almost certainly. Two other men were working on the guttering of the house, standing on precarious-looking tall ladders. Another four men were on their hands and knees, laying the blocks of a new driveway. These workers looked as though they were from South-Eastern Europe or Central Asia, Doc assessed, judging by their dark colouring and the sound of the language they spoke. The men had a downtrodden, desperate air about them and at a glance, looked far older than they probably were. In the middle of a threadbare lawn, one man was cutting a block with a handheld angle-grinder, spewing out clouds of white dust that enveloped the other men and made them cough. He wasn't wearing safety goggles or gloves of any sort. Doc grimaced but kept his head down as he ambled slowly past.

Without warning, the bald man turned from his tit-themed bantz with 2Tone and marched quickly to the youngest-looking of the block workers, whose cough was ominously deep and rattling. He thumped him so hard on the side of his head that the lad keeled over. Still clutching his chest. Still coughing violently.

'Stop fucking coughing, you useless shite. You're not here to mince about like a poof. You're here to work. So, fucking get on with it before I twat you one properly.'

The other men said nothing. Kept their eyes on their own patch of the driveway. Only one of the men on the ladders said something in his own tongue to the coughing lad.

'Hey! You! Get on with them gutters and mind your own fucking business!' Anthony said, making for the ladder.

By now, Doc had moved beyond the house and was two doors down. No cars at home. He took his chances, squatting behind two wheelie bins. Watched as the pocket-sized landscaper grabbed the foot of the long ladder and started to shake it.

'No! Please! I work. I work.'

Though Doc couldn't see the man's face clearly, he could hear he was terrified, clinging on to the guttering with the ladder and his legs swaying improbably from side-to-side beneath him.

'The plot thickens,' Doc muttered quietly to himself, his stomach in knots.

His own memory of lying on the cold tarmac of the school playground was suddenly vivid. Doc saw the delighted faces of the other boys, standing over him, enjoying the spectacle of Tim Carson's size eights finding their way home in the soft tissue of a fourteen-year-old Doc's stomach.

Get up, Shufflebotham. Take your beating like a man, you fucking weirdo poof.

Carson's voice still rang in his ears as though Doc was not a grown man, squatting behind paper- and green waste-recycling bins in Whitefield, but still a schoolboy, lying on that unforgiving tarmac.

'Oi! What the hell are you doing?' A hostile voice cut through the reminiscence.

Doc was taken by surprise when he was dragged to his feet by his overalls.

CHAPTER 26
Bev

'You can't go back,' Doc said, placing a territorial hand on the driver's seat of the Morris.

Bev tried to shoulder him out of the way but his hand stayed put. She could feel the warmth of his breath on her left ear.

'Stop leaning forward like that, for Christ's sake,' she said in a friendly sing-song voice. Still smiling, lest Sandra from the charity shop, who was sitting comfortably in the passenger seat, cotton onto their argument. 'And I don't want to talk about work while I'm doing Sandra's shopping run.'

Bev patted the old lady's arm.

Sandra turned to her and smiled. 'Thank you, dear. This is very good of you.'

'But 2Tone's dodgy as hell. I'm telling you,' Doc persisted. 'And so is that prick you're sleeping with.'

Torn between wanting to hear Doc's tale a second time and wanting him to shut his mouth and drop the subject, Bev opted to mask her hurt and frustration by ignoring him and focusing on her car-donor. The Polo was a write-off and the insurance were playing hardball, refusing to accept that she'd been the victim of a third party's reckless driving, since she'd not given the police a valid number plate from the Sprinter van and there had been no sign of a wayward sheep, ram or anything else on four legs. She needed Sandra's Morris more than ever. And Sandra needed her.

'All right, Sandra,' she shouted, annunciating clear enough for the woman to read her lips. Pointing to her ears. 'We'll take you for new batteries first and get those hearing aids sorted out. Then Sainsbury's. OK?'

Sandra nodded and glanced back at Doc. 'Very good. Batteries. Yes.'

The parking bays were all full on The Downs. Typical. Sticking the Morris on a double yellow, Bev got out to help Sandra from her seat.

'*You* can stay where you are,' she told Doc, not bothering to hide the irritation in her voice.

'Why?'

'Shout if you see a Traffic Warden. Do you think you can do that without going off-piste?'

She slammed the door on his passive-aggressive retort. Bloody man! Who the hell did he think he was, stalking Archie like that? As she ushered Sandra in through the door to the hearing aid centre, she exhaled heavily through her nostrils, privately admitting that Doc had only proven what she'd already suspected. The foreman was a scumball and a bully, related to and working for an unscrupulous abuser of the vulnerable, at best and a slaver, at worst.

'Can I help you?' the impatient-sounding receptionist seemed to have asked the question several times already, but Bev's mind was elsewhere.

'Yes. My friend here needs new batteries for her hearing aids. Will you sort her out, please? Poor sod's deaf as post.'

As the girl fussed around Sandra, Bev stood in the window of the shop, looking out at Doc. Sitting on the back seat of the Morris, he was oblivious to her watching him. Gawping down at his phone, in all likelihood. What the hell had possessed him to spend all that money on taxis and risk life and limb by spying on potentially dangerous men in a clearly incendiary situation?

She shook her head. Knew the answer, of course, and felt warmth spreading across her chest at the thought of what Doc was prepared to do for her. But then, Bev reflected, with her experience of men, she ought to know better than to have Mills & Boon sensibilities. How was Doc any different to Rob? Regardless of whether he'd uncovered a hotbed of criminal intrigue or not, the fact was that his following Archie had been a deliberate act of control. He'd set out to malign her bedfellow in a bid to influence her sexual choices and curb her freedom. *Oh, shut up, you cynical cow,* a voice said from deep within her. *Maybe the guy's just hopelessly in love with you and jealous as hell.*

At that moment, Doc looked in at her and gave her a timorous wave.

He's quietly controlling and just like all the others, the more familiar voice of inner Bev spoke. *He'll break your heart the moment you let your guard down. At least if you never let him in, he can't hurt you. None of them can as long as you push them away.*

She flipped him the bird and turned back to Sandra.

The trawl round Sainsbury's was excruciating. Doc pushed the trolley while Bev grabbed the items on Sandra's list from the shelves. The elderly charity-shop worker trudged along at the side, clearly struggling with her swollen ankles and feet stuffed inside overly tight shoes.

'Why don't you go back to the car and rest?' Bev asked her. 'Leave me and Doc to do this. Honestly, we're more than capable.'

'Are you?' Sandra asked. She took the pack of spring cabbage from Bev's hand and raised her glasses to her forehead to allow her to read the 'use by' date. 'Well, that's on the turn for a start. Buy the stuff on the bottom, for heaven's sake. And why are you glaring at James? What has he done?'

Bev felt like a kid who'd been copped smoking behind the sixth form blocks by a strict teacher that saw everything. 'I'm not.'

'Tomatoes!' Sandra said, grabbing the side of the trolley and almost rolling it over Bev's feet.

'She's not glaring at me,' Doc said, unexpectedly leaping to Bev's defence. 'We've got a difficult case on our hands. We've reached a point where we need to involve the police.'

'Oh dear,' Sandra said. Again, she snatched a packet out of Bev's hands. Squeezing the produce beneath the plastic with gnarled, arthritic fingers. 'These aren't firm. Put them back.'

It was all Bev could do to keep her cool. She checked her watch. 'Look, Sandra. I've got my daughter turning up in just over an hour. Can we crack on?' She turned to Doc. 'And can we not discuss our confidential case with other people please? Show a bit of bloody professionalism.'

'Ooh, mind your language!' Sandra said.

'Glad your new batteries are working so well.' Bev dumped the tomatoes in the trolley and strolled off towards the meat aisle.

As Sandra poked and prodded a variety of value chickens, Doc manoeuvred the shopping trolley and his lanky body so that Bev was sandwiched between him and the refrigerated display with no escape. 'Call Curtis and Owen at GMP,' he said. 'Give them the lot. Higson's a dangerous dealer – potentially a murderer. Anthony's into all sorts. You've got to know when to hold 'em and know when to fold 'em, Bev. We can pick up some insurance-fraud work instead.'

Sorely tempted to ram the trolley into her business partner and tell charity-shop Sandra where to shove her fussy shopping habits, Bev opted to do neither. More unwilling than unable to articulate her frustrations, she conducted the rest of the shopping in silence. Dutifully, she drove Sandra home to Timperley, helped Doc to carry in the shopping, put it all away in the cupboards of Sandra's stipulation and set the old woman up with a cup of tea, a slab of fruit cake and *Countdown* on the television.

'See you in three days,' she said, heading back out to the car. Checking her watch again to see that she had enough time to shower off the day's grime before she picked Hope up.

As she made her way down Sandra's draughty hall, she heard the charity shop worker dispensing wisdom to Doc.

'You're barking up the wrong tree there, James.'

'What do you mean?' Doc spoke in a half-whisper.

'She's not for you. I see the way you look at her and she's nice enough, but I've met girls like her over the years. She'll chew you up and spit you out because it's all she knows.'

There was a brief pause. Bev imagined Doc standing there, clasping his hands before him like a chastised little boy. Would he badmouth her?

'Er, I'm sorry, San, but I'd prefer not to discuss it with you, if you don't mind. Bev's the best person I know. She's just . . . Listen. I'll drop round tomorrow. Enjoy your pie.'

By the time he caught her up, Bev was already halfway down the garden path, pretending she'd heard nothing. Biting back resentful tears at Sandra's harsh judgement.

Hating that the old lady was so very, very right. How could Bev know how to love a man when the only men she'd loved had treated her so badly? Only with her daughter did Bev feel sure-footed and even then, she constantly doubted her quality as a parent compared to other mothers.

It wasn't until they arrived back at the flat that she broke the anguished silence.

'I've thought about what you've told me,' she said, peering wistfully into the fridge at the chocolate mousse she'd bought for Hope and the bottle of cheap gin that was chilling in the vegetable compartment. 'If what you say about the school visits and the Spice-busts is true, I'm going to report Higson. I can't have addicted, overdosing kids on my conscience. But Anthony . . . well, I'm hanging fire on that until I'm sure. He's off to Abersoch for a week soon and he's left me a stack of cash to house-sit. Money's money. I need to buy Hope some new uniform and it costs an arm and a leg. Also '

'Also, he's using trafficked workers on his jobs!' Doc said, grabbing a packet of Jaffa Cakes from the Sainsbury's bag on the kitchen table, opening it and shoving four in his mouth at once.

Bev took out the gin bottle and held it close. Thought better of it and returned it to the fridge. 'We don't know that until we've spoken to those men. They might just be casual labour, treated badly. There's no proof. There's no law against speaking to employees like they're shit when they're almost certainly cash-in-hand workers. God knows, I've been verbally abused and used as a whipping boy at legitimate companies over the years! Nobody gave a shit about it at a blue-chip like BelNutrive, so why's it such a big deal for a bob-a-job landscaper?'

201

'The neighbour that copped me spying behind his wheelie bins said Anthony's workmanship is shoddy.' Doc spoke with his mouth full, chewing noisily. 'He's done a few jobs round there. Luckily, the neighbour was more pissed off with 2Tone for fucking up his sinking drive than with me for trespassing. I told him I was from Trading Standards.'

Bev could smell the orange in the Jaffa Cakes and snatched the box from the table, taking two from it and staring hard at the sweet junk she knew she shouldn't be eating. She shook her head. Ate the cakes anyway. 'I'm hanging fire on Anthony. But you had no right to go after Archie like that. What the fuck were you thinking?'

Doc's noisy chewing felt like an affront. He stood up suddenly. 'I was watching your back. I was doing due diligence because I know you've got too personally involved. And turns out I was right to.'

Forging her response in the flames of her anger, she spat the words out like molten steel. 'Who do you think you are? Seriously, Doc. You're being weird. You've overstepped a mark.'

'Fuck you. I was doing you a favour. You're too good for that bonehead.'

'I don't need you to school me in what constitutes a bad man, Doc. I can find them easy enough. I've got a knack for it, haven't I? I'm well aware Archie is wrong for me and actually, deeply unpleasant. Right? But if I want to fuck him, I will. Because I'm a single woman and I'm not doing anybody any harm.'

'But you're hurting yourself, Bev. I don't want you to see you get your heart broken or worse.'

'Why do you care so much?' She'd been shouting, she realised. But she was about to elicit the very response she didn't want to hear. She couldn't cope with that level of honesty. She held her hand up. 'In fact, don't bother. Don't say a word.'

But Doc was on his feet. Unexpectedly, he grabbed her by the upper arms and pulled her to him, kissing her squarely on the lips. They broke apart. 'I love you.'

Stunned, she looked into his eyes momentarily. Found she started to kiss him back passionately as though she were driven from within by a woman she'd never met before. Her tongue was entwined with Doc's. Lights sparked behind her eyelids.

What had she done?

CHAPTER 27
Hope

'Young lady! Have you been listening to a single word I've just said?' Mr Carr said.

Hope looked up, yanked from her daydream by the irritation in her teacher's voice. She'd been lost in an imaginary world in which all the popular girls were her friends, and in which her dad didn't have a new girlfriend who clearly disliked Hope, judging by the fact that she'd never even asked her what year she was in at school or what hobbies she had. Now, Mr Carr was standing right by her desk, looming over her with arms folded; his eyes boring into the side of her head.

'Yeah,' Hope said, wishing she could hide beneath her desk.

'*Yeah?* "Yeah," what? What did I just say, Hope?'

On any other day, she might be able to cope with being singled out by her notoriously strict teacher and she might easily shrug off the sniggers of ridicule rippling across the class towards her from that big pink-faced pig, Olivia Dodds and her gang, but today, she was running on empty. She'd gone to bed at 11.00 p.m., thanks to Dad having his girlfriend round for dinner for the first time and her turning up late because she'd, 'been busy and couldn't just drop everything to fit in with some kid'. The stupid skinny girlfriend hadn't eaten any of her food, even though

Hope had helped Dad to make the pasta sauce. She'd just pushed it round and around her plate, playing with a lock of her blonde hair like the populars did at lunch to make the boys like them more. Then, when Hope had eventually turned in for the night, she'd heard Dad and his boring, bad-breathed new girlfriend doing gross snogging noises and apparently jumping up and down on the bed (Hope suspected this was what sex sounded like but she hadn't liked to bring up the subject).

'Yeah, I mean, no. Eh? What was the question?' She accidentally yawned in Mr Carr's face and knew she'd made a mistake when his eye started twitching.

'See me after school, Hope Mitchell.'

Olivia Dodds and the others started to giggle, clearly savouring every minute of her being in trouble.

Just as the realisation dawned that this was going to be another stinker of a day during the worst year she'd ever endured at school, Hope spotted the nice supply teacher peering in at her through the glazed door to the classroom. The woman smiled and waved, holding up a small white box. She pressed her index finger to her lips, as though her presence was her and Hope's little secret.

Suddenly, things were looking up. What did the friendly teacher have in the box? Could it be something cool that she wanted to show Hope?

When the bell rang, signalling the start of lunch, Hope was buffeted out of the classroom by the other kids, all starving hungry and desperate to see if chips were on. She immediately spotted the supply teacher sitting in the cloakroom area, rendered almost invisible among the coats and mess.

'Hi, Hope. How are you?' the teacher asked, patting the empty space beside her on the bench.

Hope sat down, glancing at the box. The box looked like the sort you got in fancy cake shops. Her stomach rumbled audibly.

'I'm OK, thanks.'

'Were you getting told off in there?' The woman spoke with a raised eyebrow as though they were about to share a secret. 'I could see your grumpy old teacher standing over you. He's got a face like an old sock.'

Hope laughed, delighted by this apparent betrayal by one teacher of another. 'Yes.' She looked down at the woman's pink fingernails and then expectantly over at the box to her right. 'But it wasn't my fault I wasn't listening. I was tired and it was boring and the other girls were being mean.'

'Well, I've got something that'll cheer you up,' she said, picking up the mystery item. 'After we last spoke, I had a feeling you might like these. I made them myself.'

She opened the lid to reveal four perfectly iced cupcakes. They were mouth-watering shades of pink and purple with pearlescent balls on top. Hope thought they looked the most delicious things in the world.

'You made these for me?' At that moment, she wanted one of those cupcakes more than to play on Doc's Xbox all day long, more than to move in with Mum-Mum, instead of having to live with moody old Dad, more than to go bowling on her birthday and score a strike without the barriers up.

The teacher nodded and passed one to her. 'Here. This will definitely perk you up.'

Nodding fervently, Hope sank her teeth into the thick, perfect swirl of the icing. The sweetness registered on her tongue immediately like a little burst of all that was heavenly. She ignored the slightly bitter aftertaste.

Smoothing her skirt over her knees, the teacher smiled and patted her gently on the shoulder. 'I knew you'd like them. So anyway, tell me. I was thinking about your mum the other day and how we used to be good friends. Does she ever talk about her work when she comes home?'

'A bit,' Hope said, barely intelligible with a mouth full of cake.

'Does she mention the cases she's working on at the time? She's got a cool job. I bet it's interesting if she does.'

Hope shrugged. 'Sometimes she argues with Doc about work. I don't really listen.'

'Doc?'

'Yeah. He works with Mum. They live together too. In the office.' Chewing away, Hope was suddenly aware of a giant, painful bubble of wind swelling in her belly. Would this nice teacher think any less of her if she farted?

They talked for a while – the teacher asking questions about Mum and the hours she kept on her job and all sorts of things about Doc and what Hope liked to do at the weekend. After the visit from Dad's horrible disinterested girlfriend, and with Mum-Mum constantly being so busy and tired and worrying about other things, Hope was loving every minute of talking to the teacher, who seemed only too willing to listen.

By the time the bell had rung, signalling the end of lunch, Hope had eaten all four of the cupcakes and was now clutching at her stomach, desperate to get to the toilet and let the giant pocket of wind go behind a closed door.

'I've got a little extra something for you,' the nice teacher said. 'Next time you're feeling down about school or your mum and dad, use it.' She slid her a little gift-wrapped rectangle. 'But open this when you're alone. It's our little secret.' She winked.

Hope nodded weakly, fingering the silky wrapping paper. It had balloons on it in rainbow colours. 'Thanks.'

Though maths was beginning, Hope was happy to pocket her gift and take her leave from the teacher. She sprinted to the mercifully empty toilets and there she sat for twenty minutes, unable to stem a bout of gut-wrenching diarrhoea. The solitude was punctuated by a creaking door. She had company.

'Mitchell! Hey, Hope Mitchell! I know you're in here, you big skiver.'

Doubled up with ferocious stomach cramps, Hope recognised the snarky voice of Olivia Dodds immediately. She sat in silence, praying the bully would give up when her taunts went unanswered.

But of course, Olivia Dodds wasn't about to give up the chance to humiliate her arch rival. 'I can smell you, you know. Mr Carr's going to go mental.'

One after the other, her tormentor slammed the doors of the unoccupied cubicles against the cubicle walls until she came to Hope's locked door. Her voice resonated on the tiled surfaces.

'I can see your shoes.'

'Big fupping deal,' Hope said. 'I've got the squits, and you can tell that to Mr Carr.' Her heart thundered away, making her voice ragged, but she knew instinctively that she shouldn't let a bully know she was intimidated. 'I'm not scared of you, pig-face. Get lost. Or are you trying to get a look at my knickers?'

'Oh, God. You're so disgusting.' The nasal voice said Dodds was now squeezing her nose.

'Go, then!'

'Right then. I will.'

Hope was alone again. Half an hour later, she emerged feeling slightly better. Mr Carr asked if she wanted to go home, clearly forgetting he'd given her a detention. But Hope said that her parents were working and that she'd rather stay in school. She didn't want to admit to either of them that she'd got sick because she'd been greedy.

At the end of the day, Hope was pulling on her coat when she saw the man in the green Puffa once again. It was the fourth time she'd seen him, standing on the other side of the playground railings, staring in at her. She rubbed her eyes, wondering if she was imagining him. But he was still there five minutes later, and Mum still hadn't shown up. The playground was starting to empty out.

Just as Hope started to panic that her parents had mixed up her school run arrangements, leaving her stranded, she caught sight of Mum, jogging across the playground, wearing a harried expression. She was scratching at her head. Hope ran out to meet her.

'Sorry I'm late, doll. That bloody Doc is going to put me in a loony bin. I could have clobbered him this morning. He's soft in the head. Anyway, never mind him.' She planted a big kiss on Hope's forehead. 'Ooh, you're a yummy girl. How was your day?' She held Hope's chin between her finger and thumb. 'You look peaky. Are you ill? You should have called me if you're ill. I hope you're not coming down with something.' She felt her forehead.

Feeling emboldened by her mum's presence, Hope wanted desperately to get a closer look at the man in the green Puffa, now. There he was, standing only metres away behind the railings, where he waited and waited. Their paths would surely cross, yet with his hood up, his face was still shrouded in shadow.

'I need to tell you something, Mum-Mum,' she said, feeling that she should have told her mum ages ago about him.

'Come on. I'm parked on double yellows. Quick!' But Mum was frog-marching her quickly towards the gate. The shoulder strap of her old handbag suddenly failed, scattering the contents on the playground.

'Bollocks! I hate that bag.'

Hope knelt to help her mum gather the mess of handkerchiefs, a purse, lipstick, battered business cards and keys back in the bag. By the time she looked up again, the Puffa-wearing pervert had vanished.

Back at Mum's place, Doc greeted her with his usual enthusiastic fist-bump, but Hope noticed that his eyes were red.

'Have you been crying?' she asked him.

Doc looked over at her mum. A shadow seemed to pass over his face. 'Conjunctivitis,' he said. 'Wanna do Lego?'

'You bet.' Hope was about to skip along the hallway to his room, when her mum grabbed her by the hand.

'You can't do Lego with him today, sweetie,' she said. 'We're going out for pizza,' Mum said.

Doc's expression brightened. He punched the air. 'Yessss! Make mine a meat feast with extra cheese.'

'Not you, dickhead,' Mum-Mum said.

The hour that they spent in Pizza Express felt like hard work, despite the extra pepperoni. Hope wasn't entirely sure what had gone on with Doc, but she knew her mother looked sad. She considered using this alone-time to tell her about the nice teacher friend and the staring man in the Puffa but opted not to. The last thing she wanted to do was frighten her mother. She didn't want her to cry or wind up looking any more exhausted than she already did.

On their return, Doc was waiting for Mum in the living room.

'We need to talk about Jim Higson,' he said, sitting in his egg chair with his long legs sticking out, like an over-sized chick trying to hatch.

'I'm not talking to you.' Mum hurled a pizza box into Doc's lap. 'You're an idiot. Have this.'

He opened it and smiled, taking out a bendy piece of left-over margherita.

'Who's Jim Higson?' Hope asked, sitting on the sheep-skin rug at Doc's feet.

'He fixes pianos,' Doc said, chewing. 'We're working for him, but it's all a bit of a mess.'

'You eat like a bloody T-Rex,' her mum told Doc. 'Stop talking with your mouth full. For God's sake! Bring it in the kitchen.'

By the time they'd all sat around the little table, the atmosphere between her mum and Doc seemed to have improved.

'You've got to call the cops,' Doc said. 'It's too big for us.'

Mum shook her head. 'But, if I do, that's it. The end of the case.'

'Is that such a bad thing?' Doc put a hand on top of her mum's arm.

Mum withdrew her arm and turned to Hope. 'Get your homework out, love. Mum-Mum's got a call to make.'

Hope pretended to do her English homework as she eavesdropped on her mum's call to a detective called Owen. Some ten minutes later, she ended the call.

'How did it go?' Hope asked.

'Fine, baby. Detective Owen knows me from my last case. I handed all the evidence over to her, so she trusts me. But I am going to have to go into the police station to give a statement.'

'Now?'

'Yes. I'm afraid so. You can stay up to watch *Bake Off* with Doc, but you have to go straight to sleep when it's

211

finished. Right? He'll tuck you in. I'll kiss you when I get back.'

Hope noticed how her mother's eyes suddenly looked heavy as they did when she'd had a night full of bad dreams or had been worrying about paying the bills. 'Is everything all right, Mum?'

Her mum shook her head. 'Yep. Course.' She exchanged a look with Doc that said everything was far from all right. 'As long as the police arrest this man and he never finds out I was behind it, I'm fine.'

Later, Hope lay in her camp bed in her tiny room, looking at the shafts of street light that found their way through chinks in the curtains, zig-zagging like lightning across the ceiling. It was then that she remembered the gift-wrapped object the friendly teacher had given her.

Rummaging in her school bag in the semi-darkness, Hope pulled the small rectangle out and tore the paper off. It was a smartphone, and with it was a note. She tiptoed over to the curtains and read it in the street light.

Dear Hope,

Here is a little something to cheer you up. It already has WhatsApp loaded onto it. I'll be in touch soon, as I'd like to make a cake for your mum. I really like to bake and I know your mum's birthday is coming up . . .

It's best not to tell your mum yet about our friendship and this phone, because your mum is so busy with work and it's meant to be a surprise.

Dizzy with excitement, Hope switched the phone on and saw that a WhatsApp message was already waiting for her. It was from the teacher.

CHAPTER 28
Bev

Lying awake in Anthony's master bed, Bev was relieved that a second night of insomnia was almost over. Three days had passed since she'd made her statement to Detectives Curtis and Owen at the GMP head offices, providing them with enough evidence to make an arrest. 2Tone had driven off to his holiday home in Abersoch with Soprano, leaving her with a roll of cash in her apron and the responsibility of house-sitting. *Still* nothing had happened at the Higsons'. But she knew it was about to. The clock said 4.02 a.m. Dawn was almost upon Little Marshwicke. Any minute now . . .

She drifted off momentarily but was woken only seconds later by a cacophony of multiple racing engines and squealing tyres, loud enough to wake the dead. Then, slamming car doors.

'This is it!' she said, scrambling out of bed and taking up position at the side window of 2Tone's bedroom, where she'd have an excellent view of the Higsons' frontage.

With a thudding heart, she looked down on the scene of mayhem that dominated the beleaguered cul-de-sac. For the second time that month, the place was littered with police vehicles: two police vans, one police car, the dog van, the crime scene investigator and the unmarked car of detectives Owen and Curtis of Greater Manchester Police's HQ.

What she hadn't anticipated, however, was Higson standing at his bedroom window in his blue pyjamas, pulling on his brown dressing gown and grinning down at the scene. Penny joined him, wide-eyed, with her hand clasped to her chest, her lips forming a perfectly round, 'ooh' of surprise. Did they think the police had finally come for Anthony Anthony? Yes. Bev was sure of it.

'You're in for a bloody surprise,' she muttered.

Sure enough, the smile slid from Jim Higson's mouth and Penny backed out of sight as Owen and Curtis marched up to the front door, flanked by five enormous uniformed officers and two dog-handlers. Meanwhile, a group of officers skulked round to the back, presumably anticipating an attempt at escape.

One of the uniforms thumped aggressively on the front door at Owen's say-so.

'Police! Open up!' he bellowed.

Within seconds, hardly waiting for a response, a battering ram was swung rhythmically against the peeling paint of the door by another uniform until the wood splintered and the door burst open. The police officers filed inside. Bev was sure she could hear Penny screaming and Higson yelling.

On the cul-de-sac, the other neighbours had started to emerge from their homes, shuffling together with coats over their night clothes and slippers on their feet – just far removed enough to avoid being sucked into the drama but close enough to get a good view of the demise of a man they'd presumably trusted for decades.

Higson and Penny were manhandled out of their house only minutes later in their bed attire with their hands in cuffs. The piano tuner's face was bright red, his expression thunderous as Curtis marched him towards the police van. Though he was talking to the detective, Bev wasn't able to hear his words with the window shut. Owen led Penny Higson, whose complexion was ashen. For a statuesque, middle-aged woman, she appeared suddenly far smaller and older, hunching further as she caught sight of the small crowd of neighbours that had gathered on the far side of the cul-de-sac.

Desperate to hear what was being said as Jim Higson wriggled and struggled to avoid being pushed into the awaiting van, Bev cracked the window at the front of the bedroom. She was pleased to find the stiff breeze and acoustics of the cul-de-sac whisked his words right to her.

'There must be some mistake!' he shouted, his naked indignation and fear almost rippling in visible waves on the air. 'It's Anthony you want! That little oik's up to all sorts of no good.'

Curtis whispered something into Higson's ear. Put a hand on his head and started to push him in earnest into the back of the van.

'This is preposterous,' the piano tuner yelled. 'Tell them, Penny! Tell them they've got the wrong man. It's a stitch-up!' He leaned backwards, trying to catch the attention of the already captive audience of neighbours. 'This is police brutality. I pay my taxes! I'm respectable.'

As uniforms came to Curtis's aid, bundling Higson into one van, Penny was fighting her own battle with Owen, trying to avoid being pushed into another. 'No! No! Get your hands off me!' she shouted. 'Let go! You're making a big mistake! I don't know what Jim's got himself into, but I'm innocent.'

Two forensics guys walked past the contretemps, carrying large white plastic evidence boxes to their van.

'It's nothing to do with me!' Penny protested, staring at the boxes.

Bev watched the dawn drama unfold, knowing she had done the right thing to inform on her client but regretting bitterly that the only money she and Doc would see from this job would be the cleaner's wage that Anthony was paying her. The £500 that Anthony had paid her for house-sitting for the week while he was in Abersoch wouldn't even touch the loss she'd made on the Polo. Thanks to sleeping with Archie, who had more than likely been responsible for running her off the road, Bev had made it impossible to inform the police in retrospect and claim on his insurance. Jim Higson may have been hoisted by his own petard – namely Beverley Saunders, Private Investigations – but Bev had done an equally grand job of sabotaging herself, thanks to an overactive libido and perennially poor judgement when it came to men. Speaking of which . . .

She called Doc, blinking hard to dispel the mental image of their clinch and the feel of Doc's tongue intertwined with hers.

He picked up on the second ring.

'It's done. They've both been arrested.'

On the other end, Doc merely breathed noisily down the phone. Finally, he spoke. 'And what about 2Tone and Archibaldy?'

'We'll see. Let me think on it. I've only got your word for it that Anthony's using slave labour.'

'Thanks a bundle for the vote of confidence. Are you coming back?'

'I'll pop back later, but only to pick some things up. For now, I'm gonna run myself a soaky bath and keep an eye on next door. The place is still crawling with coppers and dogs and forensics types.'

'I'll do fish-finger butties for lunch. I know they're your favourite. Or beans? I could do beans.'

Bev sighed, feeling Doc's kind words wend their way out of the phone and wrap themselves around her neck like a noose. 'Jesus, Doc. You know I'm house-sitting. I said I was only picking some bits up. I'll be back when I'm back, OK?'

'But I thought—'

'You don't have to make my tea like I'm a kid . . . or your girlfriend.'

'Oh, suit yourself.'

He hung up, leaving Bev staring dolefully out at the cul-de-sac full of other people's drama that could barely compare with her own.

Later that morning, lying in the deep foam bath that she'd run for herself in Anthony's lavish en suite, Bev realised that the case she'd hoped would rescue her from financial bedlam and help her to reclaim control over her own life had resulted in her becoming nothing more than a domestic skivvy in a wig, driving somebody else's car and inhabiting somebody else's life. Her law-abiding client had turned out to be a criminal mastermind with a vendetta against his possibly blameless wide-boy neighbour. Perennially misguided Doc had turned out to be right that neighbour disputes were trouble, *and* despite Bev not fancying him one iota, he'd proven himself to be a surprisingly good kisser. Down was up and up was down. Her world no longer made any sense whatsoever and she desperately needed to numb herself to this surreal reality.

Closing her eyes, Bev ran her hands over her breasts in the warm foamy water; stroking her newly trim body until her hand came to rest between her legs. Could she find Doc attractive? Had the man she really needed been under her nose all along? Imagining her business partner naked and on top of her, she slowly rubbed herself until the silken flow of her own arousal merged with the bathwater. Felt her nipples harden in the steamy bathroom air as she pursued the hot rush of climax. Saw Doc in her mind's eye, coming inside her as she breached her own tipping point. Bev cried out and bucked up, splashing far too much water and suds over the side of the bath.

The moment she had come, all she could feel was embarrassment and annoyance that the unsavoury fantasy had been such an incredible turn-on.

Clambering out of the bath, Bev dried herself roughly, mopped up the semi-flood with her towel and donned a fluffy robe. She'd never felt so dirty after a long bath.

Trudging to the window, she peered out. The view that greeted her was unexpected.

'Penny!' she said. 'Penny fucking Higson!'

The mousy wife of an unlikely master criminal was paying a taxi driver. She turned around and looked towards Chateau d'Antoine. Bev backed away from the window, wondering what to do. She wanted answers, but she didn't want to unmask Gail's true identity.

Donning her clothes, shoes and coat as quickly as she could, Bev slipped out of the front door and waited until Penny had retreated inside her house. Allowing a couple of minutes to elapse, she waited behind the garden wall, crouched behind a large rhododendron bush. With Mrs Nosy Slippers dead and the other neighbours all gone, she hoped nobody else had eyes on her. Taking a deep breath, she emerged from her hiding place and strode up the drive. Pressed the bell. Knocked briskly on splintered woodwork of the busted door for good measure. Held her breath when she realised that only the Morris was parked on the cul-de-sac. With the cops all gone and no other visitors' cars in view, would Penny Higson deduce that her own PI was the scruffy-haired, bespectacled interloper who had recently been appearing most mornings in the Morris Traveller, carrying a Vileda bucket?

'Beverley. Oh.' Penny had opened the door only a fraction. She peered down at Bev through the gap wearing a sour, disappointed expression. Her sharp features seemed extra-taut with stress. 'You should have called. Now's not a good time, I'm afraid. I'll be in touch. Goodbye.'

As she started to slam the front door in her face, Bev wedged her foot in the way. Registered the sting as the force of Penny's anti-social intent almost crushed the bones inside her inadequate canvas pumps. Not like in the movies.

'Move your foot, Beverley. I want to be alone.'

'Christ almighty, Penny. You nearly took my toes off!' Bev pushed at the door until she got a good view of her employer's look of irritation. 'Let me in! A birdie told me Jim's been arrested, and it's not for nicking sweets from Tesco. I want answers. I think you owe me that much.'

Inside, the place smelled strongly of potpourri and dust. Bev sneezed with gusto, following Penny into a living room that should have been a snapshot of 1990s chintz and *Antiques Roadshow* clutter, but which was in disarray. Beyond the living room in what might have been intended to be the dining room, she glimpsed a grand piano with a wide stool, big enough for two.

Bev sat on the edge of a jacquard sofa that looked like Multiyork's best but which had seemingly been slashed open during the police search to reveal the fat white stuffing inside.

'Look at the state of this place! What a mess!' Penny said, looking ill at ease in an easy chair and smoothing down her pleated skirt. Her eyes were glassy; her lip trembling. 'I feel brutalised. It'll take me weeks to clear up.'

'It's not so bad,' Bev said.

'It *is*. Anyway, how do you know about Jim?' She reached for a box of tissues, lying on its side on the floor and blew her nose daintily. 'Was it you?'

'Was it me, what?'

'Did you rat out my husband?'

'Of course not!' she lied. 'But I do know he's been carted off to the cop shop. How I found out doesn't matter.' She noticed the crooked pictures on the walls of grown sons. They all looked like their father but with their mother's blonde, wavy hair. Wondered what the sons would make of their category A villainous dad. 'I'm a PI. Let's just say things travel down the grapevine pretty quickly. Look, I can see you're upset. I don't mean to pry, Penny, but with Jim being arrested, my job's not worth the contract you signed. I understand all that. The main thing I want to know, though, is why the hell did your husband hire me if he had so much to hide himself? I just don't get it.'

Suddenly, Penny's body started to heave. The wracking sobs erupted from her as though tectonic plates were shifting at the core of her being. Tears rolled onto her cheeks, dripping from her square jawline onto her twinset. 'I c-can't believe it myself. My Jim. A common criminal. Our business will be ruined. How could he have done this to me, Bev? All these years, I've devoted myself to that man. I brought his children into the world. And l-look at how he's bet-trayed me.'

Feeling her client's anguish as a tight ball inside her own chest, Bev approached her and put her arm around her. 'Aw, come on, now. It'll be OK. If you didn't know anything about his shenanigans, you'll be fine. You'd be surprised by the number of women I come across in this game who haven't got a clue about the terrible crap their husbands are into.'

Penny looked at her with red-rimmed eyes full of sorrow. 'Really?'

'Men are liars, Penny.'

'How could he be manufacturing drugs in his own workshop all this time and I didn't even know about it?' She shook her head. 'But I think Anthony must have found out, and that's why Jim insisted we get a private investigator – to dredge up dirt as an insurance policy, maybe. That's my guess.' She shrugged. 'He's insanely jealous of him next door, is my Jim. He can't stomach the thought that such an uncouth loudmouth should be so popular.'

'Is Jim normally the envious type?' Bev looked at the wedding photo that took pride of place on the mantelpiece above the reproduction Victoriana fireplace. There was Jim Higson, a good twenty years ago or more, dressed in a three-piece suit, looking like a poster boy for boring suburban respectability.

'Jim has always liked to be top dog,' Penny said quietly. 'When we first met, I was a concert pianist with a bright career ahead of me.' She looked momentarily wistful. 'He'd enjoyed a couple of appearances in the orchestra pit of some theatre in the West End, but his career as a performer hadn't really progressed beyond that. Back then . . .' There was the flicker of a smile on her masculine face. 'He'd just started up in business and was tuning the piano at the Hallé, when the orchestra was still in the Free Trade Hall. I'd turned up for a rehearsal at the right time on the wrong day. It was a chance meeting and we hit it off immediately. He wooed me. Made me feel like a star. His star. And then the moment he realised I'd fallen for him, it started. The denigration. The chipping away at my confidence. The control.' Her smile was gone, now. In its place was a sneer. 'We got engaged. I was already four months pregnant with our firstborn. Jim said I didn't really have what it took to be a virtuoso pianist. He reckoned so far, I'd made it on my looks because there weren't many five-foot-eleven natural blondes in music. If I was a big, fat pregnant brood mare, barely able to reach the keyboard, I'd find the work drying up, so it was best to preserve my dignity, quit while I was ahead and devote myself to my family. And I believed him. I believed him when he said I got my place at the Royal Northern College of Music because they were filling quotas.' She seemed to return to the room after a meander down her bitter Memory Lane. 'Anyway. Anthony likes to be top dog, too. So, there's a problem for a kick-off. Two alphas, living cheek by jowl. My Jim can be very petty-minded.'

'But if your husband paid me to start investigating someone else on his own doorstep, there was always the chance that *I'd* accidentally unearth his own secrets and lies.' Bev swallowed hard.

Penny regarded Bev through narrowed eyes.

Bev quickly added, 'Clearly, someone else beat me to it.' If Penny Higson was to find out she was the one who had handed her husband over to the police, Bev wanted to be safe on the far side of the M60 when she did so.

Penny's tears started to flow anew. 'He obviously thought he was so darned clever, nobody would ever suspect a quiet, intelligent man like that of peddling poison to school kids. Oh, the shame of it! How can I ever go into the village with my head held high?'

'But if it's all down to him, and you knew nothing about what was going on . . .' Bev saw shades of Angela

Fitzwilliam in Penny Higson. Another woman duped into thinking she'd married a fine, upstanding man who could provide and protect. 'People will understand.' Not that she was feeling particularly bloody understanding at that moment. She rose from the sofa, wishing she could ask to be compensated for her car, at the very least. Knowing she couldn't possibly. 'What will you do now?'

'I'm going to go away for a while,' Penny said, dabbing at her eyes. 'I have a friend I can stay with. I really don't want to be here alone.'

Bev nodded. 'I guess this is it, then. Look, I hope you manage to sort this mess out and get back on your feet.'

She shook Penny's hand and left. She was out of work and skint again. She was back to square one.

CHAPTER 29
Bev

I tell you what. If I mean that little to you, don't bother coming back at all 'til I've moved out. How about that? Then you can install Archibaldy, the racist landscaper.

Doc's bitter words rang in Bev's ears as she stared up at the ceiling.

'Damn you, you pain in the arse!' she said aloud.

Turning onto her side, she looked at 2Tone's digital clock yet again. The glowing red display said it was 3.17 a.m. She'd tried to clear her mind of all thoughts, but the harder she tried to fall asleep in the strange house with its strange noises, the more defiantly sleep seemed to evade her. Anthony's emperor-sized bed had been too firm. So, she'd moved room. Then, she'd moved room again. Finally, she'd returned to the master bedroom to no avail. Now, her brain was awhire with the last exchange she'd had with Doc on the day that Jim had been arrested. The echoes of his disappointed, bitter words had become louder with every minute that passed until they coursed around her body like strong caffeine.

'Go to bloody sleep, woman!' Bev said, pulling the pillow on top of her head so that all light was blocked out from the window in the en suite.

Her jumble of thoughts continued to roll around in her tired mind. *Should I be working for a man who profits from slave labour? Maybe I should find out a bit more and then tell Curtis and Owen everything. Maybe Higson's not the only rotten apple in the Little Marshwicke barrel and I'm turning a blind eye for the wrong reasons.* She thought about her only income stream disappearing and her self-respect dying if 2Tone and Archie were carted off by the cops. *I'm a graduate and a skilled professional. Should I even be working as a cleaner under a false identity? Is it right that I should be treating house-sitting like a mini-spa break while my daughter's having to endure Rob the Knob? Should I dump Archie? Have I been a shithouse to Doc?*

Her ruminations took her to 4.02 a.m. She rolled onto her back and practised the slow breathing she'd been taught to use when her anxiety got the better of her. Felt the sudden urge to make an origami model.

'Oh, I've had enough of this crap!'

Finally, she switched on the bedside lamp, flung the bedclothes off and sat at 2Tone's dressing table, surrounded by expensive and dreadful crystal knick-knacks, folding a piece of monogrammed Chateau d'Antoine notepaper into a frog. She was instantly absorbed in the task – so much so, that she didn't immediately notice the sound of smashing glass coming from downstairs. Then, there was a hefty thump, followed by the tinkling of more broken glass. It was enough to catch her attention.

Freezing mid-fold, with the blood pulsating in her ears, Bev now wished Tony hadn't taken Soprano away with him. If she listened hard, she could hear movement in the kitchen. Someone had definitely broken in.

Oh, you're joking. No, no, no.

She had only moments to decide what to do. Fight or flight? She opted for the latter, switched off the lamp and ran into the en suite. There was nowhere to hide, but the bottle of Flash at the side of the toilet caught her eye. She snatched it up and grabbed the toilet brush as backup. Returning to the bedroom with her makeshift weaponry, she could now just about hear the stairs squeak beneath the weight of the intruder.

He was coming for her!

She scanned the vast room for a hiding place. The walk-in wardrobes!

Almost tripping on the sheepskin rug, she scurried across to the door that led to the warren of shelving and racks that held 2Tone's extensive collection of suiting and casual gear. Bev stepped inside, closing the door quietly behind her. The claustrophobic space was lit only by the small window at the far end. Thankful for the moonlight that streamed in, casting long shadows that might conceal her, Bev wedged herself behind some rubber dresses that surely didn't belong to the diminutive landscaper. Or, judging by the giant stilettos by her feet that almost sent her flying, perhaps they did.

Please don't let them come in here, she silently prayed. *Please let them nick the stereo or telly and bugger off. Why didn't I put the sodding alarm on downstairs? Stupid cow!*

Clutching the toilet brush and Flash so tightly, she thought her knuckles might break apart, Bev held her breath, listening for footsteps beneath the din of her own tinnitus. It was only when the footsteps were on the other side of the partition that separated the master bedroom from the walk-in wardrobe that Bev knew the intruder was inevitably heading her way.

Fuck off! Fuck off! Fuck off! Don't come in here!

The door creaked as it swung open. She could make out ragged breathing, now. Sensed the intruder's presence among the neatly hung and folded garments. Fight or flight. Fight or flight.

'Aaaaaagh!' Bev sprinted out from behind the rubber camouflage, brandishing the bristled toilet brush like a lance with her left hand and spraying the Flash bathroom for all she was worth with her right.

She had the two-pronged advantage of being familiar with the space and having the element of surprise. The moonlight shining through the window reflected at precisely the right moment off the glassy surface of the intruder's eyes. Her aim was true; her trigger-finger fast.

What came from the burglar's mouth was unexpected. A string of words Bev didn't recognise. He rubbed his eyes and lunged at her, grabbing her arm and pulling her to him. It was then that she realised he was holding a crowbar. In a bid to free herself, she punched his ear hard with the bristles of the brush. The sound of the crowbar swooshing through the air as though it were no heavier than a cane gave Bev just enough warning to wriggle her way into the clothes. The rubber dresses bore the brunt of the impact.

Bev broke free and ran back into the bedroom. Sprinted out onto the landing, getting as far as the stairs. But the intruder was upon her.

'Where is Anthony?' he yelled, grabbing at her pyjama top and pulling her backwards so that she almost lost her footing.

She swung the Flash bathroom around and hit him squarely on the wrist with it, but it wasn't hard enough to loosen his grip on the crowbar. He smashed it down towards her. It glanced painfully off her shoulder, hitting home on the bannister where it splintered the wood.

'Where is Anthony?' His voice was gruff and full of venom as he bellowed in her ear.

Unable to get a clear look at his face, Bev kicked her bare foot backwards into his shin with all the might she could muster. Anything to unbalance him or else give herself a brief physical advantage. She swung around and poked him in the nose with the sharp, soiled bristles of the toilet brush. Squirted Flash foam into his mouth.

He gagged. Swore in his own tongue. Stumbled several steps downwards, clinging to the handrail. Bev took the opportunity to hurtle past him, taking the stairs at a dangerous two at a time.

But he recovered quickly and descended hot on her heels, still carrying the crowbar.

'Where is Anthony?'

Bev didn't look back. Her bare feet squeaked on the marble floor of the hallway, which she'd buffed to a treacherous shine only that morning with Mr Sheen and a brand new duster. She made straight for the front door.

'Help!' she shouted, realising that there was nobody there to hear her. She slammed on the lights as she ran past the switch, squinting as darkness gave way to the blinding super-light of the LED chandelier.

'Stop where you are!' the intruder said. 'Or I'll kill y—'

Her pursuer's sentiment transformed mid-word into a yowl. There was a slap, slap, thump. Hand on the front door's night-latch, Bev had glanced behind just in time to see him slip on the marble and skid. His legs flailed uselessly for one step, two steps . . . and then he collapsed flat onto his back. His head hit the deck with a toe-curling crack. The crowbar went scudding across the marble floor, coming to rest by a giant potted palm.

Bev seized the moment to pounce on the prone intruder, spraying him directly in the eyes with the Flash. No reaction beyond tears streaming down the sides of his face. He was out cold. She pulled his collar aside. Felt for a pulse in his neck. Nothing.

'Oh, shit. He's dead.'

CHAPTER 30

Bev

'He can't be dead. He can't be. That's ridiculous. Please don't let him be dead.' Bev felt her way along the intruder's neck, desperate to find a pulse; not willing to believe a man had died because of her. But as she probed, all she found was a dressing that looked like it had recently been applied by someone who knew their way around first aid. Had the man had his throat cut? She lifted a loose corner of the bandage and saw black stitches holding together a florid, seeping puncture wound.

Gagging, she shuddered. 'Ugh. Grim! Come on, Bev! Pull yourself together. You can't be done for manslaughter. He's got to be alive. Mirror. You need a mirror.' She remembered how her aunt had held a mirror to her uncle's mouth to be certain that the cancer had indeed taken him. When no steaming breath had appeared on the glass, she'd known he had finally slipped away.

But Bev couldn't leave a violent burglar unattended – even if he seemed dead.

'Got to be sure. This can't be happening.'

She grabbed his wrist and pressed down on the underside. Finally found a strong pulse and gasped with relief. Felt tears threatening.

'Are you faking?' she asked the prone intruder. 'Hey!

You!' Prodding him in the cheek with the toilet brush as a precaution, she decided he wasn't. She had to get him secured before he came to. Then she had to call an ambulance and the police.

Hastening to Anthony's office, she ripped the extension cord from the socket. Returned to the hall with a thudding heart. But her pounding heart seemed to hang still in her chest when she looked at the spot where the intruder had been lying, out cold.

He was gone.

'Where are you, you bastard?' she yelled, holding the Flash out in front of her, as if she could lure him from his hiding place and cleanse him into submission. Clutching the cable and toilet brush in her left hand, Bev tried to slow her ragged breathing, taking the first tentative steps towards the place she was sure he'd hidden – the entrance to the basement, handily concealed behind the staircase. It was the only place he could have gone in a matter of seconds. Wasn't it?

Show no fear. He's wounded. You can do this. Attack is the best form of defence. Feeling fear starting to snuff out her bravery, she darted towards the door to the cellar, expecting to surprise the intruder.

'Got you!' She held the Flash out with a shaking hand, poised to fire.

But there was nobody there.

'To hell with this,' Bev whispered.

She had to get out. House-sitting was one thing, but risking her life to protect Chateau d'Antoine was another. £500 didn't cover that kind of self-sacrifice. What was she thinking? Running towards the front door, praying she'd be able to unfasten the multiple locks before the intruder was upon her, Bev yelped when he leaped out from behind the giant bushy parlour palm by the front door.

Before she could react, he had her in a vice-like grip from behind.

'Let me go,' she screamed, struggling uselessly in his arms. The smell of his sweat stung her nostrils. Was he going to rape her? *No, no, no!* She tried and failed to reach up and hit him on the head with the detergent bottle. 'Don't hurt me!'

'You're Anthony's wife,' the man said, squeezing her painfully across her middle.

'No! I'm the cleaner.'

'You're lying. Where is Anthony?'

Bev shook her head vehemently. 'I swear. I'm the cleaner. I'm house-sitting. He's away.'

She spied the crowbar, peeping out from beneath Soprano's dog bed. It was just within reach of her right foot. If she could only swipe it towards her and reach downwards. Just for a split second . . .

'Let me go,' she said. 'You're hurting me. Let me go and I'll give you the address where he's staying. Please. I want to help you. You've got no argument with me.'

The intruder loosened his grip on her just long enough for Bev to lunge for the crowbar. She dropped her make-shift cleaner's weaponry. Snatched up the heavy iron bar and swung it backwards against the man's ribs with a sickening thwack.

Clutching his chest, he crumpled to the floor, gasping for breath.

'Put your hands up where I can see them or I'll use your head as a piñata,' Bev said, staring down at the dishevelled man. Though her whole body shook, it trembled with adrenaline, now. The fear had dissipated, and she was emboldened further when she saw his eyes were bloodshot but unfocused. He was concussed.

'Do it, or this finishes here. I'm not afraid of you,' she lied.

'I just want Anthony,' he said, finally relenting and holding his arms up to allow her to bind him. His English had a heavy Eastern European accent. 'I've come a long way to speak to him.' There was a hint of London twang to his accent, too.

'Do all of your social calls start with a crowbar?' Bev asked, daring to set down the crowbar – well out of reach of her captive – while she tied his hands together with the extension lead.

There was malicious intent in his face as he narrowed those drunken eyes. 'You were sleeping in his bed.' He tested his bonds as if having second thoughts about having surrendered. But the fight went out of him instantly. 'You're no cleaner.'

Spraying a small amount of Flash onto his nose, Bev said, 'Fuck you. I *am* his cleaner. Sort of. Now, tell me why you broke in?' She brandished the bottle at point-blank range above the man's watering left eye. 'What the hell do you want?' She pressed the toilet brush against the dressing on his neck, feeling only slightly cruel when he yelped with pain. 'Let's start with your name.'

'My name is Mihal,' he said, gasping. 'Mihal Kazaku. Me and my brothers, Bogdan and Constantin, were Anthony's slaves.'

'Slaves?' Bev thought about Doc's recent field trip to one of 2Tone's building sites and his alleged discovery of trafficked workers being brutally treated. Whilst she'd been reluctant to take a jealous man's word without proof, surely Mihal's accusation lent credence to everything Doc had said. Didn't it?

'We were trafficked from Romania. Anthony bought us. He beat us. He took everything from us. Bogdan is dead. Constantin is missing. Now, I want answers.'

CHAPTER 31
Bev

'Oh, you're kidding me,' Doc said, lurking by the front door.

How long had he been standing there behind the closed door? Bev beckoned Mihal forwards.

'Have you been waiting for me to put my key in the lock for three days?'

'Don't flatter yourself. I heard the Morris's engine.' Doc had wedged himself between Mihal and the hallway beyond. He was speaking quickly; tight-lipped and looking at his feet. 'Now, who the hell is this guy, and why have you brought him here? I hope you don't think I'm cool with—'

Bev pushed him in the chest. 'Come on, man. Move it. I've not brought him here to fuck. It's a story you're gonna want to hear.' She grabbed their visitor by the arm and steered him into the kitchen. 'Get the kettle on, Doccington.'

'Stop trying to butter me up,' Doc said. His normally sloping shoulders were almost skimming his ears. He filled the kettle with jerky, exaggerated movements, slamming it back onto its base. Turned to Mihal. 'Who are you and why are you sitting at my table?'

'*Our* table, you territorial tit.' Bev took a seat next to the bewildered-looking Romanian. 'This is Mihal. Go on, Mihal. Tell Doc what you told me.'

For almost an hour, Mihal retold the story of how Anthony Anthony had taken his freedom while the Thai Dragon's Spice had taken the rest.

Doc whistled long and low as he finished his tale. 'That's some tragic shit, dude. You could make a film out of that.'

Mihal shrugged. 'I don't think so. It's not as unusual as you think. Look around you at some of the men who work on building sites and the girls in the brothels and nail bars.'

Doc rammed a Jaffa Cake into his mouth, speaking with his mouth full. 'Yeah. OK. But I still don't understand why you're sitting in *our* kitchen.' He glanced at Bev and raised his eyebrows.

Mihal ran his hands through black hair that looked as though it hadn't been washed for some time. 'I've been looking for Anthony since I came out of prison. I knew his name. I knew what his fist felt like against my jaw and how his boot felt in my ribs. But I never had the chance to find out where he lives. His address is not in the phone book. Not on the electoral roll. His business is registered to a builder's yard ten miles away.

'Couple of days ago, I went to a squat, looking for a bed for the night and maybe some information. A junkie stabbed me in the neck with a broken bottle, and I would have bled to death if someone hadn't called an ambulance.' He pulled his collar aside to reveal the dog-eared dressing. 'But before I passed out, I overheard a guy saying Anthony's connected to the Thai Dragon. When I came to and the hospital discharged me, I finally got hold of his address. I came looking for him in Little Marshwicke but found Bev instead.'

'Don't you mean, Gail?' Doc asked, looking to Bev for an explanation.

'He knows,' Bev said. 'I explained about the undercover gig. He knows about Higson too and how you followed

Archie to the building site.' She caught Doc's eye and saw hurt there. 'Listen! You wanted to bring Anthony and Archie down for the shady shit they're into? Well, this is our chance to do the right thing. Mihal is gonna help us gather enough intel to pass onto Curtis and Owen. He's going to reach out to those men you saw, and then we hand everything over to the cops. Right?'

Doc closed his eyes momentarily. His brow furrowed. 'And what does he get in return?'

Bev smiled uncertainly, realising that many obstacles lay in her way – most of them putting her safety in jeopardy – before she could bring some semblance of order to this mess. 'I'm going to help him find his little brother. Or at least find out what happened to him once Mihal left for London.'

'So, you're going to get hard evidence, condemning someone we've not found a scrap of dirt on so far, and you're going to track down a missing trafficked man, who might either be dead or maybe doesn't want to be found. How, precisely?'

'Bev-magic.'

'And what do you propose we do with a homeless Romanian ex-con?' Doc turned to Mihal. 'Sorry mate, I get your predicament. I do. I've got a record, myself, but . . .'

Bev rolled her eyes. 'It's only for a couple of days. He swears he's clean. He can sleep in the stock cupboard.'

Doc's laughter took her by surprise. 'What? The stock cupboard with my extremely valuable Lego collection in? Have you banged your head? Listen! You're the one with an ex who's constantly got a stick up his arse about how this place isn't suitable for your daughter. How's he gonna feel when he finds out you've got a complete stranger with a drug problem and a conviction for burglary staying?'

Searching Doc's eyes for the soft spot that led to his heart, Bev hoped she could convince him. She'd taken some convincing too, but how could she let her baby girl grow up in a world where modern-day slavery was allowed to flourish in the suburbs, unchecked, while Manchester was being pumped full of a drug that turned its most vulnerable sons and daughters into zombies? 'I'm skint, Doc. So skint that I'm scrubbing somebody else's toilets for cash. But I can't take wages from a man who profits from suffering.'

'Oh, but you can sleep with one?'

She punched Doc's upper arm. 'Pack that in right now! That's my judgement call. Not yours.'

'But I thought we—'

'And I won't stand idly by and let this poor guy wonder indefinitely about the fate of his youngest brother. I know where *my* family is. My parents are in the cemetery. My daughter's down the road. But I can imagine what it must be like to not know and I can't think of anything worse. Two days max. Hand over what we find to Curtis and Owen. Then, whether we're winning or not, Mihal goes on his way.'

'You are so kind, Beverley. I won't betray your trust,' Mihal said.

Doc exhaled heavily. He regarded her with the same concerned expression she'd seen in her favourite English teacher and her first boss and her dad, when he'd been well enough to see that his daughter was prone to poor judgement and impulsive behaviour. Doc turned to their visitor. 'I don't mean to sound uncool, mate, but if you touch my Lego, I'll kill you.' He pointed to the smear of brown on Mihal's jaw that Bev knew was evidence of her self-defence with a toilet brush. 'And get a shower. You honk even by my standards.'

'Are you sure they're the ones?' Bev asked Mihal. 'I don't know how you can see anything in this crappy light. It's going to hammer down.'

As she spoke, pain lanced through her forehead. Trying to sleep with only two walls and a snoring Doc between her and a potentially dangerous stranger had taken its toll. For the umpteenth night in a row, she'd lain awake, tossing and turning and worrying about her future. If she led the police to Anthony Anthony and he found out, would she face retribution from either him or Archie or both? Would Hope be safe? Would Rob find out about this temporary addition to her unconventional household?

At 3.00 a.m., she'd wondered how she could she be sure Mihal wasn't a psychopathic liar, intent on murdering them both as they lay in their respective sofa beds. By the time the clock had insisted it was time to head for the hills to tail Archic on his rounds, though the sun hadn't yet received the memo that the day had dawned, Bev's head felt as though it had been cleaved in two by Mihal's crowbar.

Now, the three of them sat in Sandra's Morris with the windows quickly fogging up. Mihal wiped the passenger side glass yet again and peered across the road at the gang of nine or ten dark-haired, olive-skinned men who were toiling away on the construction site of a large house in Alderley Edge. Mixing concrete, pushing wheelbarrows, carrying hods of bricks on their backs up precariously-balanced ladders to the second storey of shoddy-looking scaffolding that had no safety rails and few visible planks.

'This is unbelievable. Are you sure this is one of Anthony Anthony's jobs?' Bev asked. 'I thought he just did gardens and drives.'

'He has his fingers in many pies,' Mihal said. 'Gangs like this working on big high rises in the City of London. Everywhere. He seems like an idiot, but don't be fooled.'

The pre-divorce trouser suit that Bev was wearing was so tight, despite losing a few pounds through her time spent cleaning, it felt like bondage gear. It dug into the soft rolls of her belly. She'd already undone the buttons on both trousers and jacket. Would she pass muster with a hard hat and steel toe-capped wellies she'd bought from B&Q? 'Let's just wait 'til Archie buggers off.' She pointed to her lover who looked in their direction at that moment.

Mihal grimaced. Made a spitting sound. Sank low in the passenger seat and pulled the cap Doc had lent him over his eyes. 'He is evil, that man.'

Bev could feel the smile on Doc's face without having to look round and see it for herself. The car seemed to brighten with his told-you-so smug satisfaction.

'How do you mean?'

Balling his fists, Mihal craned his neck to get another glimpse of the foreman. His freshly shaven top lip visibly glistened with sweat. 'He's the one who gets the slaves for Anthony. Anthony does the business and agrees a price with the trafficker. That bald beast collects new men in his van, takes any personal possessions – even photos of your family. If you complain, he beats you and beats you until you pass out. To make an example for the others. After a while, even if you can get away for a few hours at night, you always go back, because he has everything you own: your passports, your money, your *brother*! He makes you think that if you try to escape, you get arrested and deported. He tells you, if you run, Anthony knows where your family is back home and they will be killed. He told me and Bogdan that Constantin would be killed. So, we never had any hope of escaping. Even when we got high and burgled that house where Bogdan fell, we were always going to go back to the building site because of Constantin. And now, I think my little brother must also be dead.'

The thought that she'd been sleeping with such a scumbag made Bev queasy. Staring through the windscreen at Archie, engaged in banter with another of Anthony's men – a legal worker, judging by the free and easy way they communicated with one another – Bev realised that if she were ever to be a good mother to Hope, she had to do more than stop frequenting sex parties. She had to stop hooking up with men she knew nothing about. Perhaps it was time to cut men from the equation altogether. Full of secrets and lies, they were an unknown quantity, and Bev knew she had form for picking the very worst of the bad ones.

'OK,' she said, watching Archie fist-bump the man he'd been talking to and make for his Sprinter van. 'He's off. This is it. I'll create a diversion, Mihal. You sneak in among the Romanians. Blend in.'

With the foreman gone, Bev donned her hard hat, grabbed her clipboard and climbed out of the Morris. She approached the man Archie had been talking to.

'Morning. I'm Sandra Morris, Building Control, Local Authority,' she said, speaking with as much no-nonsense authority as she could muster, though her bowels and bladder insisted she should have stayed home, locked in the bathroom. 'I've come for a spot inspection.'

The builder looked her up and down. She shivered and not just from the freezing, gusting wind that threatened to strip her excess flab off by force.

'Hello, love. I haven't seen you before. What did you say your name was?'

'Sandra Morris. And your name is?'

'Terry.'

Brandishing her clipboard, she took down his details. *Keep on the offensive. Remember, as long as he buys your story, you're the one in control, here.* 'Thank you, Terry. Now, I want to talk to all of your men, and I want to start with that group over there.' She pointed to the Romanian workers.

The builder's body language became suddenly combative as he stood legs akimbo and puffed out his chest; shoulders forward. He took his phone out of his pocket. 'I'm gonna have to phone the boss.'

Stand your ground! Stand your ground! Bev tried to mirror his movements, glad that she'd worn Doc's anorak on top of her suit. She was far shorter than the builder but matched him in bulk. 'Put your phone away, Terrence. If you need to call your boss for me to talk to those men, over there, I'd say you're hiding something. Have you got anything to hide, Terrence?'

He grinned, revealing a mouthful of rotten teeth. 'Hiding? You're a piece of work, aren't you, love? Maybe I'll call Building Regs and make a complaint.' He started to dial a number on his phone.

Bev's heart galloped away inside her chest. She imagined she could feel the adrenalin speeding to her brain. *Think, Bev! Think!*

Without warning, she held up her phone and took several photographs at close range of the builder. He squinted at the bright flash and tried to grab the device from her, but Bev was quick and took a step backwards, out of reach. She could hear the tinny voice of somebody answering on the other end of his phone – perhaps a receptionist in the local council. She was mere seconds away from being exposed as a fraud.

'If you're unwilling to let me speak to *all* of your work-force, Terrence . . .' she said, locking eyes with her adversary, 'why don't I call HMRC?' She waved her own phone at the visibly blanching builder, then dialled Doc. 'Seems to me, you've got something to hide. Are you declaring all of your earnings? Is Anthony Anthony charging VAT on this job? Maybe those men aren't legally employed at all and that's why you don't want me to inspect them and the site.' She looked up at the scaffolding. Knew enough from her own father, who had spent thirty years of his working life tiling bathrooms and kitchens in new-builds just like this, that the set-up was dangerous. 'Maybe after I've spoken to HMRC, I can call my superiors and have a word about your on-site safety. This looks like criminal negligence to me. If you're in charge of all these men during the working day, that makes you liable. Do you earn enough to make that level of responsibility worth your while, Terrence? Could you afford to pay all those legal fees out of your own pocket if you're sued by any of these men or HMRC pursue action against fraudulent declarations of income?'

Terry, the rotten-toothed builder put his phone back in his pocket. He scanned her face, seemingly trying to decide if she was full of bullshit or not. 'Ask 'em what you want. They won't understand you. I'll be in my van, having a brew if you want me.'

Bev was certain that the moment he climbed into the cab of his flatbed truck that he would be on the phone to either Archie or even Anthony himself. She had a small window of opportunity before they turned up to see who was threatening them.

'He's gone,' Mihal said, pretending to shovel building debris, along with another Romanian man, into a wheelbarrow. 'He didn't even notice me. Good diversion.'

Some of the other Romanians were looking at Mihal with undisguised suspicion. A handful smiled in recognition. Had these men really been enslaved to Anthony all this while, Bev wondered?

Mihal spoke to them in their own tongue, keeping his voice low and even. Not looking up at anyone. They started to move towards him, still carrying out their individual tasks, but soon within earshot. He led them surreptitiously to a spot behind a new breeze-block wall where they were beyond the line of sight of Anthony's henchman in his van.

Bev stood with her clipboard held high. 'Tell them to make it look like they're still working,' she said. 'And let's be sharpish about this. Go on, Mihal, explain we're here to help them and then ask them about Constantin.'

There was a hurried exchange as Mihal filled the men in on Bev's intentions and identity. Some of the younger men started to speak animatedly, waving their hands.

'They don't trust me,' Mihal told Bev. 'They think this is a test. That they'll end up in trouble with Anthony if they talk to me.' He turned to the older workers, whom he clearly knew. The word, 'Constantin' came up several times.

Bev watched Mihal's expression change from one of hope to dejection, like a heavy cloud scudding over the wintry sunshine in the stiff wind. 'Nobody has seen my brother since me and Bogdan left for London. One day he was there. The next, gone.' He pressed his lips together.

'Tell them I can help them get free, but I need to know anything extra they can tell me about the sort of stuff Anthony's involved in. They must hear gossip. Some of these guys must be able to understand English. Quickly!'

Mihal nodded. Spoke rapidly to one of the oldest-looking men in the group. 'My friend, Gavril, here, says Anthony is still getting them hooked on Spice.'

The two Romanian men continued their exchange. Mihal nodded and turned to Bev.

'He's getting some of his British builders to commit crimes like stealing and fighting so that they get put in prison but not for long. A few months here and there. Gavril says he's heard them boasting when they get out that they've been paid well. Really well.'

'I don't get it. How does it benefit him to have his legitimately employed guys inside?' Bev studied Gavril's weather-beaten face to see the sincerity there. Was it possible he was making up such an outlandish tale?

Mihal translated and awaited the response. He relayed it to Bev. 'The womenfolk go to visit Anthony's men in prison. They're taking Spice stuffed inside hollowed out chocolate bars . . . any treats they can smuggle in.' He shrugged. 'The value of that stuff on the inside is sky-high.'

Bev considered the narcotic semi-buried treasure in Jim Higson's workshop. Owen had told her, after the sniffer dogs had uncovered everything of criminal note in the inspection pit, that the workshop held enough raw ingredients to produce half a million pounds' worth of the drug.

'Anthony's a distributor,' she said, nodding at Mihal. Looking back towards the Morris where Doc was sitting in the back. 'The piano tuner next door has got to be the Thai Dragon – the client I told you about. My God! What a tangled web,' she said softly, trying to revise the motive she'd ascribed to Higson for having Anthony snooped upon.

'But you said he'd been arrested,' Mihal said.

Nodding, Bev heard the door of a vehicle slam. Doc was still in-situ in the Morris, so it wasn't him . . . though he was waving and pointing frantically towards where the truck was parked. 'He's coming back,' she said.

Gavril took up his spade. Said something in Romanian to Mihal as a parting shot. Started to distance himself, clearly afraid.

'The supply hasn't stopped,' Mihal said, glancing towards Anthony's henchman who was striding towards them carrying a scaffolding pole like a baseball bat. 'We need to get out of here.'

'What do you mean the supply hasn't stopped?' Bev was slow to realise that Terry, the rotten-toothed builder, was making straight for her.

Mihal grabbed her and started to drag her towards the Morris. 'Higson can't be the Thai Dragon.'

'Oi, you cheeky bitch! I wanna word with you!' Terry started to sprint towards them, brandishing the scaffold pole, clearly intent on denting who or whatever it came into contact with.

'Run!' Doc yelled from inside the Morris, slapping his palms pointlessly against the glass.

Bev turned around just as the scaffolding pole whistled through the air towards her.

CHAPTER 32
Bev

'Terry Smith,' Archie said, laying back and dragging on his cigarette. 'He normally supervises Tony's sites down south.'

'Oh yeah. What was he in for?' Bev asked, toying with his chest hair.

Archie smiled, as if wistfully recalling a fond family memory. 'Well, not fencing bent gear, that's for sure. Terry's handy with his fists, like. He went down for GBH. This feller looks at Terry's bird the wrong way in the pub. Right? Terry was playing pool at the time. Notices this cheeky wanker. Next minute, he's doing a Mr Miyagi with the pool cue on the feller's head.' Archie mimed some Kung Fu moves, dropping ash all over the duvet cover. Blithely swept it onto the carpet. 'He did a year for that.'

As Archie continued to wax lyrical about Anthony's second-best foreman, Bev considered the near miss she'd had with Mihal on the building site.

Terry, the psychopathic builder with a smile that would have looked at home in the 1700s, had tried to bring the scaffold pole down on Bev's head. The only thing that had stood between Bev and concussion had been Mihal, who had wrenched the pole out of his opponent's hands, using it to take him out at the knees. Praying that the old Morris wouldn't fail her, Bev had turned the stalling engine over three times, managing to pull away from the building site only moments before her attacker had scrambled back to his feet, retrieving the metal pole and going in for a second swing. He'd taken out the Morris's tail light and in doing so, Bev had realised that not only would she have yet another repair on her hands, but using the Morris any longer to travel to Anthony's or Archie's had been rendered a no-no. The vintage, half-timbered burgundy car stuck out like a sore thumb in a city full of recently manufactured silver saloons and hatchbacks. Even if Terry would never be able to pick Bev out of a line-up once she'd shed the suit, the wig and the hard hat, the car enjoyed no such easy anonymity. Had her cover been blown entirely? Would Terry describe her as 'A bird in a burgundy Morris'? If confronted by Anthony, could she claim a connection with the distinctive car as a figment of 2Tone's overactive imagination?

She'd travelled to Archie's place from Altrincham on public transport. It had taken her the best part of three hours. Happily, he'd not mentioned the suspicious Building Inspector as having an identical car. They'd had perfunctory sex, which he'd apparently enjoyed and which she'd found uncomfortable. It had been the first time Bev had faked an orgasm since she and Rob the Knob had been on the skids. Now, however, she was reaping the rewards of her self-sacrifice, taking a hefty down-payment in incriminating pillow talk.

'That's dead funny,' she said, faking a giggle. 'Terry sounds such a rum bugger.' She twirled her index finger around in Archie's chest hair, as though lying in this modern-day slaver's arms was her idea of heaven. All the while, thinking of Mihal sitting at her kitchen table, sobbing at the thought that his brother had been murdered; his remains perhaps casually buried in the concrete cast of Anthony Anthony's kidney-shaped swimming pool. 'Tell me about the other blokes you work with. You know . . . the real characters. I love hearing all the stuff they've got up to. They sound like the biggest laugh.'

Archie dragged hard on his cigarette and passed it to Bev. 'They're a cracking bunch,' he said, nodding and smiling. 'I love my job. There's always something going on. Like, Steve Cooper, the brickie. He's a right card, he is! He had this run-in with another builder before he started working for Tony. Right? And this builder wouldn't pay him what he was owed from the last job. Anyway, Christmas is coming and all that. So, Steve builds this wall with no ventilation block, knowing the place'll get damp as hell. But that's not all. He gets so fucked off with this feller that he nicks his dog. Next minute, dog's head winds up in this feller's bed like summat out of *The Godfather*.'

Bev clasped her hand to her mouth, imagining the absence of any kind of empathy or moral compass that would make someone capable of killing and dismembering a family pet. But then, she reasoned, these men were doing far worse to other human beings. Mihal had explained that Spice was notorious for causing heart failure in the otherwise healthy. How many trafficked workers had keeled over on the job, died of hyperthermia as they slept in tents in winter or been beaten senseless to teach the others a lesson? Perhaps it was Steve, the brickie's job to dispose of the collateral damage of a modern day slave racket. 'Shitting Nora,' she said. 'That takes some balls. But hang on. Anthony's got a dog. Wasn't he worried that if he pisses Steve off, Soprano will go the same way?'

Archie laughed, stubbed the cigarette out and started to kiss Bev's neck. His breath was rancid and eggy when he spoke. 'Tony doesn't lose sleep about Soprano. Cos he knows that when one of the lads goes down for summat, he looks after everyone proper. Makes sure the wives and mams and dads have got enough to live on, like. Nobody has to go cap in hand on the tap. And Tony pays well. If them lads need time off, they get it. We knock off early on a Friday and go to the pub. It's all on him. Benefits, like what you get in a big office and that.' He winked. 'Once you work for Tony, you're in it for life. It's a bond.'

Sensing a plan forming inside her from the flotsam and jetsam of gathered information, like a planet slowly coalescing from the dust in a galaxy, Bev pressed on. 'Sounds like you lot are a right bunch of hard nuts! So, how many are inside at the moment, then?'

Exhaling slowly, Archie's eyebrows bunched together. He ran a hand over his shining head. 'Hey! You're asking a lot of questions all of a sudden.'

Bev held her breath, aware of the quickening of her pulse. Had Terry's run-in with a Morris-driving imposter in a wig reached Archie's ears after all? She searched for an excuse that would throw him off the scent. 'Well, is it any wonder? The most exciting thing that ever happens to me is Harpic being on half price at Asda.' She tittered. 'I love listening to the stuff you lot get up to. It's funny and exciting. All that ducking and diving.' Grabbing his craggy face, Bev forced herself to plant a passionate kiss on his lips. 'I've never met a man like you before, Archie.' She stared into his eyes with feigned wonder and adulation. 'You're like James Bond with a big dick and green fingers. You turn me right on.'

Would he buy her flattery?

He fondled her left breast. 'Show me how much I turn you on again.' Flicked back the duvet to reveal another erection.

One hand job and three minutes later, his suspicions seemed to have subsided sufficiently to answer Bev's question as to how many of 2Tone's crew were currently doing time:

'Three. Steve, the brickie, like I said. A lad called Alan. Alan Doherty. He normally lays the turf. He's in for doing over a builder's yard, the daft twat.' He chuckled. 'They're good lads, really. And then there's Darren Titchmarsh.'

'Destined to be a gardener?!' Bev offered.

'Eh? Darren's a spark. He's just gone down for credit card fraud. I went in to see him last week and he's got the most amazing tat inside.'

'A tattoo?' Bev committed the names to memory. Steven Cooper. Alan Doherty. Darren Titchmarsh. 'Cool.'

Shuffling up the bed, Archie was suddenly animated. He flung back the duvet cover, revealing his naked body. Held his leg in the air, twisting it so that Bev could see the tattoo on his calf muscle. 'See that? I got that when I was doing a stretch.'

Bev already felt weighted down by her recent discoveries. The news that Archie had a criminal record made her suddenly feel more leaden and despondent than ever. 'It's a corking tat,' she lied, eyeing the poorly executed image of a baby. The features were all wrong, made even more out of proportion by the bulge of his overdeveloped muscle. Below the baby was the word, 'Canel'.

'Do you have a daughter?' Bev asked, realising that in the handful of times she'd spent the night with Archie, she'd never asked him about his past or any other family members apart from Anthony.

'It's my niece.'

'Canel's a really unusual name. It's Dutch for cinnamon isn't it? I love reading ingredients in foreign, me. You learn all sorts from a packet of biscuits. What a lovely thing to call your little girl after. Sugar and spice and all things nice!'

Archie rubbed his muscle. 'Oh no! Ha. It's meant to be Chanel but the lad who did the tattoos when I was inside is a fucking knob. He can't spell for toffee.'

What had put Archie behind bars? Bev swallowed hard, waiting for the inevitable sucker punch where she was bound to discover she was sleeping with a monster even worse than she'd imagined. She could almost hear Doc shouting, 'Told you so!' She clutched the duvet back around her, covering her nakedness.

'What were you inside for?' Searched her lover's weather-beaten features for any sign of goodness. Found none.

'Armed robbery.' He grinned and winked. 'I did a ten-stretch. It was a long time ago, though. I was a kid, running with the wrong crowd. Thought I could make a killing without any graft. We all did.'

'Did you use a real gun?' Armed robbery. Of course he was a damned armed robber. Why would Bev opt to shag anybody with better credentials?

Archie turned to her, suddenly wearing an expression that oozed suspicion from every pore. Wordlessly, he swung his legs out of bed and padded out of the bedroom. Returned moments later carrying a large pistol that looked incredibly like the real deal. The sinews in his forearms strained with the weight of it in his hand, and he was pointing it straight at her.

'For a cleaning woman . . .' he said, peering down the sights, taking off the safety catch. 'You're definitely asking a lot of fucking nosy questions.'

CHAPTER 33
Bev

'OK, Beverley,' Mihal said, shuffling in the passenger seat of the freezing cold Morris to get a better look at the red-brick gothic spires and towering walls of HMP Manchester – visible from where they'd parked in the neighbouring street. 'The guy you are visiting is Petru Tarus. It's all arranged. I've spoken to him. He's going to say you are his girlfriend. The men you have mentioned are also due visits.'

'All three? Are you sure?'

'Absolutely. Just give Petru the bag of crisps. I put your fifty pounds inside and glued it back shut.'

Bev examined the crisp packet she'd bought from a Polish shop for signs of tampering. She privately admitted that Mihal had done an excellent job of resealing it. 'What happens if the guard susses I'm trying to smuggle something in?'

'Then, the guard gets fifty pounds and a bag of gherkin-flavoured chips all the way from Romania.'

'Will I get arrested?'

'It's unlikely.'

Bev looked around at Doc for a show of encouragement, but all she got was an eyeful of her business partner sitting on the back seat with his arms folded tightly across his chest. 'Don't look at me for approval,' he said. 'You don't have to do this, man. I don't know why you're happy with this level of personal risk. I'm not.'

Grabbing the crisps, Bev opened the driver's side door. 'Wait here,' she said to Mihal, ignoring Doc. 'I'll be back soon. Strong people just feel the fear and do it anyway, right?'

Bloody Doc. Always bloody preaching on how she should run her life. Mr Arbiter of Good Taste and Judgement. Yellow-toothed tit.

Dressed as Gail in her badly bleached blonde wig, Bev bent her head against the wind and drizzle, praying that for once, Doc would be proven wrong. He'd run when the heat had been on during the Fitzwilliam case, and now, despite his initial protestations (which had been a thinly disguised opportunity to have a dig at Archie), he was prepared to walk away from exposing a drugs- and slave-labour cartel that was flourishing on Manchester's doorstep. *Prick!* Her legs felt like jelly. That was Doc's sodding fault too for putting the fear of god into her. *Personal risk, bollocks.* She stumbled twice on the walk to the prison's visitor centre, wondering if the CCTV that hung from every high wall around the sprawling campus had marked her out as a fake.

Barely able to speak, lest her trembling voice give her away, Bev made it through security, armed with her charm-offensive bag of gherkin-flavoured crisps. She scanned the depressing visitors' room which smelled of poverty and stale cigarettes. Tried to pick out Petru. Initially, she smiled at a man who matched Mihal's vague description of 'tall, black hair, slim build' but realised when the man sat down at a table to speak to a woman in a glittering salwar kameez, that the man was Asian, not Romanian.

'Gail.' A man's deep voice cut through her confusion.

She pinpointed its owner. 'Petru.' A handsome Romanian awaited her at a bolted-down table. Mihal's contact was in his thirties, by the looks, with thick black lashes that ringed large brown eyes. She wondered what he was in for. Maybe he wasn't *that* dangerous and unpleasant.

Petru held his hands out. Bev offered hers, acting the dutiful girlfriend.

'No. I want chips.' He pointed to the gaudy bag of gherkin-flavoured crisps, not even giving her the once-over.

Bev took her seat, feeling the bite of implicit rejection. She wasn't here for this man, in any case. She turned her attention to the other people seated at tables in the room, conjuring the memories of photos Doc had turned up from his trawl through a maze of the internet's lesser nooks and crannies. After an initially fruitless search, he'd ended up hacking into Archie's laptop hard drive, where he'd found some old A.A. Developments' Christmas party snaps that featured the three men she sought.

'Just talk,' Petru said. 'You don't have to make conversation. Only make it look like a real visit.'

Nodding, Bev started chattering inanely about what she'd watched on television, which mainly amounted to some kids' programmes she'd seen with Hope on CBBC and the odd Netflix offering she'd viewed with Doc – hold the 'and chill'. As she gabbled away at the handsome Romanian, she watched the couples that were flirting, bickering or merely exchanging boring domestic information at the other tables. There were Steve Cooper and his large, washed-out wife, Alan Doherty and his much younger, overly made-up girlfriend and Darren Titchmarsh, with his very own far older Charlie Dimmock, complete with ginger curls and tits on her waistband. She looked familiar. In all three instances, she saw the women handing over treats and gifts. Were they even allowed to do that? Bev observed the guards who seemed to be looking anywhere but at the couples in question. Was it possible the prison staff were complicit in the smuggling of the Spice? Surely not.

The prison visit wouldn't yield the evidence she'd need for Curtis and Owen. All she'd witnessed so far was that Anthony's men were in prison together and that they received visits from their womenfolk. Bev needed more.

'Thanks for seeing me,' she told Petru when her time was up. 'Enjoy your crisps.'

The disengaged Romanian upped and left without a smile, leaving Bev to follow her quarry outside. Did the women who had visited Anthony's workers even know one another?

On the street outside the high walls and fortress-like security of the visitor centre, the women all lit cigarettes and walked separately down the road. Some ten paces apart, they made their way past the Salford Van Hire depot to the bus stop on Bury New Road. Bev followed at a respectful distance, observing their body language. It wasn't apparent that they were connected in any way.

But the moment the women converged at the bus stop, she saw them smile warmly at one another. Laughing and nudging. Yes, they knew each other all right. And Bev wanted in.

'Are we going for a brew then, girls?' she heard Steve Cooper's large, matronly wife ask.

Charlie Dimmock stamped from foot to foot in her fishtail parka with its pink fur hood. 'I'll say. It's bleeding freezing out here. I know it's only twice a month, but fucking hell . . .'

'It's so depressing and all.' The glamorous blonde who sported enough contouring to paint an entire mountain range on her cheeks dragged hard on her cigarette. Her lipsticked mouth pruned around the smoke, hinting at the lived-in woman she'd become in a decade's time – perhaps less. 'I hate coming to see Andy. I never bring our Michaela.'

'Have you left her with your mam?'

The younger woman nodded at the sympathetic-looking matriarch of the group. 'She gets bored. Andy moans at me, though.'

'Bugger what he thinks. It's no place for kids. Anyway, he's in there, toasting his arse at Her Majesty's leisure. You're out here, making money and holding everything together. Come on. I'll treat you to a muffin.'

'I'm watching my figure.'

'Arseholes to that,' Charlie Dimmock said.

The group scuttled across the road and disappeared into the warren of litter-strewn streets that housed the almost exclusively Asian wholesale shops, flogging everything Manchester didn't really want or need, from tiles to clothes and electronics. Bev texted her intentions to Doc and followed, jogging to keep up.

They repaired to a greasy spoon in a back street and stood a while, gawping at the wall-mounted menu. The place reeked of frying bacon and the vinegary tang of brown sauce and ketchup. The windows were steamy. It was busy enough for Bev to slip into the queue ahead of the women and order a tea. She sat at a table for two, stacked with the remnants of somebody else's congealed full-English and strong tea. Though it made the tense tangle of her stomach lurch, Bev calculated that it was worth sitting here, given it was adjacent to the only available table for four.

'I think I'll have an egg butty, me,' Charlie Dimmock said, loud enough for the rest of the café's clientele to hear.

'I'm having a sausage barm,' the young blonde said.

The two repaired to the table for four while the chubby matriarch of their little clique cogitated loudly over whether to have a full English with a tea or a super-sized mixed grill with a can of diet Coke, since she was trying to lose weight. Finally, the three were sitting within earshot of Bev.

Charlie Dimmock slipped out of her parka and tossed her ginger curls over her shoulder. 'I was at a pub lock-in 'til two last night. I feel like dogshit.'

'Tell me about it,' the matriarch said. 'It's our Kieran's birthday, so I was up 'til all hours trying to find the Nikes he wants on eBay. They're limited edition ones. Over a grand!'

'Fucking hell,' the blonde said. 'You gonna pay that for a sixteen-year-old? I wish I'd got a grand's worth of birthday present when I turned sixteen. My mam got me a set of heated rollers and a bikini wax.'

The matriarch shrugged, as her plate of food was set before her by the café owner. She waited until the owner had retreated behind the counter before saying, 'Yeah, but your mam wasn't one of Tony's Angels, was she? I'm earning it, aren't I? We all are.' She primped her hair and impaled a disk of black pudding on the end of her fork. Shovelled it in sideways, speaking as she chewed. 'I can't be tight, me. No pockets in a shroud.'

'Did I tell you about that new Louis Vuitton weekend bag I bought from Selfridges?' Charlie Dimmock chimed in.

As she sipped her tea, Bev listened to the women discuss the long list of luxury and completely useless items they'd recently spent obscene amounts of money on. Studying their attire, she could see that their wardrobes consisted of supermarket polyester offerings teamed with top-end designer accessories and coats. They smacked of grey council estate daily grind, splashed with the colour and optimism of recent cash injections. Tony's Angels, indeed.

Though the hairs on her arms stood to attention at the thought of what she was about to do, Bev dug her nails into her palms and took a deep breath. She leaned over, cleared her throat. Spoke with a whiff of same Pennine-town accent that the women had – enough to ingratiate herself. 'Is there room for one more on that table, girls?'

The matriarch glowered at her, clearing sizing her up. 'Who the fuck's asking?'

'One of Tony's Angels.' Bev grinned. 'I'm Gail. I'm going out with Archie, Tony's brother. I clean for Tony.'

Hostility froze the other women's faces into caricatures of suspicion.

Bev was only moments away from ruining the case she'd risked so much to build. She needed to say something that would salvage her plausibility, and fast. *Bluff it before they eat you for pudding.* 'I met Archie, waitressing at one of Tony's parties.' She aimed the comment at Charlie Dimmock. Praying for the gods of coincidence and half-remembered chance meetings to shine on her. 'I'm sure we met there. Didn't I ask you where you got your amazing shoes?'

The sceptical look on Charlie Dimmock's hard face softened slightly into curiosity and then melted into a proud smile. 'Yeah. That's right. You had a crushed velvet black number on and I said I thought your tits were to die for.'

'You got your shoes at . . .' Bev noticed the MK label on Dimmock's handbag and took a wild guess. 'Michael Kors.'

'Bingo!' Dimmock snapped her fingers and laughed raucously as though Bev had cracked the best joke in the world.

The frost had all but left the group now, allowing the spring shoots of womanly camaraderie to burst forth. They all seemed to straighten in their seats. Blondie and Charlie Dimmock were full of *Hiya, love,* delivered with near-reverence. Bev clearly scored points for being so closely connected to the top.

'I heard Archie was seeing someone new,' the matriarch said, her smile not quite meeting her tired eyes. 'You just been to the nick?'

Bev nodded. 'My brother's inside for shoplifting. Tony said it made sense to make the most of the visits.' She winked.

The other women exchanged glances. Had they smelled a rat? Was Gail's time up?

'He's not daft, is Tony,' Charlie Dimmock said, taking a giant bite of her sausage barm. Licking the ketchup from her lips. 'Getting new people in on . . . you know.' She winked back at Bev.

The matriarch nudged her. No hint of warmth in her stern expression now. 'Hey! Keep your gob shut, for Christ's sake. How do we know she's not a copper or a grass? You daft cow!'

'I'm not,' Bev said, tittering. *Think fast, dammit!* She took out her phone and brought up some selfies of her and Archie together, which she'd taken in the dreadful local pub. 'See?'

The three women scrutinised the photo as though they were a jury, considering vital evidence. The tension hung thick as grease on the air. Finally, though, as if they were communicating by signals sent through their thick, pencilled-in eyebrows, they relaxed in their chairs and unfolded their arms.

'She's not a bloody grass.' Dimmock delivered the verdict, wrinkling her freckled nose. 'No way! Archie's not mug enough to get involved with a copper. I'm not daft, either. I can sniff coppers and grasses a mile off.'

It was enough. The matriarch let down her guard and all three began to talk openly about the cash-in-hand king's ransom they earned, thanks to Tony and his smuggling racket.

'Mars bars are the best,' matriarch said. 'You can pack quite a bit in the big ones and that caramel's brilliant for shoving it all back together. I'm an artist, me.'

'I'm just worried I'll get my collar felt,' Bev said. 'I mean, the guards know Spice is getting in cos the papers write about it, don't they? I bet they know who's behind it too.

They're not stupid. What happens when Tony and the Thai Dragon – what's the Dragon's real name again? Archie told me but I can't remember.' Blank faces and silence said if the women knew the true identity of the Spice-empire's kingpin, they weren't about to share the secret with a newcomer to their inner circle. 'What happens if Tony and that get nicked? We'll all go down, won't we?'

The matriarch shook her head. 'It's all cash. There's no proof.'

'Apart from his ledger, Andy said,' the blonde chimed in.

Matriarch nodded and cocked her head to the side, thoughtfully. Dunked a chip into the yolk of her fried egg. 'Yeah. He keeps a ledger full of names of who's involved and who gets paid what. My Steve seen him writing in it. But Tony's got it hidden, under lock and key. Sherlock Holmes couldn't find it.' She shrugged and shovelled the eggy chip in. Washed it down with tea. 'As long as the money keeps coming in and I can keep our Kieran in Nikes, I don't give a shit, me. I just don't think about it.'

A ledger. The proof was out there somewhere – perhaps it revealed the Thai Dragon's name. Could it be in the house, despite her having searched high and low for exactly that kind of evidence of criminal wrongdoing? 'He doesn't keep the ledger in the house. It better had be safe if my name's in it.' Bev nonchalantly sipped her tea, though she felt three sets of narrowed eyes staring at her, recalculating her threat potential. 'Where do you reckon he's got it stashed?'

'Hang on a fucking minute, lady,' matriarch said, dropping her knife. Her lips had thinned to a line. She pointed her fork in accusatory fashion at Bev.

Her time was up.

CHAPTER 34

Doc

'I don't think this is a good idea,' Doc said, taking a bite of his soggy bacon sandwich. He stared out at the horizontal rain as the sodden seafront was buffeted by gusting winds. The skies were leaden and the sea, a charcoal, roiling mass, like hell's own coastline with the colour and heat turned down all the way to zero. It should have been picturesque, with the long stretch of golden sand and the cottage-studded hillside, but it wasn't. Not to Doc. 'I've never liked Wales. My parents brought me here in a caravan when I was two. The seats were upholstered in red tartan. They gave me a headache and it did nothing but piss down for a fortnight, so there was no escape.'

'Jesus. That's traumatic. Tartan upholstery. No wonder you've spent years in therapy.' There was no trace of sympathy in Bev's words. Only ridicule. 'You should try being ganged up on by three tough old birds in a greasy spoon when they're convinced you're a *Sun* reporter, doing an exposé. I narrowly avoided being forked to death to get this information.' She exhaled heavily. 'I'm playing with fire, you know. Archie thinks it's funny to threaten me with a gun. The only thing standing between me and death, at the moment, is people's love of boasting and flattery.'

But Doc wasn't listening. 'Why couldn't 2Tone have a holiday home in bloody Salcombe or something?'

Bev warmed her hands on her mug of steaming coffee and yawned, her feet tucked beneath her on the holiday let's flowery armchair as though she were a cat, perfectly at home in its surrounds. Swathed in her dressing gown, she showed no signs of having tossed and turned all night, of course, because she hadn't. She had got the bed, while Doc had done the gentlemanly thing and had opted for the uncomfortable, short sofa. Slept with his long legs dangling over the side. Now, he felt stiff and damp, having slept in yesterday's cold, clammy clothes.

'Don't punish me because you didn't have the sense to pack properly. I told you to bring something to sleep in.' She met his gaze. Wry amusement tugged at the corners of her mouth. 'Did you think you'd be spending the night in the nip, warmed by yours truly?'

Shaking his head in the most disapproving manner he could muster, he tore a mouthful off his bacon sandwich and chewed noisily in her general direction. Swallowed, licking his lips. 'Don't flatter yourself. It was pure oversight. I wouldn't sleep with you if . . .'

'If what?' She raised an eyebrow.

'Forget it.' Doc reasoned that there was no point dredging up the kiss. She'd clearly regretted it the moment it had happened. All he could do was rescue the last remaining shreds of his dignity and pretend it had been a foolish impulse on his part, not to be repeated. She didn't need to know how deep his feelings for her really ran. 'We're here now. We've come to spy on Tony.'

'When the cat's away . . .'

'What makes you think he'll play in Abersoch?'

Bev took a bite of the cheese on toast she'd opted for for breakfast. Chewed thoughtfully. 'There's nothing at his house in Little Marshwicke. I've had that place upside down. We're looking for a ledger and I nearly got my head stoved in with a ketchup bottle to get that information.'

'You said it was a fork.'

'Oh. So you *were* listening. I told you. I'm treading on very thin ice with 2Tone's inner circle. Very thin. We've used up eight of our nine lives.'

'*You've* used them, you mean.'

'Gail's used them, *actually*.' She shut her eyes tightly and waved at him dismissively. 'Nobody knows who the hell Gail is. And she's still got one life left. I'm not gonna waste it. I haven't heard a word from Archie since gungate, apart from dick pics. Whatever suspicions Tony's Angels had about me when I started digging, they've obviously not said anything to him, else I'd have heard. Maybe those women in the café don't have a direct line to the top. I bet some underling drops the Spice and cash off for them and they never speak to the mighty 2Tone or his brother. It's all good.' She blinked hard and pulled her dressing gown tighter around her. 'Anyway. Ledger. Chances are, Tony's got it here, in his holiday home. So, we get the ledger, somehow, and hand everything over to Curtis and Owen. Job done.'

'This job was done when Higson was arrested,' Doc said. He pointed the last corner of his sandwich at her. 'When I said I'd be a silent partner in Beverley Saunders, Private Investigations, I never signed up to burglary and spying that involved leaving the safety of my desk chair. I don't do people. I'm not Jack Reacher and neither are you. We don't even have a plan!'

Finishing his unsatisfying breakfast, Doc watched a dog-walker in the distance, braving the foul weather. The man was wearing head-to-toe waterproofs and wellies, while his greyhound or whippet or whatever the hell it was streaked at full pelt along an otherwise deserted beach into the gusting banks of torrential rain.

'How far are we from 2Tone's holiday cottage?' he asked, feeling as though the sight of the dog walker had finally switched a light on, illuminating the gloom in his mind.

Bev rose from the armchair, carrying her mug. Approaching the window, she peered out and scanned the view of the sea and picturesque homes, clinging to the coastline. 'He's in that modern one with the big windows,' she said.

'You sure?' Doc asked, standing close enough to her to smell the scent of the holiday let's bedding on her hair. He breathed in deeply and closed his eyes momentarily, savouring the proximity.

'I've seen pictures of it on the side in Chateau d'Antoine.' Bev pointed to the white-rendered new-build. 'Why?'

'Well, this is his nearest stretch of beach and it's just gone 8.00 a.m. Unless we've already missed him, he's going to be out there soon, walking that dick of a dog. I bet he'll come out when the rain stops. It's what dog owners do by the seaside, isn't it? Ponce around with wellies on, pretending to be all outdoorsy and shiz.'

'So?' Bev moved away, returning to her seat.

'That's where we can keep tabs on him at close quarters. On the beach while he's walking the dog. He doesn't know me, does he? I can find a way to distract him while you go to the house. You've got a key, haven't you?'

Bev snatched up the bunch of keys that she'd left lying next to her handbag. She jangled them at Doc. 'Spares are on the same keyring as the keys to his Little Marshwicke castle. He's even labelled the buggers and I know the code for the alarm. He writes everything like that down and hides it under a cereal box in a kitchen cupboard.'

'OK then. We've got a plan. Get me those binoculars and get dressed. You're going to do some burglary and I'm going to do some bullshitting.'

'Nice doggy,' Doc said, already uncomfortable, thanks to the freezing wet sand that seeped uncomfortably into his trainers. At least the rain had abated, finally.

The giant of a dog jumped up at him, covering his damp stonewashed jeans with filthy sodden paw prints. 'Oh, you're, erm . . . Ha. Excitable.'

'He's just being friendly,' the dog's teenaged owner said, laughing. 'Maybe he can smell meat on you. He goes mental when somebody's had bacon. Ha ha.'

Yes, that's right. You laugh at the bloody spectacle of a computer nerd being attacked by a Dulux dog that looks like it eats steroids. Doc smiled at the kid, deciding he couldn't be more than fourteen or fifteen. He wasn't one of Doc's number. On his feet, he wore expensive-looking walking shoes. A Canada Goose jacket on top. The kid was materialistic. It was perfect.

'Do us a favour,' Doc said. 'Lend us your dog for fifteen minutes and I'll give you twenty quid.' He glanced over nervously at Anthony Anthony, who was frolicking at the far end of the beach with his own outsized ball of fur. It was now or never.

The boy frowned. Rubbed a hand through his gelled hair that was impervious even to the stiff wind. 'Why?'

'Reasons. You can stand here and watch me. No funny stuff. I just need to spend time with a dog.'

The kid laughed and grabbed his dog by the lead, pulling it away from Doc. 'You're a pervert, aren't you?'

Doc shoved his hands in his pocket and felt the half-eaten pork pie he'd stashed in there. The Dulux dog strained at its leash to be with him. For once in his life, Doc knew he had all the magnetism of a processed meat product. 'Please, man. I lost my dog a month ago to . . . cancer of the . . . snout.'

'Jesus, bruv. I'm so sorry. Make it thirty quid and you've got him for ten minutes. I ain't standing here, freezing my tits off for longer than that. He's called Chewbacca.'

Handing over the cash, Doc grabbed the lead and was dragged down the beach in the opposite direction to Anthony Anthony by Chewbacca, the four-legged wookie.

'This way, Chewbacca!' He tugged at the truculent dog's lead.

In the distance, 2Tone flung a stick high in the air. Soprano pelted after it. Close, but still no cigar.

Doc broke off half of the pork pie and lobbed it in the direction of the landscaper. Sure enough, Chewbacca flounced after it. Amid a riot of excited barking, the Dulux dog and Soprano met, quietening only to sniff each other's rears.

Anthony Anthony was red in the face with watering eyes. 'Nice dog. I love them Dulux dogs, me. They remind me of being a kid. You know? The adverts for paint and that. My aunty used to have one called Norman, after Norman Bates.'

'Yeah. Cool.' Doc nodded, wondering who Norman Bates was and what he should say next. He had to keep the conversation going for a full ten minutes; prayed that Bev was using this window of opportunity to gain entry to the house. 'I like yours. He's . . . furry.'

Anthony rubbed his hands together and blew on them. 'Aye. Our Soprano can't feel the cold, but I'm bleeding freezing, me.' He sized Doc up with undisguised curiosity etched on his windswept face. 'You live round here or just on holiday?'

Now was Doc's chance to shine as a pathological liar! Finally, he could try to walk a mile in Bev's TK Maxx stripper shoes. 'I've got a house here. Yeah. I only come a few times a year though, because I'm just, like, really busy in London.'

'What do you do?'

'IT. I'm big in IT. I develop systems and shiz for big corporates. Those stiff arses in their suits haul the likes of me in when they need something clever doing.' He threw his head back and laughed at the outlandish fib he'd just told and the fact that Anthony seemed to have swallowed it whole.

'Computers and all that?' The landscaper studied Doc's face thoughtfully. 'Aye, I can see someone like you doing that. You look like one of them boffins. No offence, like.' He seemed to switch off, then, his curiosity satisfied. Examined his ball and put it into the throwing stick.

Doc dug his hands into his pockets, feeling the remains of the pork pie crumble at his touch. Realising he was losing Anthony's attention, he plucked an untruth out of the brisk briny air that might appeal to the landscaper. 'I also dabble in property development.'

'Oh aye? What do you develop?'

'Flats. That sort of thing.'

'Round here?'

'No.'

'Well, where then?' said 2Tone, fully engaged, now. He took a business card out of his anorak, clearly about to proposition Doc in some professional capacity, when a tall figure in a bright green Puffa jacket shouted his name. The figure was walking towards them at a brisk pace, wearing jeans and wellies.

'Tony!' It was a woman's voice.

Soprano barked twice at the approaching figure and then proceeded to mount the Dulux dog. At first, Doc was so distracted by the sight of the male German Shepherd, humping the male borrowed dog that he almost failed to notice who the woman was.

Taking the chunks of pork pie out of his pocket, Doc threw them towards the water's edge in a bid to distract the clearly pansexual Soprano from his amorous task.

'Hello, darling,' the woman said, kissing Anthony on the lips in a way that implied more than just friendship.

Finally, Doc looked around to take note of 2Tone's girlfriend. He almost blurted her name out loud.

Penny Higson.

CHAPTER 35

Bev

'What makes you think you can find my brother if you can't even find Anthony's ledger?' Mihal asked, as they headed in the Morris towards a twilit Manchester city centre.

Bev looked at her accidental lodger and considered her answer. 'The only difference between success and failure, when you're a PI like me, is persistence and good gut instincts.'

'But your instincts aren't good. You didn't know Penny Higson was the Thai Dragon. You didn't work out that she was involved with Anthony.' He balled his fist and ground his knuckles into the palm of his left hand. 'And Doc told me you've been sleeping with that bastard, Archie.'

Bev gasped as his words hit home – a body blow knocking the air from her lungs. The Morris suddenly felt like a cage and she was trapped inside with an angry predator. Wounded Mihal may be, but he still had the smell of blood in his nostrils and Bev was within striking distance. She gripped the steering wheel hard so he wouldn't see her hands shaking.

'Listen, I may be far from perfect, mate, but I managed to uncover a drugs empire as well as a trafficking ring. There's still work to do, though. You want revenge? You wanna do it properly? We need to put these pricks behind bars. And if your brother's out there, we need to find him or at least, find out what happened to him. Now, just trust me to do my job. OK?'

As she approached the concrete tangle of the Mancunian Way, with newly built glass-fronted skyscrapers looming before her, she considered all that the past couple of days had revealed. Her best efforts at searching 2Tone's Abersoch holiday home had been cut short by Penny strutting out of the house, just as Bev had been poised to break in. Since a hapless Doc had been marooned on the beach with two dangerous criminals and a borrowed dog, Bev had had to abandon her ambitions to find the ledger . . . for the time being.

They'd fled Wales but returned home to deduce – thanks to a little more light hacking by Doc of the Outlook calendars of the 'Spice scandal schools' – that the diary entries *Higson: piano* had not just been referring to Jim. Penny had also been employed in each and every location as a music supply teacher, teaching piano to the kids. Either Penny and Jim were in cahoots, or the wife in this Bonnie and Clyde set-up had used her unwitting husband as a patsy for her narcotic misdeeds.

But possibly the most disconcerting element of discovering the connection between Anthony and his lying lover had been Mihal's reaction to the news. The Romanian had snatched up a hammer from the kitchen knick-knacks drawer and had smashed a hole in the wall, screaming that he was going to kill the landscaper and the music teacher. Bev had known then that they had to find Constantin as a priority and get Mihal out of the flat, fast. He was an angry, unknown quantity, and she wasn't about to put her daughter in harm's way.

She swallowed hard at the thought of Hope being on the receiving end of Mihal's grief and rage. 'Right, our first stop is Barnabus in the Gay Village,' she said, pulling into a parking bay in China Town.

The homeless charity, Barnabus, was a non-descript-looking building sandwiched between Krunchy Fried

Chicken and a Middle Eastern eaterie. At just after 5 p.m., the staff seemed to be preparing to pack up for the day. Mihal showed several people a photo of Constantin, taken before the brothers had left Romania.

'Do you recognise him?' Bev asked, hopeful that such a centrally-based place would enjoy steady footfall of the city's destitute.

They were met with apologetic shakes of the head. Moved onto the next place and the next . . . and the next. There were nine organisations for the homeless within a square mile, roughly, but most of them seemed to shut up shop around 4.30 p.m., meaning Bev and Mihal were greeted by locked doors and dark buildings.

'I thought shelters would have dormitories or something,' Bev said, her feet throbbing from the pace at which Mihal was marching her around Manchester's streets. 'Where the hell do these poor sods sleep?'

'Anywhere they can keep dry. I slept in a squat miles away from the city centre when I first got out of prison and came up here.'

'We need to take this to the people,' she said, trying to stay positive though her optimism was fizzling like a bulb on the blink. 'Come on! It shouldn't be hard.'

The city changed as they moved from the Irwell back towards Piccadilly. Crossing the tram tracks by Marks & Spencer and the Royal Exchange onto Market Street, the suited corporates and smartly dressed shopworkers were replaced by doughy-faced people in leisurewear. Amid the gaudy high-street stores and chewing-gum spattered pavements and buskers, it was hard to differentiate the homeless from the merely down-at-heel. But it was only once they reached Piccadilly that Bev felt they'd reached the epicentre of the city's homelessness crisis.

At the side of Debenhams, six or seven had gathered with their sleeping bags. They were already either stoned or steaming drunk. People were walking past them, head down, studiously avoiding any kind of interaction.

'Excuse me,' Mihal said, approaching the motley band that were arguing amongst themselves, right next to an upmarket flower stall. He held out the photo, shouting above a heated debate about who had bought the last four-pack of Tennents Extra. 'Have you seen my brother? Please. Look at this photo. It's my brother. He might be on the streets. I'm looking for him. He's Romanian. Twenty-six-years-old. He was only twenty-one in this photo, so maybe he's aged now. Last time I saw him, he was using Spice.'

A woman with straggling greasy hair and more gaps than teeth laughed at him. 'Aren't we all, mate? Bung us a tenner!' She spoke with a guttural Mancunian accent. Could have been anywhere from her mid-twenties to her fifties.

'Do you recognise him, lady?' Mihal asked, hopefully. 'His name is Constantin.'

Glassy-eyed, the woman pushed the photo aside. 'Listen, cock. This is Manchester.' Bev could smell the alcohol on her breath from several paces away. 'If he's here, he's getting looked after. Right? This city's full of love.' She raised her can to him. Three sheets to the stiff northern wind.

'We're not getting anywhere,' Bev said, grabbing Mihal by the elbow and leading him away to Piccadilly Gardens.

The place thronged with all of Manchester's lower demographic echelons. Students and workers, scurrying from shop to shop or mounting the concrete ramp to the Market Street tram stop. Mothers in full burka with toddlers in pushchairs – the handlebars laden down with Primark bags. The elderly, the young, the stony-faced queens of the local council estates in their onesies and Uggs. Outside

Superdrug, hope flourished anew in the form of a young man, burrowed into a filthy sleeping bag in the doorway. His dark hair poked out the top in a matted clump. His skin was olive though his face was angled towards the ground, making it difficult to see his features clearly.

'Constantin?' Mihal reached out to touch the man. His voice was timorous, disbelieving.

'What do you want?' The man in the sleeping bag was suddenly awake, swiping Mihal away. His accent was clearly west-country. Definitely not Constantin. 'You trying to nick my gear? Fuck you! Can't a feller grab a kip around here?'

Superdrug's customers merely stepped over him as if he were nothing more than a dislodged flagstone or piece of trash, lying in their way.

Mihal backed off, raising his hands in surrender. 'Sorry. I thought you were someone else.'

Torrential rain brought the search to an abrupt end. With a heavy heart, Bev realised that trying to locate Constantin was like trying to find a dirty needle in a haystack.

The following day, after an exhausting, sleepless night where Bev had lain awake, half expecting Mihal to leave for Abersoch, with murder on his mind, they hit the streets yet again. This time they arrived earlier, visiting the organisations that had been shut the previous evening. In one bland drop-in centre after the other, well-meaning staff shook their heads as they looked at the battered photo of Constantin.

'Sorry. We get so many people come through here,' one woman said, smiling sympathetically.

'But not many Romanians! You must remember a Romanian man,' Mihal insisted.

'You'd be surprised. We get people from all walks of life in here. Workers who have missed one too many mortgage payments and got themselves into debt. People with mental health problems. Runaways. Lots of runaways. The young kids break my heart.' She touched her chest. 'There's immigrants from all over the world, love. Asylum seekers from places like Africa generally go to the Boaz Trust. But they all come in their droves from these far-flung destinations thinking Manchester's going to be the land of plenty. What a flipping joke!'

Bev placed a hand on Mihal's arm. 'Come on. Onwards and upwards. The fat lady hasn't sung yet.'

The sun was setting. Behind Piccadilly station, beneath the arches, they found a warren of backstreets that all showed signs of having been inhabited by the homeless after dark. Abandoned, flattened cardboard boxes were propped against walls. McDonalds wrappers and empty cups sprouted from the ground like optimistic weeds. For now, though, the doorways and nooks that offered shelter were empty. Bev and Mihal scoured the area, looking for anyone who might examine Constantin's photo.

Only as darkness fell in earnest did the streets started to fill up.

'No, love.'

'Sorry, love.'

'Have you got any spare change?'

'Never seen him, mate.'

Scores of beleaguered wraiths with cracked lips and wind-burnt cheeks almost remembered him. They even argued among themselves over whether they'd ever spoken to Constantin or not.

Just before 8.00 p.m., a mobile soup kitchen arrived and set up. The homeless were appearing from every corner of Piccadilly, it seemed. Now, this unglamorous part of the city thronged with the destitute. With hot food on offer to

273

go with the cold-combatting properties of their extra strong alcohol, they seemed less interested in Mihal's plight.

'I think we should go,' Mihal said, lighting a cigarette and exhaling through his nostrils. 'You're cold.'

'I'm not.'

'I can see you shivering, Beverley. No. It's time to go. Constantin is dead. I feel it here.' He balled his fist and touched the place beneath which his broken heart lay.

But Bev felt frustration niggle. Was it merely the after-effects of the kebab she'd had a couple of hours ago at Mihal's insistence? 'You're giving up too easily.' She looked down at her numb feet to avoid his wounded expression.

'Don't judge me!' he shouted. 'Don't offer to help me and then get on your high horse, saying—' He grabbed her roughly by her forearms and pinned her against the wall.

Bev opened her mouth to yell for help, but when she saw the pain in Mihal's eyes, she held her tongue.

'Hey! Let her go!' An authoritative woman's voice pierced the tension between them. Mihal and Bev both turned to the interloper. It was the woman who was in charge of the soup kitchen. She peered at Mihal through bifocal glasses. Waited until Mihal had released Bev and mumbled an apology. 'Now, are you the Romanian man who showed me the photograph?'

'Yes,' Mihal said, casting his cigarette butt aside. 'Why? Do you know where my brother is?'

'Show me the photo again,' she said, smoothing a finger over the edges of her hijab.

Mihal handed the dog-eared snap over.

The woman studied it beneath the streetlight and nodded. 'I thought I recognised the mole beneath his eye and those eyebrows. Very distinctive. Yes. I can tell you exactly what happened to this man.'

CHAPTER 36
Bev

'Tell me!' Mihal pleaded, snatching the photo back. 'Is he dead?'

Against all odds, the woman who ran the soup kitchen pointed to a ramshackle-looking man with overgrown black hair and a bushy beard that made him look some two decades older than he was. 'He told me he'd been trafficked and then ran away. He's been coming here for years.'

Mihal ran towards the figure who stood in the queue for soup. Bev followed close behind, watching as Mihal tapped the hirsute figure on the shoulder. The man turned around, his bushy eyebrows bunched together in curiosity. Mihal's mouth fell open.

'Constantin!' He reached out to embrace his long-lost brother. 'You're alive!'

Constantin pushed Mihal backwards, no flicker of recognition immediately obvious in his eyes. But suddenly, Bev saw realisation dawn on the ragged man's face.

'Mihal!' There was desperation and longing in that one word of greeting.

The search was over.

*

An hour and a half, an extremely smelly drive home and a dinner of ready-made pizza later, Bev was staring into the black thatch of Constantin's freshly washed hair. 'I can't bloody well cut *that*!' she said.

Now, against her better judgement, her office-cum-flat was occupied by not one, but two destitute Romanian men. She was overjoyed that Mihal had been reunited with his long-lost baby brother, rather than being faced with the prospect of having to bury the last of his siblings, but *this*?!

'Why the hell should he cut his hair, man?' Doc shouted from the adjacent room. 'Samson cut his hair, and look at what happened to him! Just leave it.'

'I'll take him to the barbers in the morning,' Mihal said.

Swinging around swiftly, Bev treated him to a disparaging look. 'With what? It's like London round here. You know they charge upwards of £15 for a bloke's haircut, don't you? Peanuts for a footballer, maybe, but are you that flush?'

Mihal shook his head in silence and shrugged at his brother.

Bev looked at Constantin's scalp and the coarse shafts of his hair, studded with tiny brown dots. She turned to Mihal and raised her eyebrows. 'They wouldn't take him at a barber's anyway. He's a walking infestation. No. It's all gonna have to come off. I'm bagging and burning the lot.'

Constantin said something in pigeon English that sounded like an apology. Scratched at his scalp, tweezed a louse between his fingers and popped it.

She swiped his hand away from his head. 'Dirty bugger. You're not a bloody chimpanzee. I'm no anal-retentive, but squishing lice is gross.' Patted him gingerly on the shoulder. 'I'll cut it as close as I can. The razor will have to do the rest.'

Doc appeared at the doorway to the kitchen. 'Just get some of that nit shampoo. Why should the dude lose his locks?' He caught Constantin's eye and pointed to his head; gave the thumbs up. 'I'd kill for hair like that, man.' Pinched some of his own lank, dark-blond hair between his finger and thumb. 'Wanna swap?'

Bev turned to him, threatening her business partner with the scissors. 'Have you seen the price of Hedrin? You wanna delouse this bugger on your dime and nit-comb him twice a day for a week, feel free. But if he stays even one night, this shit is going up in flames. I'm not giving Hope nits. She's got hair like rope. I'd be nit-combing for a year!'

'Cut it,' Mihal said, sentencing the hair to history. 'Just cut.'

Bev twisted her own braid high onto her head and donned one of Hope's rubber swim-caps, rolling it down over her hair as makeshift protection against the blood-thirsty, wandering parasites. She grabbed a handful of Constantin's lice-infested thatch and brandished the shears. 'Here goes. While I'm doing this, get your brother to show us those photos. He shares what's on the phone, or we kick him back onto the street.'

During the emotional car journey back up the M56, Constantin had revealed that he'd collected damning photographic evidence on an old phone. It was this with which he'd tried to blackmail Anthony, just prior to his disappearance. But frustratingly, he'd been reluctant to share it, as if Bev and Doc would rob him like some thug on the street.

Mihal now spoke to his brother in their own tongue, clearly pleading for his brother to let them examine the phone. Finally, Constantin's shoulders dropped. He nodded.

As Bev started to hack away at the wild growth, quaking and itching as she watched the lice scurry deeper into the hairy thicket, away from the blades, Constantin plucked an old phone from the pocket of the stonewashed jeans that Doc had lent him. The Motorola's screen was so badly damaged with an intricate spider's web of fissures, that it was hard to imagine it still worked. But he powered it up, his overly long thumbnail still ingrained with dirt despite two hot showers.

'Give that to me, man,' Doc said, approaching. He held his hand out for the phone, which Constantin reluctantly handed over. 'I'll download what's on it.' He examined the device. 'It's on 4 per cent. It won't display properly. We'll have to wait.'

Minutes passed as Bev hacked away at Constantin's hair. Barely able to control her gag reflex, she watched the tresses fall onto the newspaper she'd spread over the kitchen floor, wondering if lice could infest slippers and crawl their way up to your hairy bits. Every few seconds, she looked around hopefully for a reaction from Doc that said the phone was charged enough to display the screen.

'Here we go,' Doc finally said.

'I took when I was make swimming pool,' Constantin explained as they all gathered around the small screen.

The first images appeared, showing Anthony Anthony and Penny Higson in various compromising poses: screwing up against the kitchen cupboards, kissing over the garden fence, together in Tony's Bentley. All of the photos had clearly been taken without the couple's knowledge. Some were a little grainy and not helped by the screen being shattered, but still clearly showed the clandestine couple.

'The files are dated,' Doc said, 'so there's proof of when the relationship was in existence.'

'You see neighbour lady make Spice,' Constantin said, his Romanian accent so much more pronounced that his brother's; his command of English far less accomplished. He gestured that Doc should scroll along.

Constantin poked at the screen triumphantly as a photo of Penny in Jim Higson's piano workshop popped up. Taken through the window, the photo showed her alone, scooping white powder out of a large sack. There was a second. Using an agricultural hand-spray, she was spraying what appeared to be herbs spread out on a long trestle table.

'We saw all this gear in the inspection pit,' Bev explained.

Mihal nodded. 'This is proof that she is the Thai Dragon. She's in charge.'

What followed was a photo of Penny handing balls of the finished product to Tony. They were looking into each other's eyes with all the subterfuge, greed and lust that Bev could imagine might power such a relationship.

'How did you take these, Constantin?' she asked, wondering that a slave labourer would be able to get hold of a phone, let alone escape the scrutiny of an ever-watchful taskmaster like Archie or, indeed, Tony himself.

'I am small and fast,' Constantin said. He spoke in Romanian to Mihal.

Mihal translated. 'He says he got the phone by picking the pocket of one of Anthony's legitimate apprentices. Constantin had seen Archie and Tony beat two other men senseless − a couple of Bulgarians. They disappeared. When he asked Archie, Archie said he'd taken them to the hospital but they never came back. Constantin thinks they might have been murdered. Then, a couple of the other Romanians dropped dead from heart attacks after using Spice. Constantin says he was scared he would be next − especially after Tony sent me and Bogdan to London. He knew he had to get hold of a phone.'

'Why didn't he use it to call the police?'

Mihal chuckled mirthlessly. 'The police? Yes. Call the police and get deported. Or maybe Archie and Tony find out and kill him. Beverley, trafficked men can't trust anybody, let alone the police. Anyway, Constantin says he knew he needed to take photos of what was going on. It was insurance; emergency currency.'

Bev took the phone from Doc, thumbing along until she found an image that made her smile. It showed Tony standing by his greenhouse at the bottom of the garden, handing small, egg-like packages to four women. They were flint-faced women, like those she'd spoken to in the greasy spoon café near Strangeways prison. 'Tony's Angels,' she said. 'They're young too. Look at them. They can't be more than nineteen. Mid-twenties, tops.'

Constantin snatched the phone back and brought up a screenshot of a newspaper article. It was the Little Marshwicke local rag, showing Anthony Anthony, dressed in his Paul Smith Sunday best, presenting a giant cheque to a young man. The caption said the donation was intended for Full Marks – the charity where Anthony was a trustee, ostensibly supporting vulnerable young men at risk of offending. 'It's all big lie.' He said something else to Mihal.

Mihal's eyebrows shot up towards his hairline. 'Constantin says the lad in this photo is the boyfriend of one of those girls. He'd seen the lad at the house with the girl a few months after Bogdan and I left for London. They were chatting with Tony in the kitchen.'

Doc whistled low. 'So, do you reckon all this charity bullshit is just old 2Tone grooming young guys for his con? He knows they already flirt with the wrong side of the law, right? And he needs to get his gear smuggled into prison, since that was his main market before it became rife on the street. Obviously, if you're skint and living on a shitty, dead-end estate and always getting picked up by the police anyway, if the local Don Pablo turns round and offers to pay you handsomely in return for doing a bit of time at Her Majesty's leisure, you're gonna be up for it. Anything to get out of Dodge, right?'

'What a little shit,' Bev said. Her hands shook with anger. She took a deep breath and surveyed her hairdressing handiwork. 'Time for the razor. Mihal, get me a bowl of warm water, the conditioner out of the shower room, a comb, some soap and a towel. Doc, give him a hand!'

As she soaked the short, shaggy mess that was now Constantin's hair in conditioner, she set about it with a cheap nit comb, trying to remove the adult lice that were still crawling around in the thicket. Wiped them on the towel. Considered that they now had almost everything the needed to take to Owen and Curtis – everything apart from the final piece of the puzzle.

Taking the razor to what was left of the hair, Bev asked blithely, 'Constantin, did you ever see Tony use or write in a ledger?'

Mihal translated. Constantin sighed. Lifted his hand to scratch at his scalp but stopped short. 'Book. Yes. Book with numbers and names. I seen.'

'Where?' The blood rushed in Bev's ears. 'In the house?'

'No,' Constantin said. 'I work at cottage. By seaside. Fixing new windows. I go down to his boat to make sand and varnish deck. On boat, he use numbers book there.'

CHAPTER 37

Bev

'Why do you have to be such a dick, Rob? I'm just asking you to have her tonight instead of tomorrow night. Is that such a big deal?' Bev spoke into the phone that Doc was holding to her ear. It wasn't easy with the Morris bumping over undulations in the road that had led them through the natural majesty of Snowdonia National Park to a rather more monotonous landscape of high hedgerows, punctuated only by the odd farm or field full of sheep.

'You can't just wander in and out of her life when it suits you,' Rob said on the other end, superiority dripping from his every vowel and consonant as he laid it on with a trowel. 'Hope needs stability and routine.'

Bev could hear her daughter merrily shouting, 'Hiya, Mum-Mum! Love you!' in the background.

She dearly wanted to see her delicious girl, but the appointments Mihal had made for Constantin with the housing officer and the GP weren't scheduled until tomorrow morning. The last thing she wanted was her daughter spending the night at the flat when two homeless men with on/off drug dependencies and sketchy criminal records were kipping down in the storeroom. Plus, there was the small problem of her being halfway to Abersoch with little chance of returning that evening.

'Don't lecture me on Hope's needs, you lump of shite,' she said, her tone tipping over from assertive into full-on losing it. 'If you gave a monkey's flying arsehole about stability and routine, you wouldn't have cut her mother out of her life for years and subjected her to social worker-supervised visits.'

She knew he was close to putting the phone down on her, which was not what she needed. Had to dial it back. Even Doc was gesticulating with his free hand that she should calm down. She batted his hand away and smacked him squarely in the ghoulish portrait of Iron Maiden's zombie mascot, Eddie, who adorned Doc's pigeon chest in the form of a worn-out T-shirt.

'Ow.'

'Who said, "ow"?' Rob asked. 'Who are you with? Are you sacking off your motherly duties to go off on a fuck-fest?'

'Shove it up your pipe. And don't talk like that within earshot of Hope, for Christ's sake. If you must know, the reason I need you to have her tonight is work-related. I'm off to Abersoch on a surveillance job with *my business partner*, and our target is in situ right now. It's a one-time-only opportunity.'

As she navigated the twists and turns of the Welsh country roads, she bickered on with her ex-husband until he eventually relented.

'I had plans, you know.'

'What? A date? With your new girlfriend, who sounds *suspiciously* like Sophie?'

'Sophie?! Don't be ridiculous. Sophie hates my guts.'

'She didn't hate your guts when you were sipping latte on that terrace after—'

'Shut up, Bev. Do you want me to have Hope tonight or not?'

She'd won. Ordinarily, she'd never rearrange her time with her daughter. Any night where Hope slept over was a hard-won victory, after all. But this expedition was time-sensitive in the extreme.

'Let's hope 2Tone's not already had the boat put in dry dock,' Doc said, once the call had ended. 'It's already getting on for late morning. We've got to get down to the harbour, find the bloody thing, pray he's not on board . . .'

'Tell me again what his calendar said,' Bev said, feeling a jolt of excitement as she drove past the stone sign that told them they'd arrived at their destination. The silver salver of the sea finally came into view on her left. 'Didn't you say he'd put 'P's B – Snowdonia' on today's entry? Wasn't there a specific time for the boat?'

Doc brought up the photo he'd taken of 2Tone's rudimentary diary system, which comprised a *Star Wars* calendar on a pinboard in the utility room. Doc had found it during a supplementary search of Chateau d'Antoine for the ledger, buried beneath various Rotary Club notices and a pinned invoice for some paving. Bev was glad Doc had had the wherewithal to take photographs of every month's badly-scrawled entries, just to be on the safe side. Turned out, her hacking sidekick was a better sleuth than she was. She opted not to tell him quite how much that stung.

'Yep. P's B – Snowdonia,' Doc said. 'I reckon it's Penny's birthday and he's taking her out for the day.'

'Might just be for lunch,' Bev said, trying to decide where to park up. Ideally, the Morris needed to be somewhere where she could make a fast getaway, if it came to it. At least, as fast as it was possible to get away in a Morris Traveller that hadn't been happy going over 75mph for decades, if ever. 'In which case, we need to get on the boat—'

'If it's there.'

'Yeah, if it's there. Get on, get in, search the bloody thing from aft to stern, or whatever the hell you call it. Get out.'

Doc checked his retro Casio watch. The suggestion of a smile played at the corners of his mouth. 'OK. Assuming they *only* go for lunch, that gives us 'til about . . . maybe 3.00 p.m?'

'Cutting it fine,' Bev said. 'Workmen eat lunch at midday. I bet 2Tone won't wait 'til 1.00 p.m., which means they could be back by 2.30 p.m.'

'If the boat doesn't get carted off with us still on it.'

Bev pulled into a parking bay in a side street. She touched her forehead, feeling the ridges that were still there thanks to Constantin's hair-cutting episode where she'd worn her daughter's overly tight swim-cap as a prophylactic against headlice. This case was making a mockery of her dignity.

Hastening down to the small harbour, she cast her eye along the row of moored boats, wondering which one belonged to Anthony.

'What's it called again?' Doc asked.

'Constantin said it was called *Corleone*,' Bev said. 'A motorised yacht, whatever the hell one of those looks like.'

'Oh, I know exactly what one of those is,' Doc said. He pointed to the row of moored catamarans and sailboats. 'Which of those do you think belongs to old 2Tone?'

Bev scanned the scene of the small vessels bobbing up and down. 'Er . . . dunno.'

'Think about the sort of materialistic twat Anthony is. Picture that blinging house that's actually only a step up from a Barratt home. And his stupid fucking 08 plate Bentley that's probably worth a damn sight less than a good, modern BWM 3 Series. The guy's a weekend millionaire with cheap cigarillos displayed in a used Cuban cigar box on his desk. He's all top show, isn't he? So, what sort of boat will 2Tone have?'

A large white blob bobbing in the distance caught Bev's eye. She squinted hard at it. It was a diminutive version of a flash fibreglass yacht. Morecambe with *Miami Vice* pretentions. 'That's it. Gimme the binoculars.'

Doc passed the theatre binoculars, which he'd tried to convince Bev were high-end bird-watching equipment but which she knew full well were old crap he'd pilfered from his parents' house.

She gazed down the fixed lenses, relieved that the back of the boat was facing towards the harbour; still visible though a mist was starting to roll in. '*Corleone*. Gotcha.'

The only problem was how to get out to it.

'The yacht club,' Doc suggested. 'His is not the only boat moored that far out. I bet they have a man who can taxi you out there or something.'

Making their way around the bay to the yacht club, which was comprised of a series of buildings, clinging to a rocky headland, it transpired that there was indeed a club shuttle service for boat owners who were moored further out. With a thudding heart and sweat pooling in her cleavage, Bev considered bluffing it out with the official shuttle operator, claiming – not entirely dishonestly – that she was Anthony's cleaner; insisting that she needed to board the boat to do a special tidy-up in honour of his girlfriend's birthday. *Come on, you can do it, Bev. Just feel the fear and do it anyway. Be Gail.*

'Do you go as far as that yacht, there?' she asked, pointing to *Corleone*. Shrouded by freezing fog that had now descended on the periphery of the bay, the pristine white vessel looked almost like a miniature iceberg, bobbing up and down on the waves.

'Oh, Mr Anthony's boat,' the manager said, unfolding his arms and smiling widely. 'Yes. Of course! He's a member here. Everyone knows him. Very successful entrepreneur from Manchester. Are you a friend?' He spoke directly to Bev's chest. Bev noticed that he was wearing a hairpiece and had the hairiest ears she'd ever seen.

'A, er, business associate,' Bev said, turning to the view through the large picture windows of misty Cardigan Bay so that the guy wouldn't notice her cheeks turn from pink to scorching red. She felt instinctively that being Gail would be a bad idea. If 2Tone was so well known in a place with a presumably limited membership, was it not likely this turd might phone ahead to Tony to double-check that his cleaner was indeed required on board the good ship Corleone? It was too risky. 'My friend, here . . .' She squeezed Doc's arm affectionately. 'Is big in IT. We're just interested in joining the club. But we'll take a leaflet. So, just give us that and we'll be in touch.'

'What kind of vessel do you have?'

'A huge one,' Doc said, taking Bev by the hand and starting to walk away. 'It's *really* big and *really* shiny. Thanks for your help.'

Outside, Bev bent over and grabbed her knees, feeling suddenly that the world was spinning too fast on its axis. 'How are we gonna get on that boat, Doc? We'll have to find a rowing boat and row ourselves out there or something. Jesus.' She straightened up. 'What do you reckon?'

Doc didn't respond. He merely stood beside her with his arms folded tightly over his chest, grimacing at the sight of two jet skis being ridden along the choppy shoreline. He'd paled visibly.

'What's up with you?' she asked, feeling that her day was about to take a turn for the even more problematic.

'I can't swim very well,' he said quietly.

'And? I'm not asking you to bloody swim out there. We need to find a boat.'

He locked eyes with her. 'You don't get it, do you? I mean, I'm a really shit swimmer. I didn't even get my twenty-five metre badge.'

'Why the fuck didn't you bring this up before we drove all the way out here?'

'I thought I'd be OK doing this. But that was before I realised 2Tone's boat was moored in the middle of the sodding bay.' He took a step away from her. 'I'm really sorry, Bev. But—'

'You're kidding me! Are you seriously chickening out, now?' Bev ground her molars together, irritated by the sight of Doc shrinking away from her and the sea and their mutually agreed goal with every step he took back towards the road.

'I'll meet you back at the car, yeah? I can be lookout! If I spot 2Tone or Penny, I'll text.' His sickly smile looked like the empty gesture it was.

'What? No! Come back here, you damn wimp!' Bev shouted after him, watching him disappear down the beach. 'Don't leave me holding the bloody baby!' But he wasn't listening.

'Fucking coward!' she shouted, kicking up sand in frustration.

Sighing, wishing she'd just delivered everything she had to Owen and Curtis, Bev found a rock to sit on by the side of the yachting club complex. She sat a while, gazing wistfully out at Tony's boat, wondering what to do. It rose and fell on the heaving swell of water that looked as though it was steaming, with the mists that swirled above it. So close, so close . . .

Briefly watching the comings and goings of the tanned, predominantly middle-aged members of the yacht club with their expensive sailing gear, wondering if any might help a pasty, poorly-clothed woman with giant tits, Bev presently noticed a silver-haired old guy row a small boat into shore. With each stroke of the oars, the sinews in his mahogany-coloured arms looked like they might snap. Was he a member of the club?

When the small boat was almost beached, the old man jumped into the water. His trousers were rolled up to the knees. He looked fit and experienced. Local, perhaps. The sort of guy that might row her out to Tony's yacht for a few quid up front.

Taking off her shoes and padding down towards him, she smiled. 'You look like a seasoned sailor,' she said.

She'd clearly caught the man unawares. He eyed her with apparent curiosity. 'I've been sailing in Cardigan Bay all my life,' he said. His rolling Welsh accent betrayed him as a local. He grabbed the prow of his boat and braced himself to haul it out of the water.

'Do me a favour, will you?' Bev said, wondering how to play this. 'If I give you twenty quid, will you row me out to that yacht please?' *Think of a good lie. Come on. Bullshit is your field of expertise.* 'It's my brother's birthday and that boat's his.' She pointed towards Tony's flashy vessel. 'He's going sailing this afternoon, but I wanted to surprise him by fixing lunch on board.' She patted her small rucksack, though it clearly wasn't bulging with food and drink fit for a celebration. 'Me and my mum and sisters are all in on it. They're coming with him, but I've got to set up. Please?'

The man narrowed his eyes at her and continued to haul his boat up the sand. 'Sailing? With the fog setting in? Better him than me. It's not good conditions, now. Anyway, how do I know you're not trying to steal that boat? It's nice. Not my cup of tea, but worth a lot of money.'

'Steal that? I wouldn't even know how to switch the engine on! I'm a landlubber. Look at me!' She held her arms out, dangling her shabby old Doc Martens on the ends of her fingers. 'Would I be trying to get on board that boat with no way back to shore if it didn't belong to my brother?'

The man sniffed the air, as though trying to catch the scent of her. 'Why don't you get the yacht club to take you out there? I don't really want to go out again today. Not with the visibility the way it is.'

It was a fair question. Bev mentally rattled through various feasible responses before settling on: 'They're a bunch of snobs at the yacht club. They treated me like crap. I'd rather pay a proper local.'

'Get in,' the man said.

Clearly she'd uncovered his raw nerve. Was this someone who'd been refused membership in the past? It didn't matter. She stowed her shoes in her bag, handed him the money and, with no sign of that spineless idiot, Doc and no text from him either, clambered into the rowing boat.

Though they moved slowly against the tide, the strokes of her sailor-for-hire were strong and sure. She texted Doc pointlessly, since her phone reception was none existent on the choppy water.

Found a ride. Am going in. Wait for me by the Morris. Bev.

Presently, the white bulk of Tony's yacht loomed above her. Her hair and clothing were damp from the mist.

'There you go, lovely,' the man said, drawing alongside the ladder that led up to the deck. 'Mind you don't slip. And you have yourself a cracking party.'

She thanked him and started the climb, realising quite how unfit she was. By the time she was faced with the inelegant task of cocking her leg over the side and flinging her body onto the deck, her ride had already been whisked halfway back to shore on a strong current. No contrite Doc, waving apologetically from the beach. No response to her text.

Taking in her surroundings, hating the way the ebb and flow of the sea made her stomach lurch, Bev was unsurprised by the luxury of this pint-sized rich-man's plaything. The deck beneath her bare feet was smooth and recently re-varnished, judging by the feel of it. A large fibreglass canopy covered an outdoor dining area, complete with a stylish long table and eight chairs. Custom-made sofas fitted along much of the gunwale. She climbed a ladder at the side just enough to glimpse a small Captain's control room above the canopy. It looked empty.

It was the interior she wanted to search first. Back down on the main deck, beyond the dining area were double-doors. She glimpsed well-appointed living accommodation beyond. Sofas. A television. Despite the gloom of the thick steel-grey cloud cover that hung over the bay, she could see it held all the creature comforts one would expect in a home. Even at sea, 2Tone didn't rough it.

The locks on the double doors were the first hurdle she'd have to overcome and it was essential to avoid damage. She took a screwdriver, two hairpins and a Swiss Army Knife out of her rucksack and set about unpicking the compli-cated mechanism. It took five minutes to faithfully recreate the stages required to crack a lock, according to the online trainee-burglars' tutorial she'd watched at home. But with the welcome click of the lock yielding, she knew was in.

CHAPTER 38
Bev

Had an idea about how you can get on the boat. Am
looking into it. D

Bev read the text that had finally reached her from Doc
thanks to a shaky one-bar signal that had been blown her
way on the wind. Too late! Had she really been expected
to sit on a wall in the freezing sea breeze, waiting for him
to grow a pair and come up with a heroic plan that didn't
involve armbands or getting wet?

Just stay put til I call you. You're a pain in the arse. Bev.

A search of the living room had yielded nothing. Now,
she moved into the tiny galley, where there was a number
of cupboards, neatly arranged in the tight space.

'Ledger. Where would I hide a ledger in here?'

Bev thought of the knick-knacks drawer in her old family
home in London. Yes. That might be the sort of place she'd
hide a ledger – underneath bobbins of cotton, only-slightly-
used birthday cake candles, matches, a measuring tape, nails,
superglue and the other flotsam and jetsam of everyday life.
One by one, she pulled open the five drawers in a stack beneath
the sink. They were almost entirely empty, but for a large set
of designer cutlery, a roll of tinfoil and some BBQ skewers.

'It's a book,' Bev said, clasping her fist to her forehead. 'Come on. Think! Where would you put a book in a kitchen?'

Shivering slightly from the cold of a boat that seemingly hadn't been inhabited for a while and also at the thought of what might happen if Anthony found her aboard, Bev looked around the galley.

'You'd hide it in plain sight. What do people have in kitchens, Bev? They have cookbooks!'

Her gaze fell upon a small, high shelf that contained a healthy-looking spider plant and tomes from Jamie Oliver and Delia Smith. There was a guide to the perfect barbecue and an old book that was so battered that the spine was hanging off and the author's name barely legible. Bev found a fold-up stepladder, wedged against a larder unit that contained only towels and bedding. She climbed the stair gingerly, hoping the boat wouldn't rise and fall on a large swell, knocking her to the ground. On closer inspection, the battered book was by Madhur Jaffrey, boasting recipes for the perfect curry. But there was no ledger, stowed cleverly between the culinary guides. The spider plant's compost was damp. The boat *had* been recently used.

'Damn it. Where could this bloody thing be?'

Bev started to feel lightheaded. She realised she was breathing too fast and too shallow. Suddenly, she remembered that *Corleone* was due to be towed into dry dock that very day. A townie like her didn't know much about nautical matters, but Bev realised she was sailing close to the wind by being on board at lunchtime.

'Sleeping quarters. They're the last places apart from the control room at the top.'

Stepping through to the double room at the back, Bev was amazed by the master bedroom. The Karndean floor of the galley transformed to thick-pile carpet that she squished between the toes of her bare feet. The place had been decked out in oak panelling and bespoke fitted furniture, making it dark until she switched on the overhead spots. But despite the hideous green velvet bedspread and gold scatter cushions, it had a genuinely luxurious feel. With a dressing table that appeared to double as a desk with an inbox, a penholder and a laptop on the shining surface, she realised the place was comfortable enough for Anthony to spend a good deal of time there. And the laptop was another clue that he'd been there only very recently. Was this the hub from which he operated his slave trade and drugs distribution business?

'Find the ledger. Get out of here, fast,' she told herself.

First, she went through the drawers of the dressing table but found only a compact printer, a hairdryer and some cosmetics – presumably belonging to Penny. Next, she rifled through the wardrobes that held a burgundy velvet smoking jacket that looked as though it had been tailored to fit a boy. Beside it hung a sparkling black evening dress. Imagining 2Tone in the smoking jacket with a cigarillo in hand as he sipped Cristal on deck was one thing. But she tried to imagine a woman as beige as Penny Higson, arriving offshore by Cannes or Montecarlo for an evening of fine dining and Casino Royale, to which she'd wear this Frank Usher bling. There were even a pair of red-soled Louboutins in the bottom of the wardrobe. Six-inch heels in a size eight black suede.

'Nah. I bet he bought this shit for her for Christmas, praying she'd wear it to keep him happy.'

She sniffed the dress. Peered inside at the lining. The tag was still attached. Picked up the stilettos. The soles were completely blemish free. Bev smiled at her own intuition.

2Tone was a wishful thinker with a mistress who was master of him. The Thai Dragon surely wouldn't be told what to do or wear.

Moving on to the bedside cabinets, Bev tried the right side first. The drawer contained a copy of *Eleanor Oliphant is Completely Fine* and a Clare Mackintosh psychological thriller. There was a pair of tweezers and a few clean cotton buds. Some Lancôme night cream for mature skin and a nail file.

In the distance, Bev could hear the thrum of a boat's engine. Did she still have time? Yes. There was no reason to believe anyone was coming for her at that moment.

On the left side of the bed, the cabinet drawer at the top revealed a cock ring, some lube, a pair of fake handcuffs and a hand-strengthening gadget.

'Ugh!'

In the drawer below, however – the last place in the bedroom Bev could feasibly search unless Tony had shoved something under the bed or the mattress or in a safe concealed behind somewhere she'd not yet considered – she found a leather-bound green and gold book with page edges that were mottled in shades of brown and blue.

'Oh, sweet Jesus, at *last*.'

The wriggling sensation in her stomach told her she'd found the treasure trove of incriminating evidence she so desperately sought. Opening the book, she stroked its creamy thick pages and cast an eye over the names, dates and numbers that were written there in 2Tone's childish hand in a mixture of biro and pencil.

'Bullseye.'

Bev could see that the records went back almost four years. She knew from her own foraging through Anthony's home office filing cabinet that he'd been involved with the

Full Marks charity that supported vulnerable youths for more than a decade. It wouldn't take much to reconcile the names in the left-hand column of the ledger (labelled, 'Doing Time') with the names of lads who had benefited from the charity's services. Beneath each man's name was the name of a woman (that column was labelled, 'Bird/Mam). It showed the weight of the Spice she'd been given, a batch number and the amount of money she'd been paid.

Bev knelt by the bed, imagining the expressions of gratitude on the faces of detectives Curtis and Owen when she handed them evidence that the prosecution would wet themselves over. The intense rush of happiness warmed her through. She was so absorbed by her hard-won reading material that she didn't notice the chummer of voices outside. She didn't hear the clank-clanking of footsteps as someone climbed the fixed metal ladder, boarding the boat. It was only when the engine of the *Corleone* started up, making the whole vessel shudder like a whale with indigestion, that Bev realised she wasn't alone. Though there was no porthole to glimpse the world outside, she could feel that the boat had hauled anchor and left its mooring.

And she was still on board.

Oh shit, shit, shit. They've come to take it into dry dock. Damn it! Why didn't I get the book and run?

She took out her phone and tried to call Doc, but there was no signal. Only a text had arrived in her inbox since she'd been on board. It was from the headmistress of Hope's school.

Hi Ms Saunders. Hope is not in school for her afternoon session. Why not? Please call me a.s.a.p.

Clutching the ledger to her chest, wondering what the hell the head was talking about, Bev looked around desperately for a hiding place that would be big enough to conceal a grown woman. The sound of the engines revving as the yacht picked up speed felt like a pneumatic drill in her head.

'Bedtime reading?' Penny Higson's voice filled the master bedroom.

Bev looked around. She could hear her worst nightmare but couldn't see her. Then, the Thai Dragon emerged from the shadows of the little hallway that separated the galley from the sleeping quarters. Her eyes glinted dangerously in the glare of the spotlights. She looked like a cougar, waiting to pounce.

CHAPTER 39

Bev

Penny lunged at Bev, pushing her painfully into the cabinets. Bev found herself pinned beneath the much taller woman.

'Get off me! You're hurting me,' she shouted. Realising the boat was putting out to sea with her trapped inside it like Jonah on a bad trip, Bev made swift mental calculations. Penny didn't know that Bev knew that she was the Thai Dragon. Might she be able to come up with a story that would put her in a good light? 'I can explain, Penny. It's all part of the investiga—'

'I don't want your bullshit. I want that book. Give it to me!'

Her attacker tried to wrench the ledger out of her hand. Bev's fingers ached with the effort of holding on. But Penny had a grip of steel. It felt like she was trying to snap Bev's wrist in two. With her head and neck crushed up against the wall at an awkward angle, Bev was gasping for breath. She tried to cry out but her words were smothered by fabric and flesh as Penny leaned into her. The Thai Dragon was reaching for something behind the headboard . . .

It happened too fast. Penny bent Bev's wrist beyond its natural limits, forcing the ledger out of her hand. It fell to the floor beyond reach at the side of the cabinet. Bev felt something hit her hard, glancing off her forehead. The force of the blow and the stinging pain was intense. Hot blood started to seep into her eye. She'd been pistol-whipped and Penny was now towering over her, holding a gun.

'Jesus, you're insane!' Bev said, dizzy with fear. She could see the satisfaction in Penny's smile. 'Put the damned gun down, Penny. I'm on your side, remember?' She thought of Hope. *Your girl needs you alive. Say anything to get this loon to back off. Get on deck. Jump in the sea before you get too far from shore to swim back.* 'You paid me to investigate.'

'The job was over when Jim got carted off in a police car,' Penny said.

'But don't you see? I'm still investigating!' Bev could hear how high-pitched her voice was. She was gabbling at speed. Hands held in the air with the gun pointing straight at her head. 'Things weren't resolved. New information cropped up. Call me a perfectionist. Call me a *feminist*! There was no way I was leaving you, a vulnerable woman, with so many dangerous loose ends. You've got a poisoner on the cul-de-sac. Your poor neighbour! I wanted to—'

'Oh, save it for someone who's interested, you lying, short-arsed bitch.'

Penny stepped around Bev, still pointing the gun at her head. She crouched down, picked up the ledger with her free hand and took several steps backwards. Clicked the safety off.

The room spun. The ends of Bev's fingers started to prickle with pins and needles. She felt consciousness start to ebb away. *No, no, no!* The last thing she needed was a panic attack. Doc. Doc was what she needed. Where was her phone? In the back pocket of her jeans. If she could only let her hands drop and surreptitiously . . .

'Keep your hands where I can see them!' Penny shouted. 'I'm trying to decide what to do with you.'

Bev heard footsteps squeaking on the steep little staircase that led below deck. Anthony Anthony appeared in the doorway, looking perplexed.

'Ah, good,' Penny said. 'Darling, we need to deal with this snooping little bitch. It's the PI I hired to get Jim out of the picture. She knows about the ledger. If she knows about that, she knows about everything.'

The landscaper's arrival was just the distraction Bev needed to snatch her phone from her back pocket and slide it up her sleeve, out of view. Could her two captors hear the thudding of her heartbeat or the way she was yelling for help in her head?

'Who the fuck . . .? Have we met?' Tony said, drawing closer to her; looking askance at his lover holding a handgun. Then he studied Bev's face and it seemed to click. 'Gail?! But your hair's dark. And you've not got glasses . . . What—? Eh—? Hang on.'

'I told you. She's the PI I hired,' Penny said, rolling her eyes but never adjusting the gun's aim from Bev's chest.

'You lied,' Tony said, scowling at Bev. 'I let you into my house. I trusted you with my dog! You've been fucking our kid!' He turned to Penny. 'Did you know she got the job as my cleaner? Was it you what put her up to it?'

Penny shook her head. 'I had no idea. I knew she'd be thorough, obviously. That's why I encouraged Jim to give her the job. I read about the politician she was investigating before. It was a high-profile exposé on a par with the Profumo scandal or Nixon. Everybody's read about Beverley Saunders and her exploits.'

'I haven't.'

'That's because you don't read, dear.' There was a hint of patronising exasperation in her voice. Was Bev observing the beginnings of a lover's tiff between two phenomenally ill-suited lovers? 'But surely you saw her on the television! Her face was all over the bloody media for weeks.'

Tony shrugged. With a raised eyebrow and a wry smile, he looked Bev over from top to toe as if reappraising her and finding he was reluctantly impressed. 'Don't get time to watch much normal telly, do I? I like old war films, me.'

'Anyway, for the rates she charges,' Penny said, 'I didn't think I'd get method acting thrown in.'

'Let me go,' Bev said to Tony, hoping she could appeal to whatever shred of humanity lurked inside him. 'I won't say anything. I promise. I'm not a grass. I took on your cleaning because I'm skint.' She pointed to Penny with the aspiration of dividing and conquering niggling away at the back of her mind. 'She knew my job would go tits up and that old man Higson would get arrested. Now, there's no money and I'm owed well over a thousand in fees. And for all he's your brother, and you're pissed off that I slept with him, Archie's no angel. We both know he recently bullied a woman off the road and into a ditch.'

'What woman?'

'Don't you remember him running into the back of a Polo on a country road? Jesus! You were in the sodding van! It was early morning. There was a big bloody sheep.'

2Tone shrugged.

'That was *me*! My car's a write-off.'

'Your car looks all right to me.'

'The Morris isn't mine. It's borrowed. I've been out of pocket from day one with this bloody job,' Bev said. She thrust her chin in Penny's direction but kept her focus on the landscaper. 'She's set me up for a fool's errand and I bet she gives you the runaround, too. Madame Hoity-Toity with her Queen's English and her teaching qualifica-tion. Slagging you off for not reading when you're a busy working man. I saw her rolling her eyes! Is that what you want, Tony? Ask yourself, why exactly has she got rid of her husband? And that neighbour?' She turned to Penny. 'Was that you, Penny? Did you poison the head of your Neighbourhood Watch for being a nosy old bugger? Are you working your way through everyone you meet, so you're the last one standing and get all the cash?'

Penny took a step forward and cuffed Bev on the side of her head, reopening the wound above her eye. 'Take no notice of this stirring little scrubber, Tony. You can't believe a word that comes out of her mouth.'

The warm blood stung as it seeped into her eye, but Bev could still see the hurt and deliberation on Tony's face as he questioned whether he was indeed being used by a woman with a sharper intellect and more deadly ambition.

But suddenly, Penny lowered the gun and adopted the air of a confessor. Her voice cracked with emotion. 'If you must know, Bev, I wanted Jim out of the picture so me and Tony could be together. I told you after he got arrested that Jim was always a terribly controlling man. I wasn't lying. I was young when I first started dating him. Seventeen years his junior. You call me "Madame Hoity-Toity", but I was a girl who had come from nothing. My parents dragged me up in a high-rise in Salford. They were dirt poor. But we moved to a council house on a new estate and they bought an old upright piano from a neighbour one Christmas. For me. Thirty quid, my dad paid, and he did the gardening and odd jobs for the old lady who taught piano at my school in return for free lessons. Penny Higson – a girl who started with nothing – got a scholarship at Chetham's music school. Me!'

'Oh, spare me the sob story,' Bev said, pressing her hand to her throbbing head. 'Are you trying to appeal to my working-class sensibilities, you damned fraud?'

'Listen, lady! I took a teaching job and consigned my international career hopes and my friends and the wonderful life I had to memory . . . because memories were all he allowed me. Dreams were reckless and indulgent.'

Tony approached his lover and put his arm around her. 'My poor chicken.'

'Couldn't you just divorce him like normal people?' Bev asked. 'Did you have to set up a bloody drugs empire and frame him for it?'

'I needed to rebel. I needed something that was mine and I wanted to steal from him, like he'd stolen my future from me. Jim Higson has shockingly poor self-esteem underneath all his grandiose self-importance and flourish. He clings to his reputation as a sought-after, respectable bloody boring piano technician and feeds off people's misery just to get out of bed in the morning. If I could snatch away his respectability by building a highly illegal business and then bring him down for it . . . that's the best punishment I could think of, and it saves the emotional fallout of the children losing their father.' She grinned and looked momentarily like a snake with its eye on a nest full of eggs. 'I'd far rather the boys shunned him than mourned him. And that leaves me free to be with Tony. No blood on my hands.'

Apart from all the poor, vulnerable junkies who have died because of your product, Bev thought. *And the countless lives that have been ruined thanks to Tony's slave-labour business.*

'And your neighbour? The one you poisoned.'

Penny shrugged. 'Collateral damage. She was a greedy fat cow who stuck her oar in where it wasn't wanted. Is it my fault she gobbled up a cake without checking its provenance first?' She smirked.

Tony threw his head back and laughed. 'That's my

303

girl. You offed the biggest bitch in the cul-de-sac with a Battenberg. I love it! You can't make that shit up.'

Jesus. What a pair. Is it worth trying to appeal to the better nature of these two monsters?

'Listen, Penny. I won't breathe a word about any of this. Client confidentiality and all that. Just let me go. I've got a kid to feed and bills to pay.'

Penny nodded. Raised the gun again. 'I know. Hope's a lovely girl.'

'Come on, Tony!' Bev continued, rattling the words off almost automatically while her overtaxed mind slowly processed what Penny had just said like some old forgotten computer programme running in the background. 'Don't you think Soprano would have chewed me to ribbons if he'd sniffed me out for one second as a grass? I came looking for this ledger to protect Archie! I knew the police were digging into the Spice bullshit. The last thing I wanted was my boyfriend to go down because you'd left incriminating evidence knocking . . .'

Bev noticed Penny looking at her with a dangerous glint in her eye at the same moment that her brain made sense of what had been said. 'Hang on a minute. Hope. You said, "Hope". What do you know about my daughter?'

That snake-like grin was widening. Penny licked her lips – her tongue, the flicking fork of an asp. 'I'm a supply music teacher, remember? You're not the only one who does thorough homework, Beverley. If I'm playing a game to win, I like to know where all the pieces are on the board.'

Bev remembered the cryptic text she'd just received from Hope's headmistress. Hope wasn't in school for the post-lunch register. If she wasn't in class, where the hell was she? Bev felt the blood drain from her lips and her cheeks. It seemed to divert to the throbbing heart of her motherly anger. 'Don't you fucking threaten my girl! What have you done to her? Is she here on this boat? Is she at your holiday home? I don't give a shit about what happens to me, but don't you dare—'

'I'm sick of this loose end, Tony.' Penny raised her voice and spoke over Bev. Pushed the gun into her forehead. 'Let's tie her up.' She locked eyes with Bev. 'One more word out of you and I pull the trigger.'

'What do you want to do with her, my love-bucket?' Tony asked, grabbing Bev's hands and wrenching them up her back. He started to pinion her arms painfully to her body, binding her with the cord from a dressing gown that had been draped over the end of the bed.

The landscaper hadn't discovered her mobile phone stashed inside the arm of her velour top. It was held in place by the sleeve's tight, elasticated cuff. That was one saving grace, assuming Bev would ever again be able to use her only link to the shoreline and the prospect of safety. She had to try. Had to get free of this nightmare. They had Hope. She was sure of it. And Hope's safety was the only thing in the world that mattered now.

Think, Bev. Think! You're not going to talk your way out of this one, but maybe, if they lock you in a room and there's a signal . . .

'I know,' Penny said, still pressing the gun to Bev's head. Talking as though Bev were already dead. 'Let's roll her up in that tarpaulin you've got up on deck. Take the boat out to deep water. The fog's getting thick. We'll throw her into the sea. Nobody will be any the wiser.'

'We'll have to weight her down, else her body will get washed back into the bay with the tide.'

'Use the stones from the sauna,' Penny said. 'Some of the bigger ones weigh a tonne.'

Tony beamed as if his lover had said the most intelligent thing he'd ever heard. 'That'll do it. I've got some empty oxygen tanks too. They must be a good couple of extra stone. Upstairs for thinking, downstairs for the tango, eh, chunky chicken?'

CHAPTER 40
Bev

The tears streamed from Bev's eyes as 2Tone, the modern day slaver packed used oxygen cylinders and large stones next to her body. She was lying on the deck of the Corleone, shaking uncontrollably. A freezing fog had settled over the choppy sea. Her breath steamed defiantly on the air. For now, at least, she was still alive.

Hope, my baby girl. I pray you don't come to harm, and that there's just been some big cock-up with the class register. If nothing else goes right in my life and this turns out to be my last day on earth, I just pray to the universe that you're alive and well.

With the duct tape pressed firmly over her mouth, she had no chance of communicating with her abductors. But she could at least think loving thoughts and wish fervently that her little girl somehow felt them, wherever they had her stashed. If Bev died, with a bit of luck, these monsters would let her daughter go. Penny had her own children. Hopefully, within that Thai Dragon's reptilian heart, there lurked more than just the greed and bloodlust of a cold-blooded killer and a hoarder of ill-gotten gains.

'That should do the trick. Let's roll up the tarp, now,' Penny said, lifting the thick material up at one end.

She folded it over Bev's bound body. The long tarp extended above her head and below her feet. Instantly, the dull grey-white light of the foggy afternoon was gone. Her faith that things might turn out well were snuffed out with it. All she could hear was the grim exchange of her captors trying to work out the best way they might package her so that her bindings wouldn't fail on impact when they threw her overboard. In the distance, she could make out the high pitched thrum of an engine too. A small motor-boat, perhaps, or a jet ski – entirely oblivious to her plight.

Tony started to roll her body and what was left of the tarp up until she was nothing more than a tight bundle of impenetrable fabric and ballast. Dizzy. Desperate. Afraid. A human enchilada to be consumed by the Irish Sea.

Trying to yell through the duct tape and layers of fabric, Bev wriggled and thrashed as they picked either end up. She felt herself being hoisted up from the deck.

'Jesus. She weighs a tonne.' Tony's voice.

'We've just got to get her up on the bench, then up to the gunwale and shove her over. Do it in two goes.'

They dropped her heavily onto a new surface, hitting her head on something hard, but the surface beneath her back and legs was more forgiving – padded, perhaps. They'd lifted her onto the benches. Shit. The gunwale wasn't much higher.

Would drowning hurt? Would it take long? Might she die of exposure first, as her warm body hit the icy water? Perhaps her heart would give out quickly. Would her parents be waiting for her in death? She might find some small measure of comfort in the thought that her dad would greet her on the other side with a bear hug. Could she watch over Hope?

Bev's preparatory thoughts in advance of her watery death were interrupted only by the high-pitched thrum of that engine getting louder and louder until it sounded like a winged insect making a beeline for the *Corleone*. She tried yet again to scream her way through the duct tape and layers of tarpaulin, knowing the driver of the nearby craft could not possibly hear her. And yet, the engine was drawing ever closer.

'Aye-aye,' she heard Tony say. 'What the hell's this? Some dick on a jet ski.'

The stress on the tarp relaxed. They had both let go . . . temporarily.

'They're a long way out, aren't they?' Penny said. 'I thought there were restrictions.'

Bev felt the tarp lifted again at one end. 'Dunno. Come on. It's foggy. Let's get this in the water before the wanker's close enough to see proper.'

She felt Penny heaving at the foot-end and the two swung Bev into the air. Her head knocked against an unyielding object that had a metallic ring to it. The brass rail. It was the only thing between her and the end, now. They rolled, hefted and shunted her bulk. She felt the bar dig into her ribs, and then . . . freefall. She bumped momentarily against the side of the bobbing boat and hit the water with a painful smack. Gasping for breath. Bev was winded. Thrashing around. The pocket of air trapped inside the tarpaulin kept her buoyant for one, two, three seconds . . . and then she was sinking, sinking, sinking.

At the same time, the whining engine of the jet ski seemed to be right beside her. There was a sickening, deafening crack and the sound of splintering hull. Shouting.

But Bev was already in her watery, icy-cold grave. Her lungs burned with the effort of holding her breath. Lights popped behind her eyes as she strained against her bonds. She knew she was wriggling like a fish on the end of a hook, fighting for its life and incapable of changing the course of fate. *Get free. You can do this. While there's oxygen in your brain, you've got a chance.*

Bev tried to shunt the dressing-gown cord down her body. Tried to shake free of the bruising ballast that was dragging her down, down, down. Her lungs felt half their size; then a quarter. Drowning did hurt. The sheer effort of resisting the temptation to inhale the sea was pain itself. There was no option but to breathe in. Her instincts demanded it. She was a dead woman thrashing.

It was too late.

CHAPTER 41

Doc

The yacht was looming closer and closer in the freezing fog. The adrenaline that whizzed around Doc's body numbed him to the cold and the wet and the pain in his balls of smacking down repeatedly on the unforgiving water's surface as the jet ski bunny-hopped over the waves. But it didn't quell his abject terror at what lay ahead. Doc had no plan other than to get to Bev. And he knew now that she wasn't alone.

Through the ghostly wreaths of mist, he could see two shadowy figures grappling at the side of the boat with a long, cumbersome object that looked like a rolled up carpet. No sign of Bev, though when he'd swept up to the beach by the yacht club on this stolen jet ski, full of apology and good intentions, the old guy who'd been fiddling with his rowing boat had told him he'd taken her out there for money. She'd clearly strung him some cock and bull story about throwing her brother a surprise party. The old guy had assumed Doc was Bev's brother, with not an inkling that he'd rowed an unarmed woman out to mortal danger with no means of escape.

Damn it, Bev. I know I acted like a berk, but I did grow a pair and I did come back! Why couldn't you trust me? And why the hell did the phone signal on the beach have to be so crap? And what am I supposed to do now?

As the stolen jet ski scudded closer, and the scene on deck became clearer, Doc realised he had to do something rash to stop the two people on board from throwing the long object into the water.

'I'm coming, Bev.'

Doc revved the engine on the jet ski and felt the thing shoot forward. Thirty metres. Twenty metres. Peering upwards to the yacht's deck, he could see the two people were Tony and Penny now. Of course! Who else would it be in this catalogue of disasters called Doc's Life but the most dangerous people in the northwest? They looked at him, clearly perplexed; exchanged a few words; heaved the object over the rail and into the water with an almighty splash.

As Doc ploughed into the fibreglass hull of Anthony Anthony's vessel at speed, hitting his head hard and almost falling off the jet ski into the water, he saw the discarded object at close quarters. It was a tarpaulin and it was thrashing around. Wasn't it? Or was he just concussed and seeing things?

With his ride wedged in the shattered hull, Doc killed the jet ski's engine. Feeling nausea wash over him, dazed as hell from the impact, he vomited into the water. The tarpaulin had slipped from sight.

'Bev! Where are you?' he shouted out but he could hear that he was slurring. His brain seemed to be running slow like an overtaxed hard-drive.

Suddenly he heard the creak and whine of the fibreglass hull cracking in half. The yacht was splitting apart in earnest, taking on water fast. It started to sink, sucking the jet ski in its deadly vortex and him with it.

'Oh my God! Bev! Bev, where are you?' Doc cried, shivering in the cold now and confused. All his heroism and determination had left him.

Peering around at the inky, roiling water, there was no sign of the tarp. Had it contained Bev or was she still on board? It didn't matter, though, because the jet ski was tipping at a sharp angle and he was sliding from the saddle into the freezing water, whether he wanted to or not.

Doc swallowed hard. Remembered thinking it a miracle when he'd finally swum a whole width at school. The last kid in the class to lose the armbands. The teenaged boy who'd eschewed the pool on holidays, preferring to stay safely on the sunbed in the shade. But there was nothing for it. Bev might be drowning. Saddo Shufflebotham was going to have to brave the waves. He stuffed his glasses into the tight coin pocket of his jeans.

'Aaaagh!' He hit the water with a splash, spluttering as salty brine flooded his mouth; stung his eyes.

With a pounding head, he thrashed around, desperately trying to remember what the swimming instructor had taught him all those years ago. Stay calm. Keep your stroke strong and even. Except Doc could only do doggy paddle even now, and the sinking yacht was dragging him down so that only his nose was above the surface. He was anything but calm. He was going to have to go under. Taking a deep breath, he pushed the fear aside.

Doc ducked below. Opened his bleary eyes and at first, saw nothing but impenetrable murk. Behind him, the yacht was bubbling and fizzing as it disintegrated under the pressure of the tide. Flotsam and jetsam everywhere, bouncing in slo-mo off his ragdoll body. Before him, there was only open sea. He came back up. Gulped a lungful of freezing foggy air. Slid back down. Kicked out. Reached into the briny soup. Felt thick fabric slip through his fingers like will-o'-the-wisp. There, one second. Gone, the next. It was the tarp. He was sure of it.

Following his instincts, he swam down after it. Didn't pause to think that he'd never succeeded in swimming underwater before. Only saving Bev mattered. *If* it was Bev. Even with his blurred vision and the stinging salt water that made his eyes smart, he could pick out the long dark shape spiralling slowly downwards. Bubbles floating up out of the top. What looked like small boulders dropping out of the bottom. Some three metres below the surface and falling.

Doc grabbed the mass and felt the strange mix of contents inside. A soft body that yielded to his touch. Hard cylindrical objects wrapped tight. He needed to untie the rope that held the tarp in a tight roll before his own lungs exploded.

Please don't be dead. Please don't be dead.

He knew it was Bev. He was sure he was too late. But he wouldn't let her sink to the bottom of the sea to spend an eternity alone in the dark. Fiddly fingers pulled at the nautical knot Anthony had tied. His concussed brain was screaming for oxygen. His legs were spasming with cramp. He had to shoot for the surface. Except the knot was coming loose and he was no diver. If he abandoned Bev, she'd sink beyond reach.

Stay with her. If you die, you'll at least die together.

The rope came loose, drifting away. The tarp unfurled around him. He felt the cylindrical weights drop and Bev's soft, limp body start to rise. Kicking the tarp away, he saw her mouth was open. Her eyes were closed. No bubbles drifting from her nose or lips. But Doc had nothing left of his own life save for one desperate kick. Would it be enough to propel them upwards in time?

As he started to black out, they surfaced. He gasped and gulped down the air, hoisting Bev's head and shoulders out of the water; feeling his own consciousness return, suffusing his body with hope and clarity of thought.

'Bev! Bev!' He patted her face with one hand, holding her above the water with the other. Beating his legs and pushing them both in the direction of what appeared to be a floating tabletop or was it a door?

Grabbing the wood, he kicked and kicked upwards and pushed until he'd propelled Bev out of the water and onto the floating remnant. Vaguely recalling the CPR he'd seen on television before, he gripped the tabletop with his left hand and with his right, he pressed down hard on Bev's chest three times. No reaction. Clinging on, though his weak muscles screamed in complaint, he stuck the fingers of his right hand into her mouth. There was nothing blocking her airways but she wasn't breathing either. Saying a silent apology, he thumped her in the chest hard once, twice. She spat up water, coughing and spluttering. Doc rolled her onto her side on the tabletop so that she wouldn't choke on whatever came up.

'Bev! You're alive!'

But his relief was short-lived. There was a deafening crack and the table's surface splintered up just by Bev's shoulder. Had they just been shot at?

Doc turned around to see Tony and Penny, teetering aboard the remnants of the yacht. Tony swayed with the swell of the sea water, clutching a book. Penny held a pistol, aimed straight at them.

The crack resounded again.

'Duck!' Bev yelled, opening her eyes suddenly.

She slapped her hand on Doc's head and pushed him under. Doc peered through the brine. He saw the bullet just as it entered the water by Bev's feet, creating a streak of white. It pelted down towards the black depths.

He had to get her away from there.

Resurfacing, kicking harder than he would have thought possible, he started to push the tabletop and Bev away from the yacht. The bullets rained down on them through the dense fog, narrowly missing them only to lodge in the floating wood.

Come on, Doc. You can do this, man. Imagine you're swimming that width again. Just keep kicking.

Glancing at Bev, he could see she'd passed out again. Her lips were blue. Was she still breathing? There was no time to stop and feel for her pulse. Looking over his shoulder it was clear he'd barely pushed them a metre further away from the sinking vessel. *Damn!*

'I'm going to kill that interfering bitch!' Penny shouted, the venom in her voice still audible even above the undulating waves and the spray they kicked up.

A rhythmic chug, chug, chug cut through the drama, however. Suddenly, Doc found himself squinting as a strong searchlight shone on him and Bev. The cone of dazzling light moved to the yacht's wreckage and a man's voice filtered through a loudhailer. With water blocking his ears, Doc didn't catch the newcomer's muffled introduction, but he did hear him demand that Penny should, 'Drop the weapon!' Was it the RNLI come to save them?

On board the sinking yacht, Penny and Tony raised their hands in the air, though Tony threw the book he'd been holding into the water as he did so. The ledger!

'Grab that book!' Doc yelled. 'It's vital evidence. Grab it before it sinks.'

A long stick with a net on the end emerged from the boat that had pulled up alongside them. It started to probe the detritus-strewn waters but scooped up only useless-looking wreckage. With the dazzling glare amplified ten-fold as it was dispersed on the frozen water particles of the sea mist, Doc found it difficult to see what kind of craft the searchlight was coming from. But when he squinted and made out

316

six letters emblazoned on the side, he was delighted to see they spelled, 'POLICE'. The whirr of a helicopter's rotary blades were now within earshot too, growing progressively louder above the blanket of fog. The sea-faring cavalry had arrived en masse, and Doc had never been so relieved to see the authorities descend on him.

'We're saved, Bev! We're saved!' he told his favourite woman in the world.

Except Bev was out cold, looking pale and heartbreakingly vulnerable on her tabletop life raft. He searched for a pulse but could feel nothing. Desperate to end this nightmare and to wake his sleeping beauty, he pressed his lips to Bev's and breathed into her mouth.

CHAPTER 42
Bev

Bev opened her eyes and sat up, as though she'd been injected with adrenaline. She made a strangled sound of protest, with Doc's lips still locked onto hers, but prized him off her, digging her fingers into his shoulders with all the strength she could muster.

'What are you doing?' she said, panting.

'Ow! Saving your life. You'd stopped breathing. I felt for your pulse—'

'Well, you were feeling in the wrong place, you dork. Drowning takes it out of you. I must have dozed off!'

He beamed at her and opened his arms wide, clearly about to embrace her, when he was grabbed from behind and hauled out of the water.

'You're under arrest, son.'

Doc was looking up into the steely face of a police officer.

'Me?' he said. '*They're* the criminals!' He pointed to Tony and Penny who were clinging to the wreckage of the *Corleone*, being cuffed by two other officers. 'One's a slaver and a dealer, one's a murdering drug lord. My partner, here, will tell you. Tell them, Bev!'

Bev opened her mouth to respond but a wave of fatigue washed over her.

The cop wasn't interested in what she had to say, in any case. He only had eyes for Doc. 'Excuse me, son, but there's the small matter of you having nicked and trashed a jet ski.' He didn't look amused or grateful or any of the things Doc was almost certainly hoping for. 'Why do you think we arrived on the scene when we did?'

'You were following *me*?' Even in the bad light, it was clear that Doc was blushing.

'My friend was acting in self-defence, officer,' Bev said, fearing that they were losing their unexpected advantage. 'Get the ledger off that man!' She pointed to Tony.

'What? You mean the book he's just thrown in the water?'

Time slowed. The cop's speech seemed slurred. Bev felt as though her world had turned to quicksand, anchoring her to her own inevitable demise; sucking her down, down, down. 'In the water? Jesus! No! I risked my life to get that ledger. It's got all the evidence you'll ever need.' She peered into the undulating mess of floating wood, clothing, chunks of fibreglass and anything else that had been on board the yacht that had been buoyant. Spotted the thing she sought by a floating lifejacket.

Ignoring her heavy limbs and waterlogged chest, Bev hoisted herself from the relative safety of the tabletop into the heaving water. With burning lungs and limbs, she swam about five metres towards the yacht.

'No!' Doc shouted. 'Come back, you loon!'

But Bev wasn't listening. She reached into a pile of mangled, sodden trash. Rummaged around. Peered into the depths beneath her and flipped herself down into the water, her pulse pounding in her ears.

'Bev!'

From beneath the waves, she could still hear Doc crying out in anguish. She felt her consciousness slipping away yet again, but her fingers finally enclosed around the silken pages of the ledger. Only moments later, Bev surfaced, clutching it like a prize. The searchlight picked her out in the mist and mayhem. She gasped for air, smiling triumphantly.

Bobbing in the water with no energy left to swim to safety, Bev waited until the police boat neared her. The officer extended a hand to pull her out. Bev passed the ledger to him and then took his hand.

'Now, you need to find my daughter,' she said, the pain of Penny's threat far more excruciating than the stabbing agony of the freezing water. 'Please. She's a little girl called Hope and she's my world. I think those two bastards might have kidnapped her and I don't know where they've got her stashed.'

'I'm sorry I didn't call earlier. It's . . . complicated,' Bev told Hope's headmistress, speaking with chattering teeth into a borrowed landline. She pulled the silver foil thermal blanket around her, quaking with cold, though it was warm in the cubicle of the local hospital's A & E department.

'Well, I'm just worried about Hope,' the head said. She didn't sound particularly worried. She sounded irritated that Bev hadn't called sooner. Perhaps embarrassed that she'd screwed up by losing an eleven-year-old. 'She didn't get her afternoon mark.'

Bev tried desperately to maintain a shred of optimism seeing as the police had grilled 2Tone and Penny about Hope on the boat back to shore and they had flatly denied knowing anything about the child's whereabouts. 'Have you called her dad?'

'Have *you*?'

The woman was beyond exasperating. 'I've been in a boating accident,' Bev said. 'You're literally the first person

I've called.' Enough of this shit. She hung up and dialled Rob, praying that he'd know where their daughter was.

'Ah, finally,' he said. 'What?'

'What do you mean, "What?"? I've not got time for this shit, Rob. I've had a call off school. Hope's missing.'

'Is she?' Though miles separated them and the reception wasn't the best, she could hear the sarcasm and guilt-laden told-you-so tone in Rob's voice. What the hell was he up to?

'Is Hope with you, Robert? Answer me, you shower of shite.'

He didn't need to say a word. She could hear her daughter singing along to music in the background. Ariana Grande, perhaps on a TV music channel. Bev's thundering heart started to slow. Her collapsing world froze, mid-tumble and started to right itself like an old VHS on rewind.

'For fuck's sake, Rob. Why the bloody hell would you sneak our daughter out of school and leave it for me to clean up the mess? Are you cracked in the head?'

'I wondered if you'd even notice,' he said. 'I was testing you. You seem to think it's OK to leave her late at school, while you're gallivanting for "work". I didn't think you were taking your responsibilities seriously, so I thought I'd give you a wake-up call.'

'Oh, you massive pain in the hole. You boil my piss. You think Hope's safety is some kind of joke? Do you know what hell I've been going through for the last couple of hours, wondering where she was? You know what kind of a job I do! How could you make me suffer like that, you lump of shit?'

He started to whinge on about priorities and being a good parent, but Bev could only see red. 'My solicitor's going to be all over this. Don't talk to me about irresponsible behaviour. You've knowingly truanted your child,

321

and I thought she'd been abducted by . . . Just put her on, you utter disease.'

The sound of Hope's voice flooded Bev with relief. It didn't matter that she'd nearly drowned. She'd recover. It didn't matter that she might have a regional drugs network on her back, seeking revenge for having cut the energy supply to their extensive lucrative business network. She could move again; change her name; become someone else. It didn't matter that she wouldn't get paid for a job that had almost killed her. Her daughter was safe. That was all that a mother could ask for. And the cherry on the top was that she was fairly certain she'd now get full custody of Hope thanks to Rob's truanting prank.

'I can't wait to see you tomorrow night, Mum-Mum,' Hope said. 'Vismaya at school did my hair in a really nice new plait thingy. You'll love it. It's sick!'

'Gorgeous! I bet it's the business. What do you want for tea?'

'Can we have enchiladas?' Hope asked.

Bev visualised being wrapped in a tarp, weighted down with sauna stones and empty gas cylinders. The human enchilada with a bitter, saltwater aftertaste. 'Anything for you, doll-face.' She thought about Mihal and Constantin, holed up in her offices. She had much to tell them on her return, and there was more that needed to be put right before Hope turned up.

'It's a deal,' Bev said. 'Be good for Dad and I'll see you tomorrow. I love you more than anything in the whole wide world.'

The curtain that shielded Bev from the rest of A & E's observation-worthy cases was wrenched aside by a harried-looking nurse. A uniform was visible just beyond her, talking quietly into his radio. She knew he was waiting for Doc, who had been wheeled off for a CT scan shortly after arrival.

'Have you finished with the phone?' the nurse asked, reaching out to take it from her before she'd even blown Hope a kiss.

Bev defiantly held onto the handpiece just long enough to fire off several more 'love you's and a flurry of kisses. 'I just nearly died, you know,' she told the nurse.

The nurse set the phone back on the side and started to record Bev's oxygen saturation score and blood pressure. 'Yeah. Well, that's why we're keeping an eye on you. Secondary drowning. You've got to watch out for that.'

'I need to go home, though. My girl wants Mexican for tomorrow night's tea.'

'I wouldn't worry,' the nurse said, smiling as she wrote numbers on a sheet of paper. 'The police want you and your friend out of here and down the station as soon as the doctor's said you're fit to go.'

The inference stung. 'I'm not a criminal, you know. I'm a victim.'

'Is that why your friend's cuffed to the bed?'

'Hey! He's not a criminal either. He's a fucking hero.'

The smile slid from the nurse's face. 'I know you're in shock, but there's no need for language like that.'

'Every fucking need, lady.'

Four hours had passed before Bev and Doc were given a clean bill of health and discharged. They were transported down to Nefyn police station near Pwllheli in a police van and grilled over the episode on the boat by local detectives. Bev knew that an avalanche of trouble was sliding her way for having broken into the yacht and having gained access to Chateau d'Antoine by pretending to be a cleaner

323

and falsifying references. She groaned; 2Tone would be hoping to use every weapon he had in his arsenal to evade conviction, and Bev had inadvertently gifted him with the legal equivalent of a rocket launcher – the dodgy methods she'd used to acquire evidence might easily blow a court case against him to pieces.

I'm in deep shit. What have I done? I'm the worst PI in the world. I'm reckless and unprofessional. Why the hell can't I just stick to the brief? What's wrong with me? What am I trying to prove?

'Explain to me again – nice and clearly for the recording, please – how you came to be on board the *Corleone*,' the Welsh female detective said. She was a woman in her thirties, dressed in smart-casual clothes. Her demeanour was relaxed, but she didn't know Bev, and the scepticism behind her eyes belied the anodyne smile on her lips.

Bev's nerve endings were tingling, telling her the detective was looking for an incriminating statement. Could they find the lock to the cabin amongst the broken apart debris? Would forensics be able to examine it and determine it had been picked? Or had the evidence sunk to the bottom of the bay?

It was so tempting to lie. But a lie could get her into even more trouble.

'Look. It's complicated.' Bev held her hands aloft. Tried to keep her voice even and authoritative. 'I'm a PI.'

'But Penny Higson says the case was closed when her husband was arrested. You were off the payroll.'

'Look. I've got a Romanian convict in my offices right now with his vagrant brother.' Bev said a silent prayer that Mihal and Constantin hadn't cleared out of the offices, taking her measly worldly goods with her. Only now did she realise the full extent of the risk she'd taken in trusting two strangers. 'They will give you chapter and verse on how Anthony Anthony enslaved them. The younger brother's got photographic evidence of Tony and Penny's illegal activities and Spice distribution network. That ledger that I fished from the water will corroborate what I'm saying.'

'Which you stole.'

'I'm Anthony's cleaner.' *Don't say too much, Bev. Take a step back. Don't dig yourself deeper by saying Anthony asked you to clean the boat. Shit. That would be a brilliant excuse. Can I say that? Damn it!* 'Am I supposed to turn a blind eye to slavery? And drugs? Look. Penny and Jim Higson came to me. Penny wanted to put her husband in the frame for heading a drugs empire and she used me to do it. But I'm not stupid and I do my job well. I know I should have handed all this over to my contacts at Greater Manchester Police. Speak to Detectives Curtis and Owen. Go on. Phone them! They know me. I handed them a pile of evidence that proved the Higsons had a Spice lab in their workshop. I was just doing what I thought was right.' Bev was pouring with sweat. Was this the time to fake secondary drowning to escape a drubbing and possible arrest? Or could she sidestep the North Wales police's questions indefinitely. 'Er, can I call a solicitor, actually?'

It was time to roll out Kandice with a K – the budget Rottweiler who had somehow managed to save Bev from a stretch behind bars last time she had overstepped the mark professionally.

The tight feeling in Bev's chest that had first manifested itself in the A & E cubicle was now akin to having one of those gas cylinders clamped to her ribs. She pulled at the collar of the dry sweatshirt she'd been given. If she was getting heat for her role in this fiasco, how the hell was Doc doing? He already had a conviction! Would their professional indemnity insurance cover all of this magically? Or was this the end of the road for Bev's business and their liberty? Might Bev's custody of her daughter slip through her fingers once and for all?

The detective nodded. 'OK. By all means, get your solicitor to come in. But right now, Beverley, all we can see is that your friend James stole a jet ski and drove it into the hull of a private individual's yacht, causing tens of thousands of pounds of damage. And you were already on board. Uninvited.'

'They shot at me! With an actual gun! I bet they didn't have a licence for that. They wrapped me in a weighted-down tarp and threw me overboard, for Christ's sake! Isn't that attempted murder?'

'There's a lot to unpick here. Let's get you settled in a cell while we sort out who did what.'

Bev felt her lips prickle cold. 'Am I under arrest?'

CHAPTER 43
Mihal

'Just let me get high,' Constantin said. He pulled the baggie of Spice out of the clean pants Doc had given to him and held it out to his big brother. 'We can do it together. Like old times. If we open the windows, she won't know.'

As non-committally as possible, Mihal opened his hand to receive the drug. 'I'm sure we can find a bottle in the kitchen that will make a good bong.' The pull of the Spice was strong for a recovering addict like him but nothing worse than the temptation he'd faced down when he'd been inside. He smiled at Constantin encouragingly. *Just give me the gear. Go on. Trust me.* 'I'll do it.'

But Constantin looked at Mihal's expectant empty palm and snatched the Spice away like Tolkien's Gollum, guarding his Precious. 'It's *mine*. *I'll* make the bong.' He pulled the waistband to his jogging bottoms wide and stuffed the baggie back in his pants.

Realising with a sinking heart that he couldn't easily undo the damage to Constantin that three years on the streets and a prolonged spell as a modern-day slave had caused, Mihal grappled to find a solution. If he could only get hold of the Spice and flush the shit down the toilet . . .

His brother desperately needed to get into rehab and yet had refused to attend his appointment with the social worker at the charity. He was badly hooked on the poison Anthony Anthony had introduced him to all those years ago. A drug that made you dependent and prone to desperate deeds. And the only remedy Mihal could think of, if Constantin wasn't going to accept proper medical help, was an enforced spell of cold turkey.

He visualised all the doors in the office complex. The storeroom in Bev's office was lockable from the outside and there was a key in the lock. Could he somehow wrestle Constantin in there? But would his long-lost brother buy the cruel-to-be-kind treatment or would he walk back out of Mihal's life – this time, for good?

Having only just been reunited after thinking Constantin dead and gone, the last thing Mihal wanted to do was to push him away. But Bev and Doc had put everything on the line for them both by investigating Anthony Anthony beyond the scope of their commission, not to mention letting them stay in their home. Mihal had sworn that he and Constantin would stay clean and stay put. He was old and wise enough to know you didn't repay kindness and trust with misdeeds and lies. Almost every man in prison had been locked up precisely because they'd abused someone's trust.

'Let's just get out of here,' Constantin said, rummaging through Bev's kitchen cupboards for an empty drinking bottle. 'They must have some money stashed away. Come on! Let's take what we can find and see where fate leads us. If we can scratch bus fare together, we can go anywhere. Or we could go back into Manchester. I know this place where we can bed down for the night. I've got friends.'

The weight of disappointment made Mihal's tired legs feel even heavier than usual, but he dragged himself from the table to where his baby brother stood and grabbed his arm. 'No. Constantin, the reason I came back . . . It wasn't just for you. I wanted to avenge Bogdan. To take an eye for an eye from Anthony.'

'So, take your eye. Kill him!' His brother wasn't even paying attention. His search for bong components was too feverish to allow a mere matter of honour to distract him.

'I would have done,' Mihal said, remembering how he'd broken into Anthony's house with the smell of the landscaper's blood in his nostrils. 'But it would have been too quick. Now, I want to make him suffer, and Beverley's given us the chance to do that. I've been to prison, Constantin. It's . . . I never want to go back. If Bev and Doc can give the police what they need and make the conviction stick, it's a good revenge. If we go now and don't testify—'

'We?' Constantin spun around. 'Wait a minute. What's all this, "we"? I'm not hanging around to testify to the police. I thought I was just giving her my phone.'

The frustration at his brother's about-turn manifested itself as acid that licked along Mihal's gullet. 'But you said! You promised her you'd make a statement.'

'I gave her the key to finding the ledger. I'll give her the phone with the incriminating photos on it. But if I said I'd help the police . . . well, I changed my mind. I don't want to be held accountable, Mihal. I need to be left in peace. And right now, I need to get high.'

He pulled an old, empty Evian bottle from a high shelf in the cupboard above the sink. 'This will do.'

Mihal wrenched the bottle from his grip. 'No! I won't let you get high. I forbid it.'

'Fuck you!' Constantin thumped him in the arm, caught in a tug of war over a makeshift bong.

Reaching into Constantin's pants with a grimace, Mihal snatched the baggie of Spice and released his brother. Sprinted to the toilet.

'You bastard! Give it back.'

His younger brother jumped on his back, clawing at his face as Mihal emptied the contents of the baggie into the toilet bowl. He tried to flush, but Constantin pulled him back from the lever with such force that Mihal lost his footing and crashed backwards onto the cramped shower room floor.

He sprang to his feet. Now he had the upper hand over Constantin as the younger man crouched over the toilet bowl, desperately trying to scoop his sodden stash from the pissy water.

Neither of them heard Bev's key in the lock. It wasn't until she stood over them with a giant of a uniformed policeman at her back that they realised they had an audience.

'I let you stay at my place and trust you with my stuff and this is how you repay me?' she said, hands on hips. Her face was ashen and she was shaking. The quiver in her voice, however, was pure wrath.

Mihal held his hands up, buckling with embarrassment and fear. Too late to try again to flush the evidence down the toilet. Constantin's stash, though he was the one who had done time. He was the one who would inevitably get done for possession and end up back behind bars. 'It's not how it looks, Beverley. I promise.' He looked beyond Bev to the cop. 'I didn't touch it. It was planted on my brother. It's all a big misunderstanding.' The cop wasn't to know there was Spice in the toilet. Not yet. But he would. There was still a green sodden blanket, floating on the surface of the water.

Constantin froze at the sight of the policeman. He was still gripping the toilet bowl, seemingly calculating the possible outcomes of the situation, depending on the choice

330

he made. Then, he pushed Mihal with some force against the tiled wall of the shower room, bounding towards the front door with the speed and agility of a cornered fox.

'Not so fast, mate!'

Constantin's attempt at escape was thwarted by the WPC who had remained behind on the landing.

He was returned to Bev's office with his arm bent up at an awkward angle against his back. Though Constantin was the taller of the two, it was clear that the woman was very strong.

Mihal felt a surge of protectiveness at the sight of his little brother, writhing in discomfort. 'Let him go!' he shouted, snatching up one of Bev's origami models that Doc had had encased in glass.

'And what are you planning on doing with that exactly, you tit?' Bev said. 'Think it through. You're supposed to be on parole and you're about to attack a policewoman with my origami T-Rex? Do me a favour!' She wrenched the shadow-box from Mihal's grip. 'It's time you stopped being angry. Both of you. Anthony and the Thai Dragon have been arrested. These guys . . .' she pointed to the cops, 'are gonna need you to testify. We're all on the same side, now. It's time to move forwards, not backwards. You're free men. Act like it. Don't screw all this up. And for Christ's sake, let go of the guilt.'

Bev nodded to the male officer who had been poised to manhandle Mihal into submission. 'It's OK. He's going to co-operate, aren't you, Mihal?'

Mihal nodded solemnly and turned to his little brother.

'It's time to start trusting them,' he said in their native tongue. 'She's right. We need to stop running and start living. None of this was our fault.'

CHAPTER 44

Bev

'I don't like this one bit,' Bev said through the driver's side window of the Morris. Gail's wig itched even more than usual, perhaps unsurprisingly since she was sweating so heavily at the prospect of what was about to happen. 'He's got a bloody gun! If this goes badly . . .'

In a hastily arranged rendezvous, Bev had pulled up alongside the unmarked car of Detectives Owen and Curtis in the street directly adjacent to Archie's T-road. Once she followed them in, there'd be no way out of the arrangement.

'Please, Beverley,' Owen said. The female detective dropped her voice to a conspiratorial almost-whisper, though Curtis could hear every word from his passenger seat. 'From one woman to another.' She was gripping her steering wheel so hard that her knuckles were standing proud like pearls. Clearly willing Bev to play ball. 'If you want to get back at Anthony and Higson for all they've done, this is your chance. Archie's a monster, but even men like him sometimes get the chance to put things right. We need him to testify.'

Bev shook her head, her stomach turning over and over with fear. Knew the sisterhood, 'one-woman-to-another' ploy was bullshit. Owen had her heart set on promotion. That much was clear. 'I don't know.'

'You're here now.'

'But I'm worried about my safety. Never mind me, in fact! What about my daughter? I found out Penny had given Hope a damned phone! She'd been grooming her. If Doc hadn't led the police to that boat, I'm fairly sure Penny would have lured my girl off somewhere and threatened to kill her if I didn't back off. These are the sorts of people we're dealing with. And if Archie or one of Tony's Angels tracks me down and comes after me . . .' She was talking rapidly, spiralling from the high of having exposed a drugs-and-slavery outfit, downwards into a suffocating whirlpool of her own catastrophic imaginings.

'You've got to do this, Bev,' Curtis said, leaning over towards the driver's side window so he could be heard.

Owen nodded her agreement. 'Look, we know your licence isn't 100 per cent bona fide. If you want us to turn a blind eye to the way you've been working outside the proper industry guidelines, you've got to do this one thing for us.'

'That's blackmail,' Bev said.

'That's the way the world works, lovey,' Curtis said, treating her to a sympathetic, totally disingenuous smile.

Glaring at him, Bev got out of the Morris and walked on trembling legs around the corner into Archie's tiny development. The bulletproof vest she wore beneath her coat weighed heavy on her shoulders. She took a deep breath and marched up to her erstwhile lover's front door. *Do this for Hope. Make sure Anthony and Penny go down.*

She pressed the doorbell.

Out of the corner of her eye, the armed officers were just about visible, concealed at the side of the house and in the attached neighbour's portico. They too were wearing bulletproof vests, guns pointed at Archie's front door, ready to pounce, should he come out shooting. Would Archie smell their adrenaline on the air or hear her thundering heartbeat from his hallway? Was it possible that, despite Owen and Curtis' assurances, Anthony had somehow got word to his brother of his and Penny's arrests in Abersoch?

A large dark shadow appeared in the hall. There was the click of locks being undone. Archie opened the door.

'Gail?' he said, smiling uncertainly. 'This is a nice surpri—'

Bev stepped aside and the police pounced all at once: squad cars and two vans entering his T-road with a squeal of tyres; armed response unit with their hardware trained on him; dogs barking at the end of their dog-handlers' leashes. Detective Owen strutted forward in her low-heeled shoes and read him his rights, listing the grim litany of offences he was suspected of committing.

Archie looked up at Bev, his face a picture of bewilderment and fear. 'What the fuck is this?'

Pulling off Gail's wig, Bev bit her lip. 'There's a chance for you to make some of this right,' she said.

'Are you one of them? A pig? Seriously? Have you been playing me all this time?'

'No.' Bev shook her head. Looked at his socks. 'I'm not police. It's much more complicated than that. You'll find out soon enough. But I just . . . Me and you were . . .' She exhaled deeply. Met his gaze. 'Tell them everything, Archie. If there's any good in you, tell them what they need to know about Tony and Penny. Make this right.'

Bent over a wheelie bin, Archie allowed Curtis to cuff him in silence. But with his head cocked to the side, he never shifted his focus from Bev. He was regarding her with the dead eyes of a shark that had a floundering seal in its midst.

'You think I'm some sort of grass?' he finally said. His face was a mask of disgust and hatred now. He breathed heavily through flared nostrils.

'Archie, what you lot were doing was unforgiveable.' Her voice was tremulous, but Bev needed to be brave. She needed to atone for having climbed into bed with the devil. 'You know that. But if you give evidence, they might cut you a deal. Don't throw your life away for Tony. I bet he wouldn't do it for you.'

He spat at her feet.

As Archie was marched to the waiting van, Bev hastily wiped away her fearful tears. She knew she was a poor judge of character and weak and easily led astray. But at least everything she did, she did with good intentions.

When she kissed Hope goodnight that evening, her conscience was clear. Almost.

CHAPTER 45
Bev

Later that week saw the return of Kandice with a K from the shitty local solicitors' firm above the bookies in Wythenshawe – the firm that every mountain-bike riding, handbag-snatching little shit had on speed dial, just in case.

'You can't keep conducting your business like this, Beverley,' Kandice said.

The budget lawyer, who had pulled a minor miracle out of her plus-sized derriere during the last job that had ended up with police involvement, was sitting in her supermarket skirt suit in Bev's office, eyeballing both her and Doc.

Bev visualised a ticker, racking up the solicitor's fee with every second that passed. Same shit, different case. This time, however, it had been Bev who had bailed Doc, using the cheque from her totalled Polo. The money had finally come in from the insurance company – not as much as she'd hoped, but enough to cover Doc's bail and hopefully, her own legal fees.

'Spare me the lecture, OK?' Bev said, slumped in her chair behind her crappy, battered desk. She slurped her strong tea, wishing it was after 4 p.m. so she could lace it with something stronger. She knew Kandice was right and hated that fact.

But Kandice sat up straight in the uncomfortable guest chair, perched right on the edge with her big knees pointing straight at Bev. 'No, Beverley. I won't spare you the lecture. I'm quite happy to get your custom, but I don't think business is brisk enough for you to be losing money on every other job and risking getting a criminal record. Do you? Is that what you had in mind when you started up a private detective agency?' She was blinking hard. Her overplucked eyebrows showed little emotion but the thin line of her mouth and the furrows in her brow said she was exasperated with her client. 'Because you told me you liked the flexibility of self-employment and were looking forward to working your job around your daughter's schooling. You can't parent your daughter if you're in Styal women's prison for the list of quite serious offences I've got written down here, Beverley.'

'Oh, come on!' Doc said. 'We've just brought down a massive drugs ring! All that crap in the papers about Manchester being Zombie Town, full of Spice-heads . . . we've stopped it! What's the quoted value of Higson and Anthony's outfit? What about Mrs Nosy Slippers and the Battenberg of Doom?'

Kandice looked at her notes. 'I don't know what you mean, James. You and I need to talk about this jet ski.'

Doc was off the sofa. A Jack-in-the-box wearing a revolting Slipknot T today with the horror-film heads of the band arranged in a ghastly circle. Bev had warned him to dress like a normal person for Kandice with a K, but the lanky berk was all about, 'sticking it to the man', as usual. Now, he was shifting his weight from foot to foot with his fists balled, trying and failing to get his words out.

'Sit down, Doc! For God's sake, you're giving me indigestion,' Bev said. 'Kandice is on our side, so don't give her grief.'

'I ain't apologising, man. I was just doing what I needed to to save my friend. That's how partners do.' Doc folded his arms, then unfolded them, then stuffed his hands in his pockets. His face turned from Cornish pasty grey to raw sausage-roll pink.

What bullshit Tarantino film or Netflix drama was he trying to sound like now? Bev felt a cold sweat break out between her shoulder blades. She remembered their kiss. The elephant in the room that still needed either nurturing or banishing at some point. He had saved her life. The jet ski theft had been an incredible act of heroism. Only now did she accept that Doc was barely out of armbands. Daft, big-hearted dork. 'Just pipe down and sit down, Doc. For Christ's sake! You're wasting billable time.'

'Now, James. Since you've got yourself worked up, let's deal with you first.' Kandice with a K put on a pair of purple rhinestone-studded reading glasses that would have suited a far older woman. She read her notes. 'You'll be glad to hear that the owner of the jet ski has heard the story and felt some sympathy for you. He's offered to drop the charges if you cover the cost of the lost vehicle.'

Doc sank back onto the sofa. The colour in his cheeks had drained away. 'How much?'

'He wants a thousand, but you're lucky. The jet ski is up for sale on eBay with a starting price of five hundred pounds and a buy-it-now of seven-fifty. I told him that would more than cover its value with a cherry on the top for inconvenience.'

'*Seven hundred and fifty quid?!* Why should I—?'

'Pay it, James, or he'll instigate proceedings. You're lucky you've got allies in Detectives Curtis and Owen and that this is now a civil matter instead of a criminal one.' She turned to Bev, glaring at her over her spectacles. 'You're both luckier than you realise. Very fortunate indeed.'

'I'm not going to prison, am I?' Bev said. 'Owen and Curtis said they'd square it all.'

'Breaking and entering. Fraud.' Kandice closed her eyes emphatically. 'You're far from blameless, Beverley. You should have let the police do their job.'

'I *did!*'

Kandice with a K rolled her eyes. 'Well, you didn't really, did you? Look. I'm on your side, here. I completely understand the chain of events that led to the showdown on the boat. But do you think Greater Manchester Police don't have undercover people? Trained operatives! Do you think the North Wales police are incapable of searching a yacht for a ledger? Warrants to search premises and make an arrest, Beverley. A paper trail that will stand up in court according to section 3 of the Criminal Law Act 1967. That's what the prosecution needs to make charges stick.'

'Oh, come on! The police don't have to go through all that rigmarole if they think some big shit is going down.'

'You're *not* the police. I had to remind you of this last time, or had you forgotten?'

'Blah, blah, blah. You say potato, I say bugger all that nitpicking, hair-splitting terminology crap.'

'You're *not* a detective. You're a private individual with no powers of state, Bev. What you've done is tantamount to vigilante justice.'

'Bollocks!' Bev blushed. Knew she was in the wrong.

Kandice picked up her heavy briefcase, opened the clasp theatrically and started to stuff her paperwork inside it. 'I can see you don't need my representation, Beverley. So, I'll send you my bill for what I've done so far.'

Bev felt a wave of light-headedness wash over her. Realised she'd forgotten to breathe. 'I'm sorry. Look. I apologise. You're right. OK? Sorry.'

'Curtis and Owen insist you finish your Institute of Professional Investigators training and get your licence in your own name. They need you to understand where the line is, Beverley. Brush up your act.'

Feeling like a Year Six schoolgirl who was being given a dressing-down by a stern teacher, Bev looked to Doc for some sign of solidarity. Sure enough, he raised his eyebrows and pushed his glasses up his nose with his middle finger – flipping the bird surreptitiously at Kandice with a K. Good old Doc.

'My, er, unorthodox methods won't jeopardise the case, will they?' Bev asked.

Kandice flicked through her notes. 'The police have rounded up the Romanian and Bulgarian slave-workers that Archie was in charge of. He might not be willing to testify, but they certainly are. Even if Anthony's and Penny Higson's defences make mincemeat of you in court because of your lies and deceit, the prosecution has quite a queue of people willing to stand up in court, including Mihal and Constantin. Constantin's photos are incontrovertible evidence. The quality's crystal clear. They're all dated.'

'Good. Good. If I'd buggered up the case after all the risks I took, I'd never forgive myself.'

She thought about Penny's threat to Hope's safety at that moment. After the showdown in Abersoch, Bev had quizzed Hope about a tall supply teacher who might have appeared at school, seeming overly friendly. Hope had showed her childishly neat handwriting in her diary entries, describing a woman who had pretended to be old friends with Bev, as well as a 'man' in the green Puffa jacket, watching Hope from afar – both Penny Higson in two different guises, trying to freak out an eleven-year-old child. The pièce de resistance had been when Hope had produced the phone that Penny had given her, loaded with WhatsApp – a terrifying grooming tactic, designed to foster intimacy and secrecy with Hope, which Penny could later exploit.

Bev felt like a parenting failure, knowing that her own daughter had preferred to confide in Dear Diary about this sinister stranger with her gifts of poisoned cake and a mobile phone instead of her own mother. But at least Penny's threats had been empty, the cake had only contained a mild laxative and Hope was safe. For now.

'What about the other people involved?' Bev asked. 'The men who have done time for Tony? Their womenfolk – Tony's Angels?' She leaned towards Kandice, holding a framed photograph of Hope for her to see. 'Is there anyone out there who's going to come after me and my baby girl? Is there a chance Penny and Tony will walk?'

'That ledger you salvaged from the water seemed to have a comprehensive list of everyone involved. The police have hauled them all in.' Kandice said, smoothing her skirt over her big knees. 'There's also the small matter of Penny having murdered her neighbour, Marjorie Wilson. She thought she'd covered her tracks by baking the lethal Battenberg in her own kitchen, boxing it in the wrapping from a renowned bakery and then booking a courier under a false name, paying in cash. But forensics gave the Higson house a second going-over and found traces of arsenic in one of her baking bowls and trapped under her built-in hob. There was CCTV in the courier's office too that showed the transaction. No doubt it was her. She was cocky.'

'You're telling me!'

'She'll go down for murder. I have no doubt of that. But for now especially as far as Anthony and Archie are both concerned, you're a key witness, Beverley.' This time, Kandice fastened her briefcase shut and stood up. '*Don't* screw it up! The police are cutting you an awful lot of slack. *Do* take that course and get yourself some watertight accreditation! I'm charging you a lot more by the hour than a careers advisor, you know. Think on!'

When Bev closed the door behind her solicitor, with Mihal and Constantin finally under the wing of a homeless charity, and with only her, Doc and Hope in the suite of offices, the place felt peaceful and safe once more.

She collapsed against the wall in the hall, trembling from the sheer effort of having held it together throughout Kandice's lecture. Tears came only moments later, falling in hot, fat beads onto her cheeks. Splashing on the vinyl black tiles of the floor.

Hope ran out from the communal living room, where she'd been doing her homework in front of the TV.

'Are we going to be OK, Mum-Mum?' she asked.

Bev nodded, sobbing silently and clasped her daughter to her chest.

Doc padded down the hall to meet them. Wordlessly, he knelt beside them and put his arms around both Bev and Hope, bringing them in close for a hug. He smelled cleaner than usual of washing powder, magnolia soap and deodorant. Bev was comforted by the warmth of his body and his complete understanding and lack of judgement.

She put an arm around him, hugging him back.

'We're going to be OK, aren't we?' she asked.

Doc kissed the top of Hope's head and then hers, lingering there a while, resting his chin on Bev's hair. 'Yeah, man. Course! We're the three amigos. Right? You, me and Hope. As long as we stick together, we're untouchable.'

Acknowledgements

This is my ninth novel in the crime-fiction genre – *NINE*!!! But at no point in my career have my books been solo efforts. I owe thanks to the following people for practical support, encouragement, comedic relief, inspiration, emotional trauma, unexplained itching and/or alcoholic sustenance, a spare bed in a far-away place and a flare-up of my hiatus hernia.

Firstly, thanks to my family for being unutterably expensive, necessitating my working 365 days per year. There is no more space in my home for sports gear, musical instruments, goldfish-maintenance equipment or Doc Martens. There is no more space in my head for hormonal bickering or excuses about unfinished homework. OK? Dial it down, for Christ's sake! (I loves ya really.)

Thanks to my Special Agent, Caspian Dennis, who still wins the prize, not just for excellence in literary agenting, but also for most eclectic topics of conversation, perfect shoe/outfit colour co-ordination, funniest anecdotes (including stunt-driving misadventures) and best beard.

Thanks to the rest of the team at Abner Stein, notably Sandy, Ben, Ray and Felicity. Never was there a better literary agency ever, ever.

Many especial thanks to the team at Trapeze/Orion, namely my editor, Sam Eades, for bringing me into her literary fold with such warmth, encouragement and enthusiasm; my interim editor, Phoebe Morgan, who is both story-savvy with bells on and runs a damned tight ship; Alainna in PR, who has worked so hard on the Bev Saunders books; Britt in marketing, whose campaigns are first class; and the sales and rights people who make all that writing worthwhile by getting it into actual shops and readers' hands. I feel very proud to have such a well-oiled machine behind me.

Thanks to the journalists and reviewers who said nice things about *Tightrope* and/or have supported me thus far in my writing journey. Barry Forshaw and Jake Kerridge in particular are always familiar and friendly faces on the crime-fiction scene and both have been true gentlemen and rare wits on each and every occasion we've met. Even if they suddenly HATE crime fiction written by noisy small Mancunians, I still think they're great. Similarly, lovely Becky Want and the hilarious Phil Trow on BBC Radio Manchester are *such* stalwart supporters (as are their wonderful producers, Helen Brown and Amy Gallagher). It's so very, very kind of them to get behind a local author, so THANKS LOADS, YOUS.

Many thanks to my readers within online book clubs, where the pace at which people read and the sheer enthusiasm for crime fiction always dazzles me. You guys are terrific, as are the folk who run those groups. You know who you are!

Huge thanks to the bloggers who support my writing and get involved in blog tours, particularly the participants in the *Tightrope* blog tour: @annecater, @writing_ie, @grabthisbook, @thebooktrailer, @kaishajayneh, @gntx, @thesundayfeel. I always get such valued support and friendship too from Bookwitch, aka Ann Giles. Bloggers are the undersung heroes of the literary community!

Finally, thanks to my friends for wise chat, encouragement and laughs when I most need it. In particular, I *must* thank Tammy Cohen, Sarah Stephens-Smith and Paulette Geelan who have made overnighters in London possible, as well as alcoholic poisoning and really bad kitchen dancing, AND Wendy Storer and Martin de Mello, who always have the answers to life's conundrums, or is it conundra? They'd know that, you see. Also, Ed James for saying exactly what I *don't* want to hear, precisely at the point where I really *do* need to hear it, like, 'Stop pissing about on eBay and write, Marnoid!'

Finally, FINALLY, thanks to my readers, who are the bestest readers in the world. If I won big on the Premium Bonds, I'd buy you all a drink. No, really. I would! But maybe just half a cooking lager because there's a whole heap of yous!

Credits

Trapeze would like to thank everyone at Orion who worked on the publication of *Backlash* in the UK.

Editorial
Phoebe Morgan
Ru Merritt
Rosie Pearce
Charlie Panayiotou
Jane Hughes
Alice Davis

Copy-editor
Loma Books

Proofreader
Kati Nicholl

Audio
Paul Stark
Amber Bates

Contracts
Anne Goddard
Paul Bulos
Ellen Harber

Design
Lucie Stericker
Joanna Ridley
Nick May
Clare Sivell
Helen Ewing
Jan Bielecki
Debbie Holmes

Finance
Naomi Mercer
Jasdip Nandra
Afeera Ahmed

Elizabeth Beaumont
Sue Baker
Victor Falola

Marketing
Brittany Sankey

Production
Claire Keep
Fiona Macintosh
Katie Horrocks

Publicity
Alainna Hadjigeorgiou

Sales
Jen Wilson
Esther Waters
Rachael Hum
Ellie Kyrke-Smith
Viki Cheung
Ben Goddard
Mark Stay
Georgina Cutler

Jo Carpenter
Tal Hart
Andrew Taylor
Barbara Ronan
Andrew Hally
Dominic Smith
Maggy Park
Elizabeth Bond
Linda McGregor

Rights
Susan Howe
Richard King
Krystyna Kujawinska
Jessica Purdue
Hannah Stokes

Operations
Jo Jacobs
Sharon Willis
Lucy Tucker
Lisa Pryde

Missed the first book in the series?

What happens when a private investigator ends up being the one uncovered?

Having lost everything after a failed marriage, Beverley Saunders now lodges in the basement flat of a house owned by her best friend Sophie and her husband, Tim. With Bev's former glittering marketing career in the gutter, she begins to do investigative work for other wronged women.

But when Beverley takes on the case of Sophie's friend Angela, who is seeking to uncover grounds for divorce from her controlling husband, she soon discovers that she isn't the only one doing the investigating . . .

Beverley has a secret history she doesn't want coming out – but will she manage to stay hidden long enough to give Angela the freedom she deserves?

'A gripping page-turner of a plot' ROZ WATKINS
'A corking thriller' ED JAMES

Read on for an extract of
Tightrope, the first book in
the Beverley Saunders series . . .

PROLOGUE

The Wolf

Pinned beneath him on the leather chaise, the girl stares up into the gaping maw of the latex wolf mask he is wearing. Despite the alcohol and cocktail of drugs they forced her to take to make her relaxed and pliant, the terror is evident in her eyes.

'You know what I'm going to do?' His voice is muffled as he speaks – hollow and otherworldly. It excites him to tell her what he has in store for her, adopting the role as narrator in this climactic scene of her own personal horror story. It is being filmed, after all. 'I'm going to squeeze the life out of you, because that's what your sort deserves.'

Her expression freezes for a brief moment. Perhaps she is deciphering the unfamiliar English. Suddenly, her face crumples into a look of sheer despair. She shakes her head from side to side. 'No! I don't like,' she says. 'Stan. Where is? I need to talk.' Her words are vodka-slurred, making her Russian accent unguent and treacly. Tears track down the sides of her face as she turns to the cameraman for a reaction. 'Please make stop.' She says something in her mother tongue. The imploring tone in her high-pitched whimper makes her sound like the little girl she really is beneath the heavy make-up.

But her needs are not The Wolf's concern, and the camera keeps rolling. He digs his knees into those slender haunches to limit her movements. Pinions her skinny arms above her head to stop her from lashing out in defence. He calls to the others to hold her down, and like her, they comply with his demands.

'No! No!' she cries, wriggling uselessly against them. 'It hurt. Where Dmitri? Get Stan! Stan! Help!'

'Stan's not here,' he says, almost whispering in her ear. 'Dmitri's busy. And so are we.'

She screams, loud enough to distort the soundtrack.

The Wolf looks up at the other men. There are five in total, all naked but for their masks. A pig. A bulldog. A horse. A cockerel. He stars as The Wolf. It is hard to infer the others' moods at this point, but they are all still visibly aroused, queuing up for a second bite of this ripe cherry.

Right now, however, it is The Wolf's turn.

He reaches over to the coffee table. Snatches up the ball gag, which he straps around her head with practiced ease, despite her wriggling. The only sounds of protest she can emit now is the gurgle of her choking on her own saliva.

'That's better. You talk too much.'

He puts his hand around the naked girl's neck and squeezes while he rides her. Invincible. In charge of her destiny, as he'd witnessed his own father, all those years ago, masterfully controlling the babysitter, the cleaner's daughter, his younger sister. The girl – silenced now; red-faced with the sheer effort of clinging to life – writhes beneath him in a bid to break free. There is pleading in her wide eyes, the veins in her forehead standing proud. She mouths the word, 'Nyet!' but the sound never quite breaks free of her compromised gullet.

The others have started shouting at him, shouting over each other. Their noise is such that it is difficult to tell if they are egging him on or protesting. But with the smell of fresh meat in his nostrils, The Wolf does not care.

When the girl's body finally lies still and her head lolls to one side, the bulldog speaks:

'Jesus! She's gone limp. Is she dead?' He approaches, pressing two fingers to her neck. 'I can't find a pulse! Am I pressing in the right place?' Unbuckling the leather straps of the gag and prising the red plastic ball from her mouth, he cocks his head and holds his ear close to her lips. 'I can't hear her breathing.'

'Try her wrist,' the horse says. He approaches and feels along the inside of her wrist for a pulsating vein. 'Nothing.' Lifting the girl's eyelids, he uselessly waves his hand in front of her glazed eyes. 'You've fucking killed her, haven't you?' he says to The Wolf. 'You absolute knob. We're buggered.' His voice is tremulous. He backs away from the scene, covering his waning erection with both hands as if he finally knows shame.

The Wolf, however, has no such compunction. Sated, he dismounts the teenage prostitute. She is nothing more to him than a spent horse after a long, hard ride. His work is done.

This is why he is the star of this little home movie, which Stan's sweaty coke-head of a cameraman is still discretely shooting.

The girl's limbs hang around her at odd angles like the arms of a broken clock, which is fitting as time no longer matters to her now.

The pig tugs at his mask as though he wants to remove it. He seems to think better of it, though. 'Why the hell did you strangle her? You prat. This is going to come back on us. My wife will find out. We'll all get nicked as accessories to murder. Christ's sake, you brutal bastard! We're ruined.' Both anger and terror are audible in his voice.

'Can you just stop panicking for five minutes?' The cockerel speaks quickly to the pig. He turns to The Wolf. 'We can't just leave her like this . . . can we? We should at least find out who she is.' He snatches up the girl's handbag, perching it on his paunch. Starts to rummage through it. Clearly agitated, he empties it out onto the coffee table of the stylish apartment, rifling through the pile of contents. Painkillers. Phone. Lipstick. Lube. Condoms. A tampon. Purse.

The Wolf picks up what appears to be ID but it is only an Oyster Card. 'Fake,' he says. He holds the photocard up. Compares the smiling girl in the photograph to the anguished death mask of the under-aged prostitute. 'Emma Davies? Not bloody likely. This silly little bitch was Russian. She's just another of Dmitri's trafficked whores. Let's face it, boys, nobody's going to miss her.'

'Look, you did this,' the horse tells The Wolf, his voice sounding nasal as it filters down the long nose of the mask. 'This is your problem.' He holds his hands up, taking a step backwards. Shaking his head. 'I'm off. I'm not getting involved. We were supposed to come here for a bit of fun. Let off some steam. But this . . .? You're on your own, bud. I've got a family. A reputation . . .'

The bulldog pulls his foreskin back over his deflating penis, his doggy head cocked to one side as he contemplates the girl. His disbelief is audible in the high pitch of his speech. 'The only way this disappears is if *she* disappears. You're going to have to get rid of her. What are you going to do with her body?'

The Wolf turns to him. 'What am *I* going to do with it? You mean, what are *we* going to do? We're all in this together, remember?'

As the others start to back away from the body and the camera, covering themselves with cushions and items of clothing that they'd discarded gleefully only minutes earlier, The Wolf moves with stealth into the kitchen. He reappears, carrying a butcher's knife block and a roll of black bin liners. Sets the block down onto the coffee table, knocking the girl's things to the floor. He pulls out a meat cleaver and a bread knife, staring down at the glinting blades through the eyeholes of his wolfish mask. Still bearing a sizeable, angry erection.

'I know exactly how to get rid of this little problem.'

The film clip ends.

The appeal of watching it over and over again in the privacy of his office never wanes, though he knows that it is now on the Dark Net for every Tom, Dick and Harry to savour too, provided they can get themselves beyond the paywall. Masturbating himself slowly, gripping the rosewood tabletop of his desk with his free hand, he muses that it makes him some sort of celebrity. He certainly feels like one, every time that piece of footage flickers into life on his laptop's screen. He is The Wolf. Everyone else is an incidental character in that unfolding drama; that perfect world, where he was the King of Everything in a penthouse in West London.

When the footage runs out, it freezes mid frame with an outstretched palm in close-up. His hand. He'd turned to Stan's cameraman, telling him to switch it off and destroy the film. Except the money-grubbing moron had done no such thing. At Stan's suggestion, to compensate for the lost income from his dead whore, he'd uploaded it onto the net instead where it could be monetised. At first, The Wolf had felt like the skies were about to collapse in on him. But they hadn't. He has nothing to fear from the authorities or that scumbag, Stan. Time has elapsed, and still, nobody knows who was responsible for the appearance of the mystery girl, bagged in pieces in the butcher's bin along with the other rotten meat. A broken Russian doll.

Cleaning himself up, he now prepares for another day as a man of unimpeachable standing. He is honourable and trustworthy and liked, just as his father was. They do not know about his starring role as The Wolf. That knowledge remains a secret which he is certain will be carried to the graves of all concerned. In those fleeting minutes captured on film, he will forever more be God's own emissary on earth, dispensing judgement and death according to his whim.

He tucks himself back in, washes his hands and checks his reflection in the mirror. All is silent but for his footfalls and the persistent voice in his head that not even the clip can drown out:

'No thanks. You're not what I'm looking for.'

Her voice on a deafening loop. The time she rejected him and humiliated him publicly. But that is nothing compared to the gargantuan lie she has been telling for more than a decade. The woman he pictures in his mind's eye has committed the ultimate act of betrayal. She has stolen from him in the worst way imaginable. But he will have his revenge.

The Wolf is watching her. He is hungry. And waiting.